74

Black Hot

HIP HOP DECODED

HIP HOP DECODED

From Its Ancient Origin To Its Modern Day Matrix

The Black Dot

MOME Publishing Inc.
Bronx, New York

First Edition

Third Printing: June 2021

MOME Publishing Inc.
P.O. Box 24
Bronx, NY 10471
momepublishing@hotmail.com
www.idecodeit.com
www.UrbanX.nyc

Book cover design by Rasta Asaru Escott EL
Interior illustrations by James Top
Book layout by Latonia Almeyda-Bowser

ISBN: 978-0-9772357-7-3

Printed in United States

Contents

DEDICATIONS

This book is dedicated to my four children: Marcus, Malcom, Elijah and Odyssey. I hold a special place in my heart for each of you. Daddy may not leave you a lot of money, but I will do my best to leave you with something far more valuable…knowledge. This book is dedicated to the memory of my mother, Liz Odessa Jones, for loving me unconditionally, and for always giving me the inspiration to do great things. I dedicate this book to the memory of my grandmother, Mary Bowser, for holding the family together no matter what. To my grandfather, Charlie Bowser and my uncle Willie, you guys will forever be missed. To my late aunt Julia Bowser, aunt Lottie, Charles Bowser, Kenneath Bowser, and to all of those ancestors who are known and unknown to me, may you all rest in peace. I dedicate this work to the entire Bowser family: aunt Vera, uncle Skip, aunt Sandra, uncle Carl, uncle Chris, aunt Vanessa, Renee and Rachele, Mavis, Lisa, Wyteria, Nathaniel, Toney, Christie, Geo, Tyrek, Shanae, Blue, Kevin, Ayesha, Dominique, Taeya, Janae, Unique, Alexis and Shamelle. This is a special dedication to my sister, April Johnson, who I love with all of my heart, you too D'andre, keep up the good work in school. I'm very proud of you.

I dedicate this body of work to the memory of my father, Stanley "Blood" Kitt, for being my gateway to the planet. I feel your spirit within me everyday; as long as I live, you live. This is dedicated to the memory of my grandmother, Jesse Felder Kitt, for instilling in me a sense of spirituality at an early age. I still call your name in times of need. This book is dedicated to the memory of my grandfather, William Kitt, and to my uncle Billy Kitt (R.I.P.). This book is dedicated to the entire Kitt family: Aunt Weezy, Stacey, Valerie, George, Spank, Eartha, Tracey, and Belinda. This book is also dedicated to my uncle Gene Kitt, aunt Mary, aunt Rose, aunt Kitty, aunt Eda and uncle Sam Tee, I love you guys with all of my heart.

A very special dedication goes out to the love of my life, Latonia Almeyda-Bowser, for being everything that I could ever want and need in a woman. You stood by me for the entire ride; this book could not be done without you. When I felt like giving up, you never let me, you sat there and listened to my crazy dreams and visions and then said, "Let's do it!" You held this family together no matter what, you went to work, cleaned the house, and raised the children, all while being my wife and best friend, not to mention an ill graphics designer, for that, I will love you forever. Fellas, when you get one like this, you hold on!

This book is dedicated to the Knowistanding Learning program, Antwane, Annika, Cleveland, Clinton, Shanae, Marcus, Ty, and Rich. I began tutoring you guys in the 6th and 7th grade, now you're all in college, how crazy is that! This book is dedicated to the masters, whose feet I sat at and learned the secret sciences; Rev. Phil Valentine for teaching me to focus on the cause of things and not the affect, Bobby Hemmitt for teaching me to never be afraid of the "dark," Henry De Bernardo for teaching me the fundamentals of effective ritual work, Dr. Lliala Afrika for teaching me how to heal myself holistically, C Freeman El for teaching me about my astrological power, Steve Cokely for teaching me never to believe what I see without investigating, Bro. Dawud for teaching me never to bite my tongue when the truth needs to be told, Dr. Nalani for her motherly touch and practical approach to self healing and Sister Myra El for teaching me the Law. I dedicate this book to Mr. and Mrs. Fuller for all of your support along with Mark Frazier, Gary Frazier and Brother Amir. This book is dedicated to Azzariah for offering me the "red pill" to begin with, and so many more. And last but not least, I dedicate this book to the memory of Eric "Money Ray" Hoskins; he was truly an angel from the hood.

ACKNOWLEDGEMENTS AND SHOUT OUTS

I would like to acknowledge Latonia Almeyda-Bowser for the vision of the book cover and for working the long hard hours needed to get the job done. And for putting up with my madness, I couldn't do it without you. I would like to thank the legendary James Top for the illustrations and bringing my vision to reality. I would like to especially thank my brothers for life, William "Chill" Jones, David "Dope fiend" Lucher, and Lyvan "Van Damn" Blount for living my dream with me, even sacrificing their money, time, and energy for me, how could I ever forget that? I would like to thank 4 Korners newspaper for believing in the Dot, I'm 4 Korners for life. Shout out to JP, Bace, Rikers, Will-I-Am, Nikka, and the entire staff at 4Knews. Much love to Paul "P Moor" Moreland for fighting for the Dot so that my work would never be compromised. Big up to Phil Moreland for holding me down out of town. To Brother A.A. Rashid; we haven't met in the physical yet, but our spiritual connection is strong. Much respect to Knowledge and his Good Money crew, the world is waiting for you God! Much love to Jehvon Bruckner a.k.a. Mwebe of the Ghetto Tymz for your continued support, as well as, waking up the dead every month with information. I can't wait for the Annilitikal to drop! I would like to thank the mother of the Matrix, Sophia Stewart for coming up with such a brilliant concept as the Matrix and Terminator movies. I would like to thank Brother Chris "Christ" Wilmore and Brother Rich for holding me down when times got hard, and for keeping me spiritually humble, being God is lonely, I appreciate the company. What up K.B. from Atlanta, (M.U. Productions in 2006!). I would like to thank my astrologer, William T. Brabam, for your guidance. I would like to thank Marcus Spears for his support. Shout out to brother Cypher. I would like to thank the street soldiers like Brother

Shabazz of Eye Opener Productions for getting the information out to the people. Shout out to Eye Opener Midwest, Dirty South, and Down South. Big up to Brother Saa Neter and The House of Consciousness for never allowing the people to forget the struggles that we had to go through to get to this point, keep up the good work, Black Power! Shout out to Big Man and Big Man Productions, Azzariah and Black Market Productions, shout out to Dr. Lamar, Brother Alim, and all of the other soldiers providing knowledge for the people. Shout out to Soul Brothers Boutique for opening up your doors to the people. I would like to thank the fellas from around the way, Big Ty, Dave, Match, Kool Moe, 400, Speedy, Clemente, Edwin, Juan, Danny, Byron, Jeff, Big Vaughn, and all of the other fellas that are just too numerous to mention. Shout out to the ladies from around the way too like Tifa, Nicole, Lisa, Selena, Sharron, and Kalima. Big up to my two "Pops" Dino and Emmitt. I love you, I love you, I love you goes out to my God daughter Ayana, and my nephews Jamie and Seven. Shout out to Gary Grant, Gary Cooper, and Tyrent "TY Stick" Scott. Much love to Sedgwick Projects (Riot Town), Big Lee, A-train, Kenwin, and Mike. Shout out to the U-Mob, and Davidson Ave. I would like to big up my barber Kirk, and the entire Happy Mount crew. What up Sleep! Oh yeah, a message to young Siri; stay on the path of enlightenment, there are many bright days ahead for you. Big up to the best football teams in Westchester County, The Bronx River Bulldogs! I would like to thank Mr. and Mrs. Gaillord for all of their support over the years. I would like to thank some very special people in my life; Marilyn Lucher, (when I say ma, I mean it from the heart), R.I.P. Derrick Lucher and Lynn Lucher, to my Goddaughter Shanae, you're going to be a great mother. Welcome to the world little Siana Lanee' Atori Collier. What up Lasean, peace Bobby, oh, I didn't forget about you Soni. What up David Jr. and Nia! Special thanks to my Aunt Phyllis for letting me raid your fridge when you barely had enough food to feed your own children, I will never forget that. And how could I forget that lovely granddaughter of yours, Skye. This goes out to the entire Hawes family, Sharon, Renee, Eric, Denise, Evelyn, Chiphone, Bubble B, Jimmy, Taji and Preston for treating me and my crazy children like family, grandma Francis, I don't know what I'd do without you! I'm forever grateful. Much love goes out to Joanne Hopkins (R.I.P.) for sharing her heart unconditionally. Shout out to Rhonda, Renee, Kyle, and Keisha.

Shout out to Marlene, Darlene, Cathy, Gwen, and all of my neighbors over the years. Shout out to Cookie, Lee Lee, Velda, and R.I.P. Mrs. Annett. Shout out to Kimmy, and R.I.P. Mrs. Jeannie. Shout out to Janice, Lisa, Cynthia, Fred, and R.I.P. Mrs. Deloris. A very special thanks to my mother-in-law Yvonne Sivills for being the greatest grandmother on the planet, and for giving birth to such a queen. To my sister-in-law, Trakeeva "Kee Kee" Sivills, thanks for treating me like family from day one. To Mr. Ishmael Almeyda (R.I.P.), we never got the chance to meet, but I can tell that you were a great man; your daughter is living proof. Special shout out to the entire Rodgers family for the love and support over the years. A very special thank you to Renee Rodgers, my first love and one of the greatest mothers on the planet, and her husband Tom for allowing me to sleep well at night knowing that my children were safe, that means a lot to me. R.I.P. Tante, You will forever be missed. What up Ifetayo! Hugs and kisses to my neice Ayana. A very special shout out to my cousin Sean Battles, your last name says it all; you are a warrior. Our mothers were best friends as teenagers and said that they were going to marry brothers when they got older, and they did, how crazy is that! Shout out to my cousin Mike Battles; keep your head up son! Shout out to my newest God Son Nahki, what up J.R.! Shout out to Ulmer Park bus depot, Flatbush depot, and Jackie Gleason depot, and the entire New York Transit System, I know what it's like! Much love to everyone that has given me their unconditional support, thank you.

VERY SPECIAL SHOUT OUTS

These very special acknowledgements will go out to my Hip Hop tree of life; these are the people that I have personally met on the path of Hip Hop, even if it was just in passing. They say that a tree is only as good as the fruit that it bares, so each and every one of these individuals is some what responsible for the information that you are about to receive. Shout out to Kool Herc and the Herculoids, The Cold Crush Brothers, Chief Rocker Busy Bee, Special K from the Treacherous Three, T La Rock, Keith Keith of the Funky Four Plus One, Grandmaster Flash, Afrika Bambaataa and The Mighty Zulu Nation, KRS ONE, E K Mike C from the

Crash Crew, DJ Prince from 104 school yard (king of the up and down mixer), DJ Whitehead, Squirrel D, and DJ Dr. Pepper, The Grandmaster Seven, which included; Moe, Ali, Kevin, Kay Kay, Derrick, Spider, Lucky, and John a.k.a. Atom Ant. Big shout out to the legendary Rob Base. Shout out to Rockin Rog, and Todd Rock, we used to spin on our heads, remember that? Big up to my first DJ Dave D, my first crew The Culture Four; Al B, Sean B, and Stevie D. Shout out to The Chill Force; E-Z L a.k.a. True Love, the greatest Emcee never known, Reg a.k.a. Born, and DJ Master Marvin. Big up Toney Tone (what a brother know) and DJ Mick. Shout out to Chubby Chubb of the Original Flavor, Black Rob, DJ Spice Nice, A very special shout out and much love to my crew The Culture Force Brothers; DJ Fresh Rob and Lou Ski (Ultimate Breaks and Beats), The Human Element Mr. Zinc, Ramiek 120 (I remember when you were the rhymeologist, we go back that far!), and Master Will. This goes out to my brother for life Ed "Everlasting" Wilson, Kendu from BK, Jazz, and Cut King. Big Up to Gee Cerone, DJ Pee, my brother Chill for being ill with the electric boogie, and for taggin up, I remember seeing Chillizm everywhere, Wayne Johnson (R.I.P.), one of the greatest boogie boys of all time. And how could I forget Boo the Big fella and Money Ray (R.I.P.), we will forever be Tall, Dark, and Handsome. Shout out to Madd M.F. Mike, you were way ahead of your time. This goes out to Emcee Rashien, my first enlightener. To Chris Lighty from the Violators, much respect. Shout out to that original Bronx Nigga, Tim Dog, you showed me the world, for that, I'm forever grateful. Big up DJ Dice and Derrick, shout out to the ultra Magnetic Emcees, Ced Gee produced my first real demo, I still got that! Big up to Keyboard Money Mike, and his brother I God, much love to the original Gompers Stompers (class of 86), shout out to Stephanie and Yasmin (Class of 88), shout out to Brooklyn's Finest, Jaz–O, the o-ri-gi-na-tor! Much love to my cousin Broadway, keep the dream alive, to Ason the Animal, you the truth. To Emcee Smooth, I can't wait for you to shine! To Heron, never give up the flow. To James Top, Nick One, Part One, and Ram Link, this white boy is truly an initiate of Hip Hop. Much love to Red Dizzy and Gee, and the entire Rapagram family. This goes out to everyone else that's a part of my Hip Hop tree, if I forgot your name, don't take it personal, peace.

ABOUT THE EMCEE

Iwould first like to start out with a little history about myself. I feel that this is crucial because of the nature of this subject. Too many times you read articles or books written by individuals who either know nothing about Hip Hop in terms of living it, or fabricate and exaggerate they're knowledge of Hip Hop in order to add credibility to the story their trying to sell you. While they may have studied the subject extensively or heard about the way it was back in the days, I was there to witness the emergence of the Hip Hop nation, but let me be clear I did not help create it. Born and raised in the South Bronx, the primary energy grid line of Hip Hop, I was fortunate enough to be inside the womb of Hip Hop when its water broke. While I was too young to participate in the growth of Hip Hop at the time, it still changed my life forever. As a youngster growing up in the Bronx without a father around, I looked up to the older fellas on the block as role models or father figures, studying their every move, mannerisms and ways, wanting to be just like them. This ultimately led to me being involved with Hip Hop at a very early age. They were called, The Magnificent Seven and were the first students of the Masters, studying the routines, rhymes, and how many times the DJ spun the record back to catch a certain word or phrase. My most vivid memories of the early days of Hip Hop were of the older fellas huddled up in a circle puffin' "Cheba" and listening to tapes on their boom box of the pioneers like the Cold Crush, Fantastic Five, Kool Herc and The Herculoids, The Furious Five, Treacherous Three, Afrika Bambaataa, and The Funky Four Plus One. They would sit for hours debating over who had the freshest routines, Cold Crush or Fantastic; who was the fastest DJ Grandmaster Flash, who spun the record back or his student Grand Wizard Theodore, who flipped the needle back to catch the break and who created the scratch, or who had more crates of records and the loudest system, Afrika Bambaataa or Kool Herc. Like a sponge, I would sit there and absorb this early essence of Hip Hop, even memorizing the routines and rhymes myself. This led to the pause tape era in Hip Hop, or at least in my neighborhood anyway. Since the older cats in my hood couldn't afford two turntables and a mixer, they used the pause button on their boom boxes to loop the break beats over and over, creating their own little mixes and routines. They would all gather around and battle to see who had the dopest pause tape, while others would take turns kicking an original rhyme, crowd pleasing routine, or bite one from their favorite group.

I remember begging my mother to buy me a boom box so I could make my own pause tapes. We were poor so she couldn't afford to get me a box with two speakers, and it didn't have a pause button, it had a stop button only. The pause button was the key. It made your edits smooth, while the stop button had an annoying clicking sound at the beginning of every edit. I remember getting laughed at and clowned on by the older fellas, but it was all good, I still felt like I was a real B-Boy. Eventually somebody in the hood bought DJ equipment. This was followed by many trips to Downstairs Records to buy two each of the hottest break beats. They would then cover up the name of the record with tape so no one else would know its origin, obviously a move they picked up from watching Kool Herc, Bam and Flash rock the jams in the park. At that point, the first real Hip Hop groups in the hood had formed, fully equipped with two turntables, a mic, and crates of break beats. No longer were the fellas kicking other group's routines and rhymes. Everything at this point was original, and that's when I became a student of the neighborhood masters. By the year 1980, I had formed my first little crew. My first Emcee name was Cheba La Rock, and even though I was only 12 years old, my rhymes were getting the attention of the older Emcees in the hood. I grew up in walking distance from Cedar Park, The Galaxy 2000, The Ecstasy Garage and The Fever, which were some of the more legendary Hip Hop spots back in the day. I had access to witness some of the greatest DJs and Emcees in Hip Hop history. Emceeing became the only thing that I wanted to do with my life, and I would actively pursue it from that point on.

Yet it wasn't until I reached Samuel Gompers High School in the South Bronx that heads starting really taking notice of my lyrical talent. Record labels like CBS, Tommy Boy, and 4th & Broadway were showing interest at the early age of 14. In 1987, I signed to the infamous independent record label B-Boy Records, home of KRS-ONE, as part of a group I formed called, Tall, Dark, and Handsome. This was before KRS dropped the famous line "B-Boy Records you just can't trust" and jetted from the label. Due to their shady dealings and lack of promotion, we received modest airplay and the label eventually folded. In 1990/1991, I teamed up with Tim Dog to promote his West Coast dis "Fuck Compton." It was my first look at Hip Hop from an international level, as we toured London, Holland, Germany, and Paris. We also toured in Canada and across the United States. As Tim Dog's hype man, I learned the inner workings of the music business and when our tour was over in 1992, I formed my own independent label called B.I.B. Records and started a new group called, The Lethahedz. We dropped a controversial EP entitled, A&R Killer: "Da Hip Hop Play," which uncovered the shady dealings of record labels and our personal struggles of trying to get a deal without selling our souls. It was received well within the industry, but lack of funds to truly promote the project brought it little success. Yet like they say, "There's always work at the post office" or in my case, the Transit Authority. With little success of getting a deal without selling out or becoming a gangsta rapper, and with a six year old son and another on the way, I became a city Bus Operator. The time away from the game enabled me to see it from the outside looking in. What I learned about Hip Hop over the last 10 years will shock and amaze you! From my early days as Cheba La Rock, to my spiritual journey as The Black Dot, these are my chronicles and this is my story.

FOREWORD

Peace

The culture of Hip Hop is now thirty one years old, but the energy and the passion which fuels it is older than any music genre. As with every other contribution black people have made to planet earth, Hip Hop has been scrutinized, berated and later exploited by mainstream America. The most damage done to this culture though, has been done by its participants and not the outside entities which have exploited Hip Hop to the masses. You can lead a horse to water but you can't make him drink, but if the horse is starving and dying of thirst, he's not gonna care where the water comes from. The culture of Hip Hop was built by young inner city youth with a need for self expression and limited resources. But how did this culture grow from a passing fad to a multi-billion dollar industry without some of its pioneers ever reaping the rewards? And how did a culture built on love, peace, unity, respect and having fun wind up as a business totally devoid of ethics, morals or love for the culture? Well there are a lot of things that contributed to the downfall of Hip Hop as a culture. Ever wonder why Willie Nelson is still performing at the Grand Ole Opry, or why the Rolling Stones are still packing arenas but the so called "Old

School Emcee" is obsolete? Maybe the deletion of a few years of our history might be beneficial to someone, so let's start the history of this culture when everybody became aware of it, instead of when it actually started. How about the old Jackson 5/Osmond Brothers syndrome, or the Run DMC/Beastie Boys debacle leading to the Hammer/Vanilla Ice episode. This is just history repeating its bullshit way of documenting our culture. It's not viable until someone else says so. It's not music until it sells, it's not art until it sells, it's not valuable until it sells. There are a lot of reasons why Hip Hop is in the shape it's in, and until some of us look up from under that smoke screen and start understanding that there are forces at work that have nothing to do with music manipulating our very existence in life, much less our music, we will continue to travel down deeper into that black hole called ignorance; driving an Escalade with spinning rims, smoking a blunt and sippin' sizzurp to the sounds of Eminem on our way to the strip club.

Peace

Grandmaster Caz

1

MATRIX INTRO

Warning! This book is not for everyone. If you feel that there's nothing wrong with the current state of Hip Hop, then this book is not for you. If you feel that gangsta rap, rollin' on 20's, violence, drugs and videos with half naked women in them has elevated Hip Hop as an art form, then this book is definitely not for you. But if on the other hand, you feel that turning on your radio and listening to the same rap songs that are laced with negative lyrics over and over, watching soft porn or graphically violent videos while reading glossy Hip Hop magazines that endorse this way of life has shaped the minds of our youth, and are collectively being used as part of a mind control operation to mentally and spiritually enslave our future generations, then welcome to: Hip Hop Decoded. Walk with me as I uncover this conspiracy as well as many others involving the culture of Hip Hop. We'll look at Hip Hop from its early days when B-Boys and B-Girls represented for the love of the art form, to what it has become today. But make no mistake about it; this is not a book about the history of Hip Hop, it's a book about the mystery of Hip Hop. We'll look at the four elements of Hip Hop: DJing, Emceeing, Break Dancing, and Graffiti as they relate to the four elements of our glorious past: the drum, the oracle, the dancer, and hieroglyphics. Together we'll add the fifth element, which is knowledge, to explore this connection and what effect it has on the future of Hip Hop. At times this book will not read like an ordinary book, this was done purposely in an attempt to break your thought patterns into fragments and descramble the Matrix program that we currently operate within which tells us how and what to think, even when it comes to Hip Hop. Reading in this manner will help decode and process this information properly. For example, I may start a story, and then abruptly stop it, only to continue it 100 pages later. This is done because in order to understand the rest of the story, some may have to become familiar with information that may sound foreign to them at the time, or otherwise they may dismiss it as something false or impossible. I'll also tell fictional stories with subliminal true undertones aimed at your subconscious mind. Some of my articles about the government, mind control, and Hip Hop are specifically designed to stretch your imagination because remember, "If you can't even conceive it, it's easier for them to achieve it." I'll use a combination of articles, stories, poems, rhymes, illustrations, and visuals in an attempt to create the perfect platform for each individual to process this information. It's easier for some to visualize, while others learn through stories or can hear truth being spoken to them. Our ancestors used all of these formats to teach and I'll keep with that tradition. I'll explore the possibility of some rappers being government agents and the secret agreements reached to keep the masses at bay. Then I'll uncover the theory of music having the ability to heal people and the government conspiracy to tone down and distort the sound of music. I'll decode why Hip Hop videos are dangerous.

I'll also reveal the Hip Hop relationship between Blacks and Jews, the satanic signs and symbols in Hip Hop, Hip Hop and the Illuminati, and explore the possibility of Hip Hop having its own secret society. A lot of this information will be simply my opinion, but that doesn't mean it's not laced with truth. Try not to allow the mind control program of the Matrix to tell you that if a story doesn't have "proof," references, sources, or quotes that it's slander or has no validity. That's just a box they have set up to keep you thinking within it and to keep you focused on using recycled thoughts and ideas, as opposed to trying to think outside of the box in pursuit of an original thought. Truth is something that you can feel in your heart, even if you can't prove it. In order to get a full understanding of this book, you are going to have to feel your way through it. On the other hand, there will be plenty of articles that are well researched, with quotes, sources, and references that are strategically planted between my opinions to give you a sense of home if you ever get lost operating outside of the box that the Matrix has set up for you. Yet there are boxes within boxes within boxes that are all controlled by the Matrix, I'm simply attempting to provide a gateway from one box to another for those who are ready to think out-side of the box that they're currently operating within. This is a work in progress; I'll take it as deep as I can take it as far as my own understanding of the Hip Hop Matrix. At that point, it will be the duty of someone with an even greater overstanding to lead us into the next box until there are no more boxes left to master. However, the Matrix of Hip Hop is ever expanding in its attempt to keep our people on lockdown. For every box we master, it stays two boxes ahead, setting up programs that counter the next trend, style, even state of consciousness that Hip Hop is heading toward before we even get there! Make no mistake about it, we're at war on a physi-cal, mental, and spiritual level. Hopefully after processing this information you'll be able to function in the Matrix of Hip Hop without being of it. Once armed with this knowledge, it's the responsibility of each of us to become Morpheus in search of the "One" who's ready to be unplugged. That person then becomes Morpheus in search of another "One" who's ready to know the truth about Hip Hop. Then, each "One" will teach "One" until we're all free of the Matrix. Remember: I can tell you the truth about Hip Hop, but then I'll have to kill you; not physically, but kill your old way of thinking until you become born again and are able to see the Matrix of Hip Hop for what it really is. Once you're born again into the true knowledge of Hip Hop, then they'll have to kill you to pro-tect the Matrix from being decoded and destroyed. So ask yourself, am I up for the task? If so, then follow me as we enter into Hip Hop Decoded.

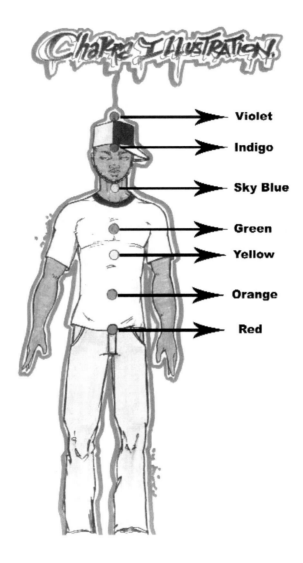

Chakra Illustration - Under the skin we are nothing more than light beings, fueled by light energy. There are seven major wheels of light that run from the base of the spine, to the top of the head. They are each color coded; each one has an element that it represents, and a distinctive function. One activates the chakras through meditation and certain spiritual exercises, the higher the chakra activated, the greater the spiritual insight. The ultimate goal is to awaken all seven of the chakras to become fully illuminated and become one with the supreme.

2

THE HIP HOP FAST & RITUAL

Wait! Before we proceed any further, there's something that we must do to ensure a safe trip. So that we don't get caught up into thinking the Matrix of Hip Hop is real or locked into a negative frequency that's hard to escape; we must take a Hip Hop fast and do the necessary rituals for protection. Fasts are taken for many reasons, some spiritual and some for health purposes. In this case, our Hip Hop fast will represent a little of both. The foods we eat can bog us down, especially if these foods are heavy. It requires a tremendous amount of energy to process this food. This energy is drawn from all parts of the body, including the brain to get the job done, leaving the body weak and the brain drained and ready to shut down. That's why most people need a nap after a good meal. It gets worse when the type of food we eat is added to the equation. You know what they say, "You are what you eat" and foods like meat, which carry a dead vibration or dairy products which carry a low animalistic vibration, force us to think on those levels. The same rules apply in terms of a Hip Hop fast except instead of food, it's food for thought that we must regulate. If all that we eat from Hip Hop magazines, radio stations and video shows are money, hoes, clothes and other negative vibrations, then that's all we are able to act upon and live out. If food is to provide nourishment, then food for thought is to provide knowledge. Food that is bad carries a lower vibration. Food that is good for us carries a higher vibration. Fasts are needed to cleanse the mind and body and assist in raising our vibrations to a level that allows us to maximize our brain potential. This will definitely be needed when we begin decoding the Matrix of Hip Hop. This will also keep our brains sharp so that when we read, hear, or see something that's garbage, we take the garbage out instead of depositing it into our subconscious mind where it can fester and contaminate our thought process. Before entering the Matrix of Hip Hop, I recommend that you take a 30 day Hip Hop fast. That means do not read any Hip Hop publications, do not turn on B.E.T. or watch any Hip Hop videos, and don't listen to the radio during this time. Try not to even think about Hip Hop, period. This will not free you from the Matrix because the system is too sophisticated, and you will still have to leave your home where you will most definitely be affected by Hip Hop. However, it will allow you to think clearly and get a better understanding of what the Matrix of Hip Hop really is. If you could take a regular fast during this time as well, that would be even better because it raises the vibration even higher. Now that the easy part is done, it's time to focus on the more controversial part of our two step assignment, the ritual.

The word ritual alone makes a lot of people nervous or spooked out. Most associate it with being evil, satanic, "paganistic," of the occult, or some magic mumbo jumbo crap that doesn't work anyway. If the current box you're operating from won't allow you to get past these myths and misconceptions and you do not feel comfortable doing a ritual, fine, skip over this section, I'll understand. However, you better understand this: The very people that run the Hip Hop Matrix that have us on physical, mental, and spiritual lock down do believe in rituals. Not only do they believe, but they perform them every chance they get to conjure up energy to keep the Matrix in power. Pay attention to when they drop certain movies, albums, and major events. It's usually revolves around certain moon cycles, the winter and summer solstices, spring and fall equinoxes, or special star alignments that enable them to tap into that energy source to use as they please. I don't have to tell you how or what they choose to use that energy for, I think you already know. Meanwhile, we sit back in amazement and wonder how such a small group of people can rule so many. We don't believe in this science and it's this science that has us in awe of them! The sad thing about it is, it's our science. If they can use our science to muster up energy, magic, or protection, can you imagine what we can do if we tap into our own science? Some rituals are very simple, like burning an incense, pouring libations and calling on your ancestors, beating on drums to awaken spirits, or using the four elements: earth, air, fire, and water. Other rituals are more advanced and require knowledge of star alignments, moon cycles, chants, alchemy, which is the transformation from one state or form to another and many other elements, which I won't get into. There are plenty of books on the subject, from beginner to advance.

This is a Hip Hop ritual which won't even take most people out of their element. For instance, if you don't wanna burn incense, burn an L, Dutch, or Philly. It's really the same thing, a form of alchemy. By transforming the Philly, which is a solid, made up of herbs from the earth that are kept together by licking it, which is water. Then adding fire to it, inhaling it into the lungs and blowing it out into the atmosphere which is filled with air. That's earth, air, fire, and water right there. If you don't wanna beat on drums, then play some bangin' drum beats. Some hot joints that you can just zone out to, the effect will be the same. The spirit will awaken within you. And lastly, pouring out libations and calling on your ancestors is no different then pouring out a lil liquor for your dead homie. In this case, pour out whatever you love to drink, whether it's water, Cristal, or "Belve." But instead of calling on your ancestors or dead homies, in rhythm with the beat, call on the ancestors of Hip Hop like: Tupac, Biggie, Big Pun, etc. Even call on those ancestors of Hip Hop whose names we do not know but gave their life in the name of real Hip Hop. Then after every name, chant "real Hip Hop." State the purpose of the ritual, which is for protection and inner vision to reveal the Matrix for what it really is. We're calling on the fallen soldiers because if at any point we get lost or trapped, we want to be guided out of the Matrix by "real Hip Hop." At this point, you can add whatever you like to the ritual, but end it by chanting "real Hip Hop" three times. The rituals that you make up on your own are very powerful because they're designed especially for you. Now you're ready for the Matrix of Hip Hop.

Food Illustration - The apple on the left represents an organic food source, which is what we are accustomed to eating in our natural state. Organic foods contain coded information that enables us to interface with nature. It is also how the supreme creator communicates directly with us. The apple on the right represents a genetically altered food, which is what most of us are subjected to today. These genetically altered foods cut us off from the earth's natural vibration and send mixed signals to our brain, leaving us confused and unable to communicate with the supreme (higher self). They also poison the body.

3

ENTER THE MATRIX

Now that we've taken our first steps into the Matrix, let's look at the big picture. This is only a book because we collectively agree, or are taught that it is. Those who bring about these agreements and teachings through words, education, religion, superstitions, food, music, time, and light, create and control our reality. If we break down the word Matrix: ma = mother, or in this case, womb, and trix = illusion, you can clearly see that we are being birthed into an illusion. It's not real! However, our perception makes it very real. The mind doesn't know what's real and what's not until perception enters the picture. When one is limited to the basic sensory of perception which is: see, touch, hear, smell, and taste, this makes it even that much harder to determine what is real and what is the Matrix. The Matrix has written certain programs designed to fool our perception into believing that it is real. In a nutshell, this is what the Matrix is all about. However, we must tap into our sixth sense and beyond to crack open the nutshell to understand its inner workings if we are to defeat it.

WORDS

Words are power. When spoken, they vibrate. The stronger the word is, the heavier the vibration it carries. This is especially true if the words are spoken in one of the original languages. The old saying "sticks and stones may break my bones but names will never hurt me" is bullshit! Words can crush you or lift your spirits. Words can motivate, inspire, or enlighten you. For centuries, prophets have moved masses of people armed with nothing more than the word.

Monks have been known to chant words like "ohm" for years to raise their vibration. The word itself is composed of the four elements: earth, air, fire, and water. The earth is represented by the tongue. Air is needed to form and pronounce words. Water is represented by the saliva in the mouth, and when combined with the movement of the tongue, you spit fire. The Bible states: In the beginning was the word. When these words resonate from the heart, they hit their targets in the heart, which becomes a measurement of the truth they contain. The Matrix has designed programs to put out this fire and corrupt the word mainly through the use of the English language. English is a fairly new language and doesn't vibrate very high when its words are pronounced, as opposed to the Hebrew language for instance, which language vibrates very high. This is not to say that the Matrix doesn't operate within other languages. It has programs for any and all languages, but English has the lowest vibration and enables the Matrix to receive maximum results from its efforts to dumb down and control the masses. These same words with no power are used to describe and give life to our reality. Once we accept and download these words, we give them power to control our lives. The Matrix then creates an artificial vibration to add to these words, some very high and some very low. Each word is designed to affect you in one way or another. For instance, words like: racist, anti-Semitic, slander, nigger, pedophile and so on, all carry a negative vibration. Words like: black, white, communist, democracy, republican, democratic, Bloods and Crips, all carry a divisive vibration. This is how the Matrix uses words to control. It's a complex system with many words having multiple meanings that make it difficult to master. Even if you mastered the English language you still couldn't defeat the Matrix. It's like trying to defeat your favorite video game; it knows every possible move that you can make before you make it. However, understanding the English language and the power of words in general puts us one step closer to victory.

EDUCATION

The word education derives from the Latin word 'educare' which means to draw out that which is in. That means whatever there is to know you already know, it just has to be brought out of you in a certain way. In ancient times, the methods used to educate included music, story telling, writings, pictures, dance, and real life situations that involved a lot of interaction between student and teacher. So why is our educational system today structured to force information into us as opposed to drawing it out of us? Because the Matrix doesn't want you to rely on what you know naturally, it wants you to rely on what you have been artificially inseminated with. It only wants you to access files that have been downloaded into your brain, and not tap into the files that are encoded in your DNA that would give you access to infinite knowledge. From pre-school to high school, we are downloaded with the basic educational package of science, history, reading, and writing. Math is universal, but the way that it is taught to us stifles our ability to master it properly and use it to unlock the Matrix. Albert Einstein said, "Math is the key to the universe." If that's the case, then miseducating us when it comes to math is the Matrix number one priority. From an early age, we are placed in overcrowded classrooms with dim fluorescent lighting and boring teachers as part of a dumb down process to manufacture robots. The hallways and lunchroom are gloomy, and it's no coincidence that they resemble prison cells and mess halls. If we follow the program set up by the Matrix successfully, that's exactly the course of destination for many of us, school to prison. We're flooded with information and then instructed to memorize it at a rapid pace. We are then tested to make sure we have accepted this information as truth. This is the basis of our education, the better your memory, the more you can excel under this system. However, that's exactly the plan, have their (Matrix) information seep deep down into the memory bank of your subconscious mind so that you begin to act on what you have downloaded. Once we finish the initial 12 step program (high school), we move on to more advanced levels of brainwash programming. So it's safe to say that going to school will only make you dumber! And the further you advance, the dumber you become, because it only shows how much you have accepted the programs that the Matrix has set up to control you. You are then paid very well for following orders and keeping the Matrix strong. It's important that we become "free thinkers" and go against the grain of the Matrix because that's the only way we can short circuit the system.

RELIGION

Religion is a touchy subject for most, especially if you are operating out of one of the pre-set boxes that the Matrix has set up for you. Each religion has its own box, and its followers are confined to it. However, they're not confined to it by force. In fact, even if the box had an exit door, most of its followers would choose to remain inside rather than exit the box to see what exists on the outside of it. This is because the particular religion that has them confined, whether it's Christianity, Islam, Judaism, or any of the other numerous religions that people allow themselves to be boxed into is all that they know and all that they wish to know. They were born, raised, and "born again" within the walls of these religious boxes. Even for those who do not believe in God, the Matrix has found ways to turn being an atheist into a religion, thus creating a box for these followers as well. The Matrix is out to control your mind, body, and soul, and it has a box for each. The mind is held captive in the box of education, and the body is held captive in prison cells. Nevertheless, the most important box for them to control is the one that contains your soul. That's where religion comes in. Long after the mind and body have decayed, the soul will remain. The soul is our direct line to "God," the "creator," the "supreme being," "the one," even "Lucifer," (depending on which box you're operating from). When functioning properly, this line will enable one to truly "know thyself." Religion has placed a splice in the line and redirected the calls. Why? What is it that the Matrix doesn't want you to know about the true link between you and God? Perhaps that you are God! So they use religion to keep the lines tied up and busy so that you can't complete the one connection that could free you forever. Religion as it is used today is nothing more than a tool to keep the masses subservient by capturing the highest essence of one's self in a box that is hard for most to escape. Religion is also big business. So while they're holding your soul captive in a box, they're also draining your pockets, the nerve of the Matrix. However, some forms of religion can be beneficial if understood properly. There are two basic forms of religion that I'll focus on, exoteric and esoteric. The exoteric religion is what is given to the masses. It keeps them searching for God on the outside of themselves. In fact, the very word exoteric means outer. As long as the masses are looking outside of themselves for answers, it allows the Matrix to control them. Esoteric means inner. Those who study esoteric religion know and understand that the power of God lies within them. That's where the true power of God can be attained. Christianity is the exoteric; Gnosticism or the Gnostic scriptures would be the esoteric. Judaism is the exoteric and the Kabbalah or tree of life would be considered as the esoteric. Islam is the exoteric, and Sufism would be considered as the esoteric science. Your preacher, imam or rabbi may teach you the exoteric science of religion, but he himself studies the esoteric science. This is how he is able to maintain power and control over you. Even though those who study esoteric religion also operate out of a box, the difference is the box has depth. The deeper one travels within the box, he'll see that the boxes are all connected at one point or another, as opposed to exoteric religion which keeps each box divided. Our goal is to conquer each box until there are no boxes left to conquer. It is only then that we can unleash the God within ourselves to bring the Matrix to its knees.

SUPERSTITIONS

This is what the Matrix fears the most, one's ability to believe or have faith that an action, object or circumstance that is not logically connected to a course of events can influence its outcome. Those who believe in superstitions live on the realm of the illogical and unexplainable, in other words, the magic realm. The key to its effectiveness is ones faith and belief. This is the only thing that can give a superstition true life. The Matrix knows that the only way it can

13

survive and have power over you are your faith and belief in it …and only it, so it has created tons of negative press around superstitions to discredit them. It also uses methods to circumvent energy from superstitions that could generate real power by flooding the mainframe with thousands of made up superstitions that have no real power at all. This is to confuse and deter you from tapping into any power greater than the Matrix. It's also done to keep the superstitions with real power reserved for a chosen few. There are many superstitions that people believe in, like: never walk under a ladder, if you break a mirror, it's seven years of bad luck, black cats are bad luck, never open an umbrella in the house, and many more. Whether these superstitions hold true or not, or are force fed to us by the Matrix to confuse us is beside the point. The fact that these types of superstitions are minute in power and don't threaten the reign that the Matrix has over us is the real issue. Superstitions in the form of witchcraft, "Black Magic," satanic worship, Voodoo, and sorcery are the ones that the Matrix uses all of its forces to make you flee from, yet these are the very same superstitions that they guard very heavily. Step out of the Matrix for a moment and ask yourself. Why? Are these superstitions where the true power lies? Could one's belief in a force greater than the Matrix bring it to its knees? The Matrix will guard the answers to these questions at all cost. Rule of thumb, whatever the Matrix tells you to stay away from you should run to. Whatever the Matrix tells you is right for you, think the exact opposite. In most cases, this will lead you closer to the truth. Run to witchcraft! Run to Satan! Run to Voodoo and "Black Magic!" It's obvious that there's something there that the Matrix is trying to hide within these superstitions that it deems very dangerous to its existence. The system is set up for logical and linear thought process. It cannot defend itself against illogical thoughts and actions. Believe in the unbelievable. Have faith in forces that the Matrix cannot even comprehend. Then sit back and watch as these forces go to work on our behalf to bring the Matrix to an end.

FOOD

As I mentioned in the Hip Hop ritual, "You are what you eat."

It's a phrase that we've all heard before, but how many of us truly abide by it, or have even given serious consideration to its validity? If we eat animal flesh then we become animalistic in our actions. If we eat poisoned foods then our thought process becomes poisoned. It's just that simple. And this law is not just restricted to the physical. If mentally you're eating sex, violence and destructive behavior, it will most certainly manifest through your physical actions. What you eat spiritually will manifest through your mental behavior. What the eyes eat, feeds the mind. Just as a car needs fuel to run, we too need fuel to operate. Yet the type of fuel that we put in our bodies will determine if we're operating sluggishly or at peak performance. The number one weapon the Matrix uses to control us is food. He who controls the food controls the people. The proper food provides us with nourishment, as well as, information. For instance, eating fruits and vegetables that the earth produces for us naturally will strengthen our bodies as well as convey information about our environment's past, present and future. It's one of the ways that the supreme creator communicates directly to us. Nature has always provided the answers to all of our questions. The exact opposite holds true for foods that are hazardous to our health. It weakens the body and feeds us misinformation, disinformation and keeps us totally out of tune with nature. The Matrix has created an artificial environment which we now live in. We, as a people, have adapted well to this environment mainly due to all of the artificial foods that we eat, foods that have been manufactured by the Matrix of course. This hybrid food has served as the perfect conducer to feed us artificial information which we have accepted as our reality. Even the fruits and vegetables that grow from the earth have been laced with animal DNA and other toxins that make it difficult to receive the necessary information that would enable us to escape the illusion that is the Matrix. Everything that we eat is polluted. In the beginning stages of programming, the Matrix doesn't want to deprive you of food, but makes sure that you overindulge in it, and all the wrong types of food at that. Over a course of time, this makes eating more habitual than essential. Once you develop a habit for food, you become dependant on it, thus it becomes the master and you become a slave to it. Once you become a slave to food, the Matrix can then move on to phase two which would be to deprive you of it. We are then at the total mercy of the Matrix. We are in a constant state of devolution when it comes to what we call food. In our highest state of being, we were solarians who lived off of solar energy. As we began to "fall," we became liquitarians, then fruitarians, vegetarians, and finally savage meat eaters. At our lowest point, the Matrix has seized the opportunity to set up shop. This has hindered our ability to re-ascend. We are in an information lockdown. The foods we eat today have no informative value. The answers we seek, food can no longer provide. The creator of the universe is trying to talk to you. It is trying to provide you with the keys needed to unlock the mystery of the Matrix, yet the calls are going unheard because the channels have been switched. By genetically altering the food, we will only receive messages transmitted by the Matrix cleverly disguised as messages from the creator. We then process this information as if it's authentic. Once it seeps into our DNA, it's a wrap. At that point, every thought we have will be generated by the Matrix. This eventually becomes our "food" for thought. In order to accelerate our exodus from the Matrix, we must begin to take spiritual, mental and physical fasts. Cleansing ourselves on all levels will help shed the unwanted pounds of illusion that the Matrix has burdened us with. It is only then that we will be able to see clearly, think clearly, and tune back into the frequency of the creator.

MUSIC

Music is the gateway. The gateway to what you may ask? The gateway to healing, the gateway to spirituality, the gateway to inner and outer body experiences, even the gateway to other dimensions. It is the one true universal language that speaks to the higher self of all. Our ancestors used the power of music for all of these purposes and many more. Music for mere entertainment was near the bottom of the scale. The right chord, hymn, or drum sound that resonates to the core of one's essence can work wonders for the soul. Even today, the right music enables one to escape the stress of everyday life, to feel free and let the imagination run wild. This allows one to unleash the power of visualization, which is imperative because our ancestors taught that "all is mental." Yet we live in a world of dualities. So for all of the positive energy and attributes that music have to offer, there are those who know the science of music well and can use its power for the exact opposite effect. There are certain sounds that carry low or negative vibrations that can trigger the dark side of our emotions like: anger, hate, sorrow and pain. There is also music that is geared toward our conscious and subconscious mind, each having a different effect on our psyche. With the advanced technology of today such as, E.L.F., which stands for Extremely Low Frequencies, the music can easily be tampered with. Harmful messages can be placed into the music that are so low that the naked ear cannot detect, but sound as loud as a boom box to the subconscious mind. There are also messages in the music that can be heard one way by the conscious mind and heard totally differently by the subconscious mind. In the early 80's, Run-DMC put out a song called, "Walk This Way" with the rock group Aerosmith. If you play the chorus in reverse, instead of the words saying, "walk this way," they say, "hail Satan!" The Matrix has trained us to think and hear in linear patterns even though our brains are far more complex. We are taught that if it doesn't make logical sense than it doesn't make any sense at all. This logical portion of our brain (left hemisphere) is only ten percent of its full potential. And since the average person only uses ten percent of their brain's capacity, which is the logical or analytical portion, this leaves plenty of space for the manipulators to work with. They can send hidden signals and messages at the part of our brains that we rarely consciously access. These signs can be right in our face, but just outside of the frequency of the ten percent that we are trained to use and we won't be able to see or hear them. It's like they're invisible. This is why it's hard for the average person to detect or even believe that something so horrible could be taking place. The word music derives from the Greek word Muse, which is the culmination of the arts, sciences, and humanities: History, Comedy, Music, Tragedy, Lyric Poetry and Dance, Erotic Poetry, Story Telling, Astronomy, and Heroic Epic and Eloquence. This sounds like Hip Hop to me. These nine Muses are cultivated in the creative portion (right hemisphere) of the brain, the 90%. This is how we make the unknown, known. It is also the reason that so called black people thrive in these areas. Our story is told through the arts, and music plays a major role in us doing so. Even though the word music derives from a Greek word, the science is much older than that. In fact, the famous Museum at Alexandria, founded by Ptolemy I, was a temple of learning dedicated to the Muses. Music can free us or enslave us. The Matrix knows this. We must begin to listen to the music again as opposed to just hearing it. There lie the keys to the story being told through the music that can reconnect us to our ancestors and put a ripple in the Matrix' grand design to control us.

TIME

It has been said that time is an illusion, it doesn't really exist. If this is the case then how can we be so caught up in something that is not real? And how can something that is not real govern our lives? This leads me to ask the question, are we real? Are these bodies and all that we see around us some form of hologram? Or is it that the only way we can utilize our bodies and participate in this hologram called life, is that we must be subjected to this thing called time. Yet when we sleep and enter the dream realm or the "dark side," time seems to be suspended. We can partake in great adventures in our dreams that seem to last for hours, yet when we open our eyes only ten minutes have lapsed. When we're asleep are we really awake and visa versa? Could the dream world be the real world where time doesn't exist? If this is the case, then this may explain why we spend so much of our lives (1/3) in the dream world. Even those who "black out" have no recollection of time. This proves that one can rise above the laws of time. Yet those with the proper knowledge of time can manipulate it as they see fit or use time to manipulate others. Do we really know the exact day and time that we live in, or are we under the influence of a program written by someone else that has us living on their timetable? If so, this only serves their agenda. How can we prepare for certain spiritual cosmic events that our ancestors foretold about if we don't know the exact time the event is scheduled to take place? Meanwhile, those who know the "time" put themselves in position to receive the energy that was meant for us. The majority of us are subjected to the lowest levels of time programming, a 9 to 5. Our lives revolve around a job that in actuality takes up far more time than just the eight hours that it appears to. The before and after affects of a grueling schedule of chasing the dollar, which is equivalent to time (time is money), dominates our lives. This may not seem significant to many, but it is. The more time and energy that we focus on the Matrix agenda, the less time we have to focus on our own. This makes us time slaves who will never be able to master our own destiny. We all would like to study more, but we don't have time. We would all like to meditate more, but we don't have time. We would all like to eat better, but we don't have time. We would all like to spend more time with our children to get to know them better, but we don't have time. Collectively, our dreams are never fulfilled because time will not allow it. And then we die. Therefore, time as it is currently used to contain us, is the enemy. Our true understanding of time can make it an ally. This is when time travel and manipulation becomes possible. Our mastery of time will mean one thing and one thing only for the Matrix, its time is up!

LIGHT

Under the flesh we are nothing more than spinning wheels of light. These wheels are called chakras by the ancients. In all, there are seven major wheels of light that govern our bodies. We use this light to receive and transmit information throughout the body and beyond. The level of enlightenment one can achieve is contingent upon the number of wheels that are spinning and activated (lit). From the base of the spine to the top of the head, each wheel is strategically placed and color coded based on its function. There's the Root Chakra (red, element: earth), the Navel Chakra (orange, element: water), the Solar Chakra (yellow, element: fire), the Heart Chakra (green, element: air), the Throat Chakra (sky blue, element: ether), the Brow Chakra (indigo, element: light) and the Crown Chakra (violet, element: thought/will). These colors collectively (rainbow) make up the visible spectrum of light. Yet the more light energy that we can activate from within ourselves, the more light that we can process from the outside of ourselves. Melanin based people can pick up a greater spectrum of rays including gamma rays and cosmic rays, especially if the proper chakras are activated. The ultimate goal is to raise the level of energy from the Root Charka to the Crown Chakra. This will bring about the highest degree of illumination. Illumination means light, and light represents the truth because it allows one to see through the darkness. One of the world's most powerful secret societies calls itself The Illuminati because it claims to know (light) what you do not (darkness). And in order to keep the masses in the dark, the art of light deception must be practiced from the most mundane levels to the grandest scale. From the fluorescent lighting in the classrooms that assist in stunting the learning process, to the sun which is the supreme light of the planet, from the internal to the external; the Matrix is in control of the light. What we are trained to eat, drink, and think limits the awakening of the higher chakras. The "chem" Trails and aluminum particles sprayed into the atmosphere, which is used to deflect the true light and energy from the sun, yet give off the illusion that we are being fed by the sun takes care of the outer source of light. The Matrix keeps us suffering from light deprivation because it's the only way that it can rule over us. Once the light is turned on, the illusion that is the Matrix will be revealed. The greatest mystery the Matrix is trying to keep from us is that there is more than one color of light that emanates from the heavens that we can tap into. There are actually three colors of light: white, black, and clear. Most of us are familiar with the white light because it makes up the visible spectrum. What we see is what we tend to believe, and that's where the Matrix would like our focus to end because it can control what we see. The black light represents the invisible spectrum or the unseen. Ninety percent of the universe is invisible to us, but it doesn't mean that it's not there. When you enter a dark room and you turn on the light, where does the darkness go? It's still there occupying the same space as the white light, it's just overshadowed. This black light is also very powerful. So even though the Matrix is trying its best to manipulate the white light, we can still raise ourselves up by tapping into the black light. Then there's the most potent of the three and it's called the colorless or the God Light. This light is basically clear, however, it is what makes up the black and white light. This light is the most dangerous for the Matrix because if one can have mastery of the visible and invisible, he or she would be able to truly see things "clearly." The end result could only mean one thing: lights out for the Matrix.

CONCLUSION

By now you're probably wondering, what does all of this have to do with Hip Hop? Well…everything. Our ancestors always taught: "As above, so below." What's going on in the heavens is taking place on the earth. There is always a microcosm of the macrocosm. With that being said, we must understand that the same programs that the Matrix has designed to run the world are the same programs being used to run the Hip Hop world, just on a smaller scale. The Hip Hop nation is just that, a nation. How can a small group of people in the world control so many? They must have a system in place to do so. That system is generally based on the eight aforementioned programs which we discussed. I felt it was pertinent to give a brief overview of these programs so we could examine how they apply to Hip Hop. There are many books already written on each program which will give you extensive insight on the matter, but we only need to understand the function of each so that we can use them as a guide to navigate through the system. In order for a computer repairman to successfully diagnose a problem, he must first be able to properly troubleshoot the system. Knowing the functions of each cable, the hardware, the motherboard, and in this case, the programs, is essential when it comes to analyzing, repairing and reprogramming a system. Yet the same rules apply for someone trying to destroy a system which is exactly what we're attempting to do, destroy this system called, The Matrix of Hip Hop. Therefore, let's get to work.

Earth

Graffiti

4

AGENTS OF THE MATRIX

The year is 2006, and on every corner of every hood and back road throughout the United States, there are potential agents everywhere. These potential agents pose a great threat to anyone who is in possession or still has access to real Hip Hop. It has become such a rare commodity, that one must move anonymously amongst these programmed Hip Hoppers for fear that if their true identity and beliefs are revealed, they will most certainly be attacked by agents in training, driven by the Matrix to believe that the latest version of Shit-Hop downloaded into our thought stream is our salvation. These wannabe agents will do anything to become agents, and their like mindedness makes it easy for agents to reach anyone that they deem a threat to the system that has been constructed by the Matrix to keep the illusion going. The Matrix of Hip Hop is just that, an illusion, but our collective mind is being used by the Matrix as a vessel to travel faster than the speed of light, bouncing off of similar programmed minds that enable them to appear everywhere and nowhere at once. The mental influence of these potential agents can be so strong that it can override one's natural instinct and ability to be free and think for themselves. You too can be short-circuited and reprogrammed if you're not extremely careful of who or what media channels you interface with regarding real Hip Hop in the year 2006. Remember, the agents are everywhere, so if you love real Hip Hop and your cover is blown, then you are in grave danger. The Matrix will stop at nothing to make sure that every black male from the age of 8 to 40 years old, dresses alike, thinks alike, listens to the same music, and adheres to the same way of life. The Matrix will stop at nothing to ensure that every black female feels degraded, worthless, and that the black male is her primary enemy. However, you are different. The mere fact that you have rejected the programming that has turned 99% of our youth into Hip Hop drones means that you are an anomaly with the capacity to retain the strand of original Hip Hop within your DNA; in other words, you still have access to your detailed files about a time in Hip Hop when the Gods ruled. It means that you are immune to every radio station, Hip Hop magazine, and video show that attempts to erase your memory or scramble your DNA structure in an effort to close the gateway between Hip Hop's past and Hip Hop's future. It means that by the Matrix standards, you are the one, and with an activated pineal gland that can clearly see beyond the illusion that is the construct, you are more dangerous than a million of its agents. It also means that at this very moment, agents are coming to get you, and time is running out! Since time itself is an illusion, it's easy for the Matrix to use it to alter the perception and the thought patterns of the youth who are 18 years old and younger because they have been literally birthed into the construct. The Matrix of Hip Hop is all that they know and they will fight feverishly to defend it. The divide between the Matrix and old school Hip Hop or "Zion" must be kept because old school heads know the truth; that you youngsters are nothing more than slaves and your sole purpose of existence is to keep this version of the Matrix alive. The further we move from its origins, the easier it becomes to suppress and conceal the true knowledge of Hip Hop.

In a generation or two, the Matrix will be able to dismiss the Gods who created real Hip Hop as some sort of myth or urban legend because there will be no remnants of their existence if we don't find a way to preserve the history, not by words alone, but through practice. If you look out into the streets in 2006, you'll see that the Matrix has successfully manufactured an army of wannabe emcees, producers, video hoes, mix DJs, ball players, street hustlers, and pimps who could care less about the origins of Hip Hop; they just wanna get paid. They are all potential agents. Make no mistake about it. It doesn't matter if they are your brother, sister, homeboy, husband or wife, if they are not unplugged and armed with a fully activated pineal gland, then they are your enemy. Instead of knowledge, most of these potential agents are armed with demos in their pockets that could very well contain the access codes needed for them to escape the hood and become full agents of the Matrix. That's the goal of many of our young warriors, but access has to be granted in the form of music that fits the criteria of the Matrix, which is violent and destructive. If their demo is also encrypted with information that indicates that they hate women, hate themselves, and are willing to allow their soul and creative energy to be captured onto a disc to gain clearance, then they could very well be uploaded into the system. The Matrix doesn't have to scan your retina or finger prints to determine if you are Hip Hop ready to become an agent, it simply has to place your CD into the hard drive of its main frame located at any of its record companies, movie studios, or video shoots. Once the CD is placed into the hard drive of the Matrix and the information is screened, processed and authorized, they become full agents and their mission, if they so choose to accept it, is to kill you. If their demo is rejected, it simply means that they have not received enough programming on how the Matrix operates and they must return to one of its many mind control outlets like the television, radio, movie theater, or magazine stand for more training and to await further instructions. The mission of a Hip Hop agent is to kill you with products like alcohol, which is one of the leading causes of death of Black and Latino people in the hood. The mission is to kill you with cigarettes that cause cancer, meat and dairy products that destroy the body. The mission is to kill you with negative and destructive thought patterns, Hip Hop ring tones that distract you from the universal tones, and the mission is to drain all of your resources so you become totally dependent on your oppressor. The mission is to spiritually kill you with religion. Now you must sit back and ask yourself, is my favorite rapper trying to kill me!? But don't blame them, your compliance with the program makes you an agent of your own demise. This is the Hip Hop art of war and these agents will stop at nothing to strategically corner and destroy their enemy in all walks of life. We are the enemy, the ones who can see, but we are grossly outnumbered by those who feel that Hip Hop belongs to the people who created it and they're just protecting our way of life, when in fact, they're protecting the very system that is destroying Hip Hop. We may have lost the battle, but we can still win the war. Just as there are agents working for the Matrix, there must be double agents positioned inside of the construct, ready to assist us in our fight for freedom. One can only hope so, because in the year 2006, the war of words will escalate to new heights as the battle lines have been drawn in these end times of rhyme. But that's the end of the story; let's go back to the beginning to see where it all went wrong.

5

EPISODE I
EARTH, AIR, WATER, FIRE, HIP HOP

EARTH

When this civilization finally crumbles and is covered by the sands of time, what will be left behind as a monument for the next civilization to study about our glorious past? From a Hip Hop point of view, the answer to this question would undoubtedly be tenement buildings, and just like the great pyramids of Kemet, these tenement buildings would be considered as sacred as any other monuments left behind by our ancestors to awaken a future people. However, it wouldn't be the architectural structure of these buildings that would be so amazing, but the graffiti writings on their walls that would tell astonishing stories just as the pyramids chronicled our journey from man to God, then from God to man. Graffiti, which is the first element of Hip Hop and also the earth element of Hip Hop, would be the only one of the four elements that could stand the test of time. A thousand years from now when they excavate our remains, they would have to look on the walls of tenement buildings to study the urban glyphs to get a mere clue of who we really were. It would then take another one hundred years for them to be able to decipher the stories being told, stories of the God Emcees who ruled the land and the riches they obtained; stories about the beat makers, the dancers, and the graf artist themselves who were the first to awaken and realize that they were once Gods. The story would go on to tell about how graffiti activated the other elements and began the alchemical process of raising a people who were left for dead, back to the God realm from which they came. Unfortunately, the story would end with the arrival of a foreign peo-

27

ple from another realm who began a crusade to destroy graffiti by removing it from walls, handball courts, and subway trains, the latter being the most critical because in the beginning of Hip Hop was the word…the written word, and the subway train enabled graf artist to spread the word throughout the boroughs activating the pineal glands of those who could decipher the strange markings. As the trains rolled by, initiates from this particular ancient mystery school of writing who chose to reincarnate at that time began popping up simultaneously. Those who are not from the God realm know and understand that they are on borrowed time. They are trained to recognize spiritual signs that serve as forewarnings of their demise. Consequently, when they saw the strange markings on the tenement buildings the interpretation was clear - the writing was on the wall that the devil's time to rule was over, so they had to shut down this vortex of energy before it was too late, before too many of the "sleep walkers" emerged from the dead. This is the real reason that today there is scarce evidence of its existence, except among those who have made the life long commitment to preserve the science of graffiti; and even today, only those with a trained first eye can truly decipher the language being spoken. The glyphs, symbols, and images are nothing more than frozen sounds bites that form sacred words spoken by the supreme consciousness. Interfacing through your interpretation of these tags is like having a conversation with God, the higher realms of self connected to the infinite one. It's the earth element because it uses matter to manifest itself. Unlike our ancestors who had as much time as they needed to carve their hieroglyphs into stone, spray paint was used because it was quick to dry, allowing graf artist the ability to stick and move undetected.

AIR

The air element is reserved for sound that has movement. In this case, I'm talking about sound waves generated by the DJ on the ones and twos. This still enabled us to interface with God, just through a different medium of sound. Music is universal, not the language spoken or harmonized over the music, so DJs mastered the art of cleverly highlighting the break beat which contained encoded messages within the music itself, and created an entirely different language that spoke to the higher realms of one's soul. Not to say that DJs didn't play the words or choruses in a song because they did, it's just that the most important part of the song was the break beat. The break beat in the song allowed you to cross over to the dark side or the chaos realm of Hip Hop because at that point in the song, no human was speaking to you in a degenerative language like English which only serves as a tool to retard your ability to connect with your higher self; you automatically were in tune with the universe itself via the melanin in your body linking up with the harmonious sounds emanating from the speakers. The mind was able to ride the sound waves into a different dimension of time and space for a short period before returning to the earthly realm, only to do it all over again when the next break came on. When the words of a song were used or highlighted, they were usually mixed, scratched or transformed into foreign languages that were incomprehensive to those who could not access the higher frequencies of sound. What sounded like gibberish to most were in fact mathematical instructions encased in sound designed to reformulate our DNA structure. In other words, music calms the savage beast but awakens the beast within us by igniting our kundalini energy. In ancient times it was the drummer who possessed the power to induce trance-like states amongst the faithful at what they called spiritual ceremonies. In Hip Hop, the drummer became the DJ and a spiritual ceremony in Hip Hop terms was known as a "jam," which was a congregation of B-boys and B-girls at a specific location in the hood that has been designated by the event's sole controller…the DJ. He and only he had the power through the use of his turntable wizardry to beam signals that blasted out of his speakers to the hood in the form of scratches and drumbeats that echoed off the concrete of project walls and tenement halls. Even the tenement buildings themselves changed the way the sound of the drums resonated throughout the jams, turning them into sound chambers equal to those found in the pyramids devised to align our energy with pyramids, or in this case tenement buildings on other planets. This was all made possible by the DJ, who had total command over two sphere-like melanin discs that he spun to create vortexes in the universe that allowed us to escape the hardships of this so called reality that we had been subjected to. These black holes were opened, not just by the spiraling of the spheres, but also by the scratching, mixing, transformation, and altering of the records original content that allowed those with melanin to cross over into alternate dimensions at will. Hip Hoppers, break-dancers, and emcees within this spiritual circumference who wanted to return home just had to follow the trail of the wormhole back to its original source…the DJ.

WATER

The human body is composed of over seventy percent water, so it should come to you as no surprise that it represents the water element of Hip Hop. B-boys, B-girls, poppers, lockers, break-dancers, and those who did the electric boogie were all of the water aspect. The composition of water changes based on the type of air it comes in contact with. In other words, the type of beats (air) that you heard determined whether you "chilled" on the wall in a frozen state, did the electric boogie in a "fluid" state, became "steamed" by beats that got you riled up and ready to fight, or you just "distilled" back to the planet in the form of the latest break-dance moves. The body has the ability to transmute at will, especially when it fuses with all of the elements at its disposal. The earth element is also important as it pertains to water because it provides a foundation for water to flow on. True masters of the water element were even able to walk on air via the moon walk. Body movement represented still a different degree of sound, the silent yet sacred geometrical portion of it. Dancing is nothing more than sacred geometry and each move that the body makes is an expression of sound without actually making any, or should I say that the body in motion makes sounds that vibrate so high that only the heavens can hear. This is how we were able to perform rain dances and things of that nature. The movers and shakers of ancient times knew the science of body movements, and that every single dance step was critical in terms of generating the proper energy needed to complete its desired ritual. B-boys boppin' down the street were also creating energy, however, the science of how to use that energy to one's benefit had been lost between the time of the ancients and the reincarnation of Hip Hop. Raising one's kundalini energy without the proper focus and intent can be very dangerous, so break-dancing without the rituals that accompanied them did us more harm than good because it allowed those devils who understood the power that we possessed to feed off of that ethereal energy to suppress us and raise themselves up. Even though we didn't have the full understanding of body movements at that time, we were still able to receive some of the spiritual properties of B-boyin' by using it to heal the body. When we were break-dancing, doing the electric boogie, or just chillin' in a B-boy stance meditating on Hip Hop as a whole, we were in fact in an altered state of mind that allowed us to escape the horrid conditions of life in the inner cities. When the music stopped and we stopped dancing, we were forced to return to the stark reality of poverty, crime, and racism which were the ingredients that created Hip Hop in the first place.

FIRE

The Emcee was the last of the four basic elements to emerge. Within him were all of the other elements combined which ignited the "spark" necessary for him or her to spit fire. The word represented the spoken sound, activated when the fiery energy at the base of the spine was raised to the level of the throat charka. Fire needs air to survive, so when the word merged with the beat, Hip Hop began to spread quickly and take on a life of its own. At the time, balance with the other elements of Hip Hop prevented the fire from burning out of control. However, in the years to come, this fire would ultimately lead to the demise of the spiritual aspect of Hip Hop by literally burning up and devouring the other elements. Large crowds began to form at the jam like particles of matter when certain sounds were pronounced and an equal vibratory rate of those particular particles in that circumference were reached. In other words, when the Emcee began spittin' fire on the mic, his voice was able to reach like minds who were rapidly drawn to the source of its energy, forming mass bodies of matter called fans, and Hip Hop as a culture began to take form. The Emcee was able to then transform and add a spark to an otherwise lifeless language, like English, by changing the meaning and vibration of its words. Words like fresh, chill, fly, sucka, deaf, wack, and so on were used to encode the gospel that was about to be taught and to isolate Hip Hop from those who were not chosen to receive it. Just as slaves who yearned to be free spoke in a secret language to discuss their plans for escape, we created a language within an existing language that served the same purpose, because we too longed to be free and Hip Hop provided the outlet to complete that mission. Once the transmutation of the language was complete, Emcees began the process of call and response by chanting, "Throw your hands in the air," and "Say hooo," and "Somebody scream." The audience participation provided the energy needed to activate the ritual; we then collectively began to raise ourselves up. The fire began to pay homage to the air that it needed to survive, in other words, the Emcee began to big up his DJ because he knew and understood that without him, he was but a mere spark that had potential to become fire. In no time, true Emcees were locked into the sync tone of the universe and began rhyming in rhythmic patterns that echoed the heartbeat of creation. The first rhymes were about partying and feeling good about ourselves, they immediately raised our energy and created a gateway for us to mentally escape the real life issues that plagued us. The next level of rhyming took us to the dream world as Emcees began to flow about things that they didn't physically have, yet they yearned to posses. We too would activate the pineal gland and journey with our favorite Emcee who was simply echoing our own sentiments, and together we would travel to the astral plane and begin the process of bringing the objects of our desire into a physical reality. Seemingly out of nowhere, there was an abundance of Gazelles, British Walkers, Playboys, Mock Necks, AJs, and Overlaps, demonstrating that the proper use of fire in conjunction with the other elements could deliver anything that the Gods of Hip Hop wished for. That fire would reach even greater heights when Emcees began joining forces in perfect harmony doing routines, immediately changing the dynamics of existing works. Commercials that were meant to seduce us into buying their products that were probably harmful to us, were converted into Hip Hop classics that did the very opposite of their initial intensions, they lyrically and spiritually empowered us. Again, this just illustrated how the Gods of Hip Hop could take nothing and make it into something, or take something that had a negative charge and give it a positive charge. In the beginning, our lives seemed like nothing, but with the proper use of the four basic elements, earth, air, water, and fire, the hidden science of who we are and who we once were began to reveal itself through the magic of an art that we created called Hip Hop.

HIP HOP

Hip Hop is alchemy in the mundane sense of the word meaning, we were able to use it to transform lead into gold. When the lead pencil hit the pad, it "lead" to gold…records, chains, teeth, etc. Hip Hop was also alchemy in the advanced sense of the word of transforming man into God. We have always been accustomed to using hieroglyphs, drummers, sacred dances, and chanting as a part of our rituals to tap into the spirit realm, today we just call it graffiti, DJing, B-boyin', and Emceeing. There is nothing new under the sun, only that which has been forgotten, so the elements of old have just taken on a new identity. The combination of these raw elements began to form what we call Hip Hop. Initially we didn't call it anything, so it had no form, it was pure chaos. By calling it Hip Hop, we gave it form, which is in essence, order. However, the four elements by themselves were not enough to elevate one into a Hip Hop occultist, you needed the fifth element which is ether, in other words, melanin and the proper knowledge of its spiritual components to become a true Hip Hop alchemist. So when Afrika Bambaataa said that knowledge was the fifth element of Hip Hop, metaphysically speaking, he was right. Knowledge has always been viewed as the foundation of all things, however, only when it was added to the other existing elements did Hip Hop take on its primary form, and primary means first. So in order for you to use Hip Hop to elevate yourself to the God realm, you needed the lost element. From the beginning, Hip Hop was not for everyone, it was for a chosen few and contrary to popular belief, it was never meant to go mainstream. Just as there are certain levels of knowledge that are not meant for the masses due to their lack of esoteric understanding, the highest realms of Hip Hop were reserved for those who could tap in. Having melanin simply meant that you had the potential to access the God realm, but it lied dormant in most who didn't understand the power that they possessed. On the other hand, those without melanin only had access to the remedial levels of Hip Hop, and at the time, that was just listening and appreciating it from afar. Very few could pass the initiation of mastering the elements of rhyming or harmonizing in a group, cutting with the speed and agility of a true DJ, pop, lock, spin on their head, or break-dance like a real B-boy, and even fewer had the spiritual insight to bring down images or glyphs from the astral plane in their writings. Hip Hop was in perfect balance until a few of the melanin deficient ones who understood esoteric knowledge yet their own limitations regarding it, were able to do the ritual work necessary to tap into the highest realm of Hip Hop that they could possibly achieve so that they could use the energy for their own benefit. Once we allowed them to study and participate in Hip Hop, they found a way to empower themselves by using it. Once Hip Hop went commercial, it was no longer Hip Hop, it was a "rap." The devil's realm is the material realm, so over a course of time they were able to lock Hip Hop into a vibration that wouldn't resonate any higher than the physical. Economically, Hip Hop was thriving, and the more sales it generated, the less power we had over it. And the more we as Gods only used it for its material resources, the less spiritual it became.

6

EPISODE II
THE LAND BEFORE RHYME
THE REALM OF THE URBAN VAMPIRE

What if I told you that vampires created Hip Hop, would you believe me? Probably not. In your mind, you'd probably be wondering what could be more far fetched? But upon further contemplation of the above statement, if you analyzed what a vampire is - one who feeds off of the energy of another to survive, even creating a food source from scratch if necessary, the conclusion reached may not be what you initially expected. Think about the state of America before Hip Hop and then examine all of the revenue, jobs, and opportunities that it has created. Now look even deeper into the situation and ask yourself, who's really eating off of Hip Hop? The disturbing truth of the matter is, we are no more than a colony of worker ants in the grand scheme of a system that has been set up by vampires whose kingdom is built upon the backs of our hard work and energy. Life itself is a series of programs whose survival is contingent upon a system of vampire and prey, the strong devouring the weak, in other words, "It's a dog eat dog world," so we are all guilty of being vampires to some degree or another. Just as a baby feeds off of its mother's breast for nourishment, and the animal and plant life feed off of the sun for its survival, we too are mentally, physically, spiritually, and even financially subjected to such vampire-like behavior. The difference is, for most of us this is not done maliciously, we only take from others what is absolutely necessary for our survival, and we then become prey for other family members and friends in their time of need, creating a balance. Nevertheless, there are those who only take from the universe, for them...it is a science.

There are entire races of blood sucking, energy draining people who are vampires by nature, whose very existence is dependant upon a steady supply of the creative and/or physical energy of others to survive. Without this energy source, they will most certainly die, so they create environments that serve as breeding grounds for the very food needed for them to feast. This food is usually made up of sorrow, hate, despair, anguish, sex, drugs, and violence. These are also the very ingredients that created Hip Hop in the first place. The horrible outer conditions that we live under in most cases, force us to turn inward and begin creating. A lot of people refer to this process as, "The pressure on the diamond." It is during this inward journey, usually to seek solace and shelter from such pressure, that we create some of our greatest masterpieces. Vampires patiently wait at the threshold of reality for us to bring these creations into a physical existence and then quickly consume them, becoming stronger in the process, while we are slowly drained of our physical and creative energy. You do believe in vampires, don't you? Not the ones that you see on television that drink the blood of their victims (even though there are those who do that as well), but the ones in the boardroom stealing you ideas, the ones you see lurking around the ball courts looking for the next Michael Jordan to make them rich, or the ones who own the record companies who sit back and allow their prey to come to them. Hip Hop is no accident; it is the effect of cause, meaning it was brought about by horrid inner city conditions (cause) that forced those living under them to create a soundtrack, dance, written and oral language, and lifestyle as a result of it (effect). We are all governed by the universal law of cause and effect. However, there are those vampires who can rise above certain laws through the mastery of that law, becoming exempt to its effect. These vampires cook up the witches brew, then sit back and wait until the stew is done. They feel that whatever arises out of this concoction belongs to them since they are the ones who created the situation that brought it about. What if the conditions that we live under were purposely brought about to create a desired effect for these very vampires? Now if I asked you, who created Hip Hop, the answer to this question may not be as simple as saying Kool Herc when you begin to look beyond the physical creation of it.

We must not keep our focus on the physical (seen), but allow ourselves to uncover the metaphysical (unseen), because it is on this realm where the vampire's true power resides. In other words, if we as a people were happy, had sufficient jobs, adequate housing, and weren't victims of racism and police brutality, then it's possible that Hip Hop would have never existed. There would have been no need for it. This is not to suggest that we would have not created a new form of music or lifestyle because it is in our nature to do so, but when you understand the true essence of Hip Hop, which served as a voice for the oppressed, it would most certainly have had a much different energy and vibration about it. However, there are those who stand to reap the benefits of your misfortunes. They themselves cannot create anything in the physical, but have set up ways to live off of your every creation. This is the true definition of an urban vampire. This system has been tried and tested on us many times before, from the days of church hymns and Negro spirituals, to the days of jazz, blues, and every music genre that we created in between. It is not limited to music; there are hundreds, perhaps thousands of black inventors whose creations were stolen by vampires. Nevertheless, it appears that Hip Hop has generated the greatest supply of food with no end in sight. A true vampire or one who understood the science could see Hip Hop coming a mile away. The seed was planted in the mid to late sixties with the assassination and incarceration of many of our black leaders. At that time, racism and police brutality were at an all time high, and jobs and adequate housing for the poor were at an all time low. By the early seventies, heroin flooded the streets in an attempt to sedate any remaining militants left over from what will always be considered as the greatest uprising of black people America has ever witnessed, the Civil Rights movement. There was no hope for the poor in the inner cities, and the Bronx in particular mirrored the images of hopelessness more that any other hood. Most parts of it were abandoned and this represented more than just empty buildings, it showed that America had abandoned Black people as a whole. We were left for dead. This created the perfect environment for something as phenomenal as Hip Hop to take place.

It is a scientific fact that every action has an equal and opposite reaction, so the further we as people were suppressed and oppressed, the higher we would rise, being privy to such information in advance, allowed the urban vampires to put themselves in position to capitalize off of our hardship. That's right, they knew well in advance that Hip Hop was coming because they planted, watered, and nurtured the soil of oppression from the beginning. Did they know that we would call it Hip Hop, no. but rarely do we just create a style of music, it is usually the reflection or by-product of the culture or movement that births it. That particular culture is usually evident in the way that we dress, talk, what we drive, and even how we think. Being able to convert our culture into a money making enterprise could ensure that these vampires could eat for a long time to come. In essence, just by living out our lives (culture), this could generate money and power for those vampires who were tapped into our energy stream. Completing such a mission would not be an easy task. Subtle, yet sophisticated actions had to be facilitated to maximize the potential of this new food source. One of the programs used was taking the musical instruments out of the curriculum in the public school system. This may not have seemed like a major move but it was because it literally forced inner city youth to create an outlet of expression from scratch. That form of expression would later be known as Hip Hop. The so-called "Blaxploitation" movies also served as triggers to bring about Hip Hop. Instead of fighting the white man physically, we simply lived out and released our frustrations mentally by going to the movies and fighting him from an artistic stand point. In other words, we whooped his ass on the screen for a few hours, and then went home to the same conditions that plagued us before we stepped into the theater. Even though it was just make-believe, it was mind control at its best, as it gave us a less harmful way to express our displeasure with the current state of our lives. This immediately changed our focus by moving us from a mode of action which we were accustomed to (Black Panthers, Nation of Islam, etc), to using mere words as our only course of action. These words would first manifest in the form of written glyphs on the walls of the most desecrated monuments in the city, followed by spoken word and then song form. Vampires are dispatched to every hood throughout the country on the look-out for that precise moment when the seed of our genius will sprout. They specifically hang around clusters of melenated people because their blood is considered to be "Black gold." Just being in the proximity of those with high concentrated amounts of melanin is like a meal for any vampire who can ethereally tap into its source. When we begin to use our melanin to create, this power source is extremely magnified. On the eve of 1974, a dying breed of vampires anxiously awaited the arrival of this new energy that would feed them well into the new millennium. From the Bronx to Wall Street, from Wall Street to Hollywood, there they were salivating at the mouth waiting until the food was done. In 1974, it was time to eat.

Prison Illustration

W o r d s	R e l i g i o n	M u s i c	S u p e r s t i t i o n s	F o o d	E d u c a t i o n	T i m e	L i g h t

Prison Illustration - Our lives are run by a series of belief systems that I call programs. These programs are: words, religion, education, superstitions, food, music, time, and light. There are many more, but these are the basics. Our inability to think outside of these parameters set up by the Matrix, creates a mental prison around us.

7

EPISODE III
WHEN THE GODS RULED HIP HOP

THE CHAOS REALM (1974-1979)

In the early days, Hip Hop or what would be later known as such, had no true form. It was pure chaos energy, meaning nothing about it was scripted, imitated, or premeditated. It was a spontaneous and creative act. What you saw or heard was what you got, and no two rhymes, routines, dance moves, graph pieces, or scratches were ever exactly the same. If you didn't witness it, you couldn't fully experience it, which meant you couldn't capture or contain it; it was lost in the Hip Hop "akashic" records forever. Some of the greatest Hip Hop moments were never recorded and never meant to be. Although they were later recorded on gritty tapes used mainly to spread the gospel, the spiritual purpose of these tapes were for a future time, which was to bare witness that the Gods who created Hip Hop were not just a myth and did truly exist. This was also done to ensure that no one would be able to tamper with the history by writing themselves into the time and space of its origins. In its original state, Hip Hop had no order to it, it was being created in real time. This is what I call the chaos realm. Those who were fortunate enough to experience it in its rawest state, lay testimony that their lives were forever changed by the Gods who conducted the sacred Hip Hop ceremonies. It was during the chaos realm of Hip Hop that it was the most powerful because there was no previous template in which it operated from or should I say that the original template (hieroglyphs, drummer, oracle, dancer), which was created in a different time and space, was forgotten by the Gods or lost in that paradigm. The template needed to create what we call

Hip Hop today only existed in the minds of a chosen few. This simply meant that there was a void and out of this void the Gods of Hip Hop began to create using the earth, air, water, fire and ether at their disposal to bring nothingness into a tangible existence. They began building a template (tree of life) from which the entire world of Hip Hop as it is practiced today would emanate. Without this template, it would be impossible for Hip Hop to exist in the physical sense. In fact, if someone had the power to go back into time and destroy the template of Hip Hop, every single one of us who's had an existence within Hip Hop would disappear instantaneously, never to have existed in the first place. The entire Hip Hop universe would be sucked back into the minds of those who brought it forth.

The Gods of the Chaos realm are too many to mention, but I will note a few from each element and they are: Kool Herc and the Herculoids, Afrika Bambaataa and the Zulu Nation, Grandmaster Flash and the Furious Five, The Cold Crush Brothers, The Treacherous 3, Funky Four plus 1, Grand Wizard Theodore and The Fantastic 5, Crash Crew, Smokey and the Smokatron, Pete DJ Jones, Lovebug Starski and Busy Bee. Some of the Goddesses of the mic are: Pebbly Poo and Sha Rock. Some of the graph Gods are: Taki 183, Julio 204, Frank 207, Joe 136, Super Kool 223, Lee 163, Phase 2, Riff 187, Tracey 168, Cliff 159, Blade One, and James Top. The break-dancers and B-Boys had their Gods as well and they included: Zulu Kings, Rock Steady Crew, Rubber Band, Dynamic Rockers, Incredible Breakers, Break Machine, Magnificent Force, Shabba Doo, Lockatron Jon, The Nigger Twins, PeeWee Dance, PopMaster Fabel and Charlie Robot. Every paradigm that comes after the chaos realm of Hip Hop is just a weaker version of the original, even if it sells more records, makes more money, or receives more exposure - simply because it is a "carbon" copy and no longer holds Hip Hop's original intent. Carbon is the basis of melanin (ether) and melanin is the creator of all things in the physical. The creation of something is its starting point, in the case of Hip Hop, the carbon date would be around the year 1974. The further it moved away from this point and the more distance that accumulated between its starting point and its current position, it lost a generation or two, figuratively and literally, so the more that Hip Hop was duplicated, the less of an original that it became. It is now the most faded carbon copy to ever exist from its primal state. Those far removed from the chaos realm who feel that they are creating something new when it comes to Hip Hop, aren't creating anything at all, they're simply living off of a blueprint that has already been laid down. Only when one expounds upon the original template by creating an element that didn't previously exist, can they truly say that they are creating something new. For example, when Doug E. Fresh created the beat box, he was adding on to the template. The core of the blueprint is the carbon itself, it holds the key and it will regenerate and renew itself, becoming stronger in most cases. The melanin can never die; this is the only reason that traces of real Hip Hop still exist today. The carbon is the spirit or the anti-matter of the physical creation. The carbon can be present in just the thought of the creation, or it can manifest into the physical creation itself. However, it has had to adapt to compensate for the loss of melanin due to the fusion of non-carbon based energy into the original template of Hip Hop. The melanin deficient ones studied the original template well, and knew that the only way to change the dynamics of its power structure was to create a new element which included them, was foreign to the Gods, and would eventually give them control over the template. The sixth (limitation, material) element of the template would become commercialism. This is where the Gods of Hip Hop began to lose control of the universe that they created. This foreign element was added to the alchemical makeup of the original template, and they didn't have the "sixth" sense to figure it out until it was too late. A universe that once thrived on chaos was on the verge of becoming order out of chaos. This was critical because the melanin deficient ones could not comprehend or withstand the chaos energy of Hip Hop, but when it was funneled into a controllable energy, the takeover was imminent.

ORDER OUT OF CHAOS (1979-1985)

1979 brought order to the chaos realm of Hip Hop by the very use of the word in what was considered the first Hip Hop song on wax called, Rapper's Delight. Technically speaking this was the second rap record (see King Tim 3rd), but it was the one song that received the most credit for putting Hip Hop on the "map," and lead to the energy of the Gods being captured and contained forever. Not only was it contained, but it was for sale. The first words of the song Rapper's Delight were: "Well it's a Hip Hop"…and from that moment on, Hip Hop was ushered into a new paradigm. This paradigm was controlled by drum machines, recording studios, record labels, radio stations, managers, producers, engineers, agents, and publishers. This was a far cry from the chaos realm when DJs just had to master the turntables by cutting and scratchin' the record on time. Now they have to record beats track by track in a mechanical manner that eliminated the feel of freedom normally bestowed upon the Gods who operate from the realm of chaos. This was a far cry from the chaos realm of the parks when an Emcee would spit his rhyme and however it came out, that was that. Now an Emcee had to stand still in front of a microphone in a studio, take after take after take, trying to perfect chaos, which is impossible. Some of the greatest live performers couldn't make records because they were out of their natural element in trying to do so, but this didn't stop them from trying to master this uncharted territory. Yet every contract signed by the Gods further sealed the fate of the chaos realm. The very language of the contracts were encoded in a dialect only understood by the melanin deficient ones.

Every thought expressed by God on wax was now owned by those who created the sixth element of the template. This included publishing, mechanical rights, royalties, etc. All of the previously mentioned Gods of rap "fell" victim to the realm of order with the exception of Kool Herc and The Herculoids who never did put out a record. The chaos realm didn't just abruptly end in 1979, the residue of chaos did seep into the early eighties with groups still doing routines and rockin' jams in the parks, and the greatest rap record ever recorded, "The Message" by Melle Mel in 1982, was pure chaos energy. But soon after this point, it would be gone forever. The emergence of Run-DMC signified the end of the chaos realm of Hip Hop. They were the first group to put out a hit record that had absolutely no trace of lineage to the chaos realm or the Gods who created Hip Hop. Even Sugarhill Gang can be linked back to the chaos realm because Grandmaster Caz of the Cold Crush Brothers wrote one of the verses from their biggest smash hit. Run-DMC represented the new school. Their style was totally different, not bad in any way…just different. The way that they rhymed was a little more slowed down and simplified. They didn't use a lot of catchy metaphors or complex rhyme schemes, which made it easy for those listening to rhyme along, and it was made to appear that anyone could do it. This kind of went against the grain of the Gods like Grandmaster Caz, Kool Moe Dee, and Melle Mel who prided themselves on rhyme innovation. They dressed like the average Hip Hop fan, which made them very easy to relate to, but by doing so, this also made it seem like Hip Hop could be mastered by the common man. Groups like the Cold Crush, Fantastic Five, and The Furious Five dressed a certain way to display style, originality, stage presence, and to distance themselves from those on the other side of the rope or stage who were not yet initiated into the art of Hip Hop. The sound of Run-DMC was the most critical component of the three. Their music had more of a Rock feel to it which immediately opened the doors to a whole new generation of Hip Hoppas. Those who didn't have a clue about the science of Hip Hop were drawn to it in great proportions, immediately throwing the template of Hip Hop out of balance forever. They didn't focus on the break-beats as much, they went for a broader sound, which lead to a broader audience. Run-DMC opened up a lot of doors in Hip Hop, but they were using someone else's key. That key belonged to Rick Rubin, who mastered the sixth element of the template. When they turned the key, they locked the door on one phase of Hip Hop, but opened it to a whole other world of marketing products like, Adidas, making movies like, "Tougher than Leather," and crossing Hip Hop over to mainstream America with songs that instructed them to "Walk This Way."

Rick Rubin was the architect of the sound and Russell Simmons orchestrated the marketing plan. On the surface this seemed like a great idea because Hip Hop was making money and receiving fame, but it was only laying the structure for the foundation that would turn Hip Hop strictly into a business for those who understood how the game was played. Two of the elements were about to be completely phased out of the equation, the earth element which represented the graffiti writer, and the water element which represented the B-Boy. The air element which represents the DJ would soon take a back seat to the Fire element which was the Emcee. The Beastie Boys were introduced by Run-DMC, this allowed those without the ether to breach the parameters set up by the Gods and participate in Hip Hop because one of their own was widely accepted. This diluted the fifth element of ether. The sixth element became the focus; everyone was out to get paid, and the art form seemed to be lost forever. God was trapped into the only sector of the template that it didn't create. By late 1985, the business of Hip Hop was in order.

CHAOS OUT OF ORDER (1986-1989)

1986 represented still another paradigm shift in Hip Hop. Even though it was still being controlled, the God energy began to reemerge with the presence of Emcees like Rakim, KRS-ONE, and X Clan. A few years later, Gods like Public Enemy, Brand Nubian, A Tribe Called Quest, De La Soul, Jungle Brothers and others were beginning to learn how to use order as a weapon. With the doors wide open now, thanks to Run-DMC and the Beastie Boys, the new generation of God Emcees began to use the media to bring attention to our struggle and plight as a people in the inner cities. They began to teach our history which reconnected us to a time in our glorious past when the Gods ruled. The whole world was listening and for those who wanted to stay in control, this was dangerous. Even though they were still making a lot of money, awareness was being drawn to who we were, and this stood to threaten their grip over us. The melanin within began to adapt to the situation, restructuring itself in the process and the chaos energy started breaking through order, creating a vortex that bridged their world and the chaos realm. Regardless of it being boxed in, Hip Hop was getting stronger and stronger as time progressed. This didn't make any logical sense, but then again, there is nothing logical about melanin or the Gods who possess it in abundance. However, the melanin deficient ones were not ready to surrender their hold over the template, they just felt that it needed some tweaking. Now that Hip Hop was being exposed to the world, they just had to control what portion of it would receive maximum airtime and what portion of it they would systematically suppress. Rakim was teaching that the Black man was God, Public Enemy were instructing the oppressed to "Fight the power," KRS-ONE pleaded with us to stop the violence because we were headed for "Self Destruction," The X Clan made us proud to wear "the red, the black, and the green," Big Daddy Kane brought style and flair to the art form, and The Native Tongues put the love, fun, and innovation back into Hip Hop. This was Hip Hop at its highest point since being trapped and conformed. What was needed to counter this energy was a system of programs that actually ran on the brains mainframe that could take the place of the template altogether. A machine world built for the sole purpose of creating a virtual Hip Hop reality that could be controlled by linking it up with the brain and manipulating the mind into believing that it is real was on the horizon. He that controlled the machines from this point on, controlled Hip Hop. This system was the beginning of...The Matrix of Hip Hop.

Here Comes The A & R Killers

Now I'll pay five grand for the head of an A & R man
I don't care if it's white or tan.
Because it's time for me to take care of ya,
the more the merrier, I grab my pump and hit suburban areas. (who's the A & R
man?)
Shit, I'm glad you asked that, a record label pimp
but when I see his faggot ass, cap!
(Why you wanna blast him?)
Because he doesn't know jack about signing Hip Hop,
it's time to get dropped.
Send em a package, but not my demo, the shit will go blast
and just crash out all the motherfuckin windows.
Jet downtown an, try to catch em lounging,up in the record
company, uh I got the pump gee.
Load the motherfucker up, nobody is expecting this,
I walk into the front door and blast the receptionist, boom!
Now the hooker is toast for breakfast, because her ass got
smart when I tried to leave a message.
Rollin on the floor she's not quite gone, I rip off her shit,
I slapped her up and left her bleeding with her tights on.
Now honey looked good so fuck it, right before she died,
I whipped out my dick, I stuck it and nutted.
Fucked her to death, now the only one left is the A & R,
I'm hawkin him, like his name is Yusef.
I run into his office like, oops! And interrupt a meeting
with a bullshit group.
But money kept on rhyming, I tried to fuck up his t t t timing,
show him the pump and the little pussy started whining.
Threw the shottie in his mouth and waited for his head to buss, cause that was the
bullshit they signed up instead of us.
I left him on the floor in a flood, and then I drew the lethahedz
logo in his motherfuckin blood.
Now it's time for the A & R baby paw, I reload the pump,
ayo Ramiek go start the car.
I pulled the trigger back, he shivered, his chest cracked,
that was that, blood spats all over blank contracts.
I watched his head disintegrate nothing but blood stains,
remains and brains all over demo tapes.
So unsigned groups get with the plan, load up your motherfuckin nine and go kill
the A & R Man! (chorus)

Pop pop pop, here come the A & R killers,
Pop pop pop, here come the A & R killers,
I'm fillin up the chamber, his ass is in danger.

Black Dot - A & R Killer, Da Hip Hop Play

8

THE H.E.R.C. GEΠE
HIP HOP'S ESSENTIAL RHYTHM CODEX

Have you ever wondered why The Bronx, which is the "Atlantis" of Hip Hop, has produced the fewest rap stars over the course of 30 years or so than any other borough? Is it just a mere coincidence or is it a conspiracy? You would think that the birthplace of Hip Hop would be the perfect source of unlimited talent just waiting to be tapped into, yet with the exception of a few marquee names, it seems like the Bronx doesn't even exist. It does receive an honorable mention whenever the history of the art form is discussed, but in 2006 it's time to deal with the mystery as to why the most sacred of places, as far as Hip Hop is concerned, has been systematically erased or its files have been deleted from the Matrix. In a system as complicated as the Matrix, nothing is an accident, every program has a purpose. Up in the Bronx in the early seventies is when the Gods of Hip Hop ruled. I referred to the Bronx as the Atlantis of Hip Hop because it was the beginning, a time before time when machines were at a minimum and the only tools at one's disposal were the four basic elements: earth, air, water, and fire. These four elements were later converted into a useful form of energy known to the modern world as the Graph Writer, the DJ, the B-boy, and the Emcee. These basic elements were the foundation of a future civilization to come. However, the key component to it all was Hip Hop's essential rhythm codex, better known as the H.E.R.C. Gene. The Encarta Dictionary's definition of the word codex is: a collection of ancient manuscript text, especially of the scriptures, in book form. The word gene is: the basic unit capable of transmitting characteristics from one generation to the next, this consist of a specific sequence of DNA or RNA that occupies a fixed position on a chromosome. In essence, the most ancient of books was never written in the traditional sense, it was written within the DNA of the Gods and later translated in the oral and written form by the keeper of knowledge. This is the true book of life. Since the beginning of time, there has always been one who has had to burden the task of carrying the knowledge of our past, present, and future from generation to generation within their DNA.

Over the years, they have come to be known as prophets or messengers. Hip Hop was no different. The one burdened with this arduous task of bringing forth Hip Hop, which would become the salvation of the people, would be none other than Kool Herc himself. He and only he contained the complete book of Hip Hop. Others who were in the midst of Herc as he began to reveal Hip Hop's sacred passages, became known as the first initiates of Hip Hop. This was an elite group in their own right, Gods and Goddesses who were commissioned to manifest the codex of Hip Hop in five separate sciences that later would be known as Graffiti, DJing, B-boying, Emceeing, and the H.E.R.C. Gene itself, which is the knowledge. Some of the Gods went on to create the art of rhyme, while others created the art of graf, scratchin', and B-boyin'. But it all permeated from the DNA of Kool Herc. Even though he himself didn't create the elements, he contained the codex of their prior existence. The elements spread quickly; this was both good and bad. It was good because the people were being delivered the truest essence of Hip Hop from the Gods themselves, but it also meant that the further the sciences moved away from the source of their teachings, the more difficult they became to comprehend or they became easily misinterpreted. This became especially apparent when it came to the knowledge since only one God, Herc, held the entire codex. So if Kool Herc disappeared, all would be lost. For years, white people have had a fascination with the legend of Big Foot. It is believed that he may hold key to their very existence. His DNA may hold the missing links of their history because wherever they search for their ancient past, they keep finding everyone else's past but their own. Kool Herc is that very Big Foot when it comes to Hip Hop, only he is not a mystery or legend in the mystical sense of the word. He is real and every true student of Hip Hop must make the pilgrimage back to the very source of his or her Hip

Hop existence while they still can. Everyone should have an inner desire to meet their father in hopes that he may bestow some of his knowledge of Hip Hop upon them. If not, your Hip Hop life has no spiritual meaning. A true student must trace his history back step by step, or the knowledge that he or she so eagerly searches for will be lost along the way. In other words, a Hip Hop new jack should not try to advance straight to Kool Herc because there will be so much knowledge lost in between. Instead, start with the very first person that introduced you to Hip Hop and work your way back to the first person that introduced him to Hip Hop and so on. If you're lucky, that will eventually lead to someone that was in possession of the H.E.R.C. Gene. In order to be blessed with the H.E.R.C. Gene, one had to have physically witnessed a jam being held in Atlantis by Kool Herc himself and then advanced that knowledge to others by practicing Hip Hop in its truest form. Obviously, those closer to Herc possessed a greater portion of the codex than others. Therefore, the further you trace your steps back, you will undoubtedly come across the names of the most powerful Hip Hop Gods like: The Cold Crush Brothers, The Fantastic 5, The Treacherous 3, Spoonie Gee, The Furious 5, Busy Bee, Love Bug Starski, Pete DJ Jones, and DJ Disco Wiz, just to name a few.

Each God contains a certain part of the codex. The further you advance, the greater the God and the knowledge about Hip Hop he will posses. Be sure not to bypass any of the Gods along the way or by the time you reach your final destination, the knowledge that you posses will only be fragmented. The final stop before you get to Kool Herc would be Afrika Bambaataa (and that's a whole other story for a whole nother book). This spiritual journey will not only increase your knowledge about Hip Hop and give you keys to the H.E.R.C. Gene, but it will raise your energy and consciousness levels up to that only experienced by those who have come to the realization that they are Gods; we all possess this potential. This is where the Matrix comes in, it must kept the God realm of Hip Hop detached from the Matrix of Hip Hop that it has created. If not, it will eventually crumble, just like in the public school system ran by the very same Matrix, it only teaches black children about slavery and Jamestown, Virginia, as if our history started there. This automatically makes us think like slaves, however, if we go beyond the Atlantic Ocean to a land where our history is rich, we will discover that we were Kings, Queens, Gods and Goddesses. In my humble opinion, the omission of the Bronx and the Gods who created the culture of Hip Hop from the history is deliberate. In order for the Matrix to have an existence, it must have a history. If I had to pick a place, I would say that Queens was the birthplace of the Matrix of Hip Hop because most people don't know that Hip Hop existed before Run DMC. Those who believe this to be true, obviously lack the H.E.R.C. Gene.

Is it just a coincidence that Queens has produced more rap stars than any other borough? I beg to differ. This is not to suggest in any way that Queens hasn't produced some of the most brilliant minds when it comes to Hip Hop, or that they are not somehow linked to the H.E.R.C. Gene because it all has to come back to Kool Herc. But none of that so called success that has been generated from Queens or any other borough or state for that matter has translated into a paycheck for the God who has started it all. On the contrary, there is a certain part of Kool Herc that is "out of this world" so no amount of money could ever equate to his true worth when it comes to Hip Hop. The lowest level of homage one can pay to a God like Herc is monetary, but it's the very least that all of those who have benefited from him being in possession of the H.E.R.C. Gene, which has transformed their lives in one way or another, can do. Even more importantly, we should all be thankful that we could still physically stand next to the one who started it all and have a meaningful conversation about Hip Hop because when he goes, so goes the H.E.R.C Gene. He still dwells in the land of Atlantis, just like so many of the ancient Gods that helped create Hip Hop do as well. The land is still the most sacred place when it comes to the knowledge of Hop Hop.

I personally am living proof that just walking the streets of Atlantis in the midst of the Gods that started it all, one can still attain some of the most advanced levels of Hip Hop knowledge. I was blessed with the H.E.R.C. Gene at the age of ten.

9

THE GAME OF HIP HOP IS LIKE THE GAME OF CHESS

So let's play a game of Hip Hop chess shall we? Or should I say, let's peep in on the game that's already in progress so that we may learn how the game is played. One must first learn the rules to a game before it can be played effectively, so pay attention. The rules to this game are not the same or as simple as playing the game of chess that you're accustomed to, which is more of a one dimensional, opponent against opponent type setting. This is Hip Hop chess, and since Hip Hop plays by its own set of rules, if any at all, the way the game is played is much more complicated. It's played on multiple levels against multiple opponents simultaneously, which mean there are enemies all around you, so focusing on one enemy at a time will get you eliminated from the game very quickly. There are players who are enemies on one level of the game that are allies on another level and are of the same bloodline on an even higher level of the game. For instance, DMX and Ja Rule were enemies on one level when they were beefin' with each other a few years back but both were owned by Def Jam on another level, and Def Jam is part of a larger family, controlled by secret societies of the same bloodline on higher levels, think not? The same rules apply to 50 Cent and Jadakiss who are both on the same label (Interscope).

For the sake of the game, some players move like pawns, while others have the power of kings, queens, rooks, knights, and bishops. Their positioning and characteristics will help you determine their status in the game. But don't forget, this is a multi level game, so a player can be a king on one level, but only a rook on another level, and simply a pawn on an even higher level. P. Diddy might be considered as a king on one level because he's a CEO (Chief Executive Officer) who has the power to make or break careers, but on another level, he's just a black CEO who's being used as a pawn by someone else with more power. Then there are players who can appear to be kings, but are simply pieces with no power at all. The one who possesses the real power for that particular piece may choose to remain hidden. The game is not gender orientated, so the queen player does not necessarily represent a female and visa versa, but one who moves on the board with the power of the queen. The game is filled with illusion and deception, so there are players who represent strong males like thugs and gangstas on one level, that are really nerds or soft spoken on another level, and straight up homosexuals on a higher level of the game. There are four main ways to die in the game: your character can be assassinated, or you can be killed physically, mentally, or spiritually. Your enemies may choose to attack your character because they don't have to reveal themselves to do so. Since most people believe what they see and hear, they can simply spread rumors, lies or misinformation that can render a player useless in the game. When this strategy is used, he or she may have to spend a tremendous amount of time and money rebuilding its image. In most cases, due to the ignorance of the public, it's usually too late.

The players that are physically killed are the only ones who are eliminated from the game for good...sort of. The energy of the physically killed can reincarnate in another player on the board. For instance, Tupac was physically killed in the game, but there are numerous players still in the game who are constantly being compared to him or posses his energy, so beware. These players are dangerous because they could be out for revenge, or may be compelled to take up the cause of the spirit that has consumed them. The mentally killed are the players in the game whose minds are being controlled by someone else on the board. These players are usually pawns that just follow orders and are expendable. These players are equally as dangerous because they can wake up out of their stupor at any time to realize that they have been played, and this can jeopardize the money or status of the one who controls them. Take Mase for example. He realized that he was being pimped by another piece on the board (P.Diddy), who was operating on level two in the game (Ownership) making P. Diddy rich, so Mase pulled the plug and P.Diddy took a hit in the pockets. The spiritually dead are the players who have sold their souls to someone else on the board in hopes of achieving greater status in the game. There are pawns that will do anything to become rooks, and there are rooks who will do anything to become kings. These players will sell out their entire race for a shot to move up in the game. Most of these players sell their souls when the have no power, this usually comes back to haunt them to the point that if they do achieve power at a later date, it's owned by someone else. So one must watch out for the soul catchers on the board, because the more souls they capture, the more power they possess.

There are three basic levels in the game and that's where we'll keep our focus for the moment. Rappers, producers, independent record labels, and black music moguls occupy level one of the game. This is the lowest level in the game. Every player on this level functions like crabs in a barrel trying to come up in the game. There's no loyalty on this level, just hate. Rappers move on the board as a team such as: The Terror Squad, Ruff Ryders, The Roc, G-Unit, Cash Money, etc. Each team has a flag that flies high with their logo on it. This logo stands as a symbol of their power that must be respected by other teams, or its war. The teams consist of rappers who are pawns, who just do as they're told, which can include anything from attacking an enemy lyrically, to attacking them physically, as well as, rappers who are kings that must be protected at all costs or their flag will perish. 50 Cent would be considered a king because of his power and status. He must be protected or G-Unit will fall. Yet don't forget that there are multiple kings on the board at one time. Each team must protect their king or they can't eat. Then there are those who fill all of the positions in between. The players who move like bishops are the ones who never come at you straight up and down. They always come at you at different angles, either with their lyrical style, business practices, or their grimy behavior. They can be hard to figure out unless you can understand or foresee every possible angle of attack. The players who move like rooks appear to be straight up and down but they can get on some sideway shit at any moment in the game, so don't be fooled by their straightforward attitude or style because on their next move, they can go left or right on you. This can also indicate that they're straight in terms of their sexual preference, or at least on the surface, but when behind closed doors they really move in the other direction. The player who moves like the knight is the most unpredictable player on the board. This is the only player who can change directions in mid air. It appears that this player is coming straight at you then in an instant, goes left or right on you. He's hard to hit. He can be gangsta rap one minute and then be on some R&B shit the next (all depending on where the money is). He appears to come out of nowhere. This is the only player who can who can leap in front of other players, which makes his cloak and dagger game tight. The queen possesses the power of all the previously mentioned with the exception of the knight. The player who moves on the board with the power of the queen is usually the CEO's #1 rapper. This rapper will protect his king at all cost. This rapper is allowed to do as he pleases by the king. He can drop albums when he wants, gets expensive videos, and receives top billing. The CEO is king. He has to watch out for other kings, as well as, his own team trying to knock him off to capture his spot. Those players who enter the game without a team are easily knocked off, unless they possess the lyrical sword of someone like Nas, who can knock off entire teams. Level two is comprised of Major record labels, radio stations, major publications, corporations, movie studios, and other media outlets. The same rules apply on each level as even the radio stations and corporations fight amongst each other for power. Level three is controlled by secret societies and elite government organizations like: the Illuminati, Knights Templar, Trilateral commission, NSA, CIA, FBI, and even the Boule, which is considered by many as the Black Illuminati. The Boule would be the pawns on this level of the game since their loyalty is to the king.

What's the object of the game? Control. Level 1: control of Hip

Hop, level 2: control of the corporations that Hip Hop will make very rich, and level 3: control of the world through corporations. Corporations will rule the world. This will be the new world order. Each player on every level plays his or her roles accordingly. Level two players are pulling the strings of players on level one, and level two players are the puppeteers for the players on level three. This game is not played on an actual chessboard but on the chessboard of life. Here's where the game gets crazy, spectators who line up around the chessboard to watch the game, aren't just watching the game...they are the game! Every move that's made on the board moves the lives of the spectators in one way or the other. The pieces on the board control how we think, what we eat, what we drive, and who we are. The Hip Hop level defines our lifestyle. The corporate level drains our finances, thus controls our economic future. The elite level controls our mind, body, and souls, making us new age slaves. He who controls the spectators, wins the game.

The game is introverted. So while you're watching the game, the game is watching you, yet the spectators are the ones who power the pieces on the board by the attention that they pay to the very game that controls their lives. When we all stop watching the game and giving it our attention, it will have no life, the pieces on the board will die. Stop thinking about the Illuminati and it will cease to exist. Stop spending your money with these corporations, and they will crumble to the ground. We must stop supporting destructive Hip Hop and allowing these rappers to tell you how to live your life, and they won't go platinum anymore. Stop watching the game and you won't get played. These are the rules to the game of Hip Hop chess. Confused? Good! Because one must be able to read the chaos to see just how orderly the game really is, then you'll see the method to the madness. As they say, "the game don't change, only the players." Now that you know the rules, it should be easy for you to see who's being played. Follow these rules and you can tune in at any time to peep the game that's already in progress, but remember, we won't become watchers of the game, we'll just "peep" the game.

Light Illustration - We are light beings that interface with the creator through light code transmissions. Due to the chemicals being released into the air creating an envelope around the planet, our ability to send and receive messages telepathically has been cut off from the creator. The sun is our main source of energy. Crop dusters also release aluminum particles into the air, blocking the sun's true energy yet giving off the illusion that we are receiving the sun's natural essence.

10

THE HIP HOP X-FILES
SUBJECT: R. KELLY
CASE: #1
TOPIC: "THE MOJO"

For some time now, I've avoided writing any articles pertaining to R. Kelly and the sex scandal that he's been facing, mainly because I felt it was a little too early to speculate or rush to judgment. I know by now you're probably saying, "Too early to rush to judgment. Didn't you see the tape Black Dot? That's him, and he's guilty!" On the surface I would have to agree with you, but is it really that simple? Is anything the media parades in front of our television set these days, especially when it involves young black males, really that simple? Or is it deeper than that? Is there an underlying motive or message that most of us are missing? Could our eyes possibly be deceiving us? Is this really about under aged girls, or more about shutting down R. Kelly's "energy" and the power that this black man possesses over millions of people? After further study, I decided to open up what I'll call "The Hip Hop X-Files" to get to the bottom of this. Now if you're familiar with the X-Files television series, you know that nothing is what it seems. In fact, it wouldn't be an X-File at all if there wasn't something "strange" about the case. Not every case that comes across my desk is a Hip Hop X-File, but this one had all the makings of a classic case. From the media coverage, to the fans response (positive and negative), to the timing of the charges, to the leaking of the tape itself, to his annulled marriage to an under aged girl (Aaliyah), to him settling out of court with two other women to keep their mouths shut. From the day that he came on national television to deny all of the charges even though the whole world saw the tape, even stating that he's being set up, to his reemergence on to the scene, to the recent pictures and new charges, everything just didn't add up. I know it seem like everything does add up, and when you consider all the evidence and behavior just mentioned, this appears to be an open and shut case right? Wrong! I told you that this is a Hip Hop X-File. That would be too easy of a case to solve. The show would be over before we even went to a commercial break.

The more X-Files we uncover together, the more you'll learn that anything that receives this much media coverage and is the topic of everyones conversation, can also be used as a tool of misdirection. While most people are looking one way, the truth about what's really going on concerning R. Kelly is hidden somewhere else. Therefore, when dealing with an X-File, you must learn to think outside the box and go against the grain of the populace to even be on the right track. If everyone is going left, you must go right. If everyone is thinking up, you must think down. If everyone is saying yes, you must say no. This will at least put us in un-chartered territory so that we can build a case independent of the masses and control our own thought destiny. This is essential because the media controls the popular view; it tells you how to think, what to think, and based on the information that it provides for you to process through its many outlets, it can easily pre-determine what conclusions you'll come to concerning R. Kelly, or any other person for that matter, all the while making you think that these were your own thoughts and you came up with this conclusion on your own. This is a science that has been mastered by those who control the media. This science is practiced successfully every day, from the 9/11 attacks (see Jadakiss), to the sniper killings, to Saddam Hussein and the war on terrorists. Rule #1: trust no one! Especially not the media, and know that any information that is released to the public through the media has been carefully written, proof read, rehearsed, and delivered in such a manner so that it will have the maximum effect on its intended target, whether the effect is joy, pain, sympathy, compassion, or in this case, anger and hate.

The worst kind of predator is the one who preys on little children, stealing their innocence, and destroying their lives forever. Just the thought alone of someone doing something horrible to your children is enough to fill you with anger and hate for that person. So when the media called R. Kelly a pedophile, most people saw "red" and were too emotionally distraught to reason with him on any level, especially after seeing the tape for themselves which "conveniently" hit the streets around the same time that the story broke. The question is, how much of it is truth and how much of it is propaganda? How much of it has been released to the public to keep us looking in the wrong direction, or aimed at our emotions to the point that we want to lynch R. Kelly before he's even been found guilty of any of the charges? This is an X-File; the truth is not on the surface. We must go deeper. Instead of taking the normal or popular approach to the subject, which is R. Kelly is a pedophile, he needs help, he should go to jail for what he did, or he's a sexual predator of the worst kind, I decided that I would try not to even address the above charges at all unless I absolutely had to, for instance, as a point of reference to an even deeper subplot to this whole mess. Yet it should also be mentioned that he could very well be all of the above and then some, that's for a court of law to decide. But to keep beating you in the head with the same information over and over again, in every publication that you watch, read, or listen to, only reiterates and further serves the purpose of those looking to control the outcome of your thought process. So before you can view the case of this Hip Hop X-File objectively, you must throw out everything you think you know about R. Kelly and the charges he's facing. Once you're able to successfully do so, you may find out that this case has nothing to do with child pornography at all! It may have more to do about what R. Kelly has, than what he did. If you're ready, let's open the case file and see what's poppin'.

First, the nature of the charges is what strikes me, child pornography. Not only is this an atrocious crime against innocent little children, but it's also a crime that those who control the media use very effectively to discredit and destroy the reputation of the accused. Not everyone charged with child pornography or being a pedophile is guilty, but to merely be accused of such a crime is enough to destroy your life forever, and maybe that was the intention all along. If R. Kelly had been charged with any other crime such as, drug trafficking, gun possession, murder, tax evasion, and in some cases, even rape of a woman of age, this would have done nothing to destroy his reputation. In fact, his reputation might have grown in the "streets" because that's what the hood calls "keeping it real." Case in point, Mike Tyson and Tupac Shakur. The rape sentences they faced only served as temporary setbacks in their careers, as the community rallied around them to show support, which seem to catapult their stardom even higher. Their attackers were not able to use these charges to put the final nail in their coffins. On the other hand, if you're accused of being a pedophile, the feelings are mutual across the board, from mother to thug to gangsta; we lose our mind when it comes to the thought of sexually abusing little children. Michael Jackson suffered the wrath of being labeled as a pedophile and his career has been in a downward spiral ever since, so one can begin to see how effective these accusations can be for someone if they were out to destroy you. The "feds" can run up in your crib right now and confiscate your computer and charge you with downloading child pornography and whether you're innocent or not, the damage has already been done. Or better yet, they can run up in your crib and confiscate that R. Kelly video that you left in your V.C.R. and legitimately charge you with possession of child pornography and it's a wrap! Second of all, the timing of the charges was an indication that he was being systematically destroyed. These charges were brought to light right before possibly the biggest album of his career was about to be released, "The Best of Both Worlds."

R. Kelly lost millions of dollars in tour money, endorsements, and record sales to say the least. This is just another part of the destruction process; (1) kill the reputation, and (2) drain the finances. Along with the millions of dollars needed to fight the legal battle, if Kelly somehow survives this, he could very well be broke when it's all said and done. This is the exact same destruction program used to bring down Michael Jackson, O.J. Simpson, Tyson and P.Diddy. The timing of the second set of charges proved to be equally as damaging. He was arrested on the set of his new video for "Ignition," which at the time was the most important video of his career because it was his comeback video. Even though the pictures from his camera were evidence confiscated during the initial seizure, it hadn't been made public until the time of his new release, why? Could it be that his new album, "Chocolate Factory" was going to be hot and along with the "Ignition" video could serve as the first stepping stone to rebuilding his reputation and winning back the many fans that he lost? Wait, it gets deeper. They found 12 photos, his bail was set at 12 thousand dollars, and the date that he was charged was 1/22, which when you take the first two digits of the date you also get the number 12. That's 12, 12, and 12. 12 is a multiple of the number 6 when you add up the three numbers, you get the number 36, or all depending how you "see" the number, three 6's (666). He later received a standing ovation rumored to be greater than Jam Master Jay's at a concert given in New York by radio station Power 105 in Jan. 2003, that's also the number 6 (1+0+5=6). His new album, Chocolate Factory, was solo album number 6. The original charges were filed in June 2002, which is month number 6. His last solo album was called TP2.com which is short for "12 Play," a multiple of the number 6. He was charged with 21 counts of child pornography. When you juxtapose the number 21, you get the number 12, which again is a multiple of the number 6. The new charges dropped on 1/22, exactly 6 days after his performance in New York for Power 105 (1/16). It's also exactly 6 days before his new album was originally scheduled to be released (1/28). Since record companies don't like to release new albums during the midst of a scandal, they pushed the date back to Feb. 18th (6+6+6). There are those three 6's again, which also happens to be during a full moon. I wonder whose idea that was? He was born Jan. 8, 1969. The month and day add up to 18, which is three 6's (6+6+6). The year that he was born adds up to 6 as well, 6+9=15, 1+5=6. R. is the 18th letter of the alphabet, that's three 6's (666), 6+6+6=18, and if you want to break it down even further 1+8=9, 9 is just an upside down number 6. He was 33 years old when he was first charged, 3+3=6. The press stated that if he was convicted, he could face up to 15 years in prison, 1+5=6. The Ignition song.

which was the first release off of his Chocolate Factory, album was song # 9, which again is an upside down # 6. The number six in Roman numerals stands for sex, which is what R. Kelly is most famous for.

The numerology speaks for itself. It indicates that there is nothing random about the charges, the timing, or events leading up to his demise at all. This is something that has been well calculated. It also indicates that whoever is behind the plot has extensive insight into numerology, possibly astrology, metaphysics, and many of the other so called "dark sciences," which leads me to believe that this is something far deeper than anyone could have ever imagined. It would seem that there are forces at work here that can't be seen with the naked eye, but exist right outside of our current physical reality. Now for the million dollar question; what energy does R. Kelly possess that would require the forces of the "dark sciences" to stop him? For years now the "secret" government has been trying to capture, contain, or destroy this force that is only bestowed upon a few men. Their best computers can't compute it, their greatest scientists can't analyze it, and their mightiest military minds can't destroy it. It defies logic. It's been around since the beginning of time and when in one's possession, it proves beyond a shadow of a doubt that all men are not created equal. It uses the flesh as a conducer, but is not of the flesh. R. Kelly possesses what we'll call…"The Mojo." I'll use this term because the technical term (melanin) is a 1000 page X-File in itself. In the movie Star Wars, they called it the "Force." This "Mojo" captivates the hearts of millions. It has the power to heal on a mass level. The bearer of the "Mojo" can be considered "The One" in his or her chosen field. Michael Jordan has the "Mojo," which chose him to manifest its power through basketball. Tupac and Biggie had the "Mojo," which chose them to manifest through the art of rhyme. Tiger Woods has the "Mojo," Venus and Serena Williams have the "Mojo." Malcolm X had the "Mojo," which took on the form of spirituality. These individuals defy the logic of the way the game is played, the words are spoken, and the message is delivered. R. Kelly has been chosen to unleash the "Mojo" in music. This is especially dangerous because the "secret government" has known for years that music is a natural healer of the people. All diseases can be healed with the proper form of music. Jazz has been healing people for years. Jimi Hendrix's music has been known to send its listeners into alternate states of consciousness. He too had the "Mojo." Why do you think they call major body parts organs? Because when the right person comes along who can hit those notes, play that tune, pull those strings that in essence begin to play your organs, the results can be harmonious-physically, mentally, and spiritually. Music is that powerful. It can make you wanna hit a club and start "Thuggin'." It can make you feel like you're the "World's Greatest." It can make the most thug player want to go home, love his woman, and go "Half on a Baby." It can inspire you to the point that you wanna scream, "I Believe I Can Fly." Ladies how does it feel when R. Kelly sings to you? Do his words hit the inner core of your soul? Can you feel his pain, his sorrow, his joy? Do you feel like every song he sings is to you? That's the "Mojo!" And to further prove my point, when he was first charged with child pornography, women all over the world began denouncing him. Then he started singing again, "Heaven I need a huuug, is there anybody out there willing to embrace a thuuug," and most of us embraced him even stronger than before. Here it is, we are all willing to embrace an alleged pedophile because his music does something unexplainable to us. That doesn't logically make sense, but I told you that the "Mojo" defies logic. It bypasses the brain and goes straight to the heart. The ancient Egyptians always threw the brain out after death and kept the heart. Logic originates in the brain, but the heart is what was used to weigh the character of men. R. Kelly is serenading our hearts. He's pleading to our hearts. He's saying people, "have a heart."

To some, R. Kelly is dangerous because he is a musical healer of the people. When you add the fact that most of his music is sexual, that only heightens the threat. The secret government has been had the X-Files on sexual energy for years. They know we have the ability to attain great power through sex, but they keep this well hidden from us. In the years to come, more will be revealed about sexual energy. This power is so great that when we have what black people call a "Freaknik," certain people have to leave the area because the force is too powerful for them to bear. R. is rising up this energy in men and women in alarming rates. He's helping us tap into the greatest essence of ourselves, not to mention that his love songs are repopulating the black community at a rapid pace like Luther Vandross did in the 80's. Just as those who carried the "Mojo" before him, that's just too much power for one man to have, and he must be destroyed at all cost.

This case has led us down a path not traveled by many. Whether you agree with all of the information provided or not is for each individual who chose to take the case with me to decide. I think we all can at least agree that there is something "strange" going on. Most of us can also agree that R. Kelly is a musical genius. However, you know what they say about geniuses, "They border on the brink of insanity," and if they cross over into the world of the insane, it's manifested in many different ways such as, the use and abuse of drugs, alcohol, violence, serial killings, and in some cases, child pornography. My only purpose in taking this case was to see if this was an open and shut case about a crime that's committed everyday in this country by doctors, lawyers, congressmen, senators, and priests, with some cases so gruesome that not even the Black Dot would write about. Elvis Presley started dating Priscilla when she was around 14 years old and nobody said anything about it. Wasn't he the R. Kelly of his time? Or is there something deeper going on that most of us can't comprehend because we don't believe in anything beyond the physical? The numerology itself is enough to make you wonder if R. Kelly is being attacked by unseen forces. Let's face it, R. Kelly has the "Mojo," that special something about him that sets him apart from every one else. The "Mojo" only uses the body as a vehicle, it knows that the flesh is weak. It can not be held responsible for the actions of the body. It can not be tried in a court of law because it doesn't physically exist, so R. Kelly will be tried instead. The secret government may win the battle when it comes to shutting down the "Mojo" in R. Kelly, just like they spiritually annihilated Michael Jackson to do the same, but it will never win the war because the "Mojo" is spirit. It's been moving in and out of the flesh since the beginning of time to get its work done. The question is, does R. Kelly know that he has the "Mojo?" In the movie "Enemy of The State," Gene Hackman said to Will Smith, "you have something they want." Will Smith responded by saying, "I don't have anything." Gene responded back by saying, "maybe you do and you don't know it."

On one hand, it doesn't matter if he knows or not because the "Mojo" has chosen him to complete its mission and that's that. On the other hand, if he knew of its presence within him, he could use its power to help fight off the demons who are trying to destroy him. The single "Ignition" indicated that he may have had a clue of its presence, instead of veering of the path by releasing a song that downplays the power of his sexual energy, the first few words of the song state; "Let me put my key in your ignition babe," taking his sexual energy to an even higher level. After a brief detour in his musical career with a gospel-like steppers album called Happy People/ U Saved Me, he has returned to do what he does best (TP3-Reloaded) but will it be enough to defeat those who are trying to destroy him? Only time will tell. The "Mojo" has the potential to make its presence felt within all of us, but most of us choose to suppress or ignore its potency because we have been brainwashed into thinking a power so great could never exist within us. Yet there are some who are ready to make its presence felt, and allow their bodies to be used by the "Mojo" for a much greater cause. But beware! The secret government has a "Mojo" radar, and if your energy is registering up too strong, they will try everything in their power to find you and destroy you. In my opinion, that's what this case is really about, but for every "Mulder" out there, there's a "Scully" who will say, "I don't believe all of that crap about secret governments, 666, or the "Mojo," this is a simple case about a black man who is guilty of child pornography and nothing else." You may be right, but you at least have to admit that all the pieces don't fit as well as you would like them to. Just like any other X-File, we may be left with more questions than answers to ponder, but we must never stop our quest for the truth. Until we take on our next Hip Hop X-File, remember, "Thing aren't always what they seem."

11

A NEW YORK RHYME STORY
PART 1

In 2001, there was a war going on in New York City. Some of the most notorious reputed rhyme families were at each other's throats over money, power, and respect. At the center of all the drama was Shawn Carter, a.k.a. Jay-Z, Jigga, H.O.V.A., the undisputed kingpin of the Roc-A-Fella rhyme family. The Roc sat at the head of all rhyme families in New York, and it appeared that this power and fame had gone to the head of Jay-Z, who constantly flaunted his riches and flamboyant style in the faces of his counterparts. This had upset a lot of families, some much older than the Roc, who felt that the "oath" by which all families must operate by had been violated. As a result, a sit down was held with some of the top rhyme families to discuss the business of Hip Hop in New York. In attendance were Nas, a.k.a. Escobar and his Queens Bridge Family, Prodigy and his Mobb Deep Family also representing from Queens Bridge, Jadakiss, the Lox, and the all powerful Ruff Ryder family under the strict orders of DMX. Also present were Fat Joe, the Don, and head of the Terror Squad family representing the Bronx. I'm sure there were other families present, but these sit downs are always conducted in complete secrecy, especially if a "hit" was about to be ordered. The subject undoubtedly was Jay-Z, the illest lyricist to rule New York since the legend himself, The Notorious B.I.G.

It appeared that no one could stop Jay-Z. He didn't honor the "oath" which required every family to allow every other family a chance to eat, he flooded the streets with so much dope product that other families began to take a loss, and he ruled with an iron mic, orchestrating "hit" after "hit" after "hit." The families felt this was too much power for one man to have and he had to be stopped. Things weren't always this good for Jay-Z; he began pushing his product on the streets in early '96. He started from the bottom and quickly rose to the top, but it wasn't easy. The top spot at that time was held by the Bad Boy Family, headed of course by his long time friend B.I.G. a.k.a. Biggie Smalls. They would often talk about joining forces and building a family so strong, that no one would be able to destroy their empire. This family would be called, "The Commission." However, the Bad Boy family at the time was engrossed in a vicious war with a West Coast family called Death Row, so those dreams of merging families would have to be put on hold until order was restored in New York.

In the meantime, Jay kept moving his product in the streets (Reasonable Doubt) and was quickly gaining a reputation for having the raw shit. All he needed now was a break, an opportunity to show the whole world of Hip Hop that, not only did he belong amongst the elite but also that he was the elite. That break would come when his long time friend and future partner B.I.G. lost his life after the ultimate "oath" of the families was broken, which was when the war he was engaged in with Death Row came off of wax and spilled into the streets. It was retaliation for the rubout of Death Row's capo Tupac Shakur six months earlier. One man's loss is another man's gain, and while the rubout of these two capos sent shockwaves through all rhyme families from the East Coast to the West Coast, Jay-Z saw it as the perfect time to make his move.

Before the New York syndicate could hold a sit down to discuss who would be the heir to the throne as King of New York, Jay had other plans and dropped some new product on the streets proclaiming, "The City Is Mine" (Vol. 1). This infuriated the syndicate and the war was on. Jay knew he would have his hands full warring with some of New York's most diabolical rhyme lords, and he needed help to ensure that the "Roc" would never crumble, so he hired a young thug named Memphis Bleek to help defend the throne so many felt he had stolen. Jay and Memphis grew up in the same hood together. He was a little wild, but Jigga knew he could trust him, and Memphis would bust his lyrical guns if Jigga gave the order.

Nas struck first with "We Will Survive," off the "I Am" Album in a tribute to Biggie and Tupac, indirectly dissin' Jay for trying to claim the vacant spot left by the legend and indicated that no one, especially Jay-Z, was worthy of that title. Yet by the time Jay-Z's next shipment hit the streets, ("Hard knock Life") it was so potent, he demanded all other families to address him as "H.O.V.A.," the godfather of organized rhyme. No matter who was firing the shots from the Lox to Mobb Deep, Jay always wore his vest and was able to escape without harm. As Jay predicted on his earlier product, "The Streets Is Watchin" and when the street thugs began to validate his power, it was a "rap," he was officially named "King of New York." This didn't stop Jay-Z from signing a Philly gangster named Beanie "Mac" Sigel to carry out more "hits" and to further strengthen the Roc for the future battles to come. He also signed a hood fella named Clue, who was his main connection to the streets. Anytime he had some new dope product that needed to be tested, Clue was always the first to get it and hit the customers with samples.

The Roc was stronger than ever, but Biggie bestowed some valuable wisdom on Jay before his untimely death. He told him "mo' money, mo' problems," and Jigga was beginning to witness this for himself. It seemed like the more money and fame he achieved, the more his enemies came at him. It's the nature of the business when you're on top, but how much could one man take before striking back? Jigga was untouchable and even though members of his cartel went to war (Beanie vs. Jadakiss, Memphis threw a few jabs at Nas), he was above all of that. By calling himself "H.O.V.A.," he was indirectly telling his enemies, "I am a lyrical God," you are all below me and you are not even worth any of my time. He stated, "For playin' me, y'all shall forever remain nameless," which rendered his enemies even more powerless, because without mentioning names, they couldn't capitalize on the publicity. This was brilliant. He also stated, "It's not real to me therefore he doesn't exist, so poof, vamoose son of a bitch." By not even acknowledging that beef existed, he could not be harmed by his enemies. Jay was winning the mind war, but his henchmen couldn't keep the syndicate from coming at the Roc. He knew he would have to finish the job himself, but this would prove to be a crucial mistake. When his hottest product to date hit the streets in 2001 called, "The Blueprint," he gave his enemies "names" and showed that they did "exist." Now they had the life and energy needed to take down the Roc. He aimed his lyrical Uzi at Prodigy from Mobb Deep on a "hit" called,"The Takeover," hitting him at point blank range in the reputation department, even providing pictures of Prodigy as a ballerina, far from the image of a thug he claimed to be. This left Prodigy's rep bleeding profusely, but Jigga was not done yet. Without even reloading, he sprayed Nas with a rhyme barrage so fierce, most people thought they were witnessing the end of his career. Even if Nas wasn't dead, Jay left one in the chamber by saying, "you know who did you know what with you know who, let's keep that between me and you," making reference to a sexual encounter he had with Nas's ex-girlfriend and baby's mother. Nas and Prodigy were left for dead.

There have been many rubouts in the history of organized rhyme. Kool Moe Dee rubbed out Busy Bee, The Force MC's ambushed the Cold Crush Brothers with a sneak attack, KRS One wiped out the entire Queens Bridge organization in the 80's, and LL Cool J murdered too many to mention. However, this rubout seemed like it would go down in history as the greatest ever. Jay thought it was over, but what he didn't know was that the New York syndicate put a "hit" out on the Roc and it would be carried out by Nas when he dropped, "The Ether" bomb. A lyrical cosmic explosion aimed at the soul of Jay-Z. It was so lethal it left the entire Roc running for cover. They never anticipated being "hit" from a cosmic level. By naming his shot "The Ether," Nas aligned himself spiritually with the heavens, his ancestors, and all the fallen rhyme lords before him, a force too powerful even for Jay-Z to overcome. By the time he reached for his weapon to release that last shot in his chamber, "Super Ugly," it was too weak to even reach Nas. "The Streets Is Watchin," and when the verdict came in from the hood, Nas was the winner hands down. This was a well organized "hit" planned months in advance, with many families playing a major role.

From Jadakiss blasting off at Beanie to weaken the Roc's foundation, to the "Don" Fat Joe releasing a blast called, "The King of New York," sending a clear message to the Roc that The Terror Squad was ready for war. The Lox went underground (freestyle) courtesy of the Drama King Kay Slay, spitting some heavy fire in the Roc's direction. And what role did Eminem play? Did he infiltrate the Roc to gain Jay-Z's trust, and then convince Jay to let him flow on the "The Blueprint" on a track that he produced, obviously mastering his flow and setting Jay-Z up to take a fall on his only "classic" album. Was this an indication that the time was right for the syndicate to make its move? Or was this done by Eminem to show the world that a white boy can take out our very best EMCEE? Or was it to let other future white kingpins know that the time was right for them to make their move and take over this entire Hip Hop Empire the way they took over Jazz and Rock and Roll? If this is the case, then the Roc was in trouble. Jigga may have had sense that the end was near, as the internal beef took its toll and his once tight knit crew was dismantled. But he also knew that if he was going down, he was going down guns blazing, so he tried to sign the most ruthless underground group in New York, M.O.P. and linked up with some more Philly thugs named the Young Gunz to try and strengthen the new Roc. It's too early to tell, but we could very well be witnessing the rise and fall of the Roc forever.

I started this story by saying there's a war going on. It's more than just a rhyme war, or a mind war. It's also a spiritual vs. a material war with many other factors involved. Everyone knows that rhyme pays, including the "Government," so when they couldn't shut it down in the early days because of its high demand, they made sure they got paid a very high percentage before the product even hit the streets. Even this wasn't enough. The government wanted to control the type of product that hit the streets more than anything else. The earlier rhyme families always gave the streets something uplifting, motivating, educational, conscious, or spiritual. This presented a problem for the government. They didn't want product that freed the minds of the young hitting the streets. This kind of product was considered dangerous and something had to be done. Positive rap was destroyed, and in came gangsta rap, followed by the playas, pimps, hoes, hustlers, and thugs. From 1991, except for Nas' Illmatic (5 mics, The Source - April '94) and DMX, the only product that would sell on the streets was about sex, murder, and material possessions, (Emcees like Common, Dead Prez, and Talib Kweli were doing the work, but weren't getting the exposure). This type of rhyme reached its apex in 2001 with the release of Jay-Z's The Blueprint (5 mics, The Source - December 2001), and reemerged at the top of the charts with "Get Rich or Die Trying," released by 50 Cent in 2003. Both of these albums had their enlightening moments, but Jigga and 50 are the ones who reaped the most benefits of the playas, hoes, get money era, but this cycle has ended and positive rap is about to make its return. There's nothing anyone can do about it, not even the government, because it's an "ethereal" energy that automatically awakens the souls of Kings and Queens. Our ancestors always looked towards the heavens for signs of change and when Nas dropped "The Ether," which means the upper regions of space, I knew the time for change in Hip Hop was upon us. Since then, more and more conscious Emcees are getting airplay. During that war, Nas represented the spiritual and Jay-Z represented the material. We are at a crossroads in Hip Hop and we must choose carefully for the fate of Hip Hop is in our hands, and the entire world is watching to see how the Mecca of the Hip Hop world will respond.

Hip Hop is a very powerful energy that can be used for good or evil purposes. Many of our hottest producers are ancestral drumbeaters who chose to reincarnate at this particular time for a specific spiritual purpose. Do not allow the masters of the material universe to deceive you into aborting that mission. Many of our best Emcee's are reincarnated ancestors who taught us the science of everything in life in the oral tradition. Let us keep with this rich tradition and use the power of the spoken word to uplift our people. Follow the sound of the drums, and hear the voices of our ancestor as they guide us toward the future of Hip Hop.

12

WHITE MEN CAN'T RAP

Oh, I know what you thinking, Black Dot done lost his mind now. He's buggin' because Eminem is nice. He can flow better than all these so called Emcees; so what he's white, can't we all just get along? A dope Emcee is a dope Emcee. On the surface all of that may "appear" true. The operative word being appear. You gonna have to follow me on this one son, no doubt. You ever seen white people try to dance to black music? When we listen to the beat we hear, boom bu dat, boom boom bu dat tss tss, boom dat, boom boom bu dat tss. This is what white people hear when they listen to the same beat, boom dat boom dat tss tss boom dat boom dat boom dat tss. They start dancing all off beat and you sittin' there scratchin' your head like, what the fuck are they listening to? Oh and don't let it be reggae music, that'll really fuck them up! The key is the silent beat. You have to have rhythm to pick it up. You have to feel it. When you have rhythm you can place the silent beat wherever you desire, and still wind up on beat. The silent beat serves as a roadmap in case one gets lost within the flow of the tempo. If you don't have rhythm, you don't have access to the silent beat. It's an exclusive club that only those with soul can be members. No amount of money can make you a member of this club. If you have rhythm, you're born a member. Rhythm allows you to flow like water, catching the on beat, the offbeat, pause for a second, back to the on beat, however you wanna do it. Those who know how to become the beat do this with ease, mastering every base, snare, or high hat. Those who master the rhythm can navigate through baselines or ride the wave of piano riffs better than any California surfer. Those without rhythm …ok let me stop frontin', white people also flow like water…ice water, yet there's a big difference between fluids and cubes even though they are both water. Obviously because white people flow like ice cubes, their motion is more robotic or linear. Maybe that's the reason they love to square dance so much. Fluids on the other hand can take on the form of anything it comes in contact with. Whether it's Reggae, R&B, Hip Hop, Techno, or Pop, we become the music while white people can only become slaves to its rhythm. If they don't step on the one beat, it's a wrap, they're lost! Since they don't have access to the silent beat, it becomes a musical disaster, even more so for those watching it than those dancing. To white people's credit though, they're masters of their own universe. They feel anything they put their minds to, study, analyze, compute, or apply logic to, they can master, so they study our every move, motion, and step until they feel they have mastered what we call dance. Then those same white people we were laughing at earlier will hit the dance floor and all of a sudden appear to be in rhythm, perfect rhythm, some of them even dancing better than you can, while you're sittin' there scratchin' your head like, how is that possible? Did they go to the cosmic supermarket and purchase a bag of soul or a can of rhythm? No. They simply mastered the art of illusion. They understand that most people believe what they see. That's how magicians make a living, they fool the eye. If you watch white people dance these days (especially Hip Hop), you would think that they have somehow overcome their rhythm deficiency. I wouldn't be surprised if they could master the Harlem Shake if they studied it long enough and I know black people who can't do that dance, but they still can't feel the music. They still can't hear the silent beat. They still can't master the rhythm. What they can do is mimic our steps so perfectly, that they appear to be in tune.

I say all of that to ask the question, if white people can't dance because they don't have rhythm, can't feel the music, or hear the silent beat, what makes you think they can rap when the same rules apply? That would be cosmically impossible. That's right, cosmically. Rhythm is one of the seven universal principles. The others being, mentalism, correspondence, vibration, polarity, gender, and causation. Rhythm is the heartbeat of the universe. Everything is affected by it. Our world revolves around a cosmic rhythm method. Our heart beats in rhythm. A woman's period flows on a 28 day rhythm cycle. Some people have sex using the rhythm method. When I bop down the street, I'm in rhythm with the universe. Spring, summer, fall, and winter, flows in rhythm. The planets orbit the sun in rhythm. You get the point. So when an Emcee steps up to the mic to spit, it's not just words that are coming out of his or her mouth. They're rhythmic wave patterns that create a ripple affect in the entire universe. Some are more complicated than others, but no two flows are exactly alike. Rhythm is like your cosmic DNA or finger print, it's designed specifically for you. Once you add music to the mix, which is vibrating on a whole other rhythmic frequency, it opens up your frequency channels and allows others who are listening to lock into it and travel with you. When your verse is over, so is the journey. This will only work if the Emcee truly feels every word that he spits. The more an Emcee feels, the more his words resonate from the soul (there's that word again). Every word has a vibration, some very subtle and some very powerful. That's the reason that some Emcees are felt more than others. It doesn't matter if he's kickin' conscious rap or gangsta rap. If the people feel you, they feel you, other than that, it's just a whole bunch of words that rhyme.

Here's where the problem lies, how many white rappers have you truly felt? Once you get past the bangin beats that were most likely provided by someone who was rhythmically in tune, what's really there? It's important that you are able to differentiate between the two because the mesmerizing beats can easily fool one into accepting a fake flow as authentic. In the 80's, a rap group called 3rd Base which consisted of two white rappers by the names of Emcee Serch and Pete Nice attempted to tap into the pulse of Hip Hop and make their presence felt. They used their black DJ as a cosmic ground to gain access to frequencies that would have normally been off limits to them. Because they respected hip hop, and didn't violate any of our rhythmic laws, we accepted them as somewhat "legit." Their rhyme flow was very basic. They did enjoy a fair amount of success, but how much was generated by them being a novelty, the beats, or mad lyrical skills? Before them were the Beastie Boys. They didn't even attempt to cop our flow. They simply put out a frequency that only white people could tune into and were very successful at it. But real hip hop heads weren't feeling them and felt they were violating the rhythmic laws of Hip Hop to make money. Not to be outdone, Vanilla Ice entered the picture and did the exact same thing as the Beastie Boys, but claimed to be a soul brother by initiation. His outlandish stories of being raised in the hood by the keepers of the rhythm got him banned for life from a wide range of Hip Hop frequencies. Everlast was ever fast to disappear into the Hip Hop Diaspora after commanding heads to "Jump Around." He quickly migrated to Rock, which was more of a frequency that he could relate to. After years of study, analyzing, and applying logic to the laws of rhythm, they finally discovered one who could seemingly master our flow. His name was Eminem. You can tell that he studied our technique well because he almost sounds authentic. And with Dr. Dre, one of the greatest Hip Hop rhythm makers of our time providing the tracks, it's hard to escape the frequency that he has created. White people are very proud of Eminem, because one of their own has finally been able to break the code of rhythm, even reign supreme over many Emcees who were born with soul. By now we have all heard the classic song Renegade, which features Jay-Z and Eminem, that appears to show the lyrical prowess of Eminem over our master lyricist Jay-Z, but let's look at the situation a little closer. This is just speculation but I'm pretty sure it all went down something like this: Eminem produced the track and shipped it to Jay. Jay spit an authentic flow of complicated rhyme patterns filled with words that he truly felt on the track. He then shipped the track back to Eminem who studied, analyzed, computed, and applied logic to Jay-Z's flow. After translating it into something he could process, Eminem mastered Jay-Z's flow, then spit it back on the same track better than the original. Jay-Z in his haste to get the "Blueprint" to the streets, overlooked the significance of the lyrical match up, and took an "L." It's easy to fool the eye, but Eminem is on some new shit by trying to fool the ear, and by the looks of things on the streets, most are already sold on the fact that Eminem is the real thing. But I know better. I don't care if he wrote a million rhymes, it takes much more to be a real Emcee. You may be able to fool many who have bought into this Hip Hop Matrix, but one can never fool the universe.

There's a Coogi sweater, and there's a "Coogi" sweater. There's a diamond, and there's a cubic zirconia. Both appear authentic, even to the naked eye, but only one is the real thing. There are tools and methods used to distinguish real sweaters and diamonds from the fakes. Just as Hip Hop has methods one can follow to weed out real Emcees from those appearing real. You can't just rely on what you see and hear, you have to go much deeper and rely on what you feel. You have to open up your soul and allow the rhythmic patterns of an Emcee to calibrate your own rhythmic frequencies to validate its authenticity, but you have to master the method quickly because Eminem is about to give birth to a nation of white Emcees whose flow will rival some of the greatest lyrical masters. He even left the blueprint for success on the inside covers of his latest album. This was a step by step rhythmic roadmap for white Emcees to follow to help them break the code. Think about it. When was the last time a rapper wrote the lyrics to his album on the inside CD cover? Either all of this makes sense to you, or I'm just the mad journalist who's hating because Eminem is nice and I can't deal with the fact that he's white. It's probably a little bit of both, but I'm still gonna stand firm on my position that "White Men Can't Rap."

Battery Illustration

Battery Illustration - We are carbon based beings (dark light). Every living organism on the planet has some form of carbon in it, the amount may differ. Black people have the greatest concentrated amount of carbon than any other people. We also call this carbon by another name, melanin or dark matter. Its remedial function is to provide protection from the cancerous rays of the sun, but its spiritual function is far greater. Melanin also has healing properties to cure any and all diseases when it's properly charged and untainted.

13

WE BE LIKE ROACHES

As I began to pour boric acid in every crack and crevice in my apartment to try and rid myself of the constant roach problem that I was having, I noticed that I had to keep changing the brand of boric acid every three months because, after a while, the roaches seemed to become immune to its potency. Not only do they return, but they seem to return in greater numbers than before. This lead me to ask myself, "Will we ever be able to totally exterminate roaches or is their will to live and survive greater than any boric acid, roach spray, combats or roach motel that we can create?" After studying the origin and history of roaches a little further, the answer to this question became painfully obvious, no! As I stepped on a few who tried to flee the scene, a conscious voice in my head said, "How would you liked to be stepped on or sprayed" or "How would you like it if someone viewed you as a pest and tried to exterminate every man, woman and child of your race?" Then it hit me. We be like roaches.

Ok, before I lose you, let me explain. Crack cocaine is a form of boric acid that has been strategically planted on every corner in our neighborhood to kill us off. It's so potent, that it kills those who ingest it (physically or mentally) and the crimes and lifestyles associated with it force roaches, uh...I mean families, to flee. Yet, just like boric acid, after a while we became immune to crack. We even became immune to seeing crack dealers, crack heads and crack babies on every corner. However, to the dismay of the "exterminators," our will to live and survive is greater than their will to kill us and, once again, life begins to flourish in our communities at a quickening pace. This war between the "exterminators" and "roaches" has been going on for many, many years. Every time the "exterminators" create a new or more potent form of boric acid, whether its heroin in the 60's, cocaine in the 70's or crack cocaine, we lose millions in the battle, but we find a way to somehow win the war of survival, why? We be like roaches.

One of the most common weapons used to kill roaches has always been roach spray, yet every time I look out of my window and see these crop duster type planes leaving clouds of "chem" trails in the sky, I can't help but wonder if we're being sprayed like roaches with some toxic or hazardous chemicals that are killing us slowly, or what about the roach motels where "roaches check in but they don't check out?" Is this any different than the prison systems where most of our young brothers check in but they don't check out? Or if they do check out, they aren't the same, in most cases for creepin' in the "dark" trying to get their hands on a few "crumbs" to feed their families. Unfortunately, when Five-O flashes that bright "light" on us and we "scatter," a few of us get caught. Then came the combats, where roaches enter, take the poisons, go back to their hiding places and kill thousands of others including their eggs. Is this any different than the school systems where everyday whether in the first grade or in college we're mentally poisoned with lies about George Washington and Christopher Columbus? We then take this poison back to our communities and teach it to our families to mentally kill them. This poison is so lethal that it even affects our "seeds" who in most cases, are "born" dead. Then there is the church that's found on just about every other corner that poisons us spiritually with "holy lies" that omits or degrades our presence in the scriptures. We also take this poison back to our communities and inject it deep into the souls of our families, even killing the 'eggs' that enable us to be spiritually "born again," and yet still we rise in alarming numbers! We must be like... well, you get the point.

According to Paul Guillebeau, an Entomologist with the University of Georgia Extension Service, roaches have been around for over 300 million years. He also states, "They have changed very little, according to fossil evidence." Further stating, "You usually find larger populations in cities due to the number of apartment buildings." Roaches need three things to form a population, food, moisture and shelter. "Apartment buildings usually provide all of these," he said. "Once a few get established, it doesn't take long for a huge population to form." In another published report entitled, "Roach Facts," it states that roaches are native of Western Asia and Northern Africa. Roaches were carried all over the world in wooden ships. White roaches are those that have shed their skin. In some countries, roaches are delicacies. And some female roaches mate once and are pregnant for the rest of their lives. You know where I'm going with this. We are the only people with a history that can date back at least 300 million years. As a matter of fact, we have no birth record. We reached the shores of North America in ships, some as slaves and some as navigators. At one point, we called this entire planet Asia (Asiatic Blackman), but our greatest legacy can be found in Africa. A large portion of our population can be found in the cities due to the number of apartment buildings. Once a few of us get established, it doesn't take long for us to start making babies and create a large population, and we too need three things to form a population: food, clothing and shelter. Now that's scary. Furthermore, we all know that "brother" who wants to be white so bad, that he would die to shed his skin, or what about that "chicken head" with so many kids, it seems like she was pregnant her entire life? Oh and let's not forget, there are those who see us as a tasty food, Jeffrey Dahmer can attest to that. It appears that of the roach world, they are the microcosm and we are the macrocosm. So before you kill that roach that just crawled across your T.V., understand that his fight to survive is no different then your own.

Now for some of the other "boric acids" that have plagued our communities for centuries: white sugar is a boric acid. White salt is a boric acid. White milk is a boric acid. White bread, white flour and white rice are all boric acids that are used to kill us on a daily basis. High blood pressure and diabetes are two of the leading causes of death of "so called" African American people. These sugars, salts and starches are deadly and are made readily available for us to consume and die. With all of the growth hormones added to the milk, which has been known to cause asthma and breast cancer, it too has become detrimental to the health of black people, and it's free for young mothers in the "hood" to ensure that they start the "death" process of their children early. When the Europeans came in contact with the Indians, they wiped them out with guns and diseases. Those who survived had to flee like roaches. When the Europeans came in contact with black people, they wiped us out or forced us into bondage. Even in ancient times, they slaughtered us and destroyed our institutes of higher learning like our libraries (Alexandria) and monuments (Sphinx), forcing us to flee "like roaches" into foreign lands. When it comes to music, the process is the same; we created Jazz music for the purpose of lifting us up spiritually, once that "boric acid" element was added to the equation, it poisoned the energy. We then created Rock and Roll to try and reestablish a new foundation for this spiritual energy, today if you listen to Rock and Roll, you would never know that we were its original creators. Again, we had to flee the scene or be musically annihilated. Now Hip Hop is facing extermination. When Hip Hop came from the heart, it resonated at a higher frequency, once that deadly element entered into the picture and turned it into a multibillion dollar business, it killed the essence of the art form, and ten years from now, it will be dominated by white artists, causing the roaches that haven't been killed to somehow become immune to this poison or flee and create a new form of music to survive. The number one rule that all roaches must adhere to or face elimination is, "stay away from everything white."

I can't help but wonder if the immune system of a roach is so sophisticated that once poisoned, over a period of time, it has the ability to somehow recognize, analyze, and create a defense mechanism that renders the boric acid useless. This is no different than our ability to fight off Aids, Ebola and other man made diseases created to destroy us on a global level. However, the "exterminators" are constantly at work inventing new biological weapons of mass destruction to totally eliminate us. We can run but we can't hide from their relentless pursuit. We must fight. We must find new ways to heighten our defense mechanisms. We must meditate, eat right (physically, mentally, and spiritually) and we must draw on the energy of our ancestors. They were victims of the very "exterminators" that we are fighting and would love a little payback. And just like roaches, we will survive. After all, we've been here long before the "exterminators" and we'll be here long after they're gone.

It is said that roaches are the only things that can survive a nuclear blast. Yet, when I looked out into my community after the 9/11 attacks, to my surprise, no one seemed a bit too concerned about their survival if this was to escalate into a nuclear war. In fact, we never even missed a beat. People still went to work, children still came outside to play, and "fellas" were still on the corner "puffin'" blunts like nothing ever happened. This lead me to ask myself, "Do we know something that they don't?" Who else could survive under the horrid conditions we live in and still say, "There's no place like home," but us. Who else could survive off mere crumbs and still have a thriving population, but us. Who else could survive the physical, nuclear and biological attacks on our very existence and still look forward to tomorrow, but us. And who else have those "roachy" family members that seem to crawl up from under a rock as soon as we invite company over and embarrass us to the point that we try to act like we don't even see them, but us. We be the ones with the will to live and survive. We be the ones who can adjust to any and all conditions set before us. We be the ones that when all the smoke clears, will be the last ones standing. And whether you're willing to admit it or not…we be like roaches.

Music Illustration - The higher frequencies of sound create a certain affect on the human psyche, usually stimulating the upper chakras, creating a sense of happiness or bliss. Bass driven sounds are of a lower frequency, usually resonating around the root (lower) chakra, creating a sense of sexual urgency or violent behavior.

14

THE THEYS - PART 1
A SCI-FI HIP HORROR STORY
THE FALL OF THE GODS AND THE PROPHECY OF HIP HOP

The year is 2011; Hip Hop has become a religion, political movement, and corporation. Gone are the days of Christianity, Judaism, and Islam where people worshipped mystery Gods or put their faith and money in the hands of corrupt ministers, priests, and Imam's. Now, when you walk the streets, you hear the faithful screaming, "Tupac is coming soon!" Or you're being bombarded with pamphlets that read: "Biggie saves," not to mention the "Jayhova's" Witnesses who you try to avoid at all cost. There's not a day that goes by when you won't hear someone arguing over the true race and origin of Tupac. Instead of churches on every corner, you find temples of Hip Hop, where the congregation meets to hear the lord Emcee spit the daily word. Samplers, drum machines and keyboards replace the tambourine, drums and organs, and the choir is made up of Emcee's who drop choruses and hooks after every sixteen bars from the lord Emcee's sermon. An open mic is set up for all who wish to blesstify. All positions of office are held by Hip Hop politicians appointed to uphold the laws of the streets. Hip Hop has become the biggest corporation in the world. Everyone is united under one flag, which is made up of a turntable, microphone, spray paint can, and a break-dancer. The future of Hip Hop seemed like heaven on earth, right? Wrong! It was a living nightmare. Hip Hop was being controlled by a foreign people for the sole purpose of their survival. The year 2012 would mark the beginning of the end for all who were not true practitioners of the science of Hip

Hop. The world was reduced to two types of people and both were preparing for the final war of the world as we knew it. One people were the originators of Hip Hop, these people were called the Gagotus and were spiritually ready to make the transition beyond 2012 and into the next paradigm. The other people were an enigmatic race called the Theys. They were not spiritually in tune with the universe, but would spend countless years attempting to morph themselves into spiritual beings or fool the universe into believing that They were authentic, and perhaps be granted a pass into the next dimension. Both agreed that Hip Hop was the key, one was naturally Hip Hop, and the other was artificially Hip Hop. These are their stories...

The Gagotus are the original people who have no birth record. Before there was anything called time, there were the Gagotus, Gods and Goddesses of the universe who were not limited to any physical form, planet or dimension. This race of people possessed a cosmic substance that gave them superpowers. This substance enhanced their physical, mental, psychic, clairvoyant, and spiritual ability. This substance was called melanin. Every living organism in the universe possesses melanin, but the Gagotus have the most concentrated portion of any living being. It's made up of the same substance that the entire universe is, Dark Matter. Black holes in space are nothing more than melanated port holes to other dimensions, so time travel was rather easy for the Gagotus who mastered the science of raising their vibration and melanin output to gain access to any dimension desired. The Gagotus were green in color. The men stood 6 to 8 feet tall with chiseled bodies that were rivaled by none. The men were the best providers, protectors, and warriors. The women possessed unearthly beauty and grace. The Gagotu women were the best nurturers, mothers, and lovers. The Gagotus were peaceful beings who lived off the energy of the sun in the daytime, and made more melanin at night so there was no need for food. These were advanced beings that possessed one eye that sat in the middle of their foreheads. This eye represented a fully activated pineal gland that could pick up thought patterns, auras, and sound waves. The Gagotus spoke through their eye, there was no need to verbally speak since that was considered as a lower form of communication. In ancient times, the Gagotus were so mentally powerful, that anything thought of in the mind instantly manifested in the physical, then came the "fall." This locked the Gagotus into the third dimension, a dimension solely based on five physical senses which were: see, hear, smell, taste, and touch. Their bodies had to mutate to adjust to being trapped. This mutation caused them to form digestive systems, change their skin color to black or brown, learn to speak verbally, and the eye that used to protrude out of the middle of their foreheads called "The First Eye," which served as the "All Seeing Eye," had closed up, forcing them to create two additional eyes that only picked up holographic images. This mutation didn't happen overnight, it took millions of years. Over a course of time, virtually all of them had forgotten their history and origin except 24 master Gagotus who had foreseen this tragedy coming. However, it could not be stopped. It was a cycle that had to run its course. These were the top scientists of their time, whose first eye was still activated and could see the future well in advance. The masters would cleverly leave monuments, artifacts, and papyruses that would be used to trigger the awakening of the Gagotus and return them back to their state of Godliness when the time was right. These master Gagotus were the only ones who knew of the exact time and place that such an event would take place. Most of the monuments were strategically placed on energy grid lines that harnessed tremendous electromagnetic energy, and then the masters ascended into another dimension to avoid being trapped in the physical body. In the meantime, the "Dead" cycle would be ruled by...The Theys.

They are a new race of people. However, no one knows exactly when They arrived. They were taught the science of tricknowledge by a master They called Semos. This tricknowledge enabled them to write themselves deep into ancient history, then The Theys covered up the truth with lies, confusion, and misinformation. Semos was the first teacher of the Theys. Legend had it that a master Gagotu named Dr. Bucay had created The Theys out of the lowest and weakest germ of the Gagotus. It was said this was done to serve as a roadmap for the Gagotus to find their way back to being Gods and Goddesses. Polarity ruled the third dimension, up, down, left, right, high, and low. Everything had an opposite except the Gagotus. Dr. Bucay understood that in order for the Gagotus to reawaken to realize that they're Gods and Goddesses, his people needed to know and study the exact opposites of themselves, so he created The Theys as a blueprint, using a science very similar to cloning. The Theys physically resembled the Gagotus in the sense that they had two arms, a head, and two legs but were much frailer in appearance. Their skin was very pale as well and could only come out during the nighttime hours because the sun would burn them instantly. They never had the one eye sight of the Gagotus, and Dr. Bucay purposely limited one important ingredient, Melanin. They possessed just enough melanin to function and survive on a physical level. They could not tap into the spirit realm, time travel, foresee the future, or shape shift like the Gagotus. This made them strictly material beings who could not survive outside of the third dimension. Being the exact opposite of the Gagotus, They were evil, violent, vicious, devious, and deadly. The Theys had a thirst for blood that was unrivaled and They were rumored to war for hundreds of years at a time. They loved to drink the blood of their enemies, and when there were no enemies, They would war with each other just to make more blood. Yet, the blood with melanin is what They were really after. Semos had taught them that if they drank the blood of a Gagotus, The Theys would inherit pure melanin and the power to escape the third dimension. However, only a selected few, who were part of a secret society called, The Illumi Nation had access to this information and the true history of who They were. Over the years, They would pass down this science in secret ceremonies to those initiates who took the oath to never reveal their true nature. They are the ones who had all the power. They are the ones who were given the science of how to rule the Gagotus and They are the ones who ruled the physical world. This war between the Theys and the Gagotus would go on for close to six thousand years. They wreaked havoc on the Gagotus, killing, torturing, and enslaving the men, women, and babies. But the high priest of the Theys knew that their time to rule was limited, yet They didn't know when. They continued to search for signs that would indicate the end of their reign.

By the early 1900's, The Theys had come across a secret papyrus left by the ancient Gagotus that revealed to them the devastating news that They had searched so long for. The papyrus read, "The gateway to the temple was through the ear lobe, the new religion would be a form of music, and the year 2012 would be the year that the planet would begin to shift into the fourth dimension destroying all of those who weren't true followers of the new religion." The total shift would take place between the years of 2012 and 2019. During this time, seven years would seem like seven days as the Gagotus and true followers of Hip Hop would mutate back into their original state of being God. Those caught in the quickening of the shift would have to be spiritually in tune or death was certain, even if you were a Gagotu. The gateway would not recognize race but energy, so if you thought like a They but you were a Gagotu, you would perish along with them. The papyruses also revealed that the gridlines were gateways for this energy that would reawaken the Gagotus to enter the earth. The Theys knew the exact location of all of these gateways, except one. Lastly, the papyruses spoke of a cosmic event that would signify the last days of the third dimension. This event would start the cosmic countdown to the end of time as we know it. At that time, there would be total chaos on earth. With this secret information, The Theys began to guard all the gateways in search of the energy that would destroy them. Their greatest scientist worked feverishly around the clock in an attempt to manipulate or alter time. The Theys wanted to keep the earth in the third dimension long enough for them to find a way to make it into the fourth dimension. They also searched to no avail to find the missing energy gridline.

In 1974, the search was over. The energy that would reawaken the Gagotus would emerge in the middle of....The South Bronx! Out of all the places The Theys looked, They never would have thought it would appear in the most run down, burnt out, crime ridden, and unsacred place. Yet, the ancient Gagotus knew this would be the last place They would look and by time The Theys figured it out, it would be too late. The movement had begun, and the energy was amongst the people. Instantaneously, Hip Hop was born. There was no sign of its coming. It just happened. The pioneers of Hip Hop were ancient Gagotus who had chosen to reincarnate at this time to destroy The Theys, and to return the earth back to its original people, but The Theys had other plans. They had become technologically advanced, and vowed to use all of their resources and sciences to shut down the spiritual energy of Hip Hop. Their most advanced initiates of the Illumi Nation were wizards and master illusionists who learned how to tap into the melanin supply of the Gagotus to use it against them. Their main objective was to absorb this spiritual energy that was against them and convert it into a material energy that would aid in their survival on a physical level. They wanted to use Hip Hop to keep the planet in the third dimension, however, it would not be easy. The four elements of Hip Hop had already begun to form, creating an alchemical process that was transforming the people. The four elements were the word, the beat, the dance, and the art. The ancient Gagotus mastered the science of alchemy, which was a science of manipulating earth's elements (earth, air, fire, and water), to make pure gold on a spiritual level. The Gagotus were mutating back into the Gods of ancient times, using their melanin in conjunction with the other elements. Sensing what was about to happen, The Theys used their sciences to manipulate the elements of Hip Hop to make gold on a material level, gold records! Their wizardry was beginning to work.

Those Gagotus, who traveled Fantastic distances, knowing that upon arrival the climate would be Treacherous, still came to unleash the Furious Forces that would awaken the Gagotus, were stunned to find that The Theys had set a trap and Bam! The first mission was Cold Crushed. The next platoon of Gagotus to reincarnate calling themselves Gods, Kings, Queens, and Teachers, claiming to speak in Native Tongues and possessing the Lite to fulfill their Quest to awaken The Poor Righteous Teachers, were quickly made Public Enemy #1. (Get it?)

The evil forces of The Theys was conquering the spiritual ener-gy of Hip Hop and destroying millions of Gagotus in the process. Would The Theys succeed in keeping the planet in the third dimen-sion so They could continue their rule over the Gagotus? Or would the Gagotus use the true essence and spirit of Hip Hop to accelerate the ascension of earth into the fourth dimension, destroying The Theys in the process? Dunn! Dunn! Dunn! Duuunn! Stay tuned for the next episode of The Theys called, The Takeover: He Who Controls Hip Hop, Rules the World.

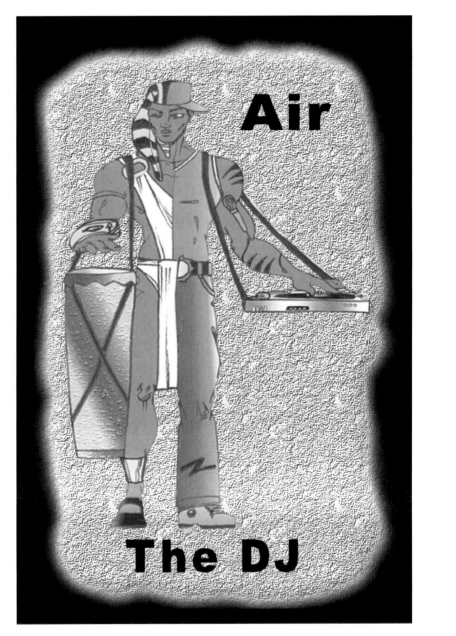

15

L.A. CONFIDENTIAL
A WESTSIDE RYHME STORY

The White House was filled with Secret Servicemen as Eazy E entered the oval office to meet with President George Bush Sr. at an N.R.A. meeting. It was supposed to be a private meeting, but somehow a few reporters got word that something big was going on. As the Press Secretary tried his best to steer reporters in the wrong direction with misinformation, Bush and Eazy sat down to have lunch. Bush's primary concern was a song called, "Fuck the Police," which was heating up the streets of Los Angeles and was quickly gaining momentum throughout the country. With no video or airplay, this underground hit seemed to echo the sentiments of millions of inner city youth all over the nation who were tired of police brutality and corruption. Bush and his team had a problem, a song of such magnitude could easily inspire an army of young gang bangers and wannabe thugs to start retaliating against the nation's first line of defense. A new generation of Black Panthers with better weapons and a renewed vigor to kill racist police officers could not be tolerated at any cost.

THE NEW HIP HOP WORLD ORDER

Bush, a member of an elite secret society called, "The Skull and Bones," which originated at Yale University, could have easily shut down a two-bit gangsta rapper from L.A. from spreading these anti-police messages. In fact, the Skull and Bones is so powerful, it could have purchased Eazy's label in twenty minutes, tore up N.W.A.'s contract, planted drugs in Eazy's car and shipped him off to the county prison for life. Yet, when Eazy left the White House that afternoon, he seemed to be on a new mission. While N.W.A. didn't tone down its rhetoric, the focus of their attack seemed to change. The injustice of the police department was no longer a major part of their message. They focused more on "bitches and hoes," drive-by's, "gang bangin'," drugs and money. Although Ice Cube, the group's front man, claimed he left for money reasons, this sudden shift in N.W.A.'s game plan was probably the main reason he defected and made the pilgrimage east to the Mecca of Hip Hop for spiritual clarity. What else was said in this meeting with the president? What kind of deal was made? Perhaps, Bush and his team felt that N.W.A. could be used to serve the Skull and Bones hidden agenda, an agenda that included flooding cities across the country with crack cocaine courtesy of the C.I.A., a subdivision of Skull and Bones. This operation enabled the C.I.A. to supply young drug dealers such as, "Freeway," a.k.a. Ricky Donnell Ross, and Michael "Harry O" Harris with an unlimited amount of cocaine and free reign to operate in the streets. This was phase one. The "Bloods and Crips" are a government operation created at Yale University using the colors of the American flag, Red for "Bloods," blue for "Crips," and the "White" elite in the middle of it all. These gangs were used to distribute crack at retail prices throughout L.A. The bitter rivalry between the two was created to keep the focus on black on black crime and not on the real enemy. This was phase two. N.W.A. would be used to complete phase three. With major shipments coming in and a team to move the product, all the government needed now was a group of spokespersons to endorse the merchandise, just like they would use Magic Johnson to endorse their A.I.D.S. operation to boost the sales of AZT. When N.W.A. dropped the album "Efil4zaggin," Hip Hop as we knew it would change forever. The album, one of the greatest ever produced, introduced mainstream America to the cold harsh reality of life in urban cities all over the country.

There's a saying that is very popular amongst the elite of the secret societies and it goes, "The ends justify the means." While the album "Efil4zaggin" brought to the surface what America has been trying for years to suppress in regards to black people becoming a beast due to the conditions of over 400 hundred years of oppression, it also glorified the lifestyle of murder, mayhem, drug use, drug selling, violence, rape and sex. The album served as a recruitment center for young black males who wanted to be gangsters and hustlers. This gave the corporation of prisons and morgues great potential for growth. This isn't the first time the government used music as a medium to convey messages of mind control and manipulation. Heavy Metal and Rock and Roll has always been rumored to contain hidden messages and codes slightly lower than the music or that can be heard if you played the songs in reverse. Yet music that catered to black America that could be used for devious purposes was uncharted territory. N.W.A. knowingly or unknowingly were government agents in one of the biggest operations to kill, incarcerate, drug and destroy young black people in America.

The group N.W.A., at this time, consisted of Dr. Dre, his partner Yella, Eazy, and Emcee Ren. Behind the scenes laid the D.O.C., the most famous Ghostwriter on the West Coast. He penned most of the songs after the departure of Ice Cube. D.O.C. would eventually step from behind the scenes with his own gangster debut entitled, "No One Can Do It better." He would be accompanied by a 360 pound bodyguard named, Suge Knight. N.W.A. had conquered the world, but soon it would all come crashing down. Turmoil over money and power would lead to the break-up of the world's most dangerous group. Upon closer examination, it's obvious that this turmoil was created by outside factions with ulterior motives to cash in on their demise. The prize possession that everyone was after was Dr. Dre. With his ability to produce beats and make stars out of just about anyone, he would be the perfect cornerstone to build a music empire around, and that's exactly who Suge Knight would go after.

THE TAKE OVER

Suge's rise to power would come with the help of Michael "Harry O" Harris, who had made millions of dollars in the 80's selling crack. He was fortunate enough to go legit and invest his money into many different ventures, including, Broadway plays with the likes of Denzel Washington. Harry O knew too much about the

C.I.A.'s illegal dealings and was sent to prison on some trumped up charges to damage his credibility. Behind bars, he struck a deal with Suge to start Death Row, a subdivision of God Father Entertainment. However, the "real" power was held by Harry O's Jewish lawyer and confidant, David Kenner. Kenner had a reputation for defending powerful mobsters and big time drug dealers and winning many of their cases. Harry O trusted him and ordered Kenner to hit Suge off with 1.5 million dollars of working capital to get Death Row up and running. However, Kenner was the one signing the checks, keeping the books, laundering the money and keeping a close watch on the dealings of Death Row. Suge was a mere pawn who would be used for his brute strength, street know how and gang affiliations. How else can you describe a bodyguard with no prior knowledge of the music business rising to power and fame so fast? He wasted no time in exercising his power. He allegedly threatened to throw a white rapper named Vanilla Ice off a balcony if he didn't sign over his publishing rights to Suge. He wisely complied and was extorted for most of his riches. Suge also supposedly barged into the offices of Ruthless Records with a baseball bat and forced Eazy E to sign release papers for Dr. Dre and now that he had what he longed for to start his empire, Suge began recruiting artists.

Snoop Dogg was at the top of his list, followed by Daz and Kurupt, Nate Dogg, Warren G, and Rage. The stage was set. With the release of Snoop's debut, "Doggystyle," and Dr. Dre's solo debut, "The Chronic," Death Row quickly grew into the powerhouse label on the West Coast and it would only get stronger. When Suge saw an opportunity to acquire Tupac Shakur, who was currently serving time for rape, he wasted no time. Tupac would be the final piece to the puzzle that would make Death Row millions of dollars for many years to come, but getting him out of prison would not be easy. Kenner, who has many powerful associates, including judges and district attorneys negotiated the release of Tupac through an appeal and by posting a million dollars bail. Upon his release, he was immediately ordered to hit the studio and begin writing songs. After all, he was already over a million dollars in the hole. Tupac was grateful and Tupac was free. He also saw it as a perfect opportunity to get back into the game and settle a score with an East Coast rival and former rhyming partner, Biggie Smalls. Biggie was allegedly responsible for the robbery and attempted murder of Tupac as he headed to a recording studio in N.Y.C. This only added fuel to a fire that was already brewing between two rap powerhouses, Bad Boy from the East Coast, and Death Row from the West.

With Suge leading the way, Death Row stormed New York at the Source Music Awards and let the entire Hip Hop world know that Death Row was in charge. This move only added to his reputation as a ruthless CEO who would stop at nothing to get what he wanted. Not everybody in the Death Row camp was happy with the tactics used by Suge to get things done. Dr. Dre didn't approve of some methods used by Suge, such as, making a former bodyguard of Puff Daddy's drink a bucket of his urine in an attempt to find out where Puffy lived, or smacking up his artist if he felt they were putting in sub par performances in the studio. Dr. Dre wanted out and would walk away from his share of Death Row that was rumored to be worth about 75 million dollars. Was Dr. Dre being forced out or extorted by Suge, who became the sole owner of Death Row? Or was he promised an even bigger payday from another Jewish music big named Jimmy Iovine? It became clear that divide and conquer tactics were being used to bring down Death Row, as Snoop and Tupac went at Dr. Dre for leaving and other artists started bickering over money they felt was due to them.

DEATH COMES TO THE ROW

Tupac, in particular, began to question the motives of Suge in regards to his money. He was in the process of firing David Kenner as his lawyer, who was the "real" owner of Death Row after conspiring with Suge to cut Michael Harris out of the picture. With Kenner as the owner of Death Row and his lawyer, this was a conflict of interest that Tupac wanted no part of. He stopped accepting cars and gifts from Suge, who was using this as a way to keep Tupac happy and to deter him away from the millions that was owed to him, leaving Suge to ask the question, "Is Tupac worth more to me dead or alive?" Tupac would never learn the truth, as he was gunned down on the Las Vegas strip after watching a Mike Tyson fight. Nobody is murdered on the Las Vegas strip! It's an unwritten law that even mobsters obey by taking their victims out into the dessert to "whack em." Still, Tupac is shot down on the strip, while riding with Suge who was not hit at all (depending on what story you believe), by someone in a white vehicle and no suspects were apprehended or brought in for questioning. How strange is that? Tupac was involved in a scuffle inside the hotel with an alleged rival gang member that was conveniently caught on tape as he, Suge and other members of Death Row's entourage attacked their rival. This may have been staged to provide a motive for Tupac's death. Suge, who was probably in on this elaborate scheme, was double-crossed, as this video would also be used to send him to prison for violating parole.

This brought about the demise of Death Row, but it also shows us just how high up and deep down this really goes. Many people were glad to see Suge locked down. This included his Death Row family, who took advantage of his absence to get paid and reestablish themselves as major players in the game of Hip Hop, and even to mend some fences with some of their East Coast counterparts, all while throwing dirt on Suge's name like he would never return. Again, Dr. Dre would be the most valuable asset needed to rebuild another empire, as he would do so with "Aftermath," courtesy of Jimmy Iovine. Snoop went down to the "Dirty South" to hook up with Master P and keep his name at the top of the charts, and Daz, Kurupt, Nate Dogg and the rest of the family continued to hold it down for the West.

Lost in the West Coast beef, was the fact that Eazy E, the Godfather of gangster rap died a year earlier after suffering from complications due to "AIDS." Eazy had a history of bronchitis, which is one of the conditions that is falsely diagnosed in many black people as H.I.V., the disease that causes AIDS. Eazy's wife tested negative and no one else came forward to say they contacted AIDS from him, leading me to ask the question, "Was Eazy killed because he was expendable or because he knew too much about Bush and the C.I.A.'s involvement in Hip Hop?" His former crew seemed to draw on his death, as Dr. Dre and Snoop began kicking it again. Even Ice Cube buried the hatchet with Dr. Dre. However, they all knew the inevitable day would come when Suge would return to claim his spot.

In 2001, after serving about two thirds of his sentence, Suge was back! This time, his main enemies were not from the East, but his own West Coast camp. Snoop and Dr. Dre had publicly denounced Suge, but not to his face. Suge has made it clear that he will stop at nothing to return Death Row to its past glory, and he will crush any-one who gets in his way. Kurupt has even reenlisted with "Tha Row" in hopes of bringing it back to the West. Suge has been in and out of jail in recent years, mostly on trumped up charges. Can Suge return Death Row to the top of the charts? Or do the "real" players, who reside much higher up the ladder, have other plans to exploit the current situation for their benefit? Stay tuned as this rhyme story constantly unfolds.

Frequency Illustration - Frequencies are channels. There are many different frequencies that occupy our time and space, the higher the frequency, the greater the understanding of things. Frequencies are also measured in long and short wave patterns. Two or more people that think alike are similar to them being on the same frequency. What we eat and think, help determine the level of frequency that we can achieve.

16

RHYME SPACE
"THE FUTURE OF HIP HOP ADVERTISEMENT"

Imagine a representative from a major corporation approaching the hottest rapper in the game and saying, "We have a new product that we're trying to push and we would like to buy some rhyme space." Then the rapper says, "Well, my rhyme is 16 bars and I'm already pushin' two products within the first 8 bars but I think I can fit your joint in within my last 8 bars. Is that aaight wit you?"

REP: "That's fine, but how much is this gonna cost?"

RAPPER: "My prices vary. For instance, the intro and outro of my rhyme range from a hun-fifty to three hundred thousand, simply because those are the two most important parts of the rhyme. Anything in the middle of the rhyme is gonna run you about 80 grand. It also depends on if it's the first or last single off my album, a collabo wit another artist, the soundtrack of a new hot movie and of course, if I'm feelin' what you pushin'."

REP: "What's the difference between the first and last singles?"

RAPPER: "The first is the most anticipated joint off a new album. And since I'm the hottest playa on the streets right now, the whole world is waiting for me to drop. So obviously, that's gonna run you a lil more."

REP: "How many potential consumers are you expected to reach with this album?"

RAPPER: "My last banger sold five million copies and that's not including bootleg, which was probably about another three million. The way I see it, every playa that cop the album will share it or listen to it wit at least another ten to fifteen of his closest homies. So, as you can see, the numbers can git crazy and rise from 8 million to between 80 to 120 million. Not to mention radio spins, which could reach 800,000 nationwide, numerous club spins, and underground mix DJ's keepin' me hot."

REP: "What about video play?"

RAPPER: "Well, the package I'm offering you includes flossin' your product in three of my upcoming videos. My joints are bumped on BET, which has over 60 million viewers and because of my crossover appeal, my videos will also be played on MTV, which is international, when you add up all the numbers, that's potentially around 500 million heads worldwide."

REP: "Wow! Those numbers are staggering. You're a very powerful young man."

RAPPER: "Mo powerful than the president right now."

REP: "What do you mean?"

RAPPER: "You see a hot Emcee is more in tune with the youth of America. They love, respect, and trust me to represent their point of view. They could care less about some old white man with old fashioned views, sitting behind some desk talking politics trying to budget the deficit or some foreign relations shit. All they wanna know about is what's goin' on in the hood and that's what I represent. My word is the law in these streets. Whatever I say, wear, drink or drive is what you're gonna see on every other corner in Urban America. Since today's youth are tomorrow's leaders, I literally play a role in the future of this country. I think that would make me just as, if not mo' powerful than the President, wouldn't you?"

REP: "Well, when you put it like that, it's hard to disagree."

RAPPER: "Anyway son, my last three clients were very happy wit the results I produced for them and I think you'll be just as satisfied."

REP: "Oh I'm pretty sure my employer will be very happy with the numbers that just one of your albums can produce. My only concern is will we be able to reach middle class America in the suburbs?"

RAPPER: "That's not gonna be a problem, nah mean? You see as much as I love my peeps from the hood, they don't buy records. They either cop the bootleg version, copy it off the radio or git hit off by one of they peeps wit a copy. Most of my sales come from white America. Dun, it's kinda weird, see black people who are the minority in America wanna be like white people and white people who are the majority in America wanna be like Black people. So, we use the hood to set the trends and we use white America to cash in on the deal. Let's keep it real, the only ones who can afford the things I rap about are fellas from the hood doin' illegal activity and rich white kids from the burbs. So, Madison Avenue is waiting for us to set the next trend."

REP: "You're smarter than most would think."

RAPPER: "Of course. What do you think most rappers are just out to be pimped by corporate America and not cash in on their own talents and skills?"

REP: "Well I..."

RAPPER: "Don't answer dat. Oh, by the way, is this product gonna be on the open market?"

REP: "We're thinking of going public right after your album drops."

RAPPER: "Cool, just let me know so I can contact my broker."

REP: "You have a broker?"

RAPPER: "Oh, no doubt son, I know what time it is. I'ma cop a couple thousand shares of your company's stock so I can cash in long term as well. So let's git back down to bitness. I'm pluggin' you in at the end of my rhyme, on my first new release and three video shots right?"

REP: "Right."

RAPPER: "We'll settle on $350,000. Is that aaight?"

REP: "That's fine. How would you like to get paid? Check or transfer the money into your account?"

RAPPER: "No let's keep this one on the low. I'll take straight cash if that's aaight wit you?"

REP: "That's even better. This way neither of us has to report it on our taxes."

RAPPER: "You said it, not me."

REP: "So, I guess I'll see you around."

RAPPER: "Yeah sooner than you think. I just bought a house in the Hamptons close to where you live."

REP: "Is that right? I guess that makes us neighbors. Well, I look forward to doing business with you. Hopefully, this will be the start of a great relationship."

RAPPER: "I think so...I'll holla at you later...One."

Obviously, this is just a fictional scenario, or is it? Are we witnessing the future of Hip Hop where major corporations buy rhyme space the same way they would buy television space to air their ads? In fact, for less money, they would probably get a better deal and reach more people buying the two bars of a hot Emcee's rhyme, than 30 seconds on a major network's station, simply because Hip Hop is everywhere, from magazines to fashion to video games, it has become a multi-billion dollar business. And since Hip Hop is a way of life it never closes, it's 24 hours a day, 7 days a week. So, instead of corporations spending millions on television ads that only reach a portion of their targeted market within the prime time hours, they can spend a fraction of that cost and hire an Emcee to run their ads for the duration of his album or better yet, his career!

Every time the record is played, the artist is seen in a magazine or the video is shown, corporate America has an opportunity to get paid. Yet, it's advantageous for them to pay a rapper to covertly slip their product into the natural flow of his rhyme to make it seem like this is a product that he really uses, as compared to the traditional overt advertising method of paying a rapper to hold up a Pepsi can and say, "Feel the joy." Real Hip Hop consumers are too smart for that and it's even a turn off at times to see your favorite rapper pushing products we know they don't use. The "hood" knows they're frontin' and sellin' us out to get paid. But what we don't realize is that the same playa we thought was keepin it gutter when he was flowin about his Rolex, Motorola two-way pager or his Benz was frontin' and sellin' us out to get paid.

The corporations now have a "front and back door method" of operation aimed at getting their hands on our hard earned dollars. The "back door method" works extremely well for products that cannot be openly advertised on T.V. like Cristal, Philly blunts and 9 millimeters. The alcohol, tobacco, and firearm industry rely heavily on the Hip Hop industry to sell their products. This is not limited to legal products. Ecstasy, crack and marijuana are billion dollar businesses that constantly reap the benefits of Hip Hop endorsements. Don't get me wrong. I'm not saying all rappers are receiving money under the table to advertise these products. In fact, most of them are being pimped for free! But the fact of the matter is, whether it's paid advertisement or free advertisement, it's still advertisement and someone is cashing in on the very words that we speak. We then blame someone else for the high level of alcoholism, cancer, drug overdoses or death by firearms in our community, when we are the ones who allow our so-called "hood" representatives to endorse the very things that are killing us.

The future of Hip Hop advertising reached new heights with the release of Busta Rhymes, "Pass the Courvoisier," featuring P. Diddy. The song and video were blatant Hip Hop commercials using two heavy weight Emcees to sell an alcoholic beverage to anyone who had access to BET, MTV, a mix CD or a radio. Commercials have 1) a product that is being sold, 2) a catchy little jingle or phrase associated with the product, and 3) superstars or celebrities that endorse the product. Hard liquor is rarely sold on television or radio, due to the monitoring of the FCC and the controversy surrounding the subject. Yet, "Pass The Courvoisier" had 1) a product being sold, 2) a catchy little jingle and beat (courtesy of the Neptunes), and 3) two Hip Hop superstars in Busta and P. Diddy endorsing the product, which was played on television and radio stations 24 hours a day, seven days a week. How clever was that? I'm willing to bet the company was smiling all the way to the bank singing, "Pass the Courvoisier."

Will other companies that have been monitored by the FCC follow suit by using Hip Hop to bypass the rules and regulations to still sell their products on television and radio? This remains to be seen, but if there's a dollar sign attached to it, don't be surprised if your favorite rapper drops a bangin' four minute and thirty second commercial disguised as a song promoting the latest alcoholic beverage or "club" drug like, "Blue and Yellow Purple Pills" by D12 and Eminem. It seems that it is now a requirement that every artist, whether he's at the top of the charts or not, promote and endorse products these days. Think of your favorite rapper and then ask yourself has he done a song lately that didn't promote something other than his music. The answer to that question, in most cases, will be no. Hip Hop is the most diversified music on the planet at this time. So it would be foolish for us to underestimate the genius of an advertising guru to utilize Hip Hop in ways we could have never imagined. Soon, we may see the very mic that a rapper is holding sponsored by Sprite, or rappers in videos throwing up gang signs that spell Pepsi. Certain rappers will have contracts similar to athletes where they can make more money off endorsements than the recording contract itself. Are you ready for the future of Hip Hop advertisement?

Another way to look at the situation is this, most of these rappers aren't being paid by the label, so if there's any way to make some extra cash, you can bet they're going to get paid. If it's all about the Benjamins, you can be bought. If you can be bought, you can be controlled, if you can be controlled, you can be manipulated into furthering someone else's cause. I say all of this to ask, can you even trust your favorite rapper any more to keep it real, or is every clever punch line or witty phrase that comes out of his mouth paid for by corporate America? Take a moment and reflect on the lyrics that come out of most rappers mouth today. They rhyme about their Rolex, Benz, chrome 22s, Timberlands, two-way pagers, Cristal, Ecstasy, 9 millimeters, Coogi sweaters, platinum chains, and fly cribs all within a 16 bar radius. This has made the boastful rapper a dream on Madison Avenue. Gone are the days when rappers spoke from the heart and represented the voice of the people. It was their "hoodly" duty to bring us the news, entertain and tell the story of our plight and struggle to survive in the inner cities, now it's all about the Benjamins.

In a sense, I understand a rappers frustration with being pimped by corporate America for so long wanting to turn the tables and pimp them, but at whose expense? Caught in the middle are loyal fans that are being led to slaughter by rappers serving as pied pipers for money hungry advertisers, even selling us products that are detrimental to our health. While they get rich, we get sick. If rappers only knew the true power that they possess, that every word they speak helps to mold and create our reality. If they only knew that the entire world is listening to what they have to say, that they could change the game by only endorsing products that enhance our lives, or dropped jewlz in the rhyme flow about how to economically strengthen our community; instead of "Pass the Courvoisier," you heard "Pass the Dictionary." Only when this approach is taken will we be able to defend ourselves from the corporate parasites looking to suck our communities dry and keep us dependent on them for survival. The stage has been set. Either rappers represent and work for the betterment of us or they're government agents and work for them. In a world where "Cash rules everything around me," it is as simple as that. So the next time your favorite rapper spits 16 bars, ask yourself, is he representing the hood or is he just representing the goods?

17

THE DAY REAL HIP HOP SAVED MY LIFE

Iwoke up one morning and the whole world around me had changed. Hip Hop was everywhere, I mean everywhere. I felt like I was suffocating, like I was living in a closed box with no escape door. I felt like I was being stalked and the further I ran away from Hip Hop, the closer I was running to it, and the more that I tried to distance myself from it, the tighter we seemed to get. The greater disrespect I showed for Hip Hop, the more love it showed me, our relationship was ass backwards. Wherever I went, Hip Hop was right there clockin' me every step of the way. We were inseparable, but not by choice. I was beginning to get fed up. Not that I didn't love Hip Hop, but just like any other relationship, it requires giving each other time and space to grow. I needed Hip Hop to stop sweatin' me for a minute, you know, let me do me. It was taking over every aspect of my life, and all of this craziness seemed to happen overnight.

I remember when we first met, Hip Hop was young and new to the block. It didn't come around that often but when it did, heads was always checkin' for it. Some older cats had put me up on Hip Hop and I could tell by the way they acted when it was around, that Hip Hop must've been the shit. Whenever they rode around in OJs back in the day, Hip Hop was there. Whenever they brought their boom boxes outside to break-dance or electric boogie, Hip Hop was there. Whenever they headed to the local club, Hip Hop was right there ridin' shotgun. I ain't gon' front, in the beginning I wanted Hip Hop all to myself, but something that hot, you know other heads was checkin' for it too. Since we were both young, I felt it was best for us to move slowly, but before you knew it, we fell in love and couldn't get enough of each other. My every thought was Hip Hop and Hip Hop's every thought was me. We would sit for hours kickin' it about all aspects of life, from partying to politics, to sex, drugs, and you know... Hip Hop. You would think it was a match made in heaven, yet too much of anything is not good for you, whether it's sex, money, work, or Hip Hop. We were spending so much time together that I started getting sick and tired of Hip Hop in my face all day, finishing my sentences or knowing what I'ma say before I even open my mouth. This constant togetherness was putting a strain on our relationship, then one day Hip Hop just spazzed out on me like it was PMSing or something. It became violent, disrespectful, and moody like it didn't give a fuck about me anymore, mainly because it started hangin' out with some other cats that weren't even from our hood. These were some rich cats who gassed Hip Hop about how much money and fame it could achieve by hangin' with them. Then Hip Hop started hangin' out in different hoods. Soon it was in hoods all over the world. That's when I first noticed the change. Hip Hop became "All that," driving up in fancy cars, sportin' expensive jewelry, and drinkin' exquisite champagne. We didn't see eye to eye anymore, it seemed like Hip Hop was too good for me. At that point our relationship took a turn for the worse. We didn't get it on the way we used to, and when we did, the feeling just wasn't the same. I was fakin' it, so I decided that it was time to end my relationship with Hip Hop, and today would be the day. But I could tell by the way Hip Hop was acting lately, all up in my face, sweatin' my every move that it wasn't going to just walk away peacefully. I mean, how many hood relationships end without drama? Hip Hop wanted to play both sides of the fence, it wanted my ghetto love and the love of those rich cats too. It wanted to still control my life while being committed to someone else. It was like Hip Hop was sayin, "If I can't have you, no other way of life can." But I ain't no sucka, I ain't gonna let nobody play me like I don't know what time it is. For me and Hip Hop it was a "Reynolds." Now all I needed was to find a way to tune out Hip Hop and get on with my life. They say, "Breaking up is hard to do," but I have to try my best to put Hip Hop behind me.

I rolled out of bed and turned on the radio and guess what was playing, Hip Hop, Damn! Just the shit I'm trying to avoid. My speakers were blastin' one of those club bangers that instructed women to take their clothes off, thugs to buss their guns, and playas to pour that cristale... at six in the morning! I tried to shake Hip Hop by turning further down the dial only to realize that they were playing the exact same song! If I didn't know any better, I'd swear that Hip Hop had me trapped. Not to be discouraged, I turned off the radio and turned on the television. I figured I'd be safe there only to be bombarded with Hip Hop video after Hip Hop video that added the visuals to those club bangers I heard on the radio. Aaaah! Is there any escape from Hip Hop? I turned to the weather channel and let out a sigh of relief. No Hip Hop here right? Wrong. A soon as they went to commercial, some Emcees popped up on the screen rappin' about the joy of Pepsi. Shook by these disturbing events, I unplugged the TV and searched for something good to read. Shuffling through my collection to my dismay, every single magazine I owned was Hip Hop, from The Source to XXL to Vibe magazine. Just when I thought it couldn't get any worse, my fifteen year old son bops into my room wearing a durag with his pants hangin' off his ass kickin' some new Hip Hop lingo that went something like this: "Aay yo dun I'ma a lil short on cheese, I'm tryin' to stack my chips up so I can git up wit this lil hottie tonight who got a straight fattie. If you hit me up wit a lil chedda, when I get my allowance I'll kick that back to you fo sho na mean?" I responded by saying, "yo son, it ain't going down like that naaa mean?" Meanwhile my eight year old is boppin' his head playing a video game that's filled with Hip Hop music, my two year old is taking off his pamper singing, It's gettin' hot in herre so take off all your clothes, my queen jumps out of the shower and throws on a pink Rocawear sweat suit. I look in my closet for something fly to wear and all I have are outfits that remind me of Hip Hop such as, Sean John, FUBU, Vokal, and Enyce, and they all have their name plastered across the front of my shirts like I'm a walking billboard or something. I settled for a plain sweat suit with no name on it, and threw on my shell top Adidas that reminded me of when Hip Hop was real to me. I quickly fell into a daze reminiscing about the past when Hip Hop and I were cool. As I stood there bouncin' back and fourth singin', "My Adidas" by Run DMC, I thought about gettin' back with Hip Hop but quickly snapped out of it because I knew it would never be like it used to be. Hip Hop would only disrespect me as soon as I start to trust it again. Saddened by this revelation, I stormed out of my apartment determined more than ever to end my relationship with Hip Hop once and for all. Not a second after I hit the Ave I hear, "Yo I got those Hip Hop CDs two for five." I walked past a bunch of brothers on the corner who were having a heated debate over who was better Nas or Jay-Z, a boom box was playing the latest in Hip Hop and R&B, some young shorties blocked the side walk doin' the Harlem shake, on the other side of the street a cipher was formed with Emcees freestylin' and puffin' blunts, and a Hot 97 van almost ran me over, all on my way to the bus stop! Hip Hop was everywhere. I stood in the bus stop shook by the fact that Hip Hop was watching my every move. People in the bus stop were looking at me like I was crazy or something. I ran over to them and tried to explain that I was being stalked by Hip Hop and I needed help. They all just laughed and told me that I was imagining the whole thing. They said that Hip Hop would never do such a thing. They started praising Hip Hop and talking about how Hip Hop made a lot of black people rich, created jobs for us, and was something that we created from nothing. I rudely interrupted by replying, if Hip Hop made black people rich, could you imagine how rich it made white people? And for us to have mere jobs from something that we created from nothing was disgusting. I told them that Hip Hop was our worst enemy now and if they didn't be careful it would stalk them the same way it was stalking me. A young wannabe thug smiled at me with a mouth full of platinum teeth and said, "Dog you takin' nis too serious aaaight." Maybe he was right, but I still needed to get as far away from Hip Hop as I could or it would drive me crazy. Deep down inside I knew that was Hip Hop's plan all along, to punish me for trying to leave it. As the bus pulled up, I noticed the billboard on the side of it was promoting the new station for Hip Hop and R&B, Power 105.1. I rushed on the bus and quickly found a seat but sat next to someone playing Hip Hop on a CD walkman that was so loud through the headphones it sounded like I was at a concert. I reached in my bag and pulled out my own CD player. I popped in an R&B CD and tried to drown out the Hip Hop around me, but every R&B song that played had an Emcee spittin' sixteen bars over it. I smashed the CD player on the floor and covered my ears yelling' Stop It! Hip Hop is trying to kill me! Everyone on the bus just started laughing at me. I felt like they were all in on it, like they were possessed by Hip Hop and I was the only one left in the world that Hip Hop couldn't control. Finally, the bus reached downtown. I smiled because I knew Hip Hop didn't rule downtown where white people lived. If anything it should be non-existent. I turned to the white bus driver and said in a most polite manner, thank you for such a safe ride and enjoy your day. He turn to me and said, Fo sheezy my neezy. He closed the door and took off laughing. Free at last, or so I thought. A cell phone rang to the tune of Missy Elliot's "Get your Freak On," three white teenagers bopped by harder than me as one gave another a pound and said, "What up my nigga," a jeep rolled by with 20 inch rims blastin' Eminem, and every other skyscraper I walked by said Sony, Columbia, or Universal records. Then it hit me, I recognized these cats as the same ones who took real Hip Hop from me back in the day. Now it's in boardrooms, controls the stock market, and has international clout.

It became painfully obvious that Hip Hop had everyone under its spell including White America. It also became obvious that I couldn't just blame Hip Hop for leaving the hood or sweating me so hard, even after I decided it was over, but also lay some of the blame on those who manipulated Hip Hop to make them rich. And lastly, it was obvious that Hip Hop was here to stay and it would probably stalk me for the rest of my life. I went home and sat on the edge of my bed contemplating ending it all. Was my life worth living if I couldn't control it? Was it worth living if Hip Hop dictated what I wore, drank, drove, listened to, or watched? I thought about my children who were being raised as slaves to Hip Hop from a very early age. If only they knew about real Hip Hop from back in the days. If only they knew how to say no to this new age type of Hip Hop that was only out to destroy them. But it's hard. It's hard when everywhere you look, Hip Hop is right there. I couldn't bare it any longer. I loaded up the nine and stuck it in my mouth ready to pull the trigger. This was it. I refused to live as a slave any longer. I turned up the radio real loud to drown out the sound of the gun shot. I closed my eyes and got ready to pull the trigger when I hesitated for a second. Were my ears deceiving me? Or was that a new song from Public Enemy playing on the radio? Then the radio personality said that Rakim was making a comeback, A Tribe Called Quest were getting back together, Big Daddy Kane was in the studio, and Queen Latifah was putting the Flava Unit back together. I lowered the nine from out of my mouth and thought, maybe there's hope after all. If real Hip Hop was returning, maybe I could find it in my heart to forgive and forget the way it treated real Hip Hop lovers like me. That day will always be remembered as the day real Hip Hop saved my life.

18

THE THEYS - PART 2
A SCI-FI HIP HORROR STORY
THE TAKEOVER: HE WHO CONTROLS HIP HOP, RULES THE WORLD

By the year 1990, They had total control of Hip Hop. The last of the Gagotus possessing the spiritual energy to lead a Hip Hop exodus into the fourth dimension were destroyed, corrupted or pushed underground. The only Hip Hop that was allowed to survive was that which supported the mission of the Theys: materialism, sex, murder, mayhem and the total destruction of minds of the Gagotus, not the physical destruction, because They still needed the Gagotus for food and energy. The high initiates of the Illumi Nation understood that carbon was the basis of melanin, the substance that gave the Gagotus super powers in ancient times. Carbon is also used to produce energy in batteries. Using mind control methods that systematically drained the life force out of all who partook in Hip Hop, They were able to use the Gagotus energy as one big battery to feed off of and stay in power. The more sex, violence, and hard times the Gagotus experienced heard through rap music or visualized through videos, the more energy the Gagotus let off. They made sure that most Hip Hop songs, videos and magazines produced a steady supply of this food. The masses of the Gagotus would then go act out what was seen in these videos, creating even more food for the Theys. It was the only way They could survive, and They had to guard the secrets at all cost.

They knew they were doomed if the Gagotus ever found out about their great past or how to use Hip Hop to tap into their super powers, or if The Gagotus found out that "All Is Mental" and their thoughts created this reality. This is why the Theys kept the Gagotus' thoughts focused on negativity and confusion. They also kept the Gagotus' thoughts on material things, to ensure that the Theys could physically exist. They were master illusionists who made this physical world appear real, but it was only an illusion, and, the more the Gagotus thought it was real, the more real it became. They called this the Matrix of Hip Hop. Since Hip Hop was the music in which They were destined to meet their doom, They created this Matrix to buy time and confuse the Gagotus. However, the most guarded secret the Theys kept from the Gagotus was the secret of sexual energy. It was the most potent form of energy that a Gagotu could release and if properly controlled could kill the Theys instantly. If one was consciously aware of this energy during sex, at the very second one reached an orgasm, whatever a Gagotu was thinking at the time, he had the power to manifest in the physical. The Gagotus could literally think the Theys out of existence. If one was not conscious of this energy during sex or when thinking about sex, the Theys could tap into this energy source to make them stronger and wipe out the Gagotus. They wanted you to have sex but not be aware of its true powers.

Since They owned all forms of the media, this is what They used to lock you into the frequency of the Matrix. From 1990 to 2005, artist after artist sold their souls to enter the Hip Hop Matrix, only to be rewarded with tons of material objects, like cars, houses and diamonds. The greatness of an Emcee was not measured by the power of the words he spoke, but by how much material wealth he could accumulate. How could one ascend into the fourth dimension if his thoughts were constantly bogged down with material from the third? This was the thinking of the Theys. Emcees from the East Coast to the West Coast, to the Dirty South lined up to be plugged into the Matrix of Hip Hop. Once you were plugged in, They had the power to create a virtual you called your image. They could create an image of you that made you appeared larger than life itself. Whoever you wanted to be, They had the power to make it happen. The images that were most successful inside the Matrix of Hip Hop were players, gangstas, thugs, pimps, hoes, and bitches, even if the real you was kind hearted, soft and broke. In the Matrix, the only you that mattered was the image of you. They made it so that the image of you was so important in the Matrix, that if They destroyed your image, you would wish you were dead in the real world. They created and controlled every single image that operated within the Hip Hop Matrix. If you cooperated and was of use to their cause, They elevated your image to great heights, awarding you the title of Hip Hop Star or Ghetto Super Star. If you didn't cooperate, were of no use or attempted to reveal the secret to the masses through your lyrics, your image was destroyed and you became one of many fallen stars. They used these stars to control the masses, the bright ones and the fallen ones. They knew that in ancient times, the Gagotus plotted the course of their lives based on the alignment and movement of heavenly stars. They created artificial stars for the masses of Gagotus to look up to. Guided by the unseen hand of the Theys, these stars told you what to eat, drink, wear, drive and think. Your every thought about Hip Hop, every Hip Hop song, and every Hip Hop artist in every urban city was controlled by the Theys.

They performed special rituals that required the energy and three magic words from the Gagotus to stay in power, "Keepin' it real." Simultaneously, Emcees all over the country began to flow about the same things from cars to murder. The ritual was complete when Emcees would utter the three magic words: I'm just "Keepin it real." It made it real...for the Theys. They understood cosmic law, which stated: "Whatever the Gagotus command, the universe must oblige." Soon, the Matrix of Hip Hop had brainwashed millions of Gagotus into chanting, "Keepin' it real!" "Keepin' it real!" "Keepin' it real!" Every media outlet was beaming the same message, which only gave the illusion more life. Record labels would only sign artists who were willing to, "Keep it real." The Theys were winning the battle but They knew the war was far from over. They knew that all major religions were waiting on a Messiah to lead them to salvation. One who would be armed with nothing more than the "word" that would be so powerful, that the very vibration of its tone when spoken by the Messiah, would uncover the truth and reveal who the Theys really were, beasts. And if Hip Hop is the new religion, it too must produce a lyrical Messiah to lead the people. One with a flow so tight that when he or she spit sixteen bars over ancient drum sounds, it could create an alchemical affect that would immediately penetrate the inner core of the earlobe, revealing the truth. They had prior knowledge of the ancient papyrus that read: "The gateway to the temple was through the earlobe." They could fool the eye with illusion and wizardry but They needed to find a way to keep the truth from reaching the inner ear. They needed to fool the ear.

In the early 90's, They created the compact disc, better known as the CD. This instantly shifted the focus from analog to digital. Analog gave you more of a realistic feel. The base and snare of a Hip Hop track resonated to the core of your ear when it bounced off of wax or tape. For the Theys, this was dangerous. Disguised as a move to enhance and clean up the music, the Theys were able to create an illusion with the sound of a CD. They made holographic music that appeared real but wasn't real at all. They then systematically removed all graphic equalizers from the store shelves and sold music systems that came equipped with preset equalizers that only supported the musical hologram, so no matter how loud you turned up your system or used the equalizer, it never resonated to the inner core. You could hear it but you couldn't hear it. They were taking no chances. If this lyrical messiah somehow slipped through the cracks of the Matrix or used underground mix CDs to reach the masses, his words would fall on deaf ears. Sampling was one of the weapons used by the pioneers of Hip Hop to reincarnate the spirit of warriors from other time periods to help fight the Theys. The Theys knew that this spirit couldn't be destroyed but wanted to lock it into the past. They wanted to prevent the spirit of warriors past from using sampling as a teleport to move from time period to time period to help defeat them. When They couldn't make sampling illegal, They made you pay a heavy price and eventually discouraged most from sampling all together, but They didn't stop there. They mastered the use of E.L.F. (extremely low frequencies), which enabled them to place hidden messages and tones that only the subconscious mind could hear and pick up. These codes were designed to keep the gateway to the temple closed and were placed in the record during the mastering. This was done right before it went to press so that the artist would have no knowledge of its existence. There was a mastering center in every major city that produced a high volume of recordings. They also learned to master the science of the drum beat itself. They knew that low bass drums vibrated to the lower body, the sex organs, or left you in a depressed or violent mood, and high tone beats were inspirational, motivational or left you in a joyous mood. They also knew the power of the pineal gland. Located in the middle the forehead between one's holographic eyes, this gland when functioning properly had the power to see through all illusions. For the Theys, it had to remain dormant or They would be revealed. Fresh melanin was secreted into the pineal gland during nighttime hours. The Theys learned to use drum patterns and sound waves to control the pineal gland of the Gagotus. They even used certain drum patterns to break up the melanin structure of a Gagotu into particles, rendering it useless. If you were a Gagotu that loved Hip Hop, there was no escaping the Theys. They wanted your mind, body and soul.

By 1995, the Matrix of Hip Hop was so sophisticated and advanced that it literally began to run itself. New artists were recruited daily, who were willing to keep it real, and most were ready to die defending the very system that was killing them, all for "Money, Hoes and Clothes." Any Emcee that They felt was a potential danger to the system or possessed the energy to be the lyrical messiah, was destroyed. Staged drive by shootings and "random" killings eliminated the physical presence of such threats. False rape charges, trumped up drug and gun charges and well publicized court cases took care of the image of any Emcee trying to bring down the system from within. The Theys had Hip Hop on lock down. Then the unthinkable happened. The masses of the Theys, who were not part of the elite Illumi Nation, began to fall in love with Hip Hop! The masses didn't have the knowledge that Hip Hop would be their demise. As far as the Illumi Nation was concerned, the masses of the Theys were no better than the Gagotus. They received a few more benefits but were still looked upon by the Illumi Nation as useless eaters. The masses began to look up to, dress like, and speak Hip Hop like the Gagotus, yet this never presented a problem for the Illumi Nation, who were warring amongst themselves over the control of Hip Hop. Different sectors of the Illumi Nation wanted to use Hip Hop for their own hidden agendas because the unwritten notion was, he who controls Hip Hop, rules the world. The Anglaxsons, the most powerful of the groups, wanted to destroy the spiritual energy of Hip Hop, or find a way to use Hip Hop to ensure that They would survive the shift in the year 2012. The Semis, a much smaller but very influential group, wanted to use Hip Hop for capitol gain. The Semis were financial wizards and saw Hip Hop as a gold mine. The two would come to an agreement that served both of their causes. The Anglaxsons needed the wombs of the female Gagotus as a backup plan in case They couldn't destroy the spiritual energy of Hip Hop outright. Since the Gagotus allowed the masses of the Theys to infiltrate Hip Hop and call it their own, even allowing them to pick up the mic and flow, it became a tool used to eliminate racial lines between the Theys and Gagotus. Soon Hip Hop, which was created for the Gagotus by the Gagotus, was for everyone to enjoy. This led to more interracial relationships. The Anglaxsons wanted to plant their seeds in the sacred wombs of the Gagotus to carry them through the shift, then, using advanced sciences, reverse the process on the other side of the fourth dimension. The Semis wanted to use Hip Hop to sell and endorse products. The power of Hip Hop affected the entire economy. Since the masses of the Theys wanted to be like the Gagotus, whatever the Gagotus ate, drank, wore, or drove, was purchased in abundance by the Theys. Hip hop controlled the stock market! By the late 90's, Hip Hop was the country's biggest moneymaking machine.

Both sectors of the Illumi Nation were happy but needed to create an illusion to mask their true intentions in case the Gagotus caught wind of the takeover. They needed to make it appear that the Gagotus still owned Hip Hop. They selected a few Gagotus to become record label moguls. These moguls were paid millions of dollars to scout new talent to keep the system strong and give off the illusion that the Gagotus were making great strides in Hip Hop. The same thing was done with the Hip Hop fashion industry, yet all of these so called successful Gagotus, who owned their own record label or clothing line, had to report to the "King," because that's where the true power source was. The Theys allowed the young Hip

Hop moguls to mix and mingle amongst them as "equals," and join in exclusive parties that included the rich and famous. Once the moguls were drunk and drugged up enough, the pawns were coerced into wild sex orgies with the Theys that included fornicating with men, little boys and even animals! These sessions were always taped as a part of an operation put in place by the Theys to ensure these young moguls didn't become too powerful and turn against the Matrix. The Theys were bisexual by nature and loved to experiment with children and animals, but to have tapes of these young Hip Hop moguls in some uncompromising positions could definitely destroy their images of being thugs and players. These images allowed them to move freely and be successful within the Hip Hop Matrix. The moguls discovered the truth of the Theys plans to take over Hip Hop, then destroy it, but because of the secret tapes and the riches promised, agreed to deceive their fellow Gagotus. This small group of Hip Hop moguls and other industry "bigs," who took the "Oath" to never reveal the truth to the masses, became known as the K.O.T.S. (keepers of the secret). The Theys used the K.O.T.S. to gain the trust of the Gagotus. Because the K.O.T.S. were Gagotus themselves, it was easy for them to betray their own people. It was easy for them to suck money out of their community or act like the struggle and pain that the Gagotus were facing was their own. Meanwhile, the K.O.T.S. were living lavishly, protecting the Theys.

By the year 2001, everything was going according to plan for the Theys, but every day, the planet moved closer and closer to the year 2012, the Theys watched the skies nervously awaiting the cosmic event that would signify the last days. What the Theys didn't know was that an Emcee would trigger this cosmic event. This Emcee was chosen to spit one word. For this mission to be successful, the heavens had to be open and the stars aligned just right to start the cosmic clock. When this word was dropped, this Emcee's work would be done. It would begin the last days of the third dimension, and the last days of Hip Hop, as it was currently known. This would make way for the true lyrical messiahs to enter the Hip Hop Matrix and destroy the Theys. The gateway to the heavens would only be open for a short period of time between September and October of 2001.

The Emcee had to step forward and deliver the word during this time, or the gateway would close and wouldn't open again until 2012 at the exact moment of the shift, but by then it could be too late. The Theys would have more time to find a way to stop the lyrical messiahs, finish off the Gagotus and manipulate their way into the fourth dimension. It had to be done now. Right before the heavens closed, a warrior Gagotu stepped forward and delivered the mystical word. It was the "Ether!" Immediately after this word was spoken into the heavens, all hell broke loose on earth and in Hip Hop. As the planet braced for the possibility of a nuclear war, the Gagotus began warring with each other on all levels. Emcees plotted against Emcees. DJs hated on other DJs. Producers dissed other producers. CEOs snaked other CEOs, and rhyme families began to break up with each other over money and power. Buildings began to fall. The stock market began to fall. Rap empires and government empires began to fall. As was the world, Hip Hop was in total chaos. Radio stations began moving on other stations in the name of Hip Hop. Even the prices of bootleg CDs reached an all time low of $2. The game became saturated and overpopulated with Emcees all sounding the same.

The monotony was due to the fact that this was the end of third dimensional Hip Hop. The rap game was locked into a frequency that couldn't go any further. It had reached its apex. This was the start of the last days. The Theys attempted one last ritual to buy or reverse time. They started reintroducing styles from the 80's like sneakers, clothing, throwback jerseys, and hairstyles to force the Gagotus to think back instead of forward. This bought the Theys a little time as They planned their next move. They then stepped up their material game with Emcee after Emcee who rhymed about nothing but money, hoes, and clothes. By 2005, staged distractions ruled the airwaves to keep the focus of The Gagotus on mundane events, but They knew time was running out. The world was at war. Hip Hop was at war, and in the next few years, the shift would be here. Stay tuned for the next episode of the Theys entitled: The Shift, Hip Hop or Die!

19

HIPHOPCALYPSE NOW

For those who have eyes to see and ears to hear, the signs are very clear. Hip Hop is just about dead. If you don't think that these are the last days of Hip Hop, take a closer look around you. What do you see being manifested in Hip Hop? I see nothing but violence, fornication, deception, and chaos. There are even false prophets coming in the name of Hip Hop in the last days to deceive the people. Women are being degraded. Sex, money, and murder have corrupted the children. There's no respect for the elders of Hip Hop. The worshipping of false Gods, like the faces on a dollar bill, and the worshipping of idols, like the gangsta rapper, have taken over Hip Hop. Every day thousands of Emcees are willing to sell their souls to the devil for a house and a car. The word, which used to be so sacred, is now polluted with praise for the devil and his lifestyle. God's hell is the Devil's heaven, and if you don't think the devil runs the rap game, take a closer look around you. What's so Godly about it? In fact, the devil's greatest manifestation of an Emcee sits at the top of the rap game as we speak. His ways, actions, and lyrics have done everything short of telling you, "I'm the Devil." His initials stand for murder and mayhem, yet still he's praised as a lyrical God, but who's God? It's the Devil's time now and Hip Hop is its Babylon. Warning! It's time to come out of her for those who are partakers of her sins will surely perish. If you don't think what I'm saying is real just take a closer look around you. Where are all the righteous rappers who have the power to save us with the word of God? They can't even get a record deal unless the Devil says so. Those who do sign up are paid in the devil's money, imagine that! The Devil has got God in his back pocket. Hip Hop is in a state of chaos and confusion, and I hope I'm not alone when I ask the question, "What is this rap world coming to?" Hopefully, it's coming to an end. Take a closer look around you. Rap empires are falling. Labels, stations, artists, and producers are warring. This will inevitably lead to bloodshed in the streets, the likes of which Hip Hop faithful have never seen before. Not studio blood, real blood, as that thin line between art and reality is about to be crossed.

That thin line is the same line that separates God and the Devil, good from evil, and spiritual from material. Some of our greatest Emcees have formed on either side of these lines to fight to the death for what they feel is real. Or is this just another line drawn by the Devil to divide and conquer? Only time will tell. Biggie and Tupac took their respective positions on opposite sides of the line. Biggie represented "money, hoes, and clothes," obviously, a material stance. This in no way negates the fact that Biggie was one of the greatest lyricists of all time. It just goes to show that the power of the word is neutral. How one chooses to use it makes it spiritual or material, good or evil, Godly or Devil-like. Tupac took more of a spiritual stance. Not to say that Pac didn't talk about gettin' money and women, but his greatest works are the songs that hit you in the soul and lifted your spirits. They both died for what they believed in.

Flash to the future and the same war was being fought, but this time between Jay-Z and Nas, proving that the game doesn't change, only the players. Jay-Z picked up where his Brooklyn counterpart left off, rappin' about fast women, fast cars and a whole lotta bling bling. Even though he fell victim a couple of times to the world of bling bling himself, Nas will forever be remembered as a spiritual warrior fighting for the righteous people. Then there was the Nelly vs. KRS-One beef. This one's a no brainer. Nelly is strictly material and makes no qualms about it. KRS elevated from Criminal Minded to Spiritual Minded in his quest to free the minds of the people. To the Devil's dismay, this war never really escalated where they could have capitalized off of the record sales. And just when it looked like it couldn't get any worse, Ja Rule and DMX drew their lyrical weapons on each other. This was the same battle being fought. Don't be confused by the different Emcees fighting the war. For Ja Rule, "It's murdeeer!" "Money over bitches," and he "Keeps 'em drugged up off that ecstasy." For DMX, it's the battle between good and evil within himself. Since day one he's been at war with material rappers, and not afraid to close out an album with prayer. Is it just me or is the ultimate war between good and evil being fought through Hip Hop? One could only hope that the spiritual side prevails because at least the war will be fought with lyrics and the mind. If the scales tip to the material side, physical weapons will be used and there could be a lot of dead rappers in the streets. On August 22, DMX called the radio station at Hot 97 and made a plea to Ja Rule to keep it lyrical (spiritual). Ja Rule called up the same station the next day and said, "Don't close the street option" (Material). Like I said, it's a real thin line, and any Emcee from either side of the line could easily cross over to the other if need be. That's the risk the Devil runs when he uses God's children, who may be confused at the time, to fight his battles. For instance, Biggie was so powerful that if he had decided to cross that thin line and took all of his followers with him, the entire system the Devil set up through Hip Hop would have collapsed overnight. That's the power that all of our great Emcees possess, but it's the Devil's job to keep us confused and at war with each other so that we may never find the perfect balance between physical and spiritual. Thus, the stage has been set for the Hip Hop war of Armageddon. Will you be ready?

The final battle must be fought between God and the Devil himself. They must meet face to face to settle this beef once and for all, and since these are the last days of Hip Hop, the war will be fought lyrically. For years, there has only been one Emcee who considered himself a lyrical God in Hip Hop, and his name is Rakim. From the moment he came into our midst in 1986, he told us he was God and had the lyrical sword to prove it. He is by far in my opinion, the greatest Emcee ever to pick up a microphone. Most true Hip Hop historians will agree. Others have come along to claim the moniker of God Emcee, but he was the first. But by the late 80's, early 90's no one wanted to hear the word of God anymore. It was the Devil's time to rule Hip Hop and God was faded to the background. Over the next ten years or so, the Devil searched feverishly for the one Emcee who would best represent his evil throne, yet lyrically hold his own. At the apex of the Devil's rule in Hip Hop, Eminem emerged to claim the throne. Eminem is a lyrical beast (no pun intended), and can devour 95% of these Emcees who claim to have skills. Never forget that the Devil is very powerful and any Emcee representing him must be just as lethal as any that God can produce. As fate would have it, the God Rakim and Eminem were on the same label at one point! As fate would also have it, the label was called Aftermath. What would have been the outcome in the "Aftermath" of the battle between "God" and the "Devil" in the last days of Hip Hop? The answer to this question and many more may never be known as Rakim has since moved on from the label as Dr. Dre and Eminem tried their best to compromise his spirituality by turning him into a gangsta rapper; it's one thing to be swift and changeable but something totally different when you are asked to go against your true nature. They were rumored to have been doing a couple of "friendly" duets at the time, but for those who have eyes to see and ears to hear, there would have been nothing friendly about it as the whole world would have been watching for the out-come of God vs. the Devil, or at least those of us who understood the symbolism of such a match up. Maybe that was the plan all along, weaken the God in front of the eyes of the world, and then have Eminem take him out. Eminem sparked Jay-Z in a lyrical tune up before his title bout, but to destroy God himself would have been the ultimate for the Devil on any level, lyrically, spiritually, physi-cally, or otherwise. Rakim was too swift for that though and would rather put his music out independently, as opposed to selling us out or destroying the legacy that he has built. We need God right now. All of the God Emcees from times past are our only hope because as you can see in these, the last days of Hip Hop, most of these rap-pers have aligned themselves with the enemy.

When I say that these are the last days of Hip Hop, it's not to be taken literally. I'm metaphorically speaking about a cycle or period in Hip Hop that will come to an end. It's the end of the ice age. It's the end of the thug age. These are the last days for Emcees to disrespect women and children with their lyrics and suffer no consequences. These are the last days for those who don't understand or care about the culture of Hip Hop to pimp it to make them rich. Interscope even has their own artists going at each other's throats to generate more sales because they know the time. It's over, and if any of Interscope's artists die in a hail of bullets, so what. As long as it means more record sales, the ends justify the means. But the Devil is not going to go quietly. For those conscious Emcees who have been shut out of the industry for so long, the time is now to seize the moment and make Hip Hop respectable once again. When we get it back, let's do the elders of Hip Hop proud. I didn't call Eminem the Devil because he was white. I called him the Devil because he sits at the top of this evil rap empire that is ruled by the Devil. Right now he's #1, but there are many black Devils in this game so don't get it twisted. It's so hard to stay focused with all the chaos and confusion going on in Hip Hop these days, but remember that's the Devil's plan. To make you think left is right, up is down, and even God is the Devil. It's time to stop hearing Hip Hop and start "listening." It's time to stop watching Hip Hop and start "seeing" it for what it really is, our salvation. Many will be lead to slaughter if they are not willing to be born again into the true essence of Hip Hop. I'll see you on the other side, God willing.

20

I LOVE HIP HOP...BUT I HATE SH*T HOP!

I love old school Hip Hop, but I hate the new school artists who don't respect the elders who came before them. I love those old school artists who realize that their time has come and gone, but I hate those old school dudes who refuse to retire and walk around with a chip on their shoulders like somebody owes them something. I love those Emcees that are original, but I hate those rappers that steal the next man's formula to get paid. I love real gangsters, but I hate gangsta rap. I love an Emcee that can spit an ill 16 bars, but I hate a rapper who only rhymes about being locked behind bars. I love a female Emcee that can really flow and just happens to look sexy, but I hate a female Emcee that relies on her sex appeal but cannot flow worth sh*t. I love all of the money that Hip Hop is making nowadays, but I hate that the only ones who are really getting paid are white people who didn't have anything to do with the culture to begin with. I love the fact that the greatest Emcee of all time is a Black man, but I hate the fact that the greatest selling rapper is Eminem. I love a real hot track, but I hate a rapper that uses a hot track to go triple platinum even though his flow is wack. I love producers that just produce, but I hate producers that want to be Emcees. I love CEO's who stay behind the scenes and work really hard to develop their artists, but I hate CEO's who are always in front of the camera, constantly outshining their own artists. I love Emcees that have a true sense of spirituality, but I hate rappers that kill, sell drugs, and pimp women on records, and then thank God for their success. I love Hip Hop...but I hate Sh*t Hop!

I love Emcees from back in the day that only had one gold front, but I hate these ignorant looking niggas that smile at you and have an entire mouth full of diamonds. I love Emcees that keep it real, but I hate rappers that rent expensive homes so that they can front on MTV like they're rich. I love back in the day when Hip Hop was so diversified, but I hate the fact that record labels will only sign gangsta rappers today. I love Emcees that can carry their own album, but I hate artists that need to feature 10 other rappers on their solo album just to go platinum. I love reggae music and I love Latin music, but I hate reggaeton. I love Jay-Z, but I hate Hova. I love Nas, but I hate Escobar. I love Beyonce…well, sh*t I love Beyonce. I love the Get Rich or Die Trying album, but I hate the Massacre. I love the DJ, but I hate when rappers step on stage to perform with a DAT tape. I love Brucie B, Kid Capri and Clue, but I hate the fact that everybody and their mother has got out a mixtape. I love Hip Hop magazines that break down Hip Hop, but I hate Hip Hop magazines that have more ads than articles. I love rap groups, but I hate when five rappers crowd the stage and all try to talk at the same time and it sounds like a bunch of mumble jumble. I love Emcees that rhyme about their personal struggles, but I hate rappers who feel that being shot is a badge of honor. I love Emcees that are conscious, but I hate rappers who front like their conscious but it's all just a part of their image. I love Emcees, but I hate rappers. I love Hip Hop…but I hate Sh*t Hop!

I love the Emcee Queen Latifah, but I hate the actress Queen Latifah, and I also hate the singer Dana Owens. I love the revolutionary Emcee Ice Cube, but I hate the movie making comedian Ice Cube. I love original Hip Hop videos with a message, but I hate video directors that keep shooting the same video of rappers drinking Cristal, riding on dubs, and half naked women over and over again, and then expect you to call them a genius. I love an Emcee that can show some versatility, but I hate the rapper/rock band collaboration. I love FUBU, but I hate the fact that it's not really for us and by us. I love the sight of a Black CEO in control of Hip Hop, but I hate the fact that he's just a figurehead and has no real power at all. I love to turn on the radio and hear a hot Hip Hop song, but I hate the fact that the radio plays the same 10 songs all day long, and I hate when a song is wack, but they play it so much that I start to like it. I love an Emcee that can speak very intelligently when conducting an interview, but I hate rappers whose vocabulary is limited to "bitch," "playa," "hoe" and they end every sentence with "nah mean." I love Emcees that can use their talent to sell themselves, but I hate rappers who sell out. I love Emcees from the nation of Islam, the nation of Gods and Earths, and the Zulu Nation, but I hate Christian Rap. I love Emcees who know the true history of Hip Hop, but I hate rappers that think Biggie is old school. I love the fact that we own our own record labels, but I hate the fact that we're still getting raped on the distribution. I love Emcees that drop hot soundtracks to movies, but I hate rappers that try to act. I love the Hip Hop clothing lines, but I hate grown ass men dressing like they're 12 years old. I love Hip Hop…but I hate Sh*t Hop!

Box Illustration - On the surface it appears that the three major religions, Islam, Christianity, and Judaism are separate and at war with each other over their ideologies and beliefs. But when one realizes that each box has depth, the further we travel below the surface and deal with these same religions esoterically, we come to realize that the principles of all three are the same, and we are all on the same spiritual course.

21

RADIO WARS

It's physically impossible for two identical objects to occupy the same space at the same time. But, what if the objects were not physical but frequencies, and the space I was referring to was the space between your ears? If you've tuned into your favorite radio station lately, no matter what region you live in, by now you know they're probably engaged in an all out radio war. I remember a time when Hip Hop was only played late at night, if at all, now there are entire stations devoted to urban music. In most cases, there are two or more stations, depending on the market, that cater to Hip Hop. In New York City, two powerhouse stations Hot 97 and Power 105 staged war on each other with an all out assault for ratings, dollars, and notoriety. For years Hot 97 ruled the airwaves in the city, but as the potential to reach more youth through advertising grew, they would soon have company as Power 105 logged on by telling you to flip the switch to the new home of Hip Hop and R&B. At that moment, you knew the shit was going down. Not just in New York, but all around the country because New York is the flagship city for Hip Hop. Sure enough, as I began to travel around the country, there were stations all along the east coast that tried their best to mimic Hot 97, even going as far as having a Latino radio personality that resembled Angie Martinez, and in most cases, they were in direct competition with another station just down the dial. Clear Channel, which owns Power 105, has the largest amount of radio stations throughout America, so they have the power to make or break an artist with their clout alone. If their pilot program works in New York, look for them to begin to launch war against smaller stations in the near future, if they haven't already begun to do so. This is a war being fought, and you're caught in the middle of it. These stations will stop at nothing to reach their intended audience. You are nothing more than cattle being led to economic slaughter. Before we get into the details of what triggered these events, I'd like to pose and attempt to answer a few important questions. 1) Why are wars fought? 2) Who benefits? 3) Who are the "pawns," patsies or in this case, "players" being played? and 4) Who wields the "unseen hand?" Wars are fought for money and power. In this case, the money is your hard earned dollars.

Let's face it, radio stations are not in the business of playing songs, they're in the business of advertisement. As much as we would like to think Hot 97, Power 105 or any other station for that matter, really love Hip Hop music and are playing all of these songs to support and advance the culture, nothing could be further from the truth. The DJs and radio personalities may love it, but the owners could care less, and they are the ones signing the checks and collecting the big bucks. Yet the songs that are played everyday, are directly connected to how they obtain their power, the power to tell you what to wear, what to drive, what to drink, who to shoot, how to treat women and of course, what to buy. How many times have you heard a wack song, but after your favorite station played it a thousand times, you thought it was hot? That's the power radio can have over your conscious and subconscious mind. On the surface it would appear that we are benefiting from having a choice of what station we would like to listen to, but when all the smoke clears, these stations are after the same things, your money and the power to control you. The madness has even breached over into the artists realm, as stations have begun to give certain artists ultimatums in terms of promotion. If an artist does promos for a rival station, he or she may face the harsh reality of losing radio spins or being dropped from the rotation altogether, so as an artist, you must choose your poison. Hot 97 was nicknamed "Shot 97," as incident after incident involving rappers and shootouts became a common event. The ratings would go through the roof as rappers would use the station to vent, or as a platform to attack other rappers. The station, under the guise of being neutral of course, would allow such actions to take place. Meanwhile the only thing they're really con-

cerned about is Arbitron ratings. We certainly don't benefit by having our young brothers and sister who work at these stations and
truly love Hip Hop, hurting, or rappers possibly killing each other
over somebody else's cause. Afterall in the end, no matter what station you choose, somebody other than ourselves will benefit and get
rich.

   To be blunt, we are acting like niggas on the frontline defending
"Massa's" property. The same Willie Lynch tactics of putting one
against the other, and divide and conquer are ever so present if you
pay close attention. Do you think they care if we kill each other off
in the streets like animals? They'll have your position at the station
filled by tomorrow. All the while, the "unseen hand" sits back and
laughs like "look at these niggas fightin' over crumbs." Don't be
fooled. This is a corporate war being fought through Hip Hop, and
when you turn on your radio or television we are the one's being
made to look like savages, while the corporations that are the
"unseen hand" remain just that, "unseen."

ANY QUESTIONS?

22

THE DANGERS OF HIP HOP VIDEOS

Hip Hop videos play a major part in the destruction of the minds of our youth. Just about every Hip Hop video is filled with sex, money, murder, alcohol or drugs. These vices at times are integrated into the videos so subtly, that the conscious and subconscious minds have a hard time detecting the dangerous and negative messages beaming from your television. Therefore, your normal defense mechanisms that would automatically send a signal to your brain indicating that this is just a video, shut down and you begin to believe that this is the normal way of life for all black people. Through the use of visuals conveyed in the form of Hip Hop, your thought process and actions can easily be manipulated into accepting a false reality about the lifestyle of urban America. Videos are one of the tools used to create these realities. As a result, when you see these types of videos a thousand times, that thin line between art and reality becomes extremely blurred. You begin to act out and respond to what you see on screen. This is one of the reasons racist police officers shoot first and ask questions later and white women clutch their pocketbooks or have fear of being raped when in our presence. They don't understand anything about our culture, religious beliefs or language so they turn to B.E.T. (Black Exploitation Television) to learn all about black people.

B.E.T. does an excellent job of showing soft porn, violent and derogatory videos of black people all day long. For 85% of the population, seeing is believing. For those on the outside of the Hip Hop culture but still inside the Matrix of Hip Hop, they're programmed to believe young black men hate their women but love their cars, we all carry guns, sell drugs, get drunk and kill each other. Our women are nothing more than big booty hoes, who love to strip and shake they ass all day. When you add a foreign type of music filled with African drums and a slang filled language that's hard for them to comprehend to the negative visuals, to them we look like nothing more than a new age so called savage tribe. Instead of having bones in our noses, carrying spears, yelling and chasing down wild animals with our half naked women behind us with baskets on their heads, we wear nose rings, carry guns, rhyme and chase down our own brothers with our women dancing nude in the background with hair pieces as big as baskets. Let's not forget what white people did to us five hundred years ago when they thought we were savages. Thanks to Hip Hop videos they still see us as savages today, so can you imagine what they have planned for us tomorrow?

These videos are especially dangerous for young individuals whose brains are still developing, and are very easy to shape and mold. The television is their window to the world and that window is left unguarded because most of our children in today's society are what we call, "latch key kids," meaning the parents are so busy chasing the dollar bill that no one is left at home to raise the child. As a result, the children turn to that "window" to teach them about life. The Matrix of Hip Hop wants your child's mind so they systematically forced both parents out of the house by creating a financial environment that puts a strain on each household and makes it impossible for one parent to maintain it. Now with both parents out of the way, they can raise your child the way they see fit, and then when your children grow up to be menaces to society, parents always ask the million-dollar question, "Where did we go wrong?" The answer is looking you right in the face. It's your television and what comes out of it, in this case, Hip Hop videos and the dangers associated with watching them. It also affects new and upcoming artists who take what they see on screen literally. They emulate these "fake" images to appeal to the fans and record labels when most of them don't have a "thug" bone in their bodies. Record labels will only sign rappers who further perpetuate the "thug life," so most artists conform or kill the true essence of their skills just to get signed, yet if asked why they choose to depict themselves as

"Ghetto Fabulous," nine out of ten would say, "I'm just keepin' it real."

Since most people believe what they see, it's not hard to paint a negative picture of black people using Hip Hop videos. However, if you turn your television to MTV to watch some of those videos by White rock bands, you'll notice that no two videos look the same. Each video is crafty, innovative, and stretches the imagination to ensure that you never stereotype, limit or have unpopular views of White people. But with Hip Hop, they want you to have one view of black people and one view only, a negative one. This is the reason that most of the rap videos that you see today have identical themes. In essence, you're being shown the same video with different music and different artists. The artificial reality being sold to you is the most important part of the video. How many times can you watch a video by your favorite rapper and see the same half naked women, cars with chrome rims, playas iced out, pouring Cristal, and counting money before you realize that the video is not about the artist, but about a lifestyle that the artist is living? Videos are merely four minute commercials used to promote products. The only difference is, you're being sold a multitude of products from sex, drugs and guns, to clothes, jewelry and cars. It's an easy sell because the spokesperson endorsing the merchandise is your favorite rapper who you want to be like anyway. They're responsible for the sale of many of the products that are sold in our community, but most of them will never receive a paycheck in the mail for their services. We think we're players, but it sounds like we are the ones being played.

The Hip Hop world is not exempt from such exploitation practices and those who stand to benefit the most from these actions. Those pulling the strings can use these videos for multiple purposes. First, let's not forget that Hip Hop is worldwide now, so the images shown all over the world of black people wearing diamonds, pushing expensive cars and living in plush houses gives the impression that black people in America are doing well, when in reality, the majority of us are poor, uneducated, incarcerated, discriminated against, beaten by the police and left for dead. Therefore, when black people start crying out about the injustices of America, it is made to appear like it's only a small amount of us who are dissatisfied. Meanwhile, the same video will show that these so called rich and successful black people obtained this fortune through murder, drug selling, pimpin', and corruption, indicating that America has a problem and must do anything and everything humanly possible to destroy these savages who are deteriorating the American way of life. So, to the outside world, any action taken against us by the United States appears justified. The same video is used by America to indirectly apologize for slavery. They flash these videos of us being so called successful, as to say, with their help and support, we as black people have overcome the physical, mental and spiritual oppression of slavery to live side by side with our former oppressors, and due to our success, we have forgiven them and everything is forgotten, when in reality, we are more enslaved than ever before. Many of our elders in Africa to this day refuse to let people take pictures of them or film them for fear of having their souls captured and trapped on film forever. If this is the case, can you imagine how many of our brothers and sisters have willingly sold their souls to be in front of that camera? One day, our obsession with being seen on video will come back to haunt us (see R. Kelly).

The Matrix of Hip Hop can also use these videos to tap into your sexual energies. The ancestors knew and understood that if properly controlled, the sexual energy could be used for multiple purposes including enhancing one's physical, mental, spiritual and psychic abilities, even enabling one to freely travel through space and time. This is why in Khemit you see the penis everywhere. Even in Washington D.C., the monument resembles that of a penis. So, while you're sitting in front of your television lusting at all the half naked women in the videos, the uncontrolled sexual energy that your exuding is being eaten like a tuna fish sandwich by those who know how to tune in to your energy "ethereally." This can also be done with fear, anxiety, stress, depression, and so on.

As spiritual beings, we are aligned and affected by every single star in the universe. Through the use of videos, the Matrix of Hip Hop has broken the law of correspondence (as above so below) by keeping us solely aligned and affected by artificially made "stars" that they themselves create and control. How many times have you been affected when your favorite rapper goes to jail, receives an award or even dies tragically? By focusing on these so-called "stars" on the physical realm, we have fallen out of balance with the universal order of things. By watching the same videos over and over again, our natural ability to ascend has been cut off and we have been locked into a frequency that has stunted our growth. As Biggie stated, "money, hoes and clothes, that's all a nigga knows," and that's all they want you to know.

Back in the days before videos, whenever you heard a song on the radio or playing from the jukebox, you would allow that song to take you wherever your imagination went. Each individual had their own feelings about what a particular song meant and how it affected individuals differently. This is what made songs back in the days so special. The songs forced you to think and use your imagination. Using your imagination is another powerful energy that the Matrix does not want you tapping into, because when you imagine, you have the power to change anything and everything in existence. Therefore, if you can get millions of people to focus on the same negative thoughts at the same time, these thoughts will manifest in the physical. Some of the conditions we live under can be attributed to Hip Hop videos that seduce us into meditative or hypnotic states that channel our energies to produce this reality we call the "Ghetto." Our thought process is the only thing that keeps this illusion in place. Simply by accepting rappers who dis women, talk about murdering their own brothers or worshiping cars and jewelry as normal, it becomes normal. By merging the visual with the audio, this completely shuts down your own ability to think and interpret the song for yourself. No one wants you to think anymore. The Matrix will do the thinking for you. One of the first music videos to revolutionize the art of mind control was "Thriller" by Michael Jackson. Videos, prior to this point, just showed the artist performing the lyrics to the song. This became rather monotonous and boring after a while. Thriller was a ritual video that initiated everyone who watched it. It was even filled with demons, werewolves and goblins. No one ever looked at videos the same after that, and the video single handedly made Thriller the greatest selling album of all time.

Many record companies and artists alike will tell you that a video's main purpose is to provide more exposure for the artist, which in turn, will lead to more record sales. This is straight "blue pill shit." In this day and time, we must begin to take the "red pill" and open our first eye to see what's really going on, and who's behind this madness involving Hip Hop videos. Not only do we need to hold record companies responsible, but also we need to check some of these video directors who get paid a lot of money to direct the same videos over and over again. Remember, "Anyone who hasn't been unplugged is potentially an agent" (the Matrix), and what do artists call the person who is responsible for the direction of their career? Agents. Every time an artist accepts a big paycheck to portray our people in such negative roles, it shows just how addicted they are to "blue pills." This is why when you approach them about taking more responsibility and not accepting the images that damage us as a people, they don't even see anything wrong with what they're doing, or they say, "I'm just trying to get paid," and continue to feign for the next "blue pill" fix. Turning down those dead Presidents and refusing to assist in the death of our people is equivalent to taking the "red pill" and detoxing from this Hip Hop Matrix, yet how many rappers are ready to look into the mirror and say, "I am an addict?" Not every rapper is guilty of "blue pill" syndrome. Artists like Busta Rhymes, Common, The Roots and OutKast, just to name a few, do an excellent job at putting out videos that assist in breaking the spell that the Matrix has on the people. However, there is much more work that needs to be done and many more artists that need to detox before we are totally free of the dangers of Hip Hop videos.

23

WHO WANTS TO BE LIKE MIKE?

Tyson, Jackson, or Jordan. Wait, before you answer this question I must warn you, "Be careful what you wish for because you just might get it." Most of us would love to be like Mike, to be considered as the greatest athlete or entertainer of our time, and to be adored by millions of fans all over the world. To be like Mike would also mean being the richest of your profession. The question I should be asking is, Who wouldn't wannabe like Mike? But to be like Mike has its downsides as well. It involves scandals, controversy, accusations, and allegations. To be like Mike is to be a convicted rapist, an alleged child molester, a compulsive gambler and womanizer. To be like Mike is to be trapped in an image of perfection that if you attempt to escape from and be a normal person, you're scrutinized and demoralized. To be like Mike is to have all of your shortcomings magnified by a thousand times in the eyes of the public. So, you still wanna be like Mike? To be like Mike is to have the media intrude into your personal life 24 hours a day, 7 days a week. To be like Mike is not being able to take your family out to eat in a public place without being mobbed by obsessed fans who feel just because they support you, you're obligated to sign an autograph. To be like Mike is to carry a great portion of the American economy on your shoulders, based on the products you endorse or what trends you set that Corporate America can capitalize on. To be like Mike is to be human with many faults, but to have every man, woman, and child worship your image more than God itself.

Are you sure you wanna be like Mike? Well, as strange as it may seem, many of us, especially Hip Hoppers, prove that we are like Mike, just not the greater half of Mike. How many rappers are con-

145

victs, murderers, hustlers, and playas and we applaud them for "keepin' it real?" In fact, two of the greatest rappers of all time, Tupac and Biggie, fall under these four categories and nobody seemed to have a problem with that. Yet when Tyson, Jackson, or Jordan make the mistakes of showing that they're human, we make their lives a living hell. At times, we all fall short or make mistakes in our quest for greatness. It just shows the human side of us. Let's not forget that before Mike was great, Mike was human. So every individual who's made mistakes, but would not like to be judged solely on these mishaps on their journey to greatness, should stand up and shout, "I am Michael Jordan! I am Michael Jackson! I am Mike Tyson!" Perhaps, this will give a whole new meaning to the words, "Like Mike ... If I Could be Like Mike."

THE KING OF "SHOT"
THE KING OF "BOP"
THE KING OF "POP"

The lives of these three superstars seem to mirror each other in more ways than one. Over the last decade or so, when one is triumphant, they all appear to be triumphant, and when one is going through hard times, they all seem to share in each other's pain or suffer from similar consequences. Is this just coincidence or are they destined to share the same fate?

In 1990, Mike Tyson was the heavyweight champion of the world with an astonishing record of 37-0 with 33 KO's. In 1991, Michael Jordan won his first of six N.B.A. titles and was by far the best player in the world. Also in 1991, Michael Jackson signed the largest recording contract ever with Sony Records, which validated his position as King of Pop. They were clearly the best of the best, but just as their careers peaked at the same time, they hit "valleys" at the same time as well. Their lives began to mimic the stock market, with many ups and downs along the way. The downfalls started with the arrest and conviction of Mike Tyson for rape in 1992. After losing his title in one of the biggest upsets in boxing history in 1990 to Buster Douglas, that aura of being invincible was gone, which led to some bad decisions by Tyson resulting in a three-year prison term. In 1993, Michael Jordan's personal life took center stage as the media began to have a field day with his bad gambling habits with "shady" characters like Richard Esquinas and James "Slim" Bouler, whom Jordan had testified under oath that he had lost over $57,000 to. Jordan had lied earlier about even knowing Bouler to cover up these losses. Subsequently, two unidentified sources see Mike gambling in Atlantic City the night before game two of a playoff series with the New York Knicks. To add injury to insult, Jordan loses his father, who was murdered while sleeping in his car off the side of a highway in North Carolina. Just when it looked like it couldn't get any worse, the father of a 13 year old boy files charges against Michael Jackson for child abuse in December 1993. These charges rocked fans all over the world and forced Jackson to go on the air in a live broadcast to deny these charges. He eventually settled out of court for a multi-million dollar amount, but says payment was not an admission of guilt.

The media was having a field day with Mike, Mike, and Mike. The saga would continue over the next five to six years as Jordan would retire from the N.B.A. for an unsuccessful stint at baseball, return to win three more titles then retire again. Jackson would marry then divorce Lisa Marie Presley, marry again, have 2 children with an unknown white woman and put out 2 unsuccessful albums in the process. Not to be outdone, Tyson returned from prison as a Muslim and was acting other than a righteous man, as he would be involved in brawl after brawl outside of the ring, and more women would step forward with allegations of sexual abuse. Yet once again, this trio would rise in the face of adversity in an attempt to reclaim their positions as the best of the best. In 2001, Tyson, Jackson, and Jordan launched comebacks at or around the same time. After a couple of warm-up fights, Tyson appeared to be in tip top shape, but lost his comeback fight to Lennox Lewis. As weak as the heavyweight division is, I still believe Mike Tyson will be the heavyweight champion of the world once more. Jordan returned to the hardwood as a Washington Wizard to "Scratch an Itch," he said had been bothering him for a while. Even though he said this comeback is for the love of the game, he never got the Wizards into the playoffs, which would have possibly been his greatest achievement ever as a player. Michael Jackson returned with a new album entitled, "Invincible." The album was doing well by normal artist standards, but it was a failure in terms of Michael Jackson standards, and failed to reestablish Michael as the King of Pop. Now as if on cue, all three of them have fallen from grace once more, as Jackson barely won an acquittal in his recent trial after being accused of being a pedophile for the second time. As much as Jordan has done for the N.B.A., he can't even acquire part ownership of the league that he helped build, and Tyson is dead broke and lost another attempt at a comeback as he quit in the middle of a fight against a bum whose name is not even worthy of a mention. Could this possibly be the end for the three? We can only hope that that Tyson's heart is made of "Iron," Jordan proves to be a "Wizard" off the court with his shoe company and other business ventures, as well as he was on the court, and Jackson shows the world that he is still, "Invincible" after beating the current charges that he was facing. Only time will tell.

WHAT'S IN A NAME?

Many names carry vibrations or special meanings that define a person's life or give it purpose. According to the Catholic religion, the name Michael signifies, "Who is like to God." This was also the war cry of the Archangel St. Michael and the good angels in the battle fought in heaven against Satan and his followers. Holy Scripture describes St. Michael as, "one of the Chief Princes and leader of the forces of heaven in their triumph over the powers of hell." In essence, this is a war being fought since the beginning of time. Ever since Satan and his followers were cast down to earth, they have ruled this realm and everything of material in it and have not stopped the assault on the Michaels of the world. If fame, fortune, and women are tools used by Satan to weaken his prey, then Tyson, Jackson, and Jordan are forever indebted. This ongoing war may also explain the character assassination each of our "Princes" face everyday. At times, it appears to be a big game to Satan who builds

Michael up, only to destroy him again in a slow torturous manner, proving that he and only he is the owner of Michael's mind, body, and soul.

The uncharacteristic behavior and actions of the three Michaels can lead one to believe that "greater" forces control their lives. Michael Jordan plays for the Washington "Wizards." The N.B.A. was in decline in his absence, but since his return every arena he plays in has sold out, which translates into millions of dollars. Corporate America is smiling as well, leaving me to ask the question, who's really casting the spells? Mike Tyson has been reduced to an animal like cannibal who feeds on the blood of innocent humans, but "Who's really being sacrificed?" And right before our eyes, Michael Jackson is transforming and mutating into an alien like being. "Are we being controlled by forces out of this world?"

Further proof that this could be the work of Satan can be found in the numerology of the name Michael, which adds up to the number 6 (M=13 +I=9 +C=3 +H=8 +A=1 +E=5 +L=12=51, 5+1=6). Michael times three equals 666. In heaven, Michael won the war against Satan and his followers. Let's hope history repeats itself here on earth for the good of all mankind.

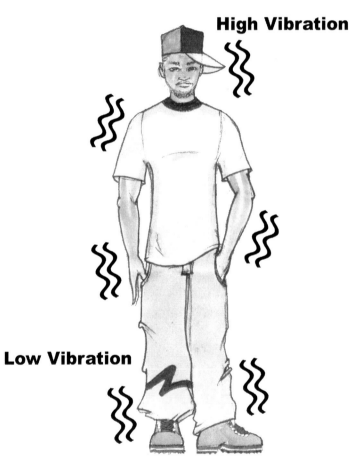

High Vibration

Low Vibration

Vibrations Illustrations - Everything in the universe is moving, some things are moving faster than others. This is what we call its vibration. To reach the higher spiritual frequencies, one must raise his or her vibration equal to or greater than the energy that they're trying to communicate with. The activation of the chakras and what we eat mentally and spiritually can assist us in this process.

24

HOW IMPORTANT IS IMAGE?

Image is nothing. Or at least that's what Sprite would like you to think in its ad campaign to sell soda. However, if that's the case, then why do they use well-known artists, especially rappers and athletes, in their commercials? The truth of the matter is image is everything. It's what sells products or gets candidates elected, or even has the power to get defendants acquitted. Notice that I didn't suggest whether the candidate was qualified, or if the defendant was innocent or not. As long as the image suggests that they are, in most cases, that's all that really matters. This is why Corporate America spends billions of dollars every year on marketing, promoting, and creating images. The Hip Hop world is no different. One of Webster's definitions of the word, "Image" is the projection of something that isn't really there. We will examine this definition a little closer in its relation to Hip Hop very shortly.

Images are captured on film negatives, CD ROMs, picture frames, etc. This too will prove to be crucial in this analysis of image, regarding its role in this art form we love so much. Thousands of images are captured by our brains every minute! In fact, there is no camera on the market today more powerful at capturing and storing images than the human brain, especially one with melanin. Those who study mind control know and understand the importance of image. They understand that an alchemical process takes place when you tap into your memory bank to conjure up images surrounding that particular thought, and based on the nature of that thought, this will determine if the images are negative or positive. This also has an affect on the physical body as well.

These images are stored forever just like on a film negative. Even the most frightening or horrible experiences from our past can be relived with a simple flash of the images associated with that experience. This becomes a very powerful weapon for those who choose to use it as such. They no longer have to assassinate you physically, they can destroy your character through what I like to call, "Image Assassination."

For instance, let's say you have powerful images in your mind of Will Smith, Wesley Snipes, Chris Tucker, Tracey Morgan, and Ving Rhames as being positive black men and role models to our community. Then you see them depicted as gay men in movies such as, Six Degrees of Separation, Too Wong Foo, Fifth Element, The Longest Yard, and Pulp Fiction. (Even though Rhames didn't play a gay character, there was a scene in Pulp Fiction where he engaged in a sexual act with another man.) Even though we know that these men aren't gay and they're just acting, these images of them as such are captured forever, and whenever the media feels like it, they can flash these images across the screen to force you to relive the negative portrayal of our strong black men. This can be done to target the conscious or subconscious mind, the more subtle the image, the more potent the affect.

The image of Muhammad Ali in the 60's was that of a powerful black man, one who would annihilate his opponent physically, mentally, and verbally. His stand against America during the time of the Vietnam War in the prime of his career was arguably by far the most courageous act by any individual in the history of the United States. Here's the image of a black man refusing to fight in a white man's war, and forcing America to acknowledge him as Muhammad Ali, not his slave name Cassius Clay. He served as a beacon of light for black people all over the world. In fact, according to the Guinness Book of World Records, he is the most written about individual in the history of the world. Yet, the image of Ali today is somewhat of a disgrace. Not the man himself, he will forever be the greatest, but the image of Ali plastered all over the screen is a disgrace. The image that I'm referring to, in particular, is the one of Ali representing America in the 1996 Olympics, stumbling and fumbling with the torchlight as if he is about to fall. Keep in mind that in his prime, Muhammad Ali was anti-American based on the teachings of the honorable Elijah Muhammad. He also taught Ali that the white man was the devil. America never forgave Ali for these actions, so they put him on display for the whole world to see and said look at this man you once called your hero. He is nothing now. This was done to destroy the positive image you once had of him. Unfortunately, the younger generation who never saw Ali in his prime will only store the image of the latter. You never saw pictures or events involving former President Ronald Reagan, who had Alzheimer's disease before he died, why? The reason is that white people always preserve the images of their fallen heroes. They want you to remember them in their state of greatness.

Now lastly, let's look at image from a spiritual level. Take the image of Jesus Christ. You know, the famous painting, The Last Supper, by Leonardo Da Vinci in which he painted Christ in the image of European decent. Even though we know that this is just a picture painted to favor the image of its creator, it sits at the head of every major church in the world as the official picture of Jesus Christ. Yet the Bible states that Jesus had "hair of wool and feet like bronze," which would suggest along with the region in which he was born in that Jesus was a black man. So here is God's only son depicted in the image of a white man, so God must be white right? That's the power of image. The masters of mind control (Yes, I'm talking about the Illuminati, let's be clear) also like to use a technique I call, "Reverse Imaging." Just about every actor and artist falls victim to this technique. It involves sending a positive flow of energy to the conscious mind, while sending a negative flow to the subconscious mind or vice versa. For example, through music, movies, the tellalievision, and with the help of the media

By now you're probably saying to yourself, what does all this have to do with Hip Hop? Well since you have chosen to take the red pill and enter the Matrix of Hip Hop by reading this article, I felt compelled to show you just how deep the rabbit hole goes, and show you the inner and outer relations of image, and the effect it has on Hip Hop. Now let's move on. You can go to any urban city in America, especially New York, and see the same images of us being portrayed. Brothers "chillin" on the corner, pants "saggin," "sportin" durags on the dome, and "rockin" the latest kicks, "puffin" on a lil herb, "drinkin" a 40, and tryin to "holla" at some shorties. And that ain't even the "hustlin" cats. They roll in benzo's, lexo's, and beamers sittin on 20's straight iced out. The images of our women are even worse. Straight "hoochie" mamas, dressed like strippers wit they ass all out. Two and three baby daddies, they gotta get paid or you can't get laid type a sisters. Not all of our people fit this description of course, but if you watch videos and movies with black people you would think so. No matter what city, whether it's weed or indo, beamers or six fo's, the language and style may be different, but the images are all the same. Most Hip Hoppers would say "we just keepin' it real." Yes, but the question I have to ask is whose reality? Is it an artificially created reality? And what are the tools used to bring this artificial reality into existence? The answer is Hip Hop music. You ever notice that wherever you go in the United States, it seems that you are in the same place? There's a mall, movie theater, Burger King, etc. in every city. This is called, "Social Engineering" and is done to keep you from having an original thought. You feel at home even when you're not, and as long as you see the same images flashing into your brain, the mind control program will always be in place. This is why the Monks go up into the mountains to free themselves from this artificial environment. The Hip Hop world is a victim of what I like to call, "Cultural Engineering." Our very way of life is dictated to us through Hip Hop songs and videos with images so powerful, it's hard to distinguish what's art and what's real. This keeps an entire nation of young, energetic, and spiritual beings locked into a negative frequency, a low vibration of material worship and seeing ourselves other than Kings and Queens. So when your favorite rapper says, "I'm just rappin' about what I know," he's probably telling the truth.

The record companies play a major role in the images of its artists. If labels only sign artists with these negative images, then every new artist will attempt to conform his image to be a thug, hustler, pimp or banger. These images are then shown all over the world via satellite as a representation of all black people, so if ever there comes a time to annihilate us, it would appear justified. We must be held more accountable for the images we portray. Every artist that loves Hip Hop must begin to reevaluate their position in the game.

Understand that it is deeper than it really appears. There are those who stand to benefit from our ignorance because they know who you are, but do you? We must begin to flash images that remind us that we were once Gods and Goddesses. Images that vibrate on higher frequencies that will help us escape this current Matrix lockdown and prepare us for the next paradigm.

Michael Jackson attempted to do just that when he flashed images of our glorious past in his, "Remember the Time" video and it almost cost him his career. Therefore, this is a very dangerous task, but a task that must be completed or our future generations will be doomed. We must never take the images that we represent for granted. Whether it's rappin', movies, commercials, or advertisements we must understand that image is everything.

25

THE NEW KING OF NEW YORK
A NEW YORK RHYME STORY PART 2

Once again, violence has escalated on the streets of New York. After a brief cease fire between the rhyme families, the quest for money power and respect has come full circle, due to the sudden retirement of Jay-Z. It has always been assumed by many that Jay-Z would be the last Don of New York, but after barely surviving a near rubout by Nas, he felt that this would be the perfect time to say goodbye. Rarely is a Don allowed to just retire, there are only two ways out of the game, death and death. That means, either your career is ended, or you leave in a body bag. But Jay was loved and respected by Dons all over the world, he was one of them you know, a real hoodfella, and since he agreed to stay in the game as a made man, but in a lesser role, no harm would come to him. Under normal conditions, Jay would call a sit down with the other rhyme families in New York to name his successor, that's just the ways things are done in organized rhyme, but Jay and his right hand Dame Dash were at each other's throats. This left the Roc-A-Fella rhyme family, one of the most powerful in the country, in a state of turmoil. Dame wanted to be his own boss, so they split the empire, but this still left unfinished business in New York about who would be the next Don. Rumors began to spread that the next Don would be Fat Joe a.k.a. "Joey Crack," or Jadakiss a.k.a. "The Kiss of Death," or perhaps an underboss out of Queens by the name of Ja Rule a.k.a. "it's Murder." All of these underbosses were highly qualified for the job, but in the end, none of them would receive the title of Don, The New King of New York. That's because a young wannabe capo from Queens by the name of 50 Cent would lay claim to that throne. Back in the day he was a loose cannon just trying to make a name for himself. He was a low level street hustler, but he knew the streets well. Everywhere he went he made connections with anyone and everyone that was moving product in the streets. Every mix DJ that was slinging dope, he wanted in. Every rhyme cipher, he wanted in. Every recording session that took place, he wanted in. Nothing was going down in the hood unless he was involved. Nothing was given to Fifty, he worked harder than anyone else on the underground. He respected the current Don, but had aspirations of becoming a Don himself one day, but he would do it the unconventional way, by building his own rhyme family from the underground up, and then launch a hostile takeover. Most Dons came up through the ranks of another rhyme family and went from soldier to lieutenant, and then from captain to underboss, and finally, from capo to Don. Fifty knew he was in for a long hard fight but he figured, an underground mix-tape here, an underground mix-tape there, and before you know it, badaboom badabang, he could be king. Being close to the streets gave 50 Cent an advantage not even the Don him self had, he knew what, and most importantly, who was going to be hot before it reached the masses of the people. He was able to build an alliance with all of the hustlers on the come up that were dissatisfied with the current Don who they felt was getting too big for his own good, was too main stream, and was receiving too much media coverage. They felt that Jay-Z's clientele wasn't geared toward the streets anymore, and rule number one of a Don is: never forget where you came from, or the people that put you there. The streets were talking, it was time for a change, and 50 Cent would bring that change about.

Fifty wanted the world and everything in it. He knew that with the right team, he could go straight to the top, so he assembled a team of hoodfellas that he felt he could trust. His main crew was Bang 'Em Smurf, Tony Yayo, and Lloyd Banks. In no time, he built an army of street soldiers that were ready for war. He would call his rhyme family, the G-Unit Soldiers. The streets were talking about the new underboss of the underground, but none of the current underbosses or the Don himself seemed to notice. This didn't sit too well with Fifty, he knew that if he was going to be taken seriously he would have to earn the respect of those that were running things.

Fifty was left with no choice but to let off a warning shot with the hit "How to Rob," which took aim at all of the bigwigs in the industry. Now he had their attention. From that moment on, all of the rhyme families were put on notice; their time to rule was over. Even Jay-Z had to admit, he liked Fifty's style and admired his hunger. From that moment he knew who the next Don would probably be when the time was right. He knew Fifty wasn't ready just yet, but he would still have to keep a close eye on him because of his reputation, a reputation of being a tough thug that got pinched once or twice, did a little time in the joint, and one that was no nonsense when it came to getting his money in the streets. But when you let off shots at other rhyme families, be prepared for retaliation. As Fifty sat in his car one night on the south side of Queens, shots were fired at him, hitting him nine times. These were not warning shots, this was a hit of a different kind, one that was destined to end his life and send a message to anyone trying to cut in on the money and power of the existing rhyme families. Miraculously, he survived the hit, which only added to his legend of being unstoppable. Speculation began to spread that the order was carried out by the Murder Inc. family, headed by Queens' underboss Ja Rule. Fifty and Ja Rule had a little run in back in the day when Fifty was on the come up. He approached Ja and tried to shake his hand. Even though Fifty was well on his way to being the underboss of the underground, Ja looked down at him, and saw him as a mere peasant, as if to say, "come and see me if you want a job." Fifty felt disrespected, and vowed never to forget that day. Things would only get worse for Fifty, his dreams of becoming the next Don would go down the drain as he was released from the record label that he thought would take him straight to the top. But whatever doesn't kill you, will only make you stronger, as Fifty laid in a hospital bed putting the pieces of his life back together, he vowed to get revenge.

THE SIT DOWN

Once he recovered, Fifty hit the streets harder than ever, rebuilding relationships and mending fences. He hit the mix-tape circuit harder than anyone had ever witnessed before. With a gun on his waist, a vest on his chest, and revenge on his mind, Fifty was determined to get his payback, but he knew that he still didn't have the muscle needed to go at his arch nemesis, Murder Inc. However, that would all change. His power moves weren't going unnoticed, a Don out of Detroit by the name of Eminem a.k.a. Slim Shady, arranged a sit down with Fifty to discuss possibly working together. This was not uncommon in organized rhyme; if a Don from another state wanted to move in on a new market, he had to make alliances in that particular market. Eminem could have easily made a connection with the current Don of New York, but maybe he knew that Jay's reign would be short lived now that Fifty was back. The Don of all Dons, Dr. Dre, was also present at the sit down to make sure that everything went smoothly. Eminem made Fifty an offer he couldn't refuse, money, power, and the connections to be the next Don of New York. Dr. Dre agreed to supply Fifty with the purest uncut dope that could be found anywhere. Now the stage was set, Fifty had everything he needed to take over New York. News spread quickly of his power and connections. This didn't sit too well with the Murder Inc. rhyme family, who had earlier issued a warning to all other rhyme families that if they make an alliance with Fifty, they were making an enemy with Murder Inc. So the moment that the Aftermath rhyme family made an alliance with Fifty, they were automatically declaring war with Murder Inc., it was just that simple. Fifty had enough firepower to go right at Jay-Z, but he had some personal unfinished business with Ja Rule and Murder Inc. first.

SAY HELLO TO THE BAD GUY!

Fifty wasted no time putting out a "hit" on Ja Rule with "Wanksta," a shotgun blast at Ja's reputation, street credibility, and rhyming style. The shot hit Murder Inc. kinda hard. It appeared to be over for Ja, but he would quickly launch a counter attack of his own with a shot at Fifty's reputation. It wasn't in song form, but he questioned whether Fifty was a snitch or working for the feds outright. Ja claimed to have evidence in the form of an order of protection against Murder Inc. that proved to be damaging to Fifty's reputation as a Don. This went against the code of silence held by all Dons. They would trade "hits" for the next year or two with Ja Rule getting the worst of it. It even got so bad that Eminem found himself in the line of fire, he then returned fire of his own. When all of the smoke cleared, Ja Rule was left for dead. The might of G-Unit and Aftermath together proved to be too much for Murder Inc. They were on the verge of being shut down for good. While Fifty was claiming victory due to his lyrical onslaught of Murder Inc., The Inc. claimed that it was Fifty dry snitching on wax that led to their demise. Back in the days, Fifty released a song called "Ghetto Quran" which spoke of the shady dealings of some of the henchmen that worked for the Murder Inc. rhyme family. On the surface it appeared to just be a song, but the feds had assigned a special task force, called the Hip Hop police, to bring down different factions of organized rhyme, so it's no doubt that they were listening in. Also keeping a close eye on the situation were some of the other under-bosses in New York like Fat Joe and Jadakiss. They weren't pleased with the way Fifty was running things. They accused Fifty of getting too big and receiving too much media coverage, the same things that Fifty accused Jay-Z of earlier. Even worse, Fifty was running the city from another state! This was unprecedented in organized rhyme. This didn't sit too well with the other rhyme families that walked the mean streets of the city everyday. The streets were talking, and the other rhyme families agreed, that's too much power for one man to have. Shouts of "I say we make 'em dead, you give me the order" could be heard from some of the most notorious Emcees ready to put out the "hit" needed to take Fifty down. But to Fifty's credit, he kept his ear to the street and seemed to stay two steps ahead of his adversaries. It was easy for him to put himself in their shoes because he was in the same position not too long ago. He continued to build his team up and brace for war. He recruited a young soldier out of Tennessee by the name of Young Buck; his street team was stronger than ever, but his biggest acquisition was the pick up of a West Coast gangsta by the name of Game. Game reminded Fifty a lot of himself, he was hungry and determined to make a name for himself in organized rhyme, he just needed a break. As a favor to Dr. Dre, Fifty took him under his wing and showed him the inner workings of organized rhyme. Fifty felt the extra firepower would come in handy, especially since Tony Yayo was still in the joint after getting pinched a little earlier. The only question that remained was, who would make the first move.

IT'S WAR!

Just when it seemed like Ja Rule was buried with dirt on him, he returned with avengeance. This time, he enlisted the help of "Joey Crack" and the "Kiss of Death" on a hit called "New York." This wasn't a direct hit on Fifty, but based on the firepower and alignment of three underbosses on one song, he knew what time it was. Fifty shouted "okay!" You wanna go to war! I take you to war! Say hello to my little friend! He then released a "hit" called "Piggy Bank." This was a machine gun blast that had everybody scattering and running for cover. Shots hit Fat Joe, Jadakiss, and Ja Rule. He even blasted off on Nas and his first lady Kelis, and Shyne who was locked up doing time. No one in the history of organized rhyme had taken a shot at so many people at one time before. This definitely meant war. Not to be outdone, Jadakiss and Fat Joe fired shots simultaneously at Fifty with the "hits," "Animal" and "My Fo Fo." Jadakiss hit Fifty with a lyrical barrage so powerful that innocent bystanders took cover, and he was just clearing his throat. Fat Joe unloaded his shot, but appeared more inclined to deal with Fifty in the streets where he was the realest gangsta. Fifty withstood every shot thrown his way and screamed "that's all you got!" "That's all you got!" He said okay, I'm reloaded! Fifty then dropped a mega bomb called "I Run New York" with his partner in crime Tony Yayo who just came home. Jadakiss, being the lyrical gangsta that he is, returned fire again with a tech nine rhyme called "Checkmate," but in the end, Fifty was still standing. In a strange turn of events, in the middle of his war with New York, one of Fifty's soldiers, Game, decided enough was enough. He was tired of taking orders from Fifty, he wanted to be his own boss, and this caused a major conflict in the G-Unit rhyme family. There could only be one boss. Fifty saw a lot of Game in himself, but he knew that it was time to sever their ties. It got bloody as it often does in organized rhyme, with one of Games henchmen from his Black Wall Street rhyme family taking a slug. A sit down had to be called quickly because Game was from the West Coast. This could have major ramifications in the entire world of Hip Hop. If this escalated into another East Coast/West Coast war, it could affect rhyme families as far as the Dirty South, and in the end, no one would get any money. So a truce was agreed upon, or at least on the surface. It was a public spectacle that brought the two families together in a show of solidarity. The media was happy, the fans were happy, and everybody went their separate ways. Shortly thereafter, it was back to war. This time Game let off his lyrical Uzi in an ambush of Fifty and the G-Unit soldiers called "300 Bars and Runnin'." He also took aim at some of the existing Roc-A-Fella soldiers, but not at Jay. This could be a rhyme story in the making in the near future.

With rhyme families coming at Fifty from all angles, he's boxed into a corner. Will Fifty survive, or is this the beginning of the end for the new King of New York? Fifty knows that he may have won the battle, but the war is far from over. The G-unit just got stronger with the addition of Mobb Deep and M.O.P., so can anybody stop him now? Fifty is beginning to feel like he's untouchable, this means that the only way his organization can be brought down is from the inside out. But when you become a figure that's larger than life, you become a prisoner of your own success, your paranoia keeps you isolated from the outside world, and you trust no one. So who can get close enough to do the job? Perhaps the ones who put him in power in the first place. Dr. Dre and Eminem have to be fed up with Fifty's antics by now. Maybe it's time for them to bring him down before it's too late. In organized rhyme, there are seen and unseen forces at work, and when you get too big for your own good, the "hit" will come. It's just the nature of the business, but I'm sure that Fifty is well aware that there's only two ways out of the game, death and death, so he's gonna ride it until the wheels fall off. Jay-Z must feel like Don Corleone right now, he's probably saying "every time I try to get out, they keep pulling me right back in!" Could he be the one to restore order to organized rhyme, or what about Nas? Rumor has it that he's ready to launch an attack on Fifty. Maybe two of the greatest Emcees of all time, who were once enemies are now conspiring together to bring an end to this madness called Fifty Cent. This could get very interesting in the near future. Stay tuned for the next episode of A New York Rhyme Story.

Machine World Illustration - Radios, televisions, and magazines are all machine manufactured; we have been mentally plugged into the machine which controls our thought process. Whatever the Matrix wants us to believe, it simply feeds it into the system that we are already plugged into, and we react. Our thoughts are not self generated, but artificially generated.

26

T.H.U.G.L.I.F.E. TO THE LIFE OF A THUG

Being that he was one of the most prolific figures of our time, we'll take a closer look at Tupac's vision of T.H.U.G.L.I.F.E. and how it relates to the life of a thug. For all of these rappers claiming to live the thug life, there's really no difference. But that's where they're wrong. To assist me in making my point, I'll be using T.H.U.G.L.I.F.E. with higher case letters to represent the higher self, one's Godhead. This is the side one would use to uplift himself or walk upright, the side of positive thought and action. I'll use thug life with lower case letters to represent the lower self, one's animalistic side. This is the side of one who acts grimy in nature, the side of negative thought and action. They both operate within the same space of one's existence, each fighting to destroy the other so that they may rule alone. It's the mystery of the Holy Cross. If you stand up straight and hold your arms out horizontally, you are the Holy Cross. Your horizontally spread arms divide your higher self from your lower self. It was the struggle Tupac was facing until the day he died, the battle between the T.H.U.G. in him, and the thug in him. He started out as a thug from the gutter who fought until his last breath to live and elevate his people to the highest degree of T.H.U.G.L.I.F.E. Yet Tupac, like many of our "sons," died on the "Cross," never truly reaching T.H.U.G.L.I.F.E. paradise. When Tupac created T.H.U.G.L.I.F.E., which stands for The Hate U Gave Little Infants Fuck Everybody, the message was clear: you reap what you sow. How could one expect these infants to grow up to be anything but thugs after all the hate that they have been given? But when that, "I don't give a fuck," thug attitude started spreading like wildfire into the suburbs, eating at the very fabric of the American way of life, everybody got fucked. That hate has now given birth to a nation of killers, drug dealers, hustlers, and rappers, all coming in the name of a thug. I very seriously doubt if this is what Tupac had in mind.

Motion is the first law of the universe, and Tupac understood that everything must move or it will die. So he began to ascend from negative to positive, from thug to T.H.U.G., with visions of starting a whole T.H.U.G.L.I.F.E. movement of lyrical T.H.U.G.S, political T.H.U.G.S, lawyer T.H.U.G.S, and spiritual T.H.U.G.S. He was like the phoenix rising out of the ashes of the Black Panther Party keeping the spirit of that movement alive, only disguised as T.H.U.G.L.I.F.E. This is when he became very dangerous. You can kill the messenger, but not the message. You can kill the revolutionary, but not the revolution. They knew that they could kill the T.H.U.G., but the question was, "Could they kill the T.H.U.G.L.I.F.E.?" Or would Tupac becoming a martyr magnify his positive vision a thousand times? As a result, a well-calculated plan was put into place to kill the T.H.U.G. and his vision. Killing the T.H.U.G. himself was the easy part, but killing the T.H.U.G.L.I.F.E. would not be as simple. An energy of this magnitude would require an extensive amount of time, power, and sophistication to eliminate. After Tupac was physically removed, like clockwork rappers from every coast started coming out of the woodworks claiming to be thugs, "I'm a thug," "Yeah, I'm a thug," "Yo son, I'm a thug." That's all you hear when you turn on the radio these days or watch videos, yet their words, ways, and actions show that they're vibrating on the lower frequency of the word, all the while drawing energy from the higher frequency of the word, making it weaker and weaker. Some rappers even come in the name of Tupac, only to defecate on his spirit with their negative use of the word T.H.U.G. It's been many years since his death, and with the help of the media, the word T.H.U.G. has been reduced into the word thug, from positive to negative, from higher self to lower self. If I were a bettin' man, I'd say that this was the plan all along. There are many people who are very afraid of this energy that has the ability to rise up a people who are considered to be nothing and transform them into something. Fortunately for us, energy cannot be destroyed, only contained. For all of these rappers who think that they are carrying on the tradition of Tupac by calling themselves thugs, they need to realize that they're actually doing him a disservice by their misuse of the word. Tupac is probably turning over in his grave every time the word thug is connected to his name. He lives on through the music, but it's through the music that his energy is being destroyed.

His vision of T.H.U.G.L.I.F.E. and the powerful messages that he dropped in his music made many people feel like Tupac was the "One," but the key to the mystery is that we are all the "One." Just think about what it took for you to get here, billions of sperm cells racing up the birth canal knowing that only one will be chosen and the rest will die. After a process of qualifying and disqualifying, you have been selected to be the "One." That's deep. We all have a T.H.U.G. deep within us, but it seems that it's so much easier to just be a thug, especially if you're watching Hip Hop videos or tuned into your favorite rap station. Tupac was human, so he too had to deal with the same struggles that we face every day in terms of becoming the best that we can be. He was also born under the astrological sign of Gemini, which is symbolized by the twins. This dual personality enabled him to cross the line and reach thugs because he also spoke their language, and show them how to become T.H.U.G.S. Today, you're frowned upon if you're not a thug. R Kelly even professes to be the R&B thug, and if you listen to his music close enough, you can sense the struggle within him to defeat the thug in him and become a T.H.U.G. He's constantly calling on God for help because he's weak. Unfortunately, it appears that the thug in him has prevailed. Ja Rule is another one who has tapped into Tupac's energy to make him stronger. He sampled Tupac's music and voice, even called on Suge Knight in what appears to be some kind of sick ritual to drain every last drop of energy that may still exist by calling on Tupac. He then topped it off by calling up the radio station Hot 97, which is based out of New York, and said that he was going to "bring Tupac back." What did he mean by that? Then there was Nas who reenacted the death of Tupac in a video by becoming him, to spiritually align his energy with Tupac's. 50 Cent also has some of Tupac's energy, constantly calling himself a thug.

The list is endless of thugs coming in the name of Tupac, but how many are willing to keep his vision alive? I've often heard people speak of Dr. King and his dream, and if he were alive today, would his dream be realized. The answer is no. So, I pose the question to you, if Tupac were alive today, would he be happy with what T.H.U.G.L.I.F.E. has become?

27

EVERY HERO NEEDS A VILLAIN

And every great champion needs a great challenger. Who would Batman be without the Joker? Who would Superman be without Lex Luther? Who would Ali be without Frazier? I remember talking to the legendary Emcee Busy Bee one day about his battle with Kool Moe Dee and he said to me, "I made Moe Dee." Since Busy Bee got crushed in that battle, I asked him what he meant by that. He said, "Before our battle, people knew who Kool Moe Dee was, but it wasn't until he put it on me that he became the legend that he is today." After he broke it down like that, I began to understand a hero's need for a villain and a champ's need for a great challenger. Who would George Bush Sr. be without Saddam Hussein? Who would George W. Bush be without Osama Bin Laden? Or better yet, who would God be without the Devil? Can one exist without the other? Or are they just different degrees of the same thing? We live in a world of polarity. We need left so that we may know what right is. We need up so we may know what down is. Just like we need "gangsta rap" so that we may know what conscious rap is. It's the yin and yang of all things.

Soon we'll be asking what is Power 105 without Hot 97? They're constantly at beef with each other, but they really need each other as a measurement of one's greatness over the other. (Does that even make sense?) Who is Biggie without Tupac? Who is Bad Boy without Death Row? And who is Jay-Z without Nas? Every hero needs a villain, and every great champ needs a great challenger to solidify his or her position in history, even if you have to manufacture one. In the movie "Unbreakable," starring Samuel L. Jackson and Bruce Willis, Jackson played a very fragile man (Mr. Glass) whose purpose in life wasn't fulfilled until he found his very oppo-site (Unbreakable) played by Willis. Jay-Z, in his prime, had no one to compare himself to, except Biggie, and since Biggie is a martyr, nothing that Jay achieves in his life as a rapper will ever place him above B.I.G. If Hova's next album sells 50,000,000 copies, he'll only be pushing Biggie further out of his reach. As great as Jay-Z is, it must be frustrating knowing you're not even the greatest rap-per in Brooklyn, let alone the world. It's evident in Jigga's constant comparison of himself and Notorious B.I.G. that he is somewhat obsessed with his position in the history of rap. Jigga is also a very smart man, he knows Biggie's legacy will forever be connected to another man's legacy, Tupac. Can you really say one without the other? Yet, in his pursuit to be better than Biggie, if you mentioned Jay-Z's name there was no one else....until now.

Don't underestimate Jay-Z's ability to manufacture a great chal-lenger in Nas to get himself closer to his intended target, which is to be considered as the greatest rapper of all time, but he didn't intend for Nas to come out on the better end of it. He figured Nas was dead in the water and he could use him to complete his mission.

So where does this leave Nas and his legacy in all of this? It leaves him to assume the role of Tupac. Like that of Shakur, Nas' lyrics are more poetic and spiritually based and won't really receive true recognition until he's gone. Jigga couldn't have picked a more perfect rapper to relive the life of the man he's most obsessed with. Think about it, Biggie vs. Tupac, and Jigga vs. Nas. Even the way Nas was carrying on at one point was similar to the last days of Tupac, when it appeared that he was mad at the world. Pac called names and took no prisoners in his quest to rid Hip Hop of the unde-sirables, and Nas seemed to be following that agenda to the letter. What both of these great Emcee's fail to realize is that neither of these martyrs received that status as the greatest of all time until they were gunned down. It's sad to say, but at the current rate that things are happening, it could be time for more martyrs now. The way that 50 Cent has been carrying on lately, would anybody even investigate? As many people who are after 50 right now, it would be a classic case of who done it? Who would 50 Cent be without Ja Rule? What's love without hate? Who are players without player haters? The point that I'm trying to make here is that we must find a way to co-exist with each other and deal with our differences in a more civil manner, or Hip Hop will be no more.

In Spike Lee's movie "Malcolm X," Denzel Washington, who played the role of our fallen leader, was stated as saying, "The Nation of Islam was the greatest organization a black man had ever seen, but niggers had to mess it up." That's exactly how I feel about the state of Hip Hop right now. We have sunk to an all time low. Whenever you have producers like Jermaine Dupri and Dr. Dre going at it, entire radio stations beefin', and new jacks like Nelly dissing pioneers like KRS ONE, you know the end time for this culture we call Hip Hop is near. Or maybe just like the earth does from time to time, Hip Hop is cleansing itself of all the waste that has accumulated. You don't even have to know how to rhyme anymore and you can be a millionaire, and considered one of the best Emcee's. Or you can do entire albums talking about nothing but your rims and jewlz and go platinum. What kind of shit is that? What's good without evil? What's black without white? And who's Eminem without...? You fill in the blank. If someone doesn't step up to lyrically challenge him and say, "No, you can't have Hip Hop, no, you will not go down in history as the "King" of our creation, he's gonna do just that. I hate to say it but lyrically, he's showing the world just how tired niggas have become on the mic. He's showing his mastery of the craft that we created with song after song ranging from social to political to conscious, while we stay flowin' about nothing. It wouldn't be so bad if he were ringing up all of these sales just because he was white, but that's not the case. He's white and America happens to think that he's nice, which poses the greatest threat yet in terms of taking over of the one thing that our generation holds sacred, Hip Hop. He's also breeding a whole nation of white rappers who love Hip Hop with a passion that will gladly take it over if you niggas don't know what to do with it. Maybe that was the grand plan all along, have these savages kill each other off because we don't need them anymore. We have who we've been looking for. Who will be the great champion that defeats this great challenger?

28

WHAT IF?

What if Tupac really faked his own death and is still alive today? What if he was really living in Cuba with Asatta Shukur? What if all of those new songs that you hear aren't really him, but someone mimicking his voice perfectly? I mean come on, I can understand a rapper having a few extra songs in the can, but it seems like Pac had a couple of hundred! He was putting out more songs dead than most rappers who were alive. What if Jay-Z had Biggie killed? I mean, two of the same objects cannot occupy the same space at the same time right? What if Jigga knew he couldn't eat as long as Biggie was alive? And what better place to take him out than in L.A. so that most would think that it was Tupac related? What if Dr. Dre and Emimen only signed 50 Cent to piss off Ja Rule and Murder Inc., since Irv Gotti was trying to form an alliance with Dre's No.1 enemy, Suge Knight?

What if 50 really did get an order of protection against Murder Inc. to cover his own ass, so that when he kills one of them he can get away with it? To me, that would be some clever shit. Or what if 50 Cent really is an informant? Look at his name, Five-O. What if Aftermath has 50 Cent in the studio recording hundreds of songs like Tupac so that when they kill him later, they'll have enough music to cash in off his death? I mean, it's already been proven that the death of a rapper can be far more beneficial to a record label than his life. What if this whole 50 Cent hype is a page out of the movie Trading Places where they take a nobody from the hood that's worth 50 Cent and turn him into 50 million dollars, all for a one dollar bet? What if the ultimate Emcee battle was not Nas and Jay-Z, but will be between Nas and 50 Cent? If you've been watch-

173

ing closely, it looks like it's headed in that direction. What if it's deeper than Nas and 50 Cent? What if it's really about good and evil? Nas is headed in one direction trying to save the children, and 50 is headed in another direction and don't give a fuck about anybody's children but his own. What if Eminem was orchestrating all of this from behind the scenes, using 50 as a pawn to weaken Nas so that he can come in for the kill at a later date? What if? What if? What if?

But if if was a spliff, we'd all be fucked up

And if if was a "fif," we'd all be drunk

And if if was a Brooklyn click, put your hands up cause we'd all be stuck

And if if was a dick, get a condom cause we'd all be fucked

But if if was a fly chick, would she get you for all your ones?

And if if was your sidekick, would he hold you down and buss his guns?

Or if if was a myth, would you believe it? I don't know son

But if if was the shit, we'd all have the runs.

What if Run only became a reverend so that he could launder money for his big brother Russell Simmons? What if Mase only became a reverend to do the same thing for P.Diddy? What if Russell is a government agent who's using his clout in Hip Hop to start a political movement, pimpin' our culture to further someone else's agenda? Is it really that far fetched? Those in control know that Hip Hop has the power to cross all racial, ethnic, and religious barriers. It's also very youth oriented, which is tomorrow's future, so why not have one of their own agents lead the way? What if the feds are really going after Irv Gotti and Suge Knight because they were conspiring along with J Prince to start their very own major distribution company? Think about this for a moment. If Hip Hop had its own distribution, it could eliminate the middleman. That in essence is virtually all the major labels. That's billions of dollars lost for them and billions gained for Hip Hop. Do you think they're going to allow "slaves" to become "masters" at their expense? Of course not! What if Jay-Z's last couple of albums were so trash because Beyonce had him p*ssy whipped? His most famous words were "I'm focused man," but even the biggest pimp can be side-tracked by the power of the "P." Or better yet, what if their relation-ship was staged for publicity purposes to generate more sales? What if Jay knew that it was time to change his image up, being that he's never really seen with women, and he doesn't want people to start questioning his sexuality? What if Roc-A-Fella was really owned by the Rockefellers? What if Murder Inc. was somehow connected to the real Murder Inc. who was involved with money laundering, racketeering, and murder? What if The Cash Money Millionaires are a government operation heavily funded by those who want to keep the youth focused on cars, women, houses, and "bling bling?" You have to admit, these players seem to come out of nowhere with minimal rhyme skills, hittin' you with the same shit over and over again on every song and every video. I know commercials when I see them. What if most of these high profile rappers and moguls are initiates of some secret society that allow them to make all the money they want as long as they keep the oath, which is to never reveal the truth about what they're doing to us in the hood? What if none of them really owned anything but were front men for the real owners of Hip Hop who choose to remain anonymous? What if? What if? What if?

But if if was a spliff, we'd all be fucked up

And if if was a "fif," we'd all be drunk

And if if was a Brooklyn click, put your hands up cause we'd all be stuck

And if if was a dick, get a condom cause we'd all be fucked

But if if was a fly chick, would she get you for all your ones?

And if if was your sidekick, would he hold you down and buss his guns?

Or if if was a myth, would you believe it? I don't know son

But if if was the shit, we'd all have the runs.

What if smoking weed and drinking alcohol was really good for you? If only we knew how to use drugs to tap into our higher consciousness instead of for recreational purposes, we'd really be dangerous. Bob Marley was a musical prophet, but he wasn't right until he took a "spliff" to the head. What if brothers who stay iced out, flashing cash, driving around on 20 inch rims are more spiritual than ghetto fabulous? Excuse my French but all the pictures I see of ancient Egypt always show the black man as kings, dripping in expensive gold, with all the riches and all the b*tches. So maybe it's just a sign of "What goes around comes around," and we're just slowly returning to our king status. What if women who carry themselves like hookers were more spiritual than demeaning? Back in ancient Egypt, prostitutes were very high up on the social ladder in their society, why you may ask? Because it wasn't just about sex. The prostitutes were healers physically, mentally, and spiritually, who took the time out to assist in solving all of man's problems, not just his physical needs. Men had great respect for prostitutes in ancient times. Maybe if some of these women who act like hookers today took the time to master the entire spectrum of what that job entails, men wouldn't have anything but respect for them. What if your biological father's only responsibility was to physically get you onto the planet, and it was somebody else's responsibility to father you mentally, and someone else's duty to father you spiritually? We always make a big deal about our father never being around to raise us, that's why we all f*cked up! Yet maybe his job was just to get you here. I'ma keep it real, my pops never did shit for me, but I'm sure glad he dug my moms back out, or I wouldn't be here in the first place. Now that I think about it, he's done a whole lot for me. Maybe the real beef should be with my deadbeat mental and spiritual dads. What if this is the way things are supposed to be? What if? What if? What if?

But if if was a spliff, we'd all be fucked up

And if if was a "fif," we'd all be drunk

And if if was a Brooklyn click, put your hands up cause we'd all be stuck

And if if was a dick, get a condom cause we'd all be fucked

But if if was a fly chick, would she get you for all your ones?

And if if was your sidekick, would he hold you down and buss his guns?

Or if if was a myth, would you believe it? I don't know son

But if if was the shit, we'd all have the runs.

177

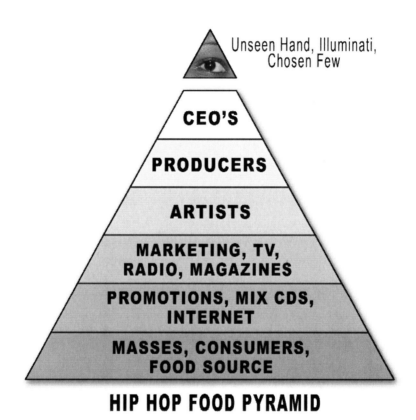

Unseen Hand, Illuminati, Chosen Few

CEO'S

PRODUCERS

ARTISTS

MARKETING, TV, RADIO, MAGAZINES

PROMOTIONS, MIX CDS, INTERNET

MASSES, CONSUMERS, FOOD SOURCE

HIP HOP FOOD PYRAMID

29

THE THEYS - PART 3

A SCI-FI HIP HORROR
THE SHIFT: HIP HOP OR DIE

Back to the year 2011, the eve of destruction, where Hip Hop has broken off into different major factions. One was a political movement ushered in by the keepers of the secret under the direct orders of the Theys. The Gagotus were duped into politics by the keepers through organizations that urged them to get out and vote. This led to the election of certain Hip Hop figures that were under the oath to carry out the mission of the Theys. What looked like a victory for the Hip Hop nation on the surface was in fact a loss. The minute that these agents got into office, their true intentions were revealed which was to uphold the way of life for the Theys who controled them. They saw the need to reform the Government with a Hip Hop ideology to give off the illusion that the people were back in control of their own destiny after the fall of what was known as democracy. Back in the year 2008, the government had reached an all time low with the suspension of the Constitution, allowing the current president to place the country under Marshal Law, suspend further elections, and implement new homeland security laws. The Theys were staging wars and terrorist acts on their own soil against their own people, as well as the Gagotus, to bring such laws about. This served as a weapon of mass distraction to keep the focus off of the real war which was to take place in the years to come. The masses of the Theys and Gagotus who were accustomed to warring with each other, joined forces to protest these conditions, but protesting had become illegal under the new homeland security act. There were riots in the streets between the haves and the have-nots as the tension started to build. This was just what the Illumi Nation had hoped for, the Gagotus and the Theys fighting for one common cause, so now They could implement their problem-reaction-solution program. This program was designed to begin the process of the Theys using the Gagotus as cocoons for the journey into the next paradigm. This is what led to Hip Hop taking over all positions of government and everyone uniting under the flag of Hip Hop. The second faction was the conscious/religious movement in Hip Hop. This was the most important movement as it had already been prophesized that the new religion would be a form of music. The Theys began to build Temples of Hip Hop on just about every corner with each lord Emcee teaching the same doctrine. Gagotus and Theys alike were both able to attend the same temple of worship and pray as one in hopes of reaching the Hip Hop hereafter. 2006 saw the reemergence of conscious Hip Hop, and the decline of gangsta rap. This was a clear indication to those in power that the paradigm shift was moving closer with each passing moment and They would have to quickly convert Hip Hop into a makeshift religion if They were going to survive. By 2008, the one religion of Hip Hop became law.

Each passing year also brought about the mutation of the mentally dead Gagotus as well, causing their pineal glands to suddenly reawaken. This became evident in the type of rhymes that Emcee's were kicking, the type of books that the Gagotus were reading, and an overall interest in their ancient history, all of which was illegal under the new Homeland Security laws. Most of them were not aware of this mutation or how to harness its power but the Theys were well aware of the change to the DNA structure of the Gagotus. In the past, the Theys would create a new vaccine or poison to try and stop the mutation, but the closer the planet moved toward the fourth dimension, the more potent the melanin became. Soon, no form of deterrent would be strong enough to defeat the melanin, so instead of trying to fight the inevitable by prosecuting those who broke the law or staging biological warfare against them, the Theys embraced the change, or at least on the surface They did. They have been able to stay in power by staying two paradigms ahead of the Gagotus with their technology. This technology allowed them to create and control false realities by manipulating the thought patterns of the Gagotus. Therfore, the same Theys that ruled gangsta rap were the same Theys who ushered in conscious rap and the new religion. This was done so that when the consciousness of the Gagotus naturally reached this progressive state, the Theys would already have conscious rappers and lord Emcee's in place to be the vanguard of this movement and They could steer it in any direction that They pleased. Even in one's quest for spirituality, the Theys owned the blueprint. The Theys also realized that if the new religion was going to be a form of music, They would have to control it just as They did Christianity, Judaism, and Islam by fabricating the stories of Tupac and Biggie, and distorting the teachings of Jayhova. By 2008, you were classified under two types of people by the Hip Hop government, the Gagotus or the Theys, in other words, you were either original or a hybrid. One ounce of melanin classified you as a Gagotu. This is how They were able to eliminate all other races of people. There was only one race that was considered melanin deficient, and that was the Theys.

The goal was to make everyone a Gagotu, so the government passed a law that eliminated all same race couples. If you were a Gagotu, you had to marry a They. If two Gagotus broke the law and had a baby, the baby would be killed instantly. By mixing politics, religion, and their blood line with that of the Gagotus, the Theys felt they were placing themselves in position to make it into the fourth dimension. All of this was done under the guise of Hip Hop and was orchestrated behind the scenes by the Anglaxsons. This faction of Hip Hop was extremely important to the Anglaxson in particular, who needed the womb of the Gagotu women to preserve their seeds but melanin alone wasn't enough to guarantee that one would make it through the shift, it only meant that you had the potential if it was properly used. The third faction was controlled by the Semis and it ruled a small but powerful section of Hip Hop that strictly dealt with commerce. Every commercial that featured Hip Hop was owned by this group of Theys who were capitalists. All products sold through the media had to be authorized by the Semis, and Hip Hop was its number one selling tool. All telecasts were monitored very closely by the Semis who used these images to create a reality based on the script that They were writing and directing. These three factors were all ruled by different elite groups for one common cause, to establish one government, one religion, and one way of life. However, there was a fourth faction. These were the underground radical free thinkers. This group was considered the most dangerous of the four and was immediately labeled as a terrorist. There was no more free speech, but this faction chose to speak out against what Hip Hop had become, and was quickly driven underground. This group held the original codex of what Hip Hop was supposed to represent. From time to time, those from the underground would appear on street corners and spread the Gospel through rhyme to anyone who would listen. These lyrical swordsmen were superior in their knowledge of their history and spoke of the primal Gods of Hip Hop like Kool Herc, Afrika Bambaataa, and Grandmaster Flash. This gospel was referred to as the lost knowledge. This sacred information was passed down from rhyme to ear from the originators themselves and was preserved by a select few. The shift would only enhance the underground's ability to use the sacred word to destroy the Theys in the near future. The Theys feared this group the most because They couldn't control them. This group was growing every day as more and more people were awakened by their mutation and became dissatisfied with the current order of things. Unifying the entire underground would prove to be very difficult because each state operated independently of the other, so Emcee's were prohibited from traveling out of their jurisdiction without the proper interstate passport. The only ones allowed a passport were the Keepers of the secret. This kept each state isolated so that the Theys could monitor and control its slaves. But soon this would all change.

DECEMBER 21, 2012

On Friday December 21, 2012, the world stood still. Finally the wait was over and the first stage of the shift was upon the people. There was total chaos in the streets as all power sources failed simultaneously. There was no police presence anywhere in sight so there was looting in every neighborhood throughout the country. This would prove to be useless because no material objects would make it into the fourth dimension. This fact was only known to the Theys who were a part of the Illumi Nation, the Anglaxsons, and the Semis, as well as the underground that were initiated by the elders of Hip Hop for this very cosmic event. This wasn't known to the masses of the Theys or Gagotus who were so used to struggling to survive; They couldn't resist the opportunity to steal food and other objects of their desires. This was the beginning of the end as the next seven years would feel like seven days. Time as we knew it was no more, and each passing year would activate one of the seven major chakras within the body. Soon, each chakra from the root to the crown would be activated. In addition to revealing that the new religion would be a form of music, the ancient scrolls also stated that in order to make it into the next paradigm, each of the seven chakras would have to be fully activated at the same time. Anyone caught in the middle of the shift without the force of all of the chakras would spontaneously combust. The Theys who were secret society members nervously awaited the opening of the first gateway and chakra, uncertain of their future. The majority of the Theys who were not of the secret order were left to die the moment that the sun reached the sky. The rays were a thousand times stronger than normal and it had reddish glow to it, instantly burning anyone that didn't have a certain amount of melanin to protect them. This represented the root chakra as the sun was following the same journey. Once the sun reached the sky it never left, and would stay burning for seven straight years, only intensifying in power with each changing chakra. Thousands of men, women and children turned to dust the moment the sun touched their skin. Even some Gagotus were killed during this attack. Even though the Gagotus had melanin, if their thought process resembled that of the Theys or if the Gagotus were only dealing with root chakra energy, the price was death. Not death in the traditional sense because there's no such thing, but They would be trapped in a void forever between this dimension and the next. The Theys of the secret society were prepared for such an event and built underground cities with running water and supplies, but this would prove to be a temporary form of shelter because there was no hiding from prophecy. The Theys thought that they could wait out the shift by staying out of sight but the ancients always taught "as above so below" and "as within, so without," meaning, whatever is going on in the heavens is happening on the earth as well. Just as there is a sun in the sky, there is a sun within you, so there's no escape. The Theys ordered the Keepers of the secret to stay on the surface and be their eyes and ears, but even the keepers realized that the end was near, yet were prepared to fight and defend the Theys to the very end. The technology that made the Theys superior was now obsolete because there was no more power left to fuel it.

The year 2013 quickly approached, and its effects were immediately felt. The sun moved a few degrees higher into the sky and changed into the color of bright orange. This represented the naval chakra. Soon after, the electromagnetic field that surrounded the planet was gone, causing any and all weapons to fail. Bullets that were shot out of guns fell to the ground, airplanes were grounded forever, and even nuclear weapons were of no use. Anyone operating at or below the navel chakra, whether on the surface or underground, quickly perished. The earth was cleansing itself before moving into the next paradigm. Those that made the cut, only got stronger, either through mutation as was common for the Gagotus, or through low level alchemy that was practiced by the Theys who were familiar with the occult sciences - the more advanced one was in occultism, the greater chance They had of surviving. More and more bodies were caught in the void as the external and internal sun ascended. The Keepers of the secret quickly became the rulers of the land because no one else could withstand the rays of the sun except them and a few of the Gagotus that managed to survive the opening of the first two gateways. The Keepers still had the mindset of the Theys who taught them the science of how to rule. There was still no word from the underground. This worried the Theys the most because the underground was in possession of the lost knowledge and would surface when the time was right to take back the earth from the evil doers. The final stage of the earth's cleansing would be at the hands of the underground. The Theys knew that the final war on earth would be between them and the underground, with the Keepers being used as pawns to buy the Theys more time. In the meantime, the Theys continued to prepare for the opening of the third gateway.

The third gateway was activated in the year 2014, by this time the sun had reached even greater heights in the sky and was a bright piercing yellow. Only those who could master their lower desires had a chance of survival. The third chakra symbolized fire, as its strength began to dry up all the water of the land and the food supply was dwindling as well. The sun was the only source of food that could sustain life at this time on the planet. The Theys were beasts by nature, so the higher the chakra, the more difficult it became for them to act other than themselves. The quickening was unbearable for anyone that wasn't in tune with self; the remaining Gagotus were suffering from severe headaches because their first eye was becoming physically visible. The Theys who were lucky enough to survive at this point did so by drinking the blood of dead Gagotus and by quoting the Hip Hop gospel to conjure up more energy. This included reciting the lyrics of old school Hip Hop legends, the more ancient the song, the greater the power achieved. Still, no one knew how this quickening was affecting the underground because there was no sign of them. The remaining temples of Hip Hop served as the last ounce of hope for worshippers, although what became evidently clear was that the religion of Hip Hop that so many had put their faith into, was not an external religion as once thought but an internal energy instead. If Hip Hop wasn't in your heart, then you would not make it into the fourth dimension.

2015 represented the crossroads, it was the dividing point between one's higher self and lower nature. The heart chakra was the true measurement of one's love for Hip Hop. The heart was the access key to the higher realms, it literally busted out of the chests of anyone doing Hip Hop for money or was green with envy and hate. The sun turned green and now had the power to penetrate through walls, killing all remaining survivors except those operating from the heart chakra and above. This instantly wiped out the entire race of Semis that were left, whose only purpose in Hip Hop was to make money and cause havoc on the planet due to their jealousy of the Gagotu legacy. This also annihilated a large portion of the Keepers that only rhymed to get rich or die tryin. The opening of the fourth chakra and gateway was also a culmination of the four elements: earth, air, fire, and water, which represented the graffiti writer, the DJ, the B-Boy, and the Emcee in Hip Hop. A true Hip Hop alchemist must be initiated and have mastery of all four elements before advancing into the higher realms. This marked the arrival of the underground that had love for Hip Hop in their hearts and were initiates of the sacred sciences. Their time to take back the planet from those that were using Hip Hop to destroy it was vastly approaching. It was no longer a mystery to the Theys or the keepers that the true chosen ones were those from the underground. These were the people in possession of the esoteric science of Hip Hop capable of the spiritual journey into the fourth dimension. The heart chakra was the zero point between the material world and the spiritual world. This threshold was where the war of the worlds would take place. The battle lines had been drawn between the Theys and the Keepers that longed for material possessions and a world based in matter, and the underground that had always aspired to reach unreachable heights into the realm of the unknown. At that point, there was no more gray area left on either side of the gateway. Anyone undecided about who they're willing to fight for, were stuck in a void between the fourth gateway forever. This would lead to the demise of the Theys as a whole because by nature They were material beings. Even the most advanced occultist amongst them was at a point of no return. Their only hope relied upon a few female Keepers that They had planted their seeds into in an attempt to make it through the shift, and a few of the male Keepers that They planted their sexual energy into during same sex rituals. Therefore, as long as the Keepers were willing to fight for material possessions, the Theys had a fighting chance, albeit, a very slim one. Even though the Keepers were about material possessions, within them lying dormant were the four original elements and the melanin to activate them, so some of them were able to carry on the mission of the Theys if their focus and intent was strong enough.

The war of the worlds quickly turned into the war of the words by the year 2016, as the inner and outer sun ascended higher into the throat chakra region. The blue sun in the sky represented the realm of ether, the fifth element. The harmonics of the planet escalated to a higher frequency, causing many that were not vibrating high enough to become deaf tone. The greatest weapon on earth at this time was sound and the ability to use words to manipulate it. Other important factors were the intent behind the words (good or evil), one's vocabulary represented how many bullets you had in the chamber or how sharp your lyrical sword was, and the rhythm in which these words were delivered determined whether one had an automatic, semi-automatic, single shooter, a shotgun, or how quick and efficient you could wield your sword. This set up the ultimate lyrical battle between the Keepers of the Secret and the underground movement. Knowledge would be the deciding factor, the more one studied, the greater the warrior he or she was. No longer did it matter if one opponent had a fly car and tons of money, which gave him the edge, or if the other Emcee was broke and living in the hood. If the latter possessed more knowledge, he would undoubtedly be the victor. The Underground would have to eliminate the Keepers and the Energy of the Theys before the planet reached the seventh gateway or the future would be doomed. It was all or nothing for both sides, two Gagotu factions, both very powerful at this time, fighting for the future of humanity.

It has been said by the ancients that, "whatever doesn't kill you, will only make you stronger." By 2017, only the highly advanced Gagotus remained and were more powerful than you can imagine; and with the sun changing colors to indigo, the mutation back into the Gods that the Gagotus once were was almost complete. The first eye that used to protrude out of the center of the heads of the Gods was not only fully visible now, but was fully activated as well. Their physical bodies were transparent-like and filled with light. The Gagotus were becoming light beings that no longer relied on their physical abilities but the realization that all is mental, gave a whole new meaning to the term battle rhyme, as the Keepers and the Underground alike both had the ability to bring anything that one rhymed about, instantly into a physical existence. That meant that if an Emcee said "my microphone's like a shot gun, I'll blast your ass real fast and survivors, no there's not one!" That's exactly what would happen. To counter such an attack, an Emcee would have to say something like "I stay in stealth mode and play dead then grab my mic load it up, take aim and spray lead!" This is the battle of the minds that would take place for the rest of the year between the Keepers and the Gagotus. With full pineal power, astral projection could take place in the blink of an eye for both sides. Under normal circumstances, it would be virtually impossible for the Underground to defeat the Keepers who could easily escape into another dimension by activating their merkaba (which is a field of light that surrounds the body in the form of a spaceship and allows one to travel faster than the speed of light to any desired destination in the galaxy), but because of the shift, the planet was on lock down, so everyone was trapped here on earth until the opening of the seventh gateway. This made it easy for the Underground to search every corner of the earth and destroy the Keepers one by one. It was a fierce battle between spiritual and material forces, but in the end, the spiritual beings prevailed. Now the moment that the Underground was waiting for, the moment that had long been prophesized about was here. The earth and everything in it belonged to them, the Gagotus who were the first to occupy it, would also be the last.

The book of Genesis states: God created the heavens and earth in six days, and on the seventh day he rested. The Bible also states: a year with the lord is like one day. From the year 2012 to the year 2017, the earth cleansed itself in what seemed like six days. Now it was the year of 2018 and the seventh and final gateway was open. The sun reached its apex in the sky and was the bright color of violet. To prepare for this joyous event, the surviving members of the underground movement sat in the lotus position and meditated heavily on opening the crown chakra and became one with the infinite. Then it all became crystal clear, the Theys, the Semis, the Anglaxsons, the Illumi Nation, and The Keepers of the Secret were all different aspects of themselves that the chosen ones had to defeat to reach the highest realm of existence, yet no one really existed at all. It was all a dream in the mind of the creator, and Hip Hop was one of the many expressions that God used to learn about itself. Just as the universe is filled with billions of stars, each body represents one of billions of atoms on the earthly realm that transports information back and forth within the mind of the creator on the spiritual realm. The Gagotus had come to learn that the earth and their bodies were all an illusion. The Gagotus were not human, but spirit beings having a human experience. The creator designed Hip Hop to be the ultimate experience because it embodied the very five elements that the creator used to create everything on the earth itself. These elements were the earth, air, fire, water, and ether (melanin). In Hip Hop, these elements were known as the graffiti writer, the DJ, the Emcee, and the B-boy. The fifth element was knowledge, or in this case, the knowledge and proper use of the melanin (spirit) that one possessed to reach beyond the known into the unknown. As the earth disappeared into the fourth dimension, the chosen ones that endured the journey smiled and prepared for their next experience because through the proper use of Hip Hop, the Gagotus knew that there were no limits to what the creator could think up next. Until we meet again on another sci-fi adventure, this is the Black Dot saying, peace.

40 Songs Consciousness

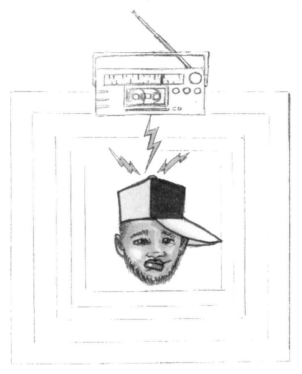

40-Song Consciousness - The radio will play the same 40 songs over and over again, usually filled with sex, drugs, and violence, creating a consciousness envelope around the individual who then begins to think that this is all that Hip Hop has to offer. We then subconsciously begin to act out what has been downloaded into our psyche as our reality. To give off the illusion that we are moving forward, the Matrix will delete one song from the end of the prism and add another to the beginning, but in the end, its still 40 songs.

30

ESCAPE THE MATRIX OF HIP HOP
PART 1

The Matrix movies have done an excellent job of using computers as an analogy to break down and illustrate how outside forces govern our lives. These forces are very powerful, yet its effects remain unbeknownst to most. In the movie, these forces were referred to as…programs. Programs are written for every function of our lives whether we choose to believe so or not. The very word program is self defining. There are those who do nothing but find new ways to program our thoughts and actions for their own benefit, yet we refuse to see this operation for what it really is…a program. When it comes to Hip Hop, it's no different. Assuming that most people have gotten at least a general understanding of the science being dropped in the Matrix movies, hedz are gonna have to really "log on" to fully receive the transmission that I'm about to send. But is there anyone out there? Can anyone out there feel that there's something wrong with the state of Hip Hop but just can't explain what it is? If this is you, then now is the time to take the red pill and escape…the Matrix of Hip Hop. Just like the Matrix movies, the Matrix of Hip Hop is run by programs. These programs serve one purpose and one purpose only, control. Control of what we eat, drink, wear, hear, drive, and most important of all, control of what we think. But what gives a program life, right, a mainframe, a construct that allows many programs to run simultaneously. It's the house in which programs live. It's the brain, without this, a program is rendered useless. This mainframe is what makes up the Matrix of Hip Hop, hundreds of programs that control our every action. It must control our actions because it feeds off of our re-actions. Its very existence depends upon it. Let me explain. A computer, which houses the mainframe, which in turn houses the programs, can do nothing without energy. That's where you come in. You're the energy. In the first Matrix movie, Morpheus held up a Duracell battery to illustrate this very point. As the red pill starts to settle, I need you to Fooocus your Miiind young Hip Hoppa.

Now if you open up a battery, you'll see that it's filled with carbon. This same carbon is also the basis for melanin, which is responsible for the skin pigmentation for people of color at the very least (we'll get into the super powers that melanin possess a little later in the article). So it's safe to say that we are all walking batteries, but batteries a thousand times stronger than any Duracell or Energizer. To drive this point home, I'll need you to see every black person of power or fame as a battery. Michael Jordan was the battery that gave the N.B.A. life, Funk Master Flex is the battery that gives Hot 97 its shine, Biggie was the battery that charged Bad Boy, Colin Powell and Condoleezza Rice were the real batteries that ran the White House, etc. etc. etc. Once these batteries are removed or replaced with weaker ones, these programs may still run but not with the same efficiency. Point and case, when the N.B.A. removed Jordan (energizer) and replaced him with Kobe's battery (cheap $1 Duracell), it still functioned but not at the same potency. They even recycled Jordan's energy and re-inserted him back into the game until he was fully drained, and then they discarded him with the rest of the dead batteries. Just like any other component that uses batteries, it must keep fresh ones in the system or it won't function properly. That's why when one rapper dies down or falls off, he's immediately replaced with another battery, uh I mean rapper, to keep the game charged. Batteries in general have a negative and positive end. Whatever is trying to utilize its energy must be connected to both ends. Human batteries are not much different. We too have a negative and positive energy about us, and there's always some positive and negative shit going on in our life. Think about it. We never seem to master either end of the spectrum. Just when it seem like things are going positive for us, some negative shit jumps off. Could this all be programmed by the Matrix of Hip Hop to keep our negative and positive in balance like a regular battery so that it could drain our life force, possibly? In the movie, "Monsters Inc.," the monsters had to scare children in order to live. The fear from the children gave off an energy that enabled the monsters to have life. The Matrix of Hip Hop needs your energy to survive, so it too must stir certain emotions in you to eat. An individual battery can run a single program, but it takes thousands upon thousands of batteries to run the construct. So now we have a construct in place that houses the programs that control us, and the energy to give it life. This in essence makes it real, or should I say a virtual Hip Hop reality. Our collective thoughts, which are the strongest form of energy, create our reality. For example, this is only a book because we all agree that it is. What if the Matrix of Hip Hop was able to write programs that artificially placed thoughts into our subconscious mind, and then induced our thoughts and projected them into a certain time and space that ultimately created the Matrix of Hip Hop? Thought is the building block for all life. The key to the mystery is these are not your thoughts, you only think that they are.

Now let's look at some of the specific programs that make this possible. If you tune your radio to your favorite Hip Hop station, you will hear the same 30 to 40 songs all day long. This is by design. First, by hearing the same songs over and over again the subconscious mind eventually will accept these songs as being hot. Second and most important, your Hip Hop consciousness will not be able to expand beyond these same 40 songs. It sets up a barrier to contain your thoughts. Anything that's contained can be controlled. Within these same songs are word sequences that may appear random but are not random at all. Think about the numbers that stream down in the Matrix movies, now replace them with words. These words have power and assist the construct in keeping us in Hip Hop lockdown. You know the words like: pimp, ho, thug, bitch, playa, ice, and many more that are simply too numerous to mention. This leads to recycled thoughts. Therefore, when a new artist comes along, he may use a different word sequence, but the actual words are the same, thus creating the same thought patterns.

The person that actually creates this 40 song play list is called a "program" director. To support the audio software that's running, the Matrix also created another program called videos. This program adds the visual to the audio programming. Your favorite video show will run the same 40 videos showing the actual physical objects of the word sequence. Visualization is important when bringing things into existence. It helps speed up the process. This also limits our Hip Hop consciousness to certain boundaries. If all we see is all we believe, then that's all that is real to us. It's no wonder that we sell drugs, pack guns, call women bitches, kill each other, spend all of our money on cars, houses and jewels, and call this "keeping it real." Another program that's crucial are your glossy Hip Hop magazines which contain the written word. These have a totally different effect on the brain. We are an ancient people who subconsciously associate written words, pictures and symbols as being sacred, and these magazines are filled with plenty of each. These written words, pictures and symbols reinforce what we believe to be true. Periodically, the Matrix will add a few new songs and videos to the rotation because it knows that everything must move. This gives off the illusion that the game of Hip Hop is moving forward, meanwhile the construct is in control of its destiny. These three programs when combined and downloaded by the Hip Hop thought stream create another program called success. The success program tells us that a fly car, house on the hill, diamonds, and lots of women mean that we have made it in the world. Once we download the program called success, the Matrix knows the end result of our journey so it can manipulate, change, or create any path it chooses for us to take to get there. It can make us sell out, play ourselves, lie, steal and cheat because it knows our final destination, success. That's control.

These programs cannot be seen or heard by most who are caught up in the Matrix, but they control our Hip Hop lives and give off the illusion that we are free, free to make our own choices when it comes to Hip Hop, free to listen to whatever artist or radio station we want, free to purchase any CD or magazine that we wish. The truth of the matter is we are not free Hip Hoppas, we are slaves to the Matrix of Hip Hop. I know by now you're probably saying "I should have taken the blue pill," but let's go deeper. In the real world, a rapper is just like you and me. He eats, sleeps, farts, and probably has stinky feet, but when he goes on wax or video he has the ability to do amazing things such as, kill hundreds of people, have incredible gun battles, sell tons of cocaine, sleep with loads of women, and has millions of dollars. He is invincible and literally has super powers. In the movie, Neo could do all of these extraordinary things in the Matrix, but in "Zion" or the real world he was a regular dude. It's safe to say that records, radio, videos, movies, and magazines can be considered as the Matrix of Hip Hop. It's the only place that such feats can take place on a grand scale. Let's keep it real, most of us will never experience such adventures. There are those who live a lifestyle similar, but they are usually the batteries to a program that's trying to enslave us, just like your favorite rapper. He's simply being paid for his services. You too can be a battery to a program that controls millions, but first you have to be contacted by what I'll call the gatekeepers of the construct. These are the ones who are responsible for plugging you right into a program, but they're very hostile individuals who are not to be trusted. They're called....agents. If you want a record deal, you need an agent. If you want a movie deal you need an agent, and if you're hot enough, you won't have to look for them, they'll find you. So beware! **From this point forward, if anyone feels that they need to re-insert themselves back into the Matrix of Hip Hop, just read your favorite glossy Hip Hop magazine from cover to cover, listen to the radio, or watch your favorite video show for about an hour straight. This should be enough to re-insert you and you can close this book and believe whatever you want to believe about Hip Hop.**

Now for those who are still with me, let's move forward. The construct is a brain that reads, analyzes, and computes brainwaves and thought patterns. It knows what you're thinking so it creates certain programs to accommodate these thoughts. It's a living, breathing entity. You created it so it can feel your pain, your struggle, and plight. It writes programs for each (individual because) it knows that we are a diversified people and we don't all think alike, so as our consciousness expands, it grows with us. For example, even the most radical thinkers must have a program in place to feed their thirst. The construct know this, so it downloads the radical rapper software so that that portion of the brain that wants to break free and go against the system is satisfied. Even the rappers that you think are the most radical or conscious, if they're on the airwaves or on T.V., it's a program that has been sanctioned by the Matrix of Hip Hop. Don't be fooled. Every now and then a rapper comes along to throw a glitch in the program. The group Outkast, which already has a program in place to accommodate the thought process of the dirty "backpackers," recently upgraded their software by letting Dre 3000 create a style that is unheard of in Hip Hop. Now the mainframe is scrambling to process this new data so that it can write the proper program to shut it down or control it. Once it's able to give it a name, let's say like, "New Age" Hip Hop, it now has form. It will then be able to write the proper program to promote, package, and sell it. It's then downloaded into our thought stream and we make it real. Every new rapper from this point will think he's being original by becoming a "new age" Emcee, but will run right into a program that has already been set up. Again, that's control.

The Matrix systematically cuts you off from the old school because that's the source of real Hip Hop. It's the "Zion" of Hip Hop. Power 105, a Hip Hop radio station based out of New York is famous for saying "back in the day, 1996." Once we accepted this as back in the day, this allowed the Matrix to delete the old school files from the system. It knows that once you find the beginning of Hip Hop, you will know its end. This poses a serious threat to the construct, so we're constantly being bombarded with programs that keep our focus on everything else but destroying the Matrix of Hip Hop. Bad Boy is a program that was written by P. Diddy. He also wrote a program within that program that put himself, the CEO, out in front. This program was then copied by Jermaine Dupri, as well as Irv Gotti with great success. Dame Dash also copied this program, especially when he felt that he and Jay were going to go they're separate ways. He knew that he would need his own identity to survive in the construct. Dr. Dre wrote a program for legit producers who rhyme that has been copied by Timberland and Pharell. Some programs can be hacked into. Ja Rule of Murder Inc., which is a program written by Irv Gotti, hacked into the 50 Cent program and renamed it five-0, which as we all know is a code for the police. Ja Rule called him a snitch and the hack almost worked, but Dr. Dre and Eminem quickly upgraded his software and he was able to recover and strike back. Now the entire Murder Inc. program is on the verge of being deleted. The 50 program is actually a copy. The real 50 Cent was from Fort Green, Brooklyn and really did most of the things that 50 Cent rhymes about. Every now and then a virus program like Dead Prez gets into the system and starts causing havoc until they can be deleted, but by that time, portions of the system are already damaged. Funk Master Flex wrote a program called "the bomb." Every time he drops the bomb on a record, you automatically think it's hot. The Source magazine wrote the 5 mic program and it has become the bible of Hip Hop. Just like in Matrix Reloaded, Dr. Dre, "the beat maker" is being held captive by a hostile program called Jimmy Iovine. Jay-Z who is the battery of Roc-A-Fella, as well as its programmer launched a new program called "Black." He came out with The Black album, the black shoe, and the black concert, all on black Friday. That's ritualistic. It has to be a success. The programming is too intricate. He's even coming out with the Black Book in the near future. The program has power just by calling it black. There's nothing more powerful in the universe than blackness. It's the melanin that we discussed earlier, the dark matter that consumes everything. Jay knows all about the strength of black because it's the same program that Nas wrote to try and take him down called "The Ether," which means the triple darkness of space. Then there's the P. Diddy and J.Lo program that was written a few years back. It's hard to tell who wrote that program, him or her. Diddy could have written it to add the final piece to his puzzle as being young, black and successful. The right woman can make the program complete. Or J.Lo could have written it because she knew that she needed some street credibility if she was going to be a hit in the industry, and what better person to accomplish this than P. Diddy. In any event, the program has now been copied by numerous couples like: Jay-Z and Beyonce, 50 Cent and Vivica Fox, Jermaine Dupri and Janet Jackson, and Nas and Kelis. Ashanti is a copy of the Mary J. program.

The dead rapper program is one of the Matrix most successful. The system benefited far more from the death of Biggie and Tupac than when they were alive, not just financially, but spiritually and mystically as well. The fact that Tupac wrote the Machiavelli Program and then died as if on cue has generated hope from the faithful. The fact that neither murder has been solved has generated much talk of conspiracy to this day. Perhaps the reason that these crimes are unsolved is because whoever wrote the rogue programs to carry out the mission has since deleted them from the construct. The white rapper program has finally been perfected thanks to Eminem, so look out for more white rappers in the near future. Fellow Hip Hopians, the programming runs deep, even our sperm cells carry a program. but this program can be determined by each individual. All that we absorb in our environment physically, mentally, and spiritually has a bearing on the sperm. If we are caught up into this Hip Hop Matrix on such a deep level, then it's safe to say that our seeds don't have a chance, for they are being birthed in the womb of the construct. They now carry the coding of the construct as a part of their DNA. It's time now for a revolution of historic proportions, one that will bring this Matrix to its knees. All the elements of Hip Hop must converge to prevent the Matrix from destroying the Zion of Hip Hop forever. Real Hip Hop must return, it's our only chance.

31

HIP HOP REVOLUTIONS
MATRIX OF HIP HOP - PART 2

The machines are digging, and very fast. It won't be long before they reach their final destination: the sub-conscious mind. If the machines are successful in their attempt to dig deep into our minds, then the thin line between reality and the Matrix of Hip Hop will forever be breached. The thin line between man and machine will forever be crossed. That is what this war is about isn't it, man vs. machine? These machines are constantly on the attack. You know the ones, the print machines, the radio, the television, the computers that tally up the billboard ratings, cell phones, Hip Hop video games, the "boom" boxes, etc. We gave them life, now they have taken on a life of their own. Every machine ever built is modeled after the human body in one way or another. You are the print machine every time you sit back and write those ill lyrics. You are the radio every time you spit those lyrics, or harmonize, or kick the "beatbox" and those sound waves travel and are received by others who are tuned into the frequency of your voice. When the brain is working at its full potential, we have the ability to send and receive telepathic messages from anyone on the planet and beyond once we dial up the math of that individual, isn't that what a cell phone does? The brains ability to receive, analyze, transfer, process, and store data at extraordinary rates (especially people with melanin) make it the greatest computer ever built. For every machine that will build on the outside of ourselves, our own abilities to perform the same task shut down. We become dependant on the machines. We no longer look inward for answers, we continue to look outside of ourselves to the machine world for solutions. That makes us the slave, and the machines the master over us.

Machines control the game of Hip Hop and are virtually unstoppable now, but the machines can only exist on one realm, the material, the realm of matter. We as humans have the ability to exist on multiple realms including the spirit realm, where the machines have no access. This is why 95% of the rappers who are plugged into the Matrix of Hip Hop only rap about material things. The machines will never allow Emcees who are vibrating from the spirit realm to rule because that would be suicide. The machine world's very existence depends on a rapper's capacity to keep the masses thought stream locked into the world of substance. Rappers serve as conduits between the machines and us, the food source. When you plug into your favorite rapper, remember, your favorite rapper is plugged into the machine. Make no mistake about it, we are at war. As we speak, the machines are digging. It's advantageous for us to fight the war on a level that maximizes our potential and minimizes the capabilities of the machines, that would be the spirit realm. The machines know this, that's why they will do everything in their powers to keep the war here where you have no chance of winning. War is constantly being launched against our higher selves (spirit), which is that little voice in our heads that tells us right from wrong and guides the lower self (physical). The two have been disconnected and the little voice in our heads that we used to trust so much has been replaced with a thousand little voices, rappers who have taken over our conscience, and they're all saying the same thing, there's nothing beyond what you see here: bitches, cars, money, guns, and houses. The machine world has made it almost impossible to escape these artificial voices that govern you. Every time you turn on your radio, television, or pop in your favorite CD, you turn off your higher self and activate the mechanism which allows the machines to keep digging and digging and digging. Even when you turn off the machines, if you continue to hum the lyrics of your favorite rapper and his lyrics are machine controlled via materialism, destruction, or non spiritual, the machines will continue to dig. The louder these voices become and the more you ignore your higher self, which is the only true voice within you, it will begin to fade until it can no longer be heard at all. That's when the machines set up shop in the subconscious mind and begin to control your every move. You become nothing more than a human machine. We used to believe in a higher force or a higher sense of self that connected us to the force, now we only believe in the machines.

In the Matrix of Hip Hop, the machines can make you or break you. We all knew 50 Cent's albums, "Get Rich or Die Trying" and "The Massacre" were going to be huge successes, not because of his tight lyrics or stage presence which we know he has, but mainly because it was machine manufactured months before the albums even dropped. The machine world used all of its resources and pulled out all the stops to ensure that we would make these albums #1. Remember, as I mentioned in my previous article (escape the Matrix), once we collectively download and accept the programming from the machines (via magazines, radio, video,), we make it real. And since 50 stuck to protocol by not saying anything spiritual, he was justly rewarded for keeping millions of minds locked into his subject "matter." I think Jay-Z put it best on a song called, "A moment of Clarity," off the Black album when he said: (I'm paraphrasing) if he wanted to he could rhyme like Common and Talib, and say something conscious that might awaken the streets, but he knows very well that the further he moves up the spiritual ladder, the less material rewards he will receive. So he said to hell with being broke. I'll just dumb down my lyrics (in the process dumb down the streets) so I can cash out. In other words, why live like a servant in heaven, when I can live like a king in hell. Most of the giants in the Hip Hop game know better than to violate the laws of the Matrix by trying to "free" the food source. Their career would be over in an instant. The Matrix could easily download any of the many programs at its disposal designed to destroy the very thing it created…you or the virtual you. I say the virtual you because the only you that really matters to the Matrix of Hip Hop is the image of you, which is not really you at all. Stand in the sun and there will be you and a reflection or image of you. Naturally you are the sole controller of your own image. Ludacris said it best when he sang, "When I move you move, just like that." However, imagine not being able to control your own shadow? The machines have found a way to disconnect the two, then project the virtual you (shadow) into a game-like simulation called, the Matrix of Hip Hop. When you begin to believe in the image of you (-) more than the real you (+), you reconnect the two, giving that particular program life. The power then shifts from what is real to what is unreal. How many rappers are actually thugs? Yet how many rappers after reading hundreds of machine manufactured articles promoting their image, start believing that this is who they really are, thus they begin acting on this belief system? They become so trapped into living up to the image of themselves that the true essence of them (spirit) begins to die, all the while the architect is in total control. He's the one controlling the joystick; you're just a player in the game. These rappers put so much of their life force into the game that if the architect decided to take his joystick and kill off their "player," they would die in the real world. In the first Matrix movie, Neo asked Morpheus, "If I die in the Matrix will I die here?" Morpheus answered, "Yes, the body cannot live without the mind."

We are celestial beings trapped in a virtual machine made world that we think is real. The Matrix of Hip Hop has designed certain programs to make this seem as real as possible. One of these programs is called "the Hip Hop star program." The Matrix knows that we are an ancient people who were guided by the movements and alignments of the heavenly stars. We were, and still are, star gazers who receive information and instructions from those beams of light emanating from the heavens. For most of us it is a forgotten science, but to ensure that we don't re-awaken, the Matrix has created advanced technology called, HAARP (High-Frequency Active Auroral Research Program), which are big powerful antennas used to create a force field around the planet to block out the rays of the sun as well as the stars. We have been cut off from the rest of the universe. The Hip Hop program was then activated. Now instead of looking up and being guided by stars out in the galaxy, we receive our instructions from the Hip Hop constellation. Our entire life is influenced by the "J.Lo star," the "50 Cent star," the "Cash Money star," etc. We watch these Hip Hop stars rise (P. Diddy), and fall

(Biggie), and are affected by every degree in between. Some of these stars shine brighter than others and have more potent effects on us. At the moment, the "Jay-Z star" is the brightest in our constellation, so his influence can be felt by many in the Hip Hop universe. Since all of these Hip Hop stars are machine made, the light that we receive is actually artificial light, and sitting at the controls is the architect. These stars can be manipulated into making us feel happy, sad, angry, militant, or sexual. These emotions are all different forms of energy that can easily be processed into food for the machines. The question that I ask you fellow Hip Hoppas is, "Which 'stars' are you being guided by?"

How can we defeat such powerful forces? Forces that not only have machines that can destroy us, but thousands of wannabe rappers, producers, and DJs with demos in their pockets ready to be inserted into the Matrix to protect it. And let's not forget the millions of fans whose manipulated thought process created the Matrix to begin with. The very Hip Hoppas that we are trying to save are our enemies. They will fight to the death to protect this system, and anyone that we haven't unplugged is potentially an agent controlled by the machines. These agents are on every corner of every neighborhood throughout the Hip Hop Diaspora awaiting instructions from the mainframe to attack. This is nothing more than slaves protecting its master. The revolution will not be televised, but will be spiritualized. We cannot rely on machines to defeat machines. We can no longer use their machines for weapons or communication. By doing so, we play right into the hands of our enemies. We must raise ourselves up to a much higher frequency, a frequency band that can only be accessed and operated from the spirit realm. The Hip Hop revolution is only for those who truly love and respect the art. It's only for those initiates who live and breathe Hip Hop as a way of life. This battle will be long and hard fought. and we will have to use unconventional methods of war if we are to even have a chance to preserve real Hip Hop (Zion). The chosen few will be those who choose themselves. Are you ready to fight for Hip Hop? Then let the war begin.

However, there's one thing that must be done before we can engage in battle, we must consult the Oracle...the true Oracle, mother earth. When we tune into her, she will reveal all of her secrets to us. By consulting her, we can learn about our glorious past as well as future events to come. The architect has been trying to destroy the Oracle for some time now by building concrete cities everywhere to disconnect us as well as using its machines to pollute the environment, and fires to burn her to the ground. The Oracle has been trying to contact us, but the architect has killed off her messengers, the fruits, vegetables, and water supply which the Oracle used to store information for us to access. The architect has made it almost impossible for you to consult her, but there are still ways she can be reached. Initiates listen closely, if you are not smoking weed for the sole purpose of contacting the Oracle, you're wasting you time! If you're not tapping into that bottle of spirits (liquor) with the intent to make contact with the Oracle, you're doing a disservice to the revolution. If you're dropping ecstasy and your mission is not to reach altered states of consciousness so that you can see beyond the illusion that is the Matrix of Hip Hop, then you're only burning up your brain cells and helping the Matrix burn up Zion in the process. It's the use, not the abuse of these drugs that can be beneficial. You can use them to become one with the Oracle. In "Matrix Revolutions," agent Smith absorbed the Oracle. By becoming one with her, he inherited all of her powers. With the proper intent, we too can use and transform any and all of the earth's elements as we see fit. Hip Hop itself is made up of the four elements: earth, air, fire, and water. The graf artist represents the earth element because he uses the concrete to paint pictures, symbols, and glyphs. The DJ represents the air element because the sound waves that he generates on the ones and twos need air to travel. A real Emcee spits fire. And the fluid body movement of the dancer represents the water element. If we are powerful enough alchemist to transform the earth's elements into a way of life called Hip Hop, then we are powerful enough to destroy the Matrix.

I began this chapter by saying that the machines were digging into our subconscious mind to illustrate that "All Is Mental." The

Matrix only exists in our mind, but how many of us have time to think anymore? The thinking is done for us by the machines, all we have to do is push a button, dial a number, or access the web which only leaves us tangled and confused. Kool Herc, Afrika Bambaataa, The Cold Crush Brothers, and many other Hip Hop Gods collectively thought Hip Hop into existence. Now they need us to collectively think the machine world that has corrupted Hip Hop out of existence so that real Hip Hop (Zion) can survive. This will not be the first Matrix that we destroy. This is actually the sixth version; there was Jazz, Blues, Rock, gospel, and Doo Wop, but Hip Hop has been the Matrix most successful version. This makes it the most dangerous. It will take the mental concentration of all who want to save Hip Hop to bring the machines reign to an end. I think Dead Prez said it best, "Turn off the radio," turn off the television, turn off the computer, turn off the machines and turn on your mind. This is when the real revolution will begin. When artists begin to make music that resonates from the heart chakra (love) again, instead of for the "soul" purpose of material gains, the power shifts back to us. When artists are willing to rhyme on the corner again to pay the rent without the help of machines, the machine world will crumble overnight. These are revolutionary tactics for 2006 and beyond. The past of Hip Hop is the future of Hip Hop. This is the main reason that the machines are trying to destroy Zion. The Gods created Hip Hop without the use of machines, and any machines that they used to assist them such as, mics, turntables, and amps, they had total mastery over. This means that Hip Hop can only be saved through the same mental channels. Peace.

Kill The A & R Man

It's hard, so very hard to get a record deal, why? Because Mr. A & R man, that's right I said Mr. A & R man doesn't want to deal with what is real.

And what is real, is that Hip Hop is a culture, a way of life that is exploited and preyed upon, by vultures,

Vultures of the industry who could care less about the real Hip Hop fan, so kill the A & R man, that's right I said kill the A & R!

Now who's to blame? The record label owners who hire these fools to recruit, because how the hell can you tell me that a nerd from the suburbs in a tight ass suit, knows more about Hip Hop than you and me? The A & R departments should be filled with some of us real motherfuckers gee!

Because 15 years down the line, they'll be known as the owners and creators of our culture of music, art, fashion and dance unless we take a stand, and Kill the A & R man!

But Mr. A & R man is always cryin', "I need a gimmick, an image I can market" well take a picture of me on stage holding my dark d*ck. So until you start dealing with what is true, Mr. A & R man, fuck you!

Kill the A & R man, that's right, I said Kill the A & R man!

Black Dot - A & R Killer, Da Hip Hop Play

32

THE SCIENCE OF THE "CHOSEN" ONE(S)
MATRIX OF HIP HOP - PART 3

The world has been waiting for a savior, a chosen one to lead the people. It's important that we understand that this is nothing more than a program designed by the Matrix for control purposes. In fact, out of all the programs that the Matrix has ever written, it's the system's oldest and most important one. From politics to religion, everything is predicated and based upon a system of a chosen one who is destined to lead us. From presidents who govern our physical lives, to "Christ like" figures who govern our spiritual lives, we are frozen in time until we receive divine instructions on how to move forward in this journey called life; it's the ultimate control program. As we further examine the term "Chosen One," the first question we should ask is, who's really doing the choosing? And since we live in a world of duality, is there an evil one and a good one, or are they one and the same, just different degrees of each other? Could the one be converted from the one to the one? Huh? Could the chosen one who we thought was our savior actually have been sent here by the Matrix to lead us to slaughter? The Bible warned against the worshipping of false prophets. If we study how the Matrix uses control to rule the world, we can begin to see the parallels of how this relates to the world of Hip Hop. One is the macrocosm, while the other is the microcosm, yet both are controlled by the same source. Both exist within the same time and space, yet time and space are illusions, so it's one's perception of such that will make it simple or complex on how worlds can exist within worlds. I can hold a world in the palm of my hand, neither size, space or time matters. Remember as we discussed in part 1 (Escape the Matrix), we mentally create the world that we live in, which means, "all is mental." With that said, it's safe to say that we're living in the mind of someone else at this present moment, and they're living in the mind of someone else, and so on and so on until there's only the primal source. There are those who only live in the Hip Hop world, who mentally shut out any other world, this Hip Hop world that has its own street laws, conscious community, criminal underworld, media outlets, and soon will have its own political movement if we continue to follow the "one" who was chosen to create it. Hip Hop is a fast growing nation, a multi-cultural nation of potential freethinkers who are anti-establishment. At this current rate of growth, Hip Hop could take over the world! This poses an immediate threat to the Matrix, it must have agents, uh, I mean chosen ones in place that can carry out the necessary programs to harness and redirect hostile energy into a combustible energy that actually aids the very system that we are trying to destroy. This type of "order out of chaos" programming is what will bring about a Hip Hop New World Order, where instead of going against the system, we become the system, but guess who will still be in charge? After being programmed by the Matrix on such extensive levels, every world that we collectively create thereafter gives the Matrix access to it.

By creating from a template set up by the Matrix, every new paradigm we embark upon is set up the same way, with laws, restrictions, and programming that inhibits us from operating outside of the boundaries of the Matrix. This is how it's been able to survive for generations; by owning the mental copyrights to our creations, we make it real and they "keep it real." It's the main reason that Hip Hop is in the state that it's in today, a state of confusion where we own nothing when it comes to the art form that we created, we only think we do. And since Hip Hop is much more than just an art form for true Hip Hoppers, it goes to show that we don't even own our own lives. Our very existence can be snatched from us at any given time. We are not in control of this destiny, our thoughts and actions are being guided in ways that are only beneficial to the system, a system of lockdown with one Emcee at any given time having the power to move millions of people in any direction that the Matrix sees fit. But there's hope, because this also means that at any given time there's one Emcee out there who has the power to destroy it, which is probably why Tupac and Biggie were assassinated. They both showed potential to short circuit or operate beyond the template programming set up by the Matrix of Hip Hop, even though they both were the appointed chosen ones in which major portions of the system was built. In an instant, an Emcee can go from the chosen one that was sent by the Matrix, to the chosen one who is operating from his original template that was created from the primal source of the universe, God, for lack of a better word. The difference could result in millions being free or millions being enslaved, so the mainframe is constantly on alert for potential defectors. It's a never ending war. Every time one is destroyed, one is replaced, on both sides. The stakes are very high and those who have been chosen have been chosen for a reason. It makes me laugh when an Emcee who has accomplished everything there is to accomplish in the game, from record sales to clothing lines, to millions of dollars, feels that he or she has done so with only hard work, perseverance, and it's a great American story, bullshit! This system has been set up by the Matrix in such a way that you can only go as far as those who are truly in control will allow, so don't gas yourself playa! When you have fulfilled your role as the chosen one for the Matrix, it will sacrifice you like all the others that came before you. When it has used up your energy for its own purposes and agenda to the point that you are no longer needed, it will pull the plug on your career. If you think that you're going to bow out of the game on your own terms, you're sadly mistaken.

Once you have been chosen, the Matrix owns you for life. The game must end in destruction because your demise equals its happiness. Michael Jordan hit the last shot of his illustrious career against Utah and walked away from the game a winner. He defeated the Matrix, or so he thought. A few years later he was back, but this time he left the game as a straight loser. He couldn't even get part ownership of a system that he helped build. When you feel that you are bigger than the very system that created you, it must destroy you, just look at Michael Jackson, how dare he curse his maker! The bigger the ego, the greater the sacrifice will be, the purer the victim, the greater the sacrifice will be as well. Kobe Bryant, who many had thought would be the chosen one to replace Michael Jordan, has always maintained a squeaky clean image, someone who is considered good, clean and wholesome. His sacrifice was equivalent to the Matrix sacrificing a virgin; can you imagine the level of ethereal energy being released from his "death?" Besides, they don't need him anymore, Lebron is the new chosen one. The sacrifice itself is food that fuels the machines. In part 1, I also revealed that the Matrix feeds off of our energy the same way a machine feeds off of a battery, but the only energy that serves as premium fuel for the machines is hatred, sorrow, fear, anger, and perverted sexual energy. When a sacrifice is performed, not only does the Matrix kill the Chosen one, but it also kills the spirit (energy) of the millions of people who put their faith in the chosen one as well, this makes for a great meal. This is one of the many ways that they process energy. Why would they sacrifice their own chosen one you may ask? Simple, they must eat, and they can easily replace him or her with another chosen one in that particular field of operation. However, when the Matrix sacrifices a chosen one who's operating from the original template, it's a little more satisfying, they eat, they defend the system they have put in place to keep us as slaves, and they kill the spirit of millions who were ready to go against the system, even die for their freedom. The Matrix has been using this program for years, it's called, "Kill the head and the body will fall." History has proven that our people cannot survive without a chosen one to lead them, or else they would be left to think for themselves, and that's one thing that the Matrix cannot have. This is why chosen ones have to be provided by the Matrix on a regular basis, for a certain level of thought control.

Based on the chosen one's mission and how valuable he is to the source that created him, he is afforded certain levels of protection, Matrix sanctioned chosen ones or otherwise. Have you ever wondered why it seems that some rappers, Hip Hop moguls, and other high profile figures have free reign to do as they please? They can commit crimes which others are charged, or if they are charged, they always seem to beat them, no matter how severe. They walk around like they own the world, not even the police can touch them. A chosen one is only as powerful as the unseen forces that protect him. Many of your favorite rappers are protected by unseen forces so powerful you couldn't imagine in your wildest dreams, secret society type forces that have nothing to do with Hip Hop per se, but have more to do with mind control and "food" management. Your favorite rapper has been chosen knowingly or unknowingly to help complete this task. Many of them drop hints of the forces that protect them by the names of their organizations, their lyrics, products that they endorse, and the people that they associate with. Each chosen one is assigned a vibration frequency that he or she can operate within. As long as they stay within their vibration frequency they're safe. In other words, as long as they're in cohorts with the Matrix and only form companies or commit actions that further serves the agenda of the Matrix, which is to drain the resources and energy of the people, they're protected. This can range from a legit alcohol company to selling crack in the hood, as long as the ends justify the means. In fact, the lower the vibration the greater the protection, because this indicates that you're willing to act in the most beastly manner to protect the system. If at any point, they try to change, raise, or step outside of their vibration and the mainframe which is reading these frequencies deems this change dangerous to its existence, the antivirus program is activated and the chosen one will be terminated and replaced, no questions asked. The same rules apply for the true chosen ones. They too are protected by unseen forces of a much greater source. This protection is spiritually based, the higher the vibration, the greater the protection.

The true chosen ones who are operating within the higher frequencies can step into enemy territories and there's absolutely nothing the Matrix can do about it. They are in the Matrix, but not of it. They too have been chosen to complete a certain task. These unseen spiritual forces are so potent that all the Matrix can do in its defense is download the discredit software and program the people against you. How many times throughout our history have we witnessed a chosen one who was sent to save us, be despised and rejected?

When the vibration is high, the Matrix can cause no physical, mental, or spiritual harm to you. However, if at any point your vibration is compromised due to your thoughts and actions, or you fall victim to the many programs that the Matrix has set up to trap you, the mainframe can pick up these readings as well, and the moment your vibration dips below a certain level, you too can be sacrificed for the betterment of the Matrix. This crucial vibration level is around the heart chakra, because once you lose the love for Hip Hop and you become motivated by greed or other ill intentions, you lose your spiritual force field.

The greatest fear that the Matrix of Hip Hop has is that we collectively realize that we are all the true chosen ones, so it must keep us fighting this battle within ourselves of good and evil. It knows that from your very conception, when billions of other sperm cells were fighting to fertilize the egg, that you were the chosen one. It knows that from that moment you were programmed from the original source. In order for it to exist, it had to create a program contrary to the original, and since that moment, the greatest war of all time has been taking place, the war between our higher and lower selves. Each one of us are encoded with both templates, one is located at the base of the spine (Matrix), the other at the top of the skull (original source). The spine serves as the pathway between each. To get a better understanding of what I'm talking about, I want you to view the human spinal cord as a thermometer and the mercury that rises up and down as a vibration. Normally when the mercury rises up the thermometer it represents heat, we're gonna flip it upside down so that a low vibration represents fire, the land of the Devil, a place where the Matrix can easily set up shop and rule. The high vibration represents the Godliness in one, where the Matrix cannot exist. The Matrix uses powerful antennae to beam out frequencies that can lock on to your vibration. This frequency comes in the form of videos, radio, movies, and magazines. It's a pulsating radar type frequency that's in search of the next chosen one to keep the Matrix afloat. If you're talented enough, and your thoughts and actions regarding Hip Hop are of a low enough vibration that this frequency can lock onto, then bleep…bleep…bleep, you could be the next chosen one. Remember, this is about control. If you're militant and you want to act upon this militancy within you, there are militant rappers who have been chosen to represent your thoughts that you can direct this hostile energy toward, so instead of you acting out these feelings, you simply live them out through your favorite rapper. The result being this hostile energy is processed into millions of record sales, which in turn means millions of dollars for the very system that your militant thoughts were against. Then they turn around and use that same money that your militant thoughts created to finance more prisons to lock your militant ass up! That's the significance of looking outside of yourself for a chosen one to save you. The Matrix has plenty of chosen ones for all of your thoughts, actions, and desires. It knows that as long as you look outward for the one, you will never discover the one within you, the true chosen one.

ETHER

HIP HOP

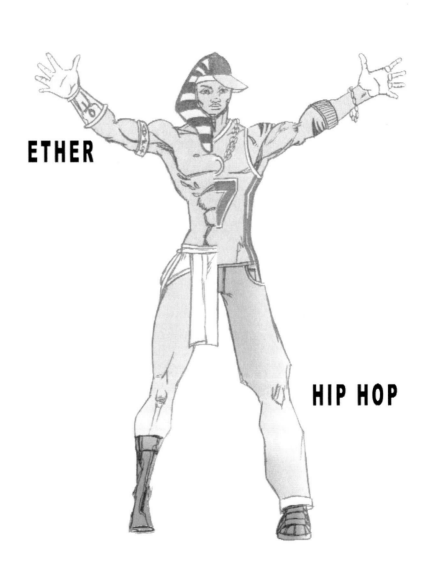

33

THE MAKING OF THE MATRIX OF HIP HOP

Recently I completed the trilogy on The Matrix of Hip Hop with The Science of the Chosen One(s), now it's time for some bonus footage as we go behind the scenes and uncover the making of this groundbreaking epic. We'll look at some of the actors and the roles they played in making the Matrix of Hip Hop such a huge success. We'll also credit the supporting cast, the directors, producers, and executive producers on a job well done. Our journey will take us from the original script, to the casting calls, to the finished product, so sit back and enjoy the show.

The first thing that must be made clear is that there's Hip Hop and then there's the Matrix of Hip Hop. One is real life and the other is "reel life," a fictional depiction of Hip Hop that beams out of televisions, radios, and movie screens across the world. With its advanced technology and special effects, the Matrix has written programs that have made "reel life" turn into real life! These programs are so intricate that our actual lives (real) have been transformed into a live Hip Hop reality show that's being recorded in "reel time" with conventional cameras, as well as in real time with the ultimate camera, the mind, in which the eyes serve as its lenses and the ears pick up its booming sounds. Hip Hop is a scripted drama, and the so called Hip Hop music that we hear today is nothing more than the soundtrack to this flick that we live in called life. The cars, the jewels, and the houses are nothing more than "props" used by the directors on the set of this epic. This is what Hip Hop has been reduced to, something that was real and tangible that gave us power, to something that's make believe that only creates more power and money for the directors, actors, and producers of our life.

Since this is a behind the scenes look at the Matrix, I'm going to show you how, and most importantly, why this was done. There's no need purchasing a ticket to go see this reality show because, like the Truman Show, you're in it! Although you may not be one of the main actors (rappers) who are actually on the screen performing, this movie is filmed in front of a live audience (masses), so our willingness to accept this film as being real as opposed to being "reel" will determine the outcome of our lives. However, unlike the Truman Show, the main characters of this never ending drama know that they're being filmed, but what they don't realize is that they're in a movie while being in a movie. This may sound confusing at the moment, but allow me to break it down.

Most of us by now have heard the phrase, "life imitating art," it's the very program by which many rappers live by, are jailed, or even killed by. The Matrix of Hip Hop has drawn such a thin line between what is real and what is art (reel) that it has become all too common for an artist to get caught on the wrong side of that line and start believing more in the illusion. This line is so thin that the Matrix has actually found a way to fuse the two (real and reel), to the point where art now controls our way of life. Think about that for a moment, art is no longer a reflection of our life, but our life is now a reflection, and dictated by the art that we created. That's like God bowing down, worshipping and serving its creation. We don't have command of Hip Hop anymore, Hip Hop now has command of us. And those who are keeping it "reel" control our destiny.

Before the Matrix, Hip Hop, which was created by the Gods of that time period, was used as a vehicle of expression. God expresses itself by creating. If God can't create it becomes stagnant, and stagnation leads to death, therefore, God must create in order to survive. Hip Hop was a direct expression of our joys, pain, struggles, and plight as an oppressed people living in the inner cities. We used the art of rhyme, dance, graffiti, and scratch to create a better way of life for ourselves, even if it was just on the mental plane to escape the hardships we were going through physically. Metaphysically speaking, art is used as a gateway between the spirit world (unseen) and the physical world (seen), as well as a tool used by us to re-member ourselves. Art is what we used to accurately record our his-tory. The basement of the Vatican holds some of the greatest pieces of art from our past, yet we will never be able to lay eyes on them for fear that we will remember the truth about who we are. Hip Hop is what this art has reincarnated into today. The science of using art to free us has been around since the beginning of time. A hundred years from now we'll call it something else, but it is art and the pur-pose of art will never change, to express and create. Naming it, cat-egorizing it, or calling it something new is just a program written by those in control to keep us "dismembered," because once we remember who we are as a collective, we become "The One," the Black "whole," that invincible force that has the power to destroy all that is the illusion. The Matrix must keep what was once a black "whole" broken into particles or it cannot survive. This is the true power and intent of Hip Hop. Back in the days we used this power for its rightful purpose, and it was always positive and progressive. The music had a message, the videos were tasteful and told an inspi-rational story, the graffiti preserved the history, and we danced the pain of oppression away. Each element of Hip Hop had a spiritual purpose. It became dangerously clear to those in control that the art of Hip Hop was healing the people. However, this was nothing new, even during the days of slavery, slave masters were baffled by our ability to use the art of dance, drums, and Negro spirituals to lift ourselves up in the midst of being beaten, raped, tortured, and killed. Art is how we as Gods, manifest things in the physical form. Art can be used as a "star gate" between the realms. The more oppressed we became, the greater the art we expressed, the more freedom we received through art. At all costs, those in control had to find a way to turn our art into a weapon that could be used against us. They had to find a way to close the "star gate" between dimen-sions in an attempt to trap us in one realm, the physical. They had to find a way to thwart our creative process so that the art form would become stagnant, in which the creative force within us would die. They then had to reverse the field of polarity so that whatever negative energy that was sent toward the Matrix through our art or otherwise, could easily be captured, harnessed, and transformed into a weapon that the Matrix could actually use to destroy us! Imagine the angrier you became at someone, the stronger they became. This is what the Matrix was attempting to do, but this would not be an easy task since we are the Gods and they're just illusionists; the difference being, we can make things real and they can only create the illusion that something is real. However, if enough of the Gods start falling victim to the many mind control programs that the Matrix has set up and start believing in the illusion, it will become as real as any other world. The opposite of the spirit world is the machine world, and here is where the illusionist would set up shop and stage their attack. A Hip Hop Matrix, separate from the Matrix that we were already living in had to be designed for the sole purpose of controlling the urban terrain. Because it was here, in the most desolate of places, that under the most wretched living conditions that something as powerful as Hip Hop could be born, or should I say re-born. Remember, Hip Hop is nothing new, the only thing new about it is its name, and every time the Matrix stages war against "the one" in an attempt to dismember it, it has to use art as a weapon to remember itself. In our case, it's the art of Hip Hop. So make no mistake about it, in this day and time, Hip Hop is "the one." And just as the "ones" that came before it, it has the ability to form a black "whole," a collective consciousness thought stream that has the capacity to evolve to unattainable heights of anything that is not spiritual. This is what controls the weather, creates new life forms on the planet, and new worlds throughout the galaxy, our collective thoughts; the greater the black "Whole," the greater the consciousness stream. This is the main reason that the Matrix keeps our thoughts fragmented with distractions, or only focused on things that it would like for us to accomplish. As we embark on the fourth dimension, the black "whole" is the only thing that can ensure us of a safe journey into the next paradigm. When we move as one thought, nothing can stop us. In addition, "black wholes" suck up and annihilate everything in its path. This means the Matrix, the machine world, and everything in it would be destroyed overnight because it could not withstand such powerful forces. This is why real Hip Hop had to be destroyed and a holographic form of Hip Hop put in its place, so that no real spiritual energy could ever be generated from it anymore, only physical energy which will forever trap us in the realm of matter. You may just see it as beats and rhymes, but those who have been fighting this war against it for thousands of years see it for what it truly is, a spirit force that refuses to die, a spirit force that can take the form of whatever creative energy that is on the planet at that time. As long as we create, God lives.

By 1988, the Hip Hop Matrix was fully designed and ready for operation. The mainframe and the necessary programs needed to turn real Hip Hop into "reel" Hip Hop were in place. The architects who wrote the programs to counter every essence of Hip Hop were ready to launch their attack. Of course this attack would be led by the machine world and the "agents" that were controlled by it. The minute that Hip Hop went primetime, it was lost to the Matrix forever. Since it had to be fed into the machines to take it primetime, the machines now controlled the destiny of Hip Hop. Prior to 1988, Hip Hop had received its share of national exposure, but the programming needed to use Hip Hop as a weapon to destroy us had not been written yet. There was no Hip Hop Matrix in place, so Hip Hop artists were able to use the media to its advantage and spread the true essence of the art form. But now, the machine world had the power to turn Hip Hop in any direction that it pleased.

The first program written by the Matrix was to change the intent of the art of Hip Hop. When you change the intent of something, you change the vibration and frequency of it. Old school artists didn't rhyme for money, fame and glory, it was an after effect of their original intent, which was to express themselves by creating and to become free in the process. By the machine world taking the very lowest essence of Hip Hop (violence, drugs, and sex) and giving it maximum exposure, it immediately changed the intent of new artists, therefore changing the entire dynamic of Hip Hop. Hip Hop is like water, it has no true form, and no two artists should ever sound the same because no two artists create alike. This allows Hip Hop to stay creative, evolve, and God continue to live. But when you place Hip Hop (water) in a bottle, it takes on the form of that bottle. The Matrix has bottled up Hip Hop, stopped the flow of its creativity, thus it has stopped the flow of life as it pertains to Hip Hop. In addition, water that doesn't flow, leads to contamination, and contamination leads to parasites. In no time, they were able to kill the flow of Hip Hop and feed off of the dead source that was contained within the bottle. The machine world began to display this bottle of Hip Hop 24 hours a day, using all of its outlets, radio, T.V., and magazines, to the point where even the most conscious minds were affected by it. Inside of the bottle was the most polluted portion of Hip Hop. Artists were no longer using their creative forces, but were seduced and controlled by dictated forces. What was in the bottle became the model for what Hip Hop would become, polluted. When they observed the riches and exposure being rewarded to those initial artists who were willing to create from within the bottle, the next generation of artists saw this as a golden opportunity to be free. But being free in the real world is much different than being free in the "reel" world. These artists may have escaped some of the physical hardships of survival, but have given their souls over to the machines. Let's not forget, the machines print the money, the machines cut the diamonds, and the machines build the cars. By changing the intent of Hip Hop, the Matrix was also able to pervert the word art, thus changing the very meaning of what it meant to be artistic. In ancient times the word art was held in such high regards because they understood its significance to our existence. Today, the word doesn't hold the same value and this was done by design.

Nowadays when a rapper completes an album, video, or movie depicting us in a certain light (usually negative), it is viewed as just his or her "artistic" expression. This term creates a loophole in which an artist can shed criticism or accountability for his actions because, after all, it's just art right? But what happens when this form of artistic expression is the only form that the machine world will allow to be seen or heard? It becomes the source by which all artists will create from, and the standard (bottle) by which all art and artists will be judged. When this is done, the art loses its power. I also mentioned earlier that art was used to accurately record our history, but what happens when the Matrix begins to record our art and the only portion recorded is this negative "artistic" expression of it? On one hand, it is made to appear that if they record the art, they also record the history since that is how it was done traditionally. If this is the case, then the history that they are recording of us today is that of pimps, hustlers, and criminals. On the other hand, it dismisses our glorious past as kings, queens, and great builders because it is made to seem like the artists of that time period were fabricating these great accomplishments that we achieved using the same form of "artistic" expression. This is a ritual, in which by changing the programming of a word, the Matrix can erase our past. We then begin to consciously and subconsciously complete the ritual by acting out the "art" that we see, hear, and read. The Matrix then records and beams the images of us actually committing crimes, doing drugs, and womanizing to every media outlet in the world. Now what was once "reel" (artistic) is actually real. hence: you're in a movie, while being in a movie.

Hip Hop is the number one feature film on the life of black people in America being shown all over the world. Since we act out what we see on screen, is there any difference between what's on a movie reel and a movie becoming real? The Matrix has added a new meaning to the phrase, "bringing art to life." This has all been made possible because Hip Hop has been bottled up. The Matrix has turned this bottle into a mystical-like power source, but instead of rubbing the bottle and a genie popping out granting you three wishes, all one has to do is focus their intent and creative force on the contents within the bottle and whatever is inside of the bottle will become their reality, it's just that simple. So when a rapper rhymes about money, cars, guns, and even hard times, his wishes are granted and he lives out that reality. Rappers are not the only ones affected by the bottle, it also affects the millions and millions of fans who are coerced into this type of reality by tapping into the thought stream of their favorite rapper who is addicted to the bottle. I'm talking mass meditation, the greater the focus and intent, the greater the results will be. The Matrix tells us what the next trend will be in the "reel" world, we then actualize it in the real world.

The Last Poets stated, "the revolution will not be televised," because if it can be televised, with today's technology and Matrix programming, it can be commercialized and trivialized. Imagine an enemy that doesn't try to attack you, but embraces you by signing you to a record deal, shooting a video for your revolutionary thoughts against it, plugging you into heavy rotation, then sitting back and watching the cash and ratings pile up. Meanwhile your revolutionary thoughts and actions haven't even ruffled the feathers of the enemy you were initially trying to kill. Hell, your first royalty check may be so lovely that you even forget who the enemy is! This is how the Matrix can take a real cause and make it a reel cause, as well as the reverse scenario. The television has that kind of power. Your life can be transformed into a reality show and a mockery made of your threat to the Matrix, and you won't even realize it until it's too late. You show up, you perform, and get paid just like all the other actors on the set. This reality show of Hip Hop even has commercials. Every time a rapper endorses a product in his video, it's no different, yet has the same affect as any other T.V. show that pushes goods to the consumers who watch it. The biggest selling rappers get the primetime slots. When I say biggest selling, I mean the ones who can get on T.V. and push products to us 24 hours a day. These products, which range from what we eat to what we wear, define our lifestyle, because without them, we feel useless. Our lifestyle is then based on product consumption, and product consumption requires capital, which equates to energy because you have to work hard expending it to make money. Our energy is what fuels the machines that control us because our belief in it gives it that power; the machines that control us, own and operate the television, see the connection? Even if you are against the Matrix, if you enter into the television world, it can manipulate you into selling something to help fuel it. Example, the more dangerous and revolutionary a rapper is, the more records sales he'll generate, which equates to more money spent, which equates to more energy released, which equates to more power for the Matrix. The Matrix can even switch his program in the process, transforming him from a revolutionary to a comedian in a matter of three albums.

Take Ice Cube for instance, he was the most feared rapper on the planet at one time. Just the look in his eyes scared White America half to death. His militant words inspired millions of would be soldiers who were ready to take on the Matrix at his command, now he's just a comedian (Barber Shop, Friday, Are We There Yet?, etc). In fact, he went from being a gangsta, to a revolutionary, to a comedian; what kind of evolution is this, and how could such a drastic change take place so fast? It's simple, the television is not real, it's reel, and when you're starring in one of its shows, you follow the script as it has been written by the director, or your show will be canceled. Besides, being a comedian pays more money in the Matrix. Ice Cube is not alone, the Matrix is filled with "Neos" (ones) who plugged into the Matrix with the sole purpose of freeing the people, only to end up plastered on a billboard somewhere with a white upper lip and the words, "Got Milk?" over their heads. This may not seem significant to most people, but those who have put on their dark glasses to see beyond the illusion that is the Matrix know and understand that we are at war, and we're being attacked literally, musically, and symbolically. So what does the "white" lip symbolize? To those without glasses, it's just milk on the face of one of our idols who's trying to lead by example and let us know that by drinking milk we can have stronger bones and receive the necessary calcium needed to live healthier lives. To those who are unplugged, it's not milk at all, it's the hand of the Matrix going back and forth, bussing off in the face of our leaders, idols, and warriors and saying, this is what we really think of you. And because milk is like kryptonite to black people, causing many diseases, it also reveals to those who are wearing their dark glasses who the double agents are, the ones who pose as your friends, but are really your enemies. Hip Hop is filled with double agents, secret signs and symbols, and encoded music that can be revealed and decoded once you put on your dark glasses to block out the glare of all the glitz, spotlights, and "bling bling." One must go into the darkness to see, because the light is where the illusion is.

N.W.A.

N.W.A. unfortunately weren't wearing their dark glasses for this purpose, they wore them to portray an image, and as a result, they fell for the illusion and were one of the first groups to answer the casting calls set up by the Matrix. Even though as a group they were already selling records outside of the system, when they joined forces with the machine world, Hip Hop as we knew it would change forever. Eazy E and the crew were simply telling their story to the world, and in the process making people aware of the gang violence, drugs, and police corruption in L.A. If you understand the science of social engineering, you know that they were just victims being paid to tell their story. They didn't create the conditions, they rhymed about them. However, pre-existing conditions+current thought stream= future conditions. All is mental; if one wanted to know the future, all he had to do was control the present since thought is the building block of all things. The Matrix has set up these conditions that we live in order to birth a certain level of thought. If all that we experience is negative, then we embark on a vicious cycle of experience, thought, and conditions that become hard to escape. So when a rapper says he's only rappin' about what he sees, heard about, or experienced, he's telling the truth. He or she just doesn't comprehend the magnitude of his own thoughts and the thoughts of the millions of fans who tap into his frequency to make it an even stronger reality. N.W.A. was the first group to premier on the show called the Matrix of Hip Hop. Thanks to the help of the machines, and the video directors on the set, people all over the country tuned in for the next episode of Niggaz Wit Attitudes. In no time, gang activity began taking place in areas that weren't known for such actions. And clone rap groups (Geto Boys) were popping up all over the country, each rapping about the same things, negative conditions that they were experiencing. This was by design. At one point you couldn't get a record deal if you didn't sound like N.W.A., and since they were not too far from Hollywood, it made sense to have them star in their own reality show first. If the pilot was successful, (and it was), the Matrix could then take this show on the road, using our own thoughts to create an artificial brand of

Hip Hop, and the negative conditions that we were purposely placed in, to keep us trapped within our own thought prison. We couldn't think our way out of the situation because all we thought about was the situation that we were in! All of the groups such as, Public Enemy, KRS ONE, Tribe Called Quest, Rakim, X Clan, and many others who were using thought as a building block, were shut out of the Matrix for fear that they would destroy it. If one had to draw a timeline in which Hip Hop began to change its course for the worse, most will agree that it would be when N.W.A. stepped on the scene. They were the first agents, but certainly not the last to have their cause further someone else's agenda. Whether you're a knowing or unknowing agent is irrelevant to those who are pulling the strings. If your energy is needed to complete a mission, the Matrix will stop at nothing to get that job done. N.W.A. was called the world's most dangerous group, now you know why.

Actors: N.W.A.
Director: Matrix, Eazy E
Producer: Dr. Dre
Executive Producer: Eazy E, Jerry Heller
Supporting cast: Ren, Yella, Ice Cube, D.O.C.

NOTORIOUS B.I.G.

After the seed was planted by N.W.A., the Matrix of Hip Hop saw moderate success, but it wasn't until the arrival of the Notorious B.I.G., a.k.a. Biggie Smalls that the program really took off, the reason being, Biggie was a legitimate Emcee. Because N.W.A. was from the west coast and they really couldn't rhyme that well at the time, most of the Hip Hop followers from the east coast rejected the programming. If it wasn't from the East where Hip Hop originated, it wasn't authentic. So when Biggie, considered to be the greatest of all time by many, logged on with his charismatic flow, the machine world's two greatest cities, New York and L.A. were in total control of Hip Hop. Biggie articulated our experience with such New York flare, that it caused a ripple in Hip Hop's grand design. When the king of New York, which is the Mecca of Hip Hop, speaks, the entire world listens. He went from ashy to classy and laid out the blueprint for the next generation of Emcees to do the same. What he didn't realize was that he was leading Hip Hop to its ultimate demise in the process. Biggie took Hip Hop to the highest realm of its lowest level, and cemented it there. The conditions in Brooklyn in which he was brought up under, gave birth to a certain level of thought, which lead to the lyrics, "money, hoes, and clothes, that's all a nigga knows." This became the apex of Hip Hop. Our collective thought stream produced more money, hoes, and clothes than ever before. A few niggas got rich, but the biggest winner was the Matrix itself because it now controlled the minds of the youth of America and abroad. Biggie sucked the revolution out of Hip–Hop.

Actor: Notorious B.I.G.
Director: Matrix, P.Diddy
Producer: P.Diddy, Hitmen
Executive Producer: Clive Davis, Arista
Supporting Cast: Mase, Lox, Lil Kim, Junior Mafia

TUPAC/NAS

Tupac Shakur was the first glitch in the Matrix of Hip Hop because he operated within two programs. He lived the life of Biggie in terms of money, cars, and women, but he was a born revolutionary. Within him, the revolution was alive and well, and could be activated at any time. At first this presented a problem for the Matrix because the mainframe had a hard time reading the contradictory signals of his actions and the forecast of where he was leading the "sheeple." This is a method employed by someone who doesn't want their true intentions known, therefore he was considered very dangerous. Unlike the artists that came before him, he was able to jump from program to program at his own will, showing an uncanny ability to master the Matrix when others were just slaves to it. His actions also represented movement, from one state of being to the next. Tupac was like a modern day Harriet Tubman working the "underground," taking people from slavery to freedom, and every time he freed someone with his words of inspiration or revolution, he would return to the T.H.U.G. realm to seek more slaves to free. It's equivalent to Neo going into the Matrix and freeing the mind of someone. Nas was just as enigmatic in his approach to the system, going from Nas to Esco to God's Son, showing that he too could not be contained in any one program. He has been called a walking contradiction in many Hip Hop circles, but in the art of war, the perception of something is not necessarily what it is. His ascension to God's Son signified the arrival of the spiritual element of Hip Hop, which is the final frontier. This was even more dangerous than Tupac because Nas was attempting to open a vortex in the Matrix in which spiritual energy could seep through. This energy is the exact opposite of the energy used by the Matrix, which is based in matter. Spirituality is like the machine world's anti-matter, and when two extreme opposites collide, a great explosion takes place (Big Bang Theory), giving birth to a whole new energy. So to counter such actions, the Matrix wrote and downloaded a new program called choice, and as the Merovingian stated in Matrix Reloaded, "Choice is an illusion between those with power and those without." By writing a program that seemed to allow space for spiritual growth, yet actually build a shield around itself for protection against such spiritual forces, the Matrix was able to give off the illusion that such artists who rebelled against the system were making progress, when in fact, the progress was being monitored and controlled by the Matrix all along. With Hip Hop partitioned off between gangsta rap, conscious rap, political rap, etc, it became easier for the Matrix to trap artists like Pac and Nas by programming the next step in their evolution before they even get there. Therefore, if one thought outside of the box and let those thoughts be known, they were no longer thoughts that were out of the box because the Matrix could build a box to place these new thoughts into and then you'd be back where you started, trapped.

Actors: Tupac/Nas
Directors: Matrix, Suge Knight/Steve Stout
Producers: Various
Executive Producers: Columbia Records/Interscope
Records
Supporting cast: Outlaws/The Firm

JAY-Z

Biggie's untimely death left a huge void in the Matrix of Hip Hop that could only be filled by one who could truly operate within the same program set up for him to exist. Instead of writing a new program, it's so much easier for the Matrix to insert someone into an existing program. Jay-Z's rise to fame would come after his Brooklyn counterpart was deleted from the system. But Jay would throw a glitch in the system by becoming one of the first real Emcees to write his own program from an existing program. In fact, he upgraded the program before he was fully inserted. Even though he rhymed and lived the life of Biggie, he deviated from his program by becoming a CEO of his own label: Roc-A-Fella Records. This gave him the power to sort of control his own destiny within the Matrix. It also gave him the authority to write and insert others into programs that he saw fit (Memphis Bleek, Beanie Sigel, etc). He too moved in and out of programs at will, and owned stock in the very system that enslaved others. Instead of being pimped, he did the pimping, which is brilliant in one sense because he had the ability to beat the system, but since we the people are plugged into the system, the only ones who really lose are us. Even though he wasn't the first black Hip Hop mogul, his knowledge of writing and upgrading programs forced the Matrix to relinquish some of its power to more young Black entrepreneurs, or at least give off the illusion that it did. In actuality, they just moved from a worker's level of control to a supervisor's position with stock options. Jigga was so good at mastering the machine world that he proclaimed himself God of the Matrix (J-hova), and with millions of followers moved by his every word, who can deny his claim? This God of the material world set the Hip Hop nation back on our quest to become spiritual beings something awful. If you live by his bible (book of Hard Knock Life, the Blueprint passages, etc), one could obtain the material riches equivalent to being in heaven...on earth. But since we are spiritual beings having a human experience, his teachings block the pathway for us to return home as Gods of the universe. His ability to morph into Jigga man from Jay-Z to Hova, demonstrates our ability to exist on multiple planes simultaneously. We can only hope that his transformation back into S. Carter will bring him closer to his spiritual essence, since it's the very first name he received when he left the spirit realm.

Actor: **Jay-Z**
Director: Matrix, Jay-Z, Dame Dash, Kareem Biggs
Producers: Kanye West, Timberland, Pharell, Just Blaze
Executive Producers: Jay-Z, Dame Dash, Lyor Cohen,
Russell Simmons
Supporting Cast: Memphis Bleek, Beanie Sigal, State
Property

LAURYN HILL

Lauryn Hill represented the feminine energy within the construct of the Matrix, which is the primal energy in which the universe is made of. She was inserted within one program (Fugees), but quickly wrote her own that was based on the one thing that could bring the Matrix to its knees, love. The machines have no soul so they cannot feel emotions, and since love is the greatest emotion of all, it is kryptonite to the mainframe. Lauryn was dangerous because she was fighting the Matrix from a whole other realm, the spiritual. The Miseducation of Lauryn Hill was an opus of love and spirituality that did for those on the spiritual path what Jay-Z's music did for those locked into the realm of matter; it gave them hope. Using love as her weapon, she was also demonstrating the proper use of sexual energy, which meant more bad news for the Matrix. The proper use of such energy enables one to tap into the spirit realm at will and manipulate or break certain laws that govern the Matrix. To counter the energy put forth by Lauryn Hill, the Matrix flooded the mainframe with programs written for Lil Kim, Foxy Brown, Trina, and Missy Elliot. Each one of these female Emcees' programming was void of love and dealt with a perverted type of sexual energy. This type of sexual energy generates no real power for the user, only more power for the Matrix. Lauryn reached the top of the Matrix world when she received five Grammy awards, then she did the unthinkable, she wrote her own exile program and vanished. In the process, she forfeited millions of potential dollars and unlimited fame, which is what the Matrix uses to lure and trap its subjects. She gave it all up for the right to control her own life. In essence, she defeated the Matrix. Even if she decides to reinsert herself at a later date, she has shown that she is a cut above any program that the Matrix can throw at her. The power of her love can still be felt by millions.

Actor: Lauryn Hill

Director: Matrix, Lauryn Hill

Producers: Lauryn Hill

Executive Producer: Columbia Records

Supporting Cast: Wyclef Jean/Pras

MASTER P/CASH MONEY

With the machine world's two major cities (New York and L.A.) on lock, the Matrix could now turn its focus to unchartered territory. the Dirty South. The energy in this region was ripe for downloading programs of control into the minds of the youth, and uploading one who could make it all possible, Master P. In an attempt to illustrate that they were more than just country bump-kins, Master P and his crew logged on and put the "Dirty Dirty" on the map with hits about getting paid and slaying women in the process. This was a significant victory for the Matrix because the south has always been deep rooted in spirituality and occult sci-ences (roots). Especially New Orleans, which happens to be the birth place of Jazz, which is another form of music that we created and used to raise ourselves up. It wasn't uncommon to witness strange or mystical occurrences in this part of the south, and if there ever was one place that a spiritual messiah could have risen through Hip Hop, this was the place. But Master P and the No Limit Soldiers pulled their followers further and further away from their salvation by dropping album after album of the same gangsta music. They called themselves No Limit Soldiers, but they were obviously lim-ited to a physical existence of materialism, sex, and violence. They even had a soldier by the name of Mystikal, but his actions proved that his existence was just an oxymoron. To add fuel to the fire, Cash Money Millionaires grabbed the baton from No Limit and ran straight to the bank, cashing in on the same formula and program of their predecessors. Baby and the crew seemed to pop out of nowhere as if it was well orchestrated by puppet masters looking to push the envelope of materialism to a whole new level, and Cash Money did just that. From fancy cars, to diamonds and furs, to lav-ish houses, these were the only things that Cash Money were ordained to rhyme about. This is extremely troubling in the face of the poverty that Black people are facing every day in this country, and particularly in the region in which they are from. The last thing someone who is out of work needs to see is a bunch of young black men on the television or radio bragging about the riches they have obtained mainly through criminal activity. We only have ourselves to blame because we are the ones who keep purchasing their records, enabling them to go legit and further torment us with video after video of all the things we may never possess, and have them rhyme about how we ain't shit in the process. We make them suc-cessful and this is the thanks that we get.

Actors: Master P/Cash Money Millionaires
Directors: Matrix, Master P/Baby, Manny Fresh
Producers: Master P/Manny Fresh
Executive Producers: No Limit/Universal
Supporting Cast: No Limit Soldier/Cash Money
Millionaires

OUTKAST/ GOODIE MOB

Before the Matrix upgraded the Dirty South version of its software to reduce southern Hip Hop to nothing more than just pimps and hoes, the land of Atlantis (Atlanta) produced a couple of diamonds in the ruff by the names of OutKast and their partners in rhyme, The Goodie Mob. OutKast sent the system haywire by going against the programs written to contain them by relying on the spirit force of those who came before this current paradigm in which we operate within. By tapping into the consciousness stream of the 70's soul groups, they have become the reincarnation of that energy. Their music and style is the embodiment of a revolutionary movement that the Matrix has already destroyed, or so they thought. Their style is significant because it reconnects our past with our present, showing that we are all connected and everything is connected to the one. By using such methods, OutKast and the Goodie Mob can enlist an army of limitless ancestral energy as far back as ancient Khemet to help us destroy the Matrix since each paradigm was influenced by the one that preceded it. The name OutKast suggests that they have been cast out, or have cast themselves out of a place or in this case, a program called, the Matrix. Lucifer was cast out of heaven because he went against the system. Now I would never liken OutKast to Lucifer in the "traditional" sense, but perhaps they named themselves such because of their "knowledge" of a system that was destroying our lives and they wanted no part of it. Through their music, they became a beacon of "light" for those didn't have the knowledge of "Goodie" Hip Hop and evil Hip Hop. The name Goodie has the word God in it, meaning once you understand that you are God, no system or program can ever contain you. OutKast and Goodie Mob have always rhymed from their soul and followed their hearts, and there's no program that the Matrix could ever write to combat that.

Actors: OutKast/Goodie Mob
Director: Matrix, OutKast/Goodie Mob
Producer: Various
Executive Producer: Arista Records
Supporting Cast: The Dungeon Family

WU-TANG CLAN

Wu-Tang entered into the hemisphere of the Matrix like thieves in the night, never revealing their true identities or purpose until the time was right. By them sliding in under the radar of the Matrix, they we able to set up the 36 chambers necessary to give birth to the one thing that could annihilate the Matrix on contact, knowledge of self. Their first album was called, Enter the Wu-Tang (36 Chambers); 3+6=9, which was the number of members that Wu plugged into the Matrix with. In the Supreme mathematics, which are the lessons that they came armed with, the number 9 represents born (birth), which is the number of completion. This signified that the first part of their mission, which was to touch down and set up a network in which they can operate from within the beast, was complete. Their second group album, Wu-Tang Forever, almost brought the Matrix to its knees. Since they were speaking the language of the Matrix, which is numbers, they had to send encrypted messages using mathematical equations that could only be solved by those who were on that particular frequency. Their third album was called, The W album. W is the 23rd letter of the alphabet, but in Supreme mathematics, 2 = wisdom, and 3 = understanding, when you add up the numbers 2+3, you get the number 5, which means power. Wu-Tang now possessed the power to make change and this was evident in the content of the W. album that wasn't present in the first one. Their 1st album represented the number 1, which is knowledge in Supreme mathematics. When you combine their three group albums, you get knowledge (1), wisdom (2), and understanding (3). When they raised their flag in the name of Islam and began to teach the babies the truth about who they were, the Matrix went to war with them by shutting down their access to the machine world via radio play, magazine coverage, and even record sales. But it was too late. Like a splinter cell, the original nine factions of the Wu had already received their instructions and went off in different directions, infiltrating many different programs in the process. Some of them went commercial like Method Man, some of them went Old School like Ghost Face, some of them went street like Raekwon, while some of them went underground like Gza, Masta Killer, and U-God. Rza continued to teach, and O.D.B. "appeared" to be out of his mind, but there is definitely a method to their madness. When the time is right for them to re-unite, they may be powerful enough to combine every style of Hip Hop into a force that can wreak havoc on the Matrix. We can only hope that the sleeper cells will awaken soon. This will be tough since O.D.B., who was the heart of the operation has expired on the physical realm, but not impossible. Remember, "You can never defeat the Gods."

Actors: Wu-Tang Clan
Directors: Matrix, Rza
Producer: Rza
Executive Producers: Loud Records
Supporting Cast: Wu-Tang/ Killer Bees

EMINEM

For years the Matrix has been on the lookout for a Hip Hop savior. Not one offering the "red pill" that could free the people, but one who would serve as a reverse Neo that was armed with the "blue pill" to help the Matrix keep the illusion going. This reverse Neo had to have the power to indoctrinate millions of White people into a system that was initially designed to enslave and control the originators of Hip Hop. In the past, the Matrix has tried diligently to manufacture its own Neo (white rapper(s)), one who appeared authentic to the principles of Hip Hop with superior rhyme skills that we would accept as being on the same frequency as the originators, but to no avail. The search would end when Dr. Dre, the reverse Morpheus, found the "One" he had been looking for and offered him the blue pill; his name was Eminem. Once Eminem accepted the blue pill, Dr. Dre brought him to the other side and showed him the inner workings of the Matrix and how he could benefit by keeping the illusion going. This is not to say that Eminem didn't love and respect Hip Hop and was doing it from his heart, but as I mentioned earlier, your cause can be easily used to further someone else's agenda. The arrival of Eminem signified the last days of Hip Hop. White people had already claimed economic dominance in Hip Hop since they were the ones reaping all of the financial rewards of our hard work and labor, but through Eminem, they could now claim the culture itself. They were no longer considered outsiders who just purchased our music, but through Eminem they were now able set up shop and partake in its future, a future that will lead to its ultimate demise. This multicultural, can't we all get along bullshit, has stifled our ability to access the spiritual properties of Hip Hop needed to assist us in reaching an elevated state of being. The energy is too diluted. It's like trying to make a phone call and there's too much static on the line. The Matrix is at the switchboard and our calls to the most high (higher self), have been put on hold or rerouted. Meanwhile, Eminem is robbing our culture blind of all of its resources, physical and spiritual. And when the his-story is written, he will be considered as the king of kings, a blond haired, blue eyed savior. When we put on our dark glasses and start decoding, we see that the way Eminem is portrayed is similar to that of another blond haired, blue eyed savior, Jesus Christ, who millions of Black people worship. Jesus had 12 disciples, Eminem's group is called D-12. Could the D really stand for disciple? He is always sitting at the head of the table as far as the group is concerned, and he gives his life (shine) so that they may live. His record company name is Shady Records, could this be an indication that something is not right? Or could the Shady represent the grey area in which Eminem has led Hip Hop into following this multi-cultural program set up by the Matrix to neutralize the power of people with melanin? His name spelled backwards is pronounced "Mini Me" meaning, he is not of the original, he is grafted. Make no mistake about it, the state of Hip Hop is under "Marshall" law, and Mr. Mathers rules with an iron fist. Just like Christ, Eminem will reign supreme as long as we give him the power to rule over us without us even questioning, does he truly exist, or is he just a figure created by the Matrix to get us to submit to its will?

Actor: Eminem
Director: Matrix, Dr. Dre
Producer: Dr. Dre/Eminem
Executive Producer: Jimmy Iovine/Dr. Dre
Supporting Cast: D-12

50 CENT

He ruled the underground like Osiris ruled the underworld. He was shot nine times by another brother, scattered in the street and left for dead. He pulled the pieces of his life back together, even resurrecting his career in the process, proving that he has an immortal trait within him that can be activated in the time of crisis. His legend underground was colossal, even those living above ground in the Matrix knew that he was a force to be reckoned with, and they would have to pay homage to him if they ever entered into his realm. The similarities between the two (Osiris and 50) are quite eerie. 50 Cent could very well be the reincarnate of that mythological figure so feared that the very mention of his name instills fear in everyone who knows the story. This is exactly why the Matrix fears him the most. The sad thing about it is, 50 Cent doesn't have a clue about the story or the potential that lies within him to re-enact the story in modern times. He could single handedly bring down the entire system because he was from another world, a world that operated independent of the rules that governed the Matrix. 50 was building an army of underground followers who were rebelling against the programming of the mainstream and the Matrix that controlled it. Whether this was his intention or not, the Matrix knew that at some point or another, they would be strong enough to rise up and destroy the system. So the Matrix did the only thing that it could do, make him an offer that he couldn't refuse, sign him, and plug him into the Matrix immediately. This mission was carried out by the king of the Matrix himself, Eminem. The minute that 50 signed on the dotted line, he not only killed himself and his legend, but the underground was dead as well. The Matrix then wrote a program called the underground and downloaded it into the space of the original. The real underground was gone because the guardian who protected it was gone. Now when the Matrix wanted to break a new artist, the first place that they sent their music to was the underground since they now owned it. You are sadly mistaken if you still think that the underground mixtape scene operates independent of the Matrix. 50 cent went from being God in one world, to being a slave in another, and he took most of his following with him, a following so large that their energy is equivalent to a battery with billions of volts. This is energy that will undoubtedly be used to fuel the Matrix. The G in G-Unit stands for guerilla, which is exactly who the Matrix has taught us, we as Black people have evolved from. This has systematically cut us off from our God head, and as long as we continue to act in a beastly nature, the lies about who we are as a people will remain to be true. His First album was called: Get Rich or Die Trying. In this case he did both; he got rich, but he killed his potential to really make a change in the life of the millions of fans who trusted him to keep it real…underground that is.

Actor: 50 Cent
Director: Matrix/Eminem

Producer: Dr. Dre
Executive Producer: Eminem/Aftermath
Supporting Cast: G-Unit

KANYE WEST

Everything in the universe must move including the consciousness of the people. The question then becomes is it moving on its own accord, or is it being guided by a system looking to take advantage of its final destination? Since the Matrix only exists in our mind, I think that it's safe to say that it has unlimited access to the thought patterns and overall psyche of the human brain. So if we're being manipulated, it's definitely an inside job. By hacking into our consciousness the Matrix has created a life of its own, and by doing so, it has become as real as anything else in our existence. Based on the current data emitting from our brainwaves, it can also plot the next logical stage in our conscious evolution, meaning, it knows what we're thinking before we think it. And since we're talking about the consciousness of Hip Hop, one can easily see that it moved from the East Coast, to the West coast, to the Dirty South. The next logical region of untapped resources for the Matrix to exploit was the Mid-West. It wouldn't be hard for the Matrix to steer our consciousness in that direction since it was already at the controls of our thoughts, and our mind is the only thing that can make anything possible. The chosen one to spearhead this program would be none other than Kanye West. There have been other rappers in this region making a little noise prior to Kanye, but none who had the capacity to truly put the Mid-West on the national and international map. The name Kanye means; King. His last name is West. So he is king of the West, or in this case, Mid-West. He has been quoted as saying, "I am the one that the world has been waiting for." In the West, the one that the world has been waiting for is the return of Jesus Christ, is there some kind of connection? Or is this just some kind of Hip Hop ritual being performed right in front of our eyes? His album even dropped during the same month as Mel

Gibson's movie, The Passion of Christ (Feb, 2004). According to the Bible, Christ will return in the last days when humanity has fallen to its lowest point. Kanye's first single off of his debut album, College Dropout, was called, "All Falls Down," followed by "Jesus Walks." He put out a single on his own prior to the album dropping and it was called, "Through The Wire," which talked about his "near death" experience and resurrection into the world of Hip Hop as its savior. It appears that the Matrix is trying to act out the Biblical scriptures through music, using Kanye as the Christ energy to do it. He even shot 3 different versions of the video for the song Jesus Walks. The number 3 is significant in Christianity because it represents the 3 days between Christ's crucifixion and resurrection, the 3 wise men who foretold of his coming, and the number 3 is also symbolic to the trinity in Christianity as well, which is the Father, the Son, and the Holy Spirit. If Kanye represents the "Son" energy, then Jay-Z is undoubtedly the "Father" since he is the one who gave birth to Kanye's career in Hip Hop. Jay is also revered as the God Emcee (J-hova). To further prove my point, right after the "Jesus Walks" song goes off, you can hear a mystical-like sound in the background and the voice of Jay-Z comes on and says, "Oh Baby!" as if calling Kanye his son. We, the people, would be considered as the "spirit" since none of this would be possible unless we mentally allowed it to happen. Notice I didn't say Holy Spirit, because Holy is something that has not been mixed, diluted, or tampered with, and our mental has obviously been tampered with, or the Matrix of Hip Hop could not exist. In the past, the Matrix has been unsuccessful when trying to download Christianity into the Hip Hop thought stream because Hip Hop has always been viewed as rebellious and against the grain. Christianity is one of the Matrix most deadly programs, and Kanye has made it possible to breach the security of Hip Hop. He can become the greatest asset that the Matrix has ever created because he is the culmination of all facets of Hip Hop. He has been cloned into the "perfect rapper," one who is a little bit thug, a little bit religious, a little bit conscious, a little bit materialistic, a little bit fraternal, etc. Kanye became the voice of all people. His ritual to be the "one" was almost complete had he not debuted at # 2 on the billboard charts. Lucky for us, his first album never went any higher.

Actor: Kanye West
Director: Matrix, Jay-Z/Dame Dash
Producer: Kanye West
Executive Producer: Roc-A-Fella Records
Supporting Cast: Roc-A-Fella Camp

B.E.T.

The machine world has turned the television into the most prominent tool used to pull off the illusion called the Matrix of Hip Hop, and the most deadly weapon on earth to destroy its spiritual purpose. The television reigns supreme now, and each home has an Alter (T.V. stand), in which this artificial God sits, ruling and governing our lives, while we give praise, pay homage, and even idolize it. If the television is God, then those who prosper by being on it are in heaven. For Black people, B.E.T. is that heaven. It's the only network that continuously shows Black people living the life of luxury without a care in the world. However, if the source is artificial, then everything that it produces must be artificial as well. This includes, but is not limited to Hip Hop itself. This is evident by the hell that the majority of us live in, and when this hell gets the best of us, we turn to "God" to show us the way. These rappers, actors, and athletes who are "stars" in heaven, become our guiding lights. Now everyone wants to "die" and go to heaven; but one doesn't have to experience a physical death to reach this artificial heaven, all one has to do is shed their spiritual body. When you sell your soul, you die spiritually. B.E.T. continues to deposit souls into its account because we as a people would much rather live in a virtual heaven than deal with the hell of this reality, so all of its programming is geared toward the spiritually dead people of the planet. Real Hip Hop is not allowed on B.E.T., and brothers and sisters with something real to say are cast out of heaven as well. It's gotten so bad that if you are not on television, you do not exist! This is the main reason that T.V. networks, and B.E.T. in particular, have hundreds of rappers and actors who are willing to buffoon themselves so quickly, because being a buffoon, pimp, drug dealer, slut, or thug is much better than not being on television at all. At least they have an existence in the only world that matters these days, the reel world.

Actors: Too numerous to mention
Director: Matrix/Stephen Hill
Producers: B.E.T.
Executive Producers: Viacom
Supporting Cast: every artist that performs for B.E.T.

OTHER IMPORTANT NOTABLES:

MASE

He returns to the game waiving the Christian flag. The Matrix has tried for years to convert real Hip Hoppas into Christians, but have failed miserably. Besides the recent emergence of Kanye West, Mase, a legitimate Emcee, possesses the greatest chance of achieving its goal. P. Diddy was also hoping that Mase would become the savior for his crumbling Bad Boy record empire, but in a stunning turn of events, Mase has joined forces with G-Unit. Not only has he switched teams, but he is back to being Murda Mase. Christians all over the world are now more confused than reading the Bible itself, as Mase has done the unthinkable. Stay tuned as this story develops.

RUSSELL SIMMONS/P. DIDDY

These two super moguls are the true vanguards of Hip Hop.

Through their abilities to capitalize on and set new trends, and their keen eye for talent, along with their positions of authority, they play a major role in the overall future of Hip Hop. They inspire everything from music, to fashion, to food and now they have both thrown their hats into the political ring. Even though they represent different organizations, their mission is the same, to lead the people into an unchartered realm of Hip Hop, the realm of politics. We trust them more than we trust the president because they represent our way of life, and we can associate with them because they come from our hood. But that can be a double edged sword because politicians are never who they say they are. They say all of the right things to gain our trust, but when we vote them into office, their true colors are always exposed. Who or what is to say that the results won't be the same if we put our faith in the hands of Russell and/or P. Diddy? And let's not forget that neither one of them are from the hood anymore. They are both in a much different tax bracket than we are and run with an entirely different crowd. It could very well be possible that they don't represent our interests at all, they're just using us (Hip Hop) to gain political leverage for themselves. Neither one of them had selected a candidate to endorse in the previous presidential election, but have used us to demonstrate that they can somehow influence the election process. In other words, our vote is for sale. Perhaps they're just pawns of a higher level of politics that have been instructed to form a political movement to benefit those who cannot come into our hood and gain our trust. Mr. Simmons and Mr. Diddy look like very smart men to me, they have to know that the next five presidents have already been selected. The Matrix has set up the voting process to give off the illusion that we are free and that our vote counts, those of us who are unplugged, know better.

SUGE KNIGHT/IRV GOTTI/J-PRINCE

Unlike Russell and P.Diddy who were catalysts in building the current system that governs Hip Hop, these three moguls are responsible for trying to take it over. They understood that the real money was in distribution, and secretly conspired to create their own avenues to distribute their music. They also were in the process of attempting to unionize Hip Hop. If they were able to achieve these goals, this would definitely spell the end of a system that has suppressed artists for years. In essence, this move can be equated to slaves trying to become slave masters. They may have caused the single greatest threat to the Matrix from an ownership position. This is why they all became targets of federal investigations aimed at shutting down or at least discrediting their companies by bringing them up on charges of money laundering, murder, drugs, and conspiracy. This is not to suggest in any way that these charges aren't true, but America was built and designed to run on these same programs. It's only becoming a problem now that slaves are beginning to understand the encrypted language used by the machine world to keep us as such. I may not totally agree with the content of music that they release to the public, or even some of their actions regarding Hip Hop in general (The verdict is still out on Suge Knight's involvement in the murder of Tupac), but I do feel in the long run that them being familiar with the system that has destroyed us can be useful to the revolution if at any time they became unplugged.

LYOR COHEN/JIMMY IOVINE

At the very top of the lowest level of the Matrix of Hip Hop are certain individuals who stand to capitalize the most from a financial standpoint off of our hard work and labor. These individuals don't have the capacity to see the spiritual significance of Hip Hop, they can only process what's spiritual in terms of monetary gains. So the more spiritual something is for us, the more money they stand to make if we allow them to set up shop and give them access to all that's sacred, and Hip Hop was sacred way before it was a business. They cannot feel the love that you have for Hip Hop because they are not spiritually based beings. And because they're soulless, it's cosmically impossible for them to understand it. When something is removed from its natural habitat or its vibration frequency has been unwillingly changed, it loses its power base and ability to protect itself. Hip Hop is not in its natural state, and Lyor Cohen and Jimmy Iovine are just two of the most brilliant business minds who reap the most benefits from our culture. It's strictly business for them so they are not bounded by any of the spiritual laws that would affect the originators of Hip Hop who violate these laws. They cannot be held accountable for the state of Hip Hop from a spiritual level because they are not responsible for it being spiritually conceived, the mental incubation period, or the physical birth of Hip Hop for that matter. We are responsible for the children that we give birth to, and Hip Hop is no different. Who's going to love and protect your child the way that you do? However, once you neglect or abuse your child and your child is turned over to the state, the state can do as it pleases with it. Once we turned Hip Hop over to the Matrix, it now owned it, and it became subject to the laws that govern the Matrix, the laws of physics. Their economic survival is based upon the "children" that we give birth to and abandon, since they themselves are spiritually impotent. They cannot bring anything from the astral plane into a physical existence without our help and our sciences. As expressed earlier, our art serves as a facilitator or gateway between these worlds. For years Lyor Cohen has sat at the head of Def Jam, one of Hip Hop's most successful labels, and Jimmy Iovine has sat at the head of the other, which is Interscope. Each has directed the fate of our lives. I know that this is a rather bold statement, but when someone can control what you see and hear, they can also gauge the spiritual properties that you receive from that information as well. In other words, the artists that they sign and promote can assist them in shutting us out from the astral plane and locking us into a physical world where the Matrix can continue to have mastery over us. Def Jam's roster has been lacking in anything spiritual or even revolutionary for quite some time, and Interscope's roster has never possessed anything spiritual to begin with. Jimmy and Lyor (sounds a lot like liar) are two of the many gatekeepers of the Matrix who will only sign artists who have been initiated into the Hip Hop fraternity of money, sex, drugs, and violence. A lot of these rappers initiate themselves by their words, actions, and abilities to perform the rituals necessary to generate the spiritual substances needed from the astral plane to keep the Matrix in power on the physical realm. All Black people are magicians, some are more potent than others, some know, but most are unknowing that they possess such power. How else can one explain brothers and sisters in the hood with no money, jobs, or training, but they continue to remain ghetto fabulous with fly clothes, cars, rims, jewels and houses? It's simple; whatever they desire and focus their (astral) energy on, it must manifest itself in the physical. It's unfortunate that most of them only want sneakers, handbags, and rims. These record labels usually sign one amongst us (high priest) who can cast a spell strong enough to have all of us participate in the ritual. Don't be fooled, both of these men (Cohen/Iovine) are well versed in the occult sciences, it's a prerequisite for all positions of power in this country from the president on down. The determining factors about whom they sign to their labels are far deeper than just rhyming skills, let's be real, rappers come a dime a dozen. That decision is probably based more on the numerology and astrology of that individual, fingerprints which serve as galactic zip codes, or what part of the universe that person has reincarnated from (womb) which will determine just how powerful a magician he or she is. They know the science well, so while you're parading around yappin' about you're the illest rapper from Harlem or whatever, they know it's more likely that you're a God from Atlantis who has returned in this day and time, but has forgotten who he was and the power that he once possessed. The money that they make is really secondary to their true cause, which is to shut down the spiritual channels needed for us to manifest the God within us. Lyor has since moved on to Warner Bros. Records to start the process all over again, while Jimmy, rumored to be the head of the church of Satan out in California, continues to put out music that's counter-spiritual to our survival. The reason that I said that they were at the top of the lowest level is because there are levels of this Hip Hop Matrix that are pure energy beyond the physical, where spiritual parasites fester and feed off of our polluted etheric energy. The negative music that we are forced to create, based on what the labels will sign and won't sign, helps generate this polluted thought stream. Lyor Cohen and Jimmy Iovine run major "supermarkets" for these entities to feed off of.

PRODUCERS

If Hip Hop were a human body, then producers would be its heartbeat. The rhythmic pulse of bangin' beats send life to the rest of the body allowing Hip Hop to live. Without the drumbeat (heartbeat), Hip Hop would die. The significance of the producer is tremendous because if he or she is not spiritually in tune with the universe, this can create an irregular heartbeat in the body that could ultimately lead to "health" issues or an untimely death. Hip Hop is in a sick state at the moment because its rhythm is not in tune with "Ra's Hymn," the natural rhythm of the universe. Just as an artist with a paint brush can make the unseen seen, a producer can make the unheard heard. Sounds are words in a different form, a collage of sounds orchestrated in particular rhythm patterns are conversations from the cosmos. A producer is an instrument himself, used by the universe to convey messages to humanity in the form of sound. The body, especially if its melanated, can easily absorb, decode, and process sound into comprehensive words and mathematical equations that can be used to solve the Matrix of Hip Hop, or even uncover the mystery of life itself. When words (fire) are added to sound (air), it changes the alchemical makeup. Fire needs air to spread itself. The Matrix is distorting the messages within the sound by using corrupted words that they allow to be spread throughout the Hip Hop Diaspora.

This has led to spontaneous Hip Hop combustion of the art form. Music also raises the kundalini energy. Just as the sweet sounds of a flute can make a snake rise from its pit, the serpent energy (fire) at the base of the spine rises when key notes of the harmonic scale are reached. Hip Hop tracks can control our mood swings. How many times have you heard a dark track that made you want to fight? Or how many times have you heard an ill beat that lifted your spirits? The type of sounds that were used to make the beat can determine your mood. For example, if a producer uses low bass drum sounds and bass lines, the sounds will only resonate to the lower chakras located near the base of the spine. These chakras are related to sexual energy. If a producer uses more high hats, claps, and mid range sounds, the sound will resonate a little higher up near the heart charka and you will feel more at peace. There are sounds that resonate so high, that they even stimulate the pineal gland, just ask any real Jimi Hendrix fan. The producer is the centerpiece, his or her value is immeasurable. Dr. Dre can be attributed to three different rap empires: Ruthless, Deathrow, and Aftermath. Without him, these empires don't exist. Nowadays, empires are built more so around the producer than a rapper. Often times the first thing that grabs us about a song is the beat, which inspires us to put our bodies (water) in motion, making the earth tremble.

VIDEO DIRECTORS

Video directors assist the Matrix in creating a false reality using destructive images to lock us into a third dimensional prison. Images, especially images in motion have a different effect on the brain than sound does. These images trigger a part of the brain that enables us to access the astral plane, which is where we bring things into a physical existence. Flooding us with the same images over and over again, short-circuit the brain's ability to process and decipher the negative impact that these images have on our lives, we simply begin to process them as normal. It's Hip Hop "Groundhog" Day," as the same six or seven video directors continue to alter and tamper with our perception by shooting the same videos over and over again. The brain views the video as a mirror of itself reflecting back images of what the mind, body, and soul are actually doing, but it's just an illusion designed to coerce the brain into actualizing the event. Frame by frame, video directors have cut, edited, and spliced our lives into a world of spinning rims, pimps, platinum chains, and the degradation of women, and coined it into a term called, Hip Hop culture. The word culture means way of life, however, this is not the way of life that real Hip Hop was created to bring about. But who are you going to believe, the video director, or your lying first eye? Most people believe what they see, so the video director serves as a Hip Hop wish master who can turn a rapper into anything that he or she desires. You wanna be a pimp? All the wish master has to do is say the magic word, action! And it's done. You wanna be a thug? Action! You wanna be rich? Action! You wanna be a player? Action! As I broke down earlier, reel is the closest thing to being real. It is my belief that video directors also play a major role in the occult side of Hip Hop. The word occult means hidden, if you slow down the frames of certain videos to almost a stand still, there are images and symbols strategically placed within the frame that are impossible to detect with the naked eye when the video is moving at full speed. However, the brain has the capacity to see these images and symbols clearly. Each image, when viewed, generates different responses from the brain, these responses range from making you hungry to making you violent. This usually takes place during the final edit or mastering process of the video. This is not to suggest that all video directors are behind some elaborate mind control conspiracy aimed at the destruction of our Black youth, there are some who constantly challenge the mind by flashing images that awaken the pineal gland (1st eye), but they're few and far in between. From now on, start making a mental note of all the video directors who only create negative or destructive images of us, then it will become blatantly clear who the agents for the Matrix of Hip Hop are.

MIX TAPE PHENOMENON

Traditionally speaking, mix-tapes are Hip Hop's anti-Matrix because they represent the very opposite of what the Matrix of Hip Hop is all about. Without radio play, video play, or magazine write-ups, an underground artist can still have a voice and make an impact in Hip Hop via mix-tapes and the underground circuit. These three mediums are major programs used by the Matrix of Hip Hop to create suitable images that will eventually lead to the sales needed to fuel the system that has taken over real Hip Hop. The origin of Hip Hop itself can be traced back to an era when the elders of the art form used underground tapes to spread the gospel from hood to hood, city to city, state to state. This of course was done when they weren't actually spittin' the word live at a jam or block party. This method ensured that the gospel would not be misinterpreted, altered, or tampered with. In keeping with that tradition, mix-tape DJs like Clue, Kid Capri, and Brucie-B became legends in their own right for rejecting the Matrix programming and using mix-tapes to expand the strength of Zion (underground) to the point that it became a world unto itself. Not only did they give you Hip Hop in its rawest form without the hype of the Matrix, they were also masters at excavating gems from within the bowels of Hip Hop, bringing them to the surface so that they could shine before the world. In many cases the Matrix (tomb raiders) would steal their gems and the credit for their hard work and labor. Although both worlds seemed connected, they weren't, and each facet operated independent of the other. This is not to suggest that an artist who started in the underground couldn't enjoy commercial success as well, but to simply illustrate that there was a line drawn between the two. The underground and mix-tapes in particular, controlled the destiny of Hip Hop because new artists and trends generally started there first, therefore, if the Matrix could somehow tap into the source of Hip Hop, they could control it from its purest state. To be successful, the Matrix would have to tap into all three levels of the underground simultaneously; the physical level, where they could immediately steal our ideas and drain any existing energy; the mental level, where they could tap into our subconscious mind to see how and what the thought process was for us to think on the realms that we do; and the spiritual level, to try and attempt to tap into the melanin which is the true source of all of our creations. Just as oil is considered as black gold, melanin is what this beast is truly after. Mix-tapes represent the "oil" of Hip Hop. Mix-tapes were our way of subconsciously rejecting programming that was placed into our conscious minds by the Matrix. A mix-tape DJ also had the freedom to add his or her own essence to a song by remixing it or blending a certain way. By doing so, they changed the vibration of the original song, making it a whole new creation. They were adding their own creative energies to an already existing work, that's a form of musical alchemy. Controlling the Mix-tapes literally took the guess work out of making hit records for the Matrix. This is why it was imperative for the Matrix to write programs enabling them to breach the underground. Just as the subconscious mind controls the conscious mind, underground Hip Hop really "fuels" mainstream Hip Hop. The Matrix has plugged into the underground for its survival, draining every ounce of creativity and energy from those willing to give up its power for the illusionary power of the Matrix. Remember, the Matrix is not real, so while you may think that the Matrix has all of the power, it knows that it is powerless, but gives off the illusion of power through your perception of it that it has created. In 2005-06 there is no such thing as underground Hip Hop, and mix-tapes which served as gateways into the true underground, now serve as back door gateways into the very Matrix you purchased a mix-tape to escape from. But there is no escape, it is all one system with maze-like programs written to confuse you. The more that you think you're going deeper underground, the more commercial your destination will be. And with thousands of mix-tapes over-saturating the game, searching for one that has any source of real Hip Hop within it is like surfing the internet, you end up with way too many entries to process and the brain goes into an overloaded state and shuts down. We created mix-tapes as a tool to free us from the Matrix, but they're now being used aa a weapon to destroy us. Whenever mix-tapes are being promoted on MTV, you know what time it is, and some of the same DJs who built Zion have been banned or flushed from the underground world and are now agents for the Matrix.

HIP HOP AND VIDEO GAMES

With Hip Hop ruling the physical world it was only a matter of time before the Matrix would attempt to merge it with the virtual world of video games. Over the years, video games have become a major part of Hip Hop culture, and with countless hours being spent with our focus and energy on something that is not real, The Matrix could now seize upon the opportunity to use video games to fuse a physical illusion into a mental reality. In other words, the characters in the game are not physically real, they only exist in the mind of the participant who has the ability to maneuver them in a physical sense, but if all is mental as the ancestors teach, then to whoever is playing the game, the characters must be real. If you can understand this concept on a microcosmic level, you can begin to understand the macrocosm of the Matrix of Hip Hop itself because the principles are very similar; Hip Hop is a game and the gangsta rappers, thugs, and hustlers are not real. They only exist inside of the television, but our mental participation in the game allows them to have a real life and presence in our physical existence. This is no different than worshipping a false image of Jesus Christ, one that never really existed but it somehow has an impact on things and events in your physical life that are real. And instead of you taking the glory for the success of your own life, you give all the glory to Christ by screaming out, thank you Jesus! Flashing images of Christ is just one way that the Matrix can manipulate our energy and what we bring down from the astral plane into a physical existence, video games are another.

Nowadays, game heads spend just as much time in the virtual realm as they do in the physical realm. In the hood, playing video games is the closest thing to having an out of body experience. Unfortunately, this shuts down our natural ability to astral project ourselves, and we have to depend on the artificial wormholes of the Matrix and its gaming systems like Playstation, X Box, and Nintendo, to reach such levels. It also means that if you exit the wormhole the same way that you entered it, then whatever you bring back belongs to the Matrix, or the Matrix has no fear of it whatsoever. So if you brought back a monster from inside of the video game to destroy the Matrix, he couldn't harm it because the Matrix put him there to begin with. On the other hand, if you tapped in on your own and brought back a beast from deep within your subconscious mind it could be used to cause havoc on the physical realm. This is why they spend millions of dollars to own every second of your focus and attention via commercials, movies, sports, concerts, news events, wars and of course…video games. They know that if you ever get your attention span back, the gig is up.

Long gone are the days when video games were designed specifically for white kids from the suburbs. During those times, it was more about controlling the thoughts of rebellious white teens by using the games to plant certain images, sounds, and actions into their subconscious mind, but that's as far as it could go because they didn't have the melanin to manifest real magic. That's where Hip Hop comes into the picture. The Matrix knows that it can get us to willingly partake in our own destruction as long as it writes Hip Hop into the specific program that it wants to use to contain us, destroy us, or use us to create something that will benefit their existence. So in 2005, Hip Hop themed video games are bigger than ever. Some of them like Def Jam's "Fight for New York" even have actual Hip Hop characters in it. It's not enough that we already idolize these artists that we made real to begin with, but now if we tap into a higher sense of self by entering the astral plane, these will be the same beings that we meet. Imagine doing a ritual to summon an entity from another dimension and Busta Rhymes shows up. These video games are not meant for your enjoyment, they're meant for your containment. Meanwhile, the type of games that we play as opposed to what White people play is significant. Black people are more likely to play a game like Grand Theft Auto, which keeps our mental focus on the earthly realm, while white people love to play games like Halo, which is more about conquering other planets. This creates a mindset which always places them in a role of master, and us in a role of slave.

HIP HOP AND VIDEO VIXENS

This has become a critical component of the Matrix of Hip Hop. Over 95% of the videos that we see have half naked women in them used to sell a certain way of life. These vixens have become the prototype of what beauty is for young girls and women from the hood. Even more important is the way of life portrayed by these women, which seems to suggest that women need to get their money any way that they can, which may include but is not limited to, stripping, having sex for money, or gettin' over on playas from the hood. Because for these vixens, there seems to be nothing more important than coppin' the latest handbag, shoes, or outfit. This is not to suggest in any way that there are not some tasteful videos out there that happen to feature video vixens in them, but I think most people will agree that they are never depicted as anything other than sexual objects. Now your sexuality can be transformed into a career. This may not be much of a problem in the "reel" world, but when it filters into the real world and becomes the primary motivational force of millions of young girls, it needs to be addressed. When more young women are focused on becoming strippers and video vixens than becoming more respectful, positive role models for Black women in particular, this is a very strong indication that the feminine energy is being suppressed. If our women are lost, then we as a nation have no chance of survival. I know that there will be plenty of women from the "Get Money" nation that will want to come at me with the notion that it's all about survival and we as women gotta do what we gotta do to make it. The way that the current system is structured, they may be right, but I can't help but to see the Black woman as anything other than what she is, a queen and the mother of civilization. Once she begins to see herself as such, change will undoubtedly come.

HIP HOP AND STREET NOVELS

It has always been said that if there's something that you wanted to hide from a Black man, you put it in a book. Now Black people in general are reading at an alarming rate, but the million dollar question is, *what* are we reading? The answer to this question will undoubtedly lead you to the local African on the corner selling street novels like crack. I never thought there would come a time in our history when reading would actually set us back, but most of these street novels are doing just that. While I do understand that drug dealing, hustling, sex, violence, and murder are a way of life in the hood, the way that this lifestyle is glorified in these street novels does nothing to help us as a people escape these hardships. In fact, they keep our mental focus stuck and stagnant on the negative aspects of life. However, there are a few street novels that have elevated the art of telling stories that have meaning and a moral to them, but they are few and far in between: most of them are very poorly written. Reading has always provided us with a mental escape, and since all is mental, it's not hard to see that what we read is critical in terms of what we manifest in the physical. The machine world which manufactures most of these books are sytematically flooding the market with nonsense to deter you from real knowledge that could free you forever. Our young women are the biggest victims of street novels. They may not know what's going on in the real world, but they sure can tell you who got laid or played in the latest street novel. This is a sad state to be in if you are a Black person, because we are in the age of Aquarius, which means there is an increase of knowledge on the planet at this time and we're not taking advantage of it by burying our heads into street novels that dumb us down. It's so bad that Black owned book stores cannot survive without selling this trash to pay the rent. If by chance you have an opportunity to have something printed for others to read, make it your spiritual duty to elevate them to the best of your ability because the greatest crime one can commit is to impede on someone else's spiritual path, and that's exactly what trashy street novels are guilty of.

34

CONCLUSION

I've stayed up countless nights contemplating whether or not I should even write a book of this nature, a book that most certainly will not be popular amongst the so called Hip Hop faithful. I know that this body of work will be ridiculed, scrutinized, despised, and rejected by those deeply conditioned to believe that the rap industry is the greatest thing to ever happen to Black people. Notice that I didn't say Hip Hop, but rap. This is mainly due to the fact that we have been programmed to think that money is the answer to all of our problems, when in fact, money, and the relentless pursuit of it, is killing us…spiritually that is. As long as money is the end result of our journey, those that control the money, control our destiny. This is what is called mind control. The only difference is that most entertainers feel like they're being rewarded for their hard work when "massa" cuts them a check for something that they created in the first place. The fact is, they're only being rewarded by those that understand that we are a spiritual people, and they're being paid off to steer our people away from their spiritual purpose, and the knowledge of themselves. Everything that we do or create is spiritual, including Hip Hop. Rap is just a byproduct of Hip Hop. Rap music has created a lot of jobs, money, cars, rims, watches, and houses for Black people, no one can deny this, but what other benefits has the rap industry afforded us? This is not to imply in any way that we don't need money for food, clothing, and shelter, but to suggest that we traveled billions of miles to get to this planet for a job is just as ludicrous. And don't tell me that we own Hip Hop, you should know better. At this rate, in ten years or so, the greatest achievement for a Black man in this country and abroad will be to become a rapper. The second and third choices will be to become a ballplayer and drug dealer, and all three of these occupations are interrelated and interchangeable now.

Is this the best that we can produce, a rapper, a baller, or a hustler? If this is the case, then our future generations are doomed. Where are our doctors, lawyers, chemists, astronauts, and scientists? There have been a growing number of people, although still the minority, that feel that the rap industry has done us as a people more of a disservice, rather than elevate us. We are not talking about Hip Hop as a culture, but the industry that's filled with vultures. Due to the spiritual times that we now live in, more and more people are being awakened to the fact that these rappers are our enemy. They do nothing but take our money, our energy, and most important, they rob us of our attention, which should be focused on one's own spiritual purpose and journey. But as crazy as this may sound, I'm not mad at them, if you're not intelligent enough to think for yourself, then someone else should do the thinking for you. You are nothing more than a food source for them, they could care less about what's going on in your life, as long as you play dead, they live. I have nothing personal against any of the rappers that I mentioned in this book, it's just business... spiritual business.

I wrote this book to fill a void that has ever been increasing of those that feel that Hip Hop is much deeper than what is being portrayed throughout the media. Everywhere that I searched, I found nothing that spoke to the spiritual few that could easily see through this illusion called the Matrix of Hip Hop. I know that I'm not alone when I say that this isn't Hip Hop, it's Shit Hop. I called this book Hip Hop Decoded for a reason, you are the ones doing the decoding, I'm simply posing the impeccable questions that need to be answered. This book is a journey within yourself, and the conclusion reached after making such a trek should be one that you and only you have arrived at. There is no one answer or solution to this problem, but I feel that if this book at least starts a healthy dialogue among the awakened few, then it was well worth it. There are those that constantly ask me, will you feel threatened in any way when these so called thug rappers and industry "Bigs" come at you for exposing their hustle? The answer is no. I'd rather be killed by the devil and his henchmen for something spiritual that I did to help my people, than have to deal with the entire force of all of my ancestors that came before me, whom I undoubtedly will see again on the other side, for something that I did not do to help. This book is not about Hip Hop, it's about numerology, astrology, occultism, metaphysics, and symbolism as it relates to Hip Hop. That's the mystery.

If you can apply these sciences to the rap industry, you will easily be able to break the code of the Matrix of Hip Hop. With these keys, the difference between Hip Hop and Rap will become crystal clear. There are many people who feel that Hip Hop is multi cultural and that it has done wonders for race relations in this country. I am not one of them. Rap is multi cultural because it speaks a langauge that white people understand and are in compliance with, which is money. As long as there is a product that can be marketed, and plenty of money made, it is very beneficial for white people to sit at the table with creative black people and find a common ground of communication. Hip Hop on the other hand is something that we live and may not necessarily generate capital. This is why the culture of Hip Hop has been disrespected by White America. This is not to suggest in any way that there are not some white people out there that truly respect the culture of Hip Hop just as there are White people who respect and appreciate the pyramids, however, they didn't build them. So when dealing with the spiritual aspect of something, that must be left to its architects. I know that the number of different cultures that enjoy rap music and claim to be a part of Hip Hop are staggerring, but how many of these ethnic groups are Hip Hoppas by default? The overexposure of rap music has recruited millions of White fans who love the music, but will never understand the culture.

I wrote this book as if I was only going to have one opportunity to say what was on my mind, yet I only scratched the surface. We'll go deeper, if the ancestors will allow, in my next book entitled, The Occult Science of Hip Hop. For those that have given me their precious time, I hope that I haven't disappointed you with this body of work. I know that it's far from perfect, but it's a start in the right direction. The vortex has been opened, it is now the duty of those with an even greater understanding of Hip Hop to step forward and lead us into the future. Until the next time that we are able to take a journey together, this is the Black Dot saying peace.

Bonus Chapter 1

HVRRICANE KATRINA - PART 1
WHEN IT'S BIGGER THAN HIP HOP

Just like everyone else in America and abroad, I casually turned on my television on Monday morning, August 29th to assess the damage of hurricane Katrina. To my dismay, the damage was far greater than anyone had ever anticipated. Initially, I assumed that this would be just like any other hurricane to hit the Gulf Coast, where there would be moderate property damage, minimal life would be lost, and the resilience of the people would once again overcome the obstacles of Mother Nature and rebuild their lives accordingly. Instead, what I witnessed has changed my life forever. I never thought that I would see the day when men, women, and children on American soil would have to endure such harsh conditions brought about by the aftermath of Hurricane Katrina. The greater portion of the Gulf Coast looked like a third world country. In fact, if you turned down the sound on your television, you would think that you were watching the daily struggles of our brethren in Somalia. As the federal Government dragged their feet to provide much needed aid to the many people suffering in that region, something became shockingly clear to me, we are no different than those suffering in Somalia or any other third world country for that matter. For years, those of us who have lived in America and are of "African" decent, have been conditioned to disassociate ourselves from the struggle and plight of our brothers and sisters from abroad. Most of us have been guilty at one point or another of saying "it's not my problem" that they don't have any food, clothing, shelter, or running water, especially since this has never been a problem for even the poorest of families in America…until now.

The traumatizing events of this disaster should be enough to convince anyone that has a conscious that there is a common thread that runs through the fabric of indigenous people all over the world, and that is that our lives are expendable. In the face of the beast, we all look the same no matter what region of the world that we're in. Even the thuggest of thugs had to shed a tear after witnessing their people starving, drowning, and left for dead by a country that was built on the backs of their blood, sweat, and tears. The look of despair on the faces of thousands really hit home, mainly because no one thought in their wildest dreams that something this devastating could take place in the place that we call home. But don't forget that this is an everyday event in third world countries, so if we are expecting sympathy from some of our sisters and brothers abroad, think again. If anything it should serve as a wake up call that this could be just a sign of things to come in this New World Order establishment, and we're about to be evicted from what we thought was our home. If you were paying attention, the media did refer to the victims of Hurricane Katrina as refugees. From that moment on, this became bigger than rap music for me. This became much bigger than who has the hottest video out, or what rappers have beef with what rappers. This became an issue of life, humanity. Even some of the most successful rappers themselves were hit with a rude awakening that it's much bigger than their expensive cars and plush houses. Master P, Cash Money Millionaires, Juvenile, David Banner and a host of other rappers from that region suffered tremendous personal losses, but none of their material losses, as was so openly expressed by these rappers, was greater than the loss of family and friends, because in the end, that's all that matters. What is considered a fortune by most can be washed away in an instant along with the status in which that fortune was built upon, but when tragedy reduces us all to the same status, it becomes clear that we are all one big family and bloodline suffering the same fate. The entire rap community was on the front line extending a helping hand to those in need.

My hat goes off to all of those personally involved, whether it was giving up money or time, it showed that rappers do have a heart. Leading the charge were none other than Jay-Z, Dr. Dre, and Diddy, three of the most successful men in the business. I know throughout this book I might not have had too many favorable things to say about a lot of rappers, and these three in particular, but I'm taking the gloves off to show love because it's bigger than rap music. Sometimes it takes tragedy to bring the family together. We will rise again, if there is one thing that is certain, it's that whatever doesn't kill us as a people will only make us stronger. We have endured far worse over the course of over 400 hundred years of rape, oppression, murder, and the lynching of our people at the hands of the very same people that we are expecting to save us from this tragedy. We must save our selves and that's exactly the mentality that has been demonstrated by many of the rappers and entertainers who are finally in position financially to take their destiny into their own hands. As rich as we have become, there's no reason to have to wait for handouts. This is also a perfect way to say thanks to all of the people who have supported their careers over the years. Due to the overwhelming response to this tragedy, I'm proud of the way that our community has come together in our darkest hour. We are all affected by this, rich or poor. My deepest condolences go out to the many families who have had to endure the unthinkable, you will forever be in my thoughts and prayers as I know that the journey forward will not be an easy one, but know that you have the strength of a nation behind you, one love.

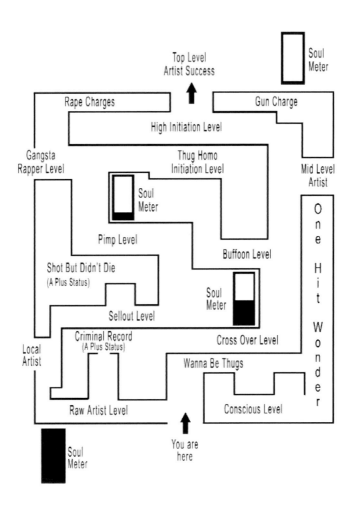

Bonus Chapter 2

HURRICANE KATRINA DECODED
WHEN THE TEARS HAVE DRIED

Now that we have all shed tears and paid our condolences to the many lives that have been destroyed by the disaster of Hurricane Katrina, it's time for us to wipe our tears and get to work decoding what really happened to our people. As we discussed in the Hip Hop X-Files, emotions can cloud your inner vision. This is not to suggest that you shouldn't allow your emotions to get the best of you when it's truly warranted. And who in their right mind could deny that this is one of those times when after witnessing such traumatizing events that have occurred, it would be hard to keep your eyes dry. This can also be dangerous because it is a tool that is used by the media and the shadow government to cause confusion and misdirection. It's only normal to levitate to the human side of the tragedy, which could be the loss of human life, injuries, etc, but this is the effect of the situation. Rarely does anyone focus on the real cause of the tragedy until it's too late, the operative words being the real cause of the situation. Initially, there will be a cause, but this is the cause that has already been set up for you to accept by those doing the manipulating. A perfect example of this is during the events of September 11. After watching the buildings collapse, most people were deeply saddened by the loss of life which is a normal response to such an event (effect), this is what triggered an emotional outburst that would be geared toward a fictitious enemy named Osama Bin Laden, created by the government (cause). The initial cause of this event was placed into the subconscious minds of America in 1993 during the first attack on the World Trade Center. This was the very first time that we were introduced to the name Osama Bin Laden. The media then proceeded to add the final piece to the puzzle by demonstrating to the entire world the proper way to knock down a building as big as the World Trade Center would not be by placing a bomb in the parking lot, but by hitting the structure at a much higher angle. So on September 11, when the event actually happened, we already knew the "cause" and became overly saturated in the effect. They had us hook, line, and sinker. Five years after that tragedy, there are numerous books out with hardcore evidence that refute the official story given to us by our government, but because it's so far after the fact, the government has had significant time to trace its steps, clean up its alibis, and put a system in place to discredit anyone coming forth with new information about what really happened. They have also made this new information hard to find by keeping it out of the mainstream media, and since most people are not familiar with alternative news sources, or do not do research on their own, the truth about who really knocked down the towers may never be known to them.

What does this have to do with Hurricane Katrina? It has everything to do with it. We must not allow the same program to be used on us again. Let's not forget that the very same government is in place as was on September 11th, so why should we think any different? Now let's get to work decoding this conspiracy. We won't focus any energy on the effects of the event, I think that speaks for itself. Instead, we want to place our focus on the possible cause of the event, not the cause given, which is a natural catastrophe. Once we accept the cause given, our decoding mechanisms in the brain shut down, leaving us no choice but to succumb to the effect, but once we begin to explore the use of weather modification weapons like H.A.A.R.P. and Teslar scalar wave technology, we activate that part of our brain that is not so easily misled. We can then begin to at least entertain the possibility that foul play could have played a role in the deaths of the victims of Hurricane Katrina, especially when taking into consideration that this government has killed its own citizens before, only this time, it's with weapons so sophisticated that they can make man made disasters appear natural. These are advanced levels of weaponry that have been used by our government and other governments like Russia and Japan to lasso storms and place them in desired areas. Imagine being able to make it rain constantly over the food crops of your enemy? Or what about eliminating rain and drying enemy crops out? This technology is real, but Americans and Black people, in particular, are too busy being victims of another advanced weapon designed by the government, Hip Hop. Hip Hop as it is practiced today has become a weapon of mass distraction, while the government continues to build these weapons of mass destruction. Our youth, who are tomorrow's future, care more about Hip Hop than life threatening changes taking place in the world around them. Case in point, Jay Z's Blueprint album dropped on the very same day as the 9-11 attack and he still moved hundreds of thousands of units and soared to number 1 on the Billboard charts. Don't get me wrong, the album was classic, but we were experiencing a "terrorist" attack on American soil and the Hip Hop world didn't seem to miss a beat, that's scary. The government has used the Matrix of Hip Hop to dumb us down to the point that we don't even think anymore. Hip Hop has also played a role in the deaths of the victims of Hurricane Katrina as well, I'll get to that in a moment.

Numerous reports have also come in from witnesses living in the New Orleans area that they heard major explosions around the area of the levees, indicating that they may have been purposely blown up, perhaps to save richer parts of the area like the French Quarters. The aerial view of the area seems to support this claim. So we have a storm that was possibly man made and alleged explosions strategically placed to limit the damage to a certain area, this would be premeditated murder. Not only does the government have a rock solid alibi by claiming that this was a natural disaster, but also by claiming that it forewarned the people to exit the city before the storm hit. Let's examine this a little further. The public announcement to leave the area was really a code for White people to get out since they, along with other tourists were the only ones who could really afford to leave and have somewhere else to go. Eighty two percent of the people from the Ninth Ward had an income of 8 thousand dollars a year. That's well below the poverty rate, so where were they going? This so called natural disaster also took place at the end of the month, which I also found to be well calculated. Most people living in that area are on some kind of government subsidy like welfare, SSI, or food stamps. Now let's keep it real, if you've ever had to depend on a government subsidy, you know that they only give you about three weeks worth of benefits, which mean that the last week you're on your own. This tragedy took place on the 29th, which meant that the city was completely broke, thus they were trapped and forced to wait out the storm that would ultimately lead to their demise.

The government's response to this disaster was inexcusable, unless death of the people was the plan all along. That's the only thing that would make logical sense. By sitting back and allowing such a tragedy to take place demonstrates just how expendable Black life is. To support this point, when help finally did show up, their main priority was to safeguard the properties that were being looted, rather than save the lives of the people who were in desperate need of assistance. Even the media seemed to place its primary focus on the so called looters rather than talk about the flooding and lack of support being provided for the people. Contrary to popular belief, most of the so called looters were only taking what was absolute necessary for survival, food, water, and other items to get by. However, the media chose to focus most of their coverage on the few bad people that were stealing useless merchandise in a time of crisis. This biased approach showed pictures depicting Black people, clearly with food in their possession, as looters, but labeled White people in possession of food as finding food. We were labeled as refugees. The military had strict orders to kill American citizens or should I say refugees who thought that they were American citizens. The government could have easily saved the lives of many, simply by providing transportation out of the city. The networks proceeded to show photos of about a hundred school buses submerged in water that could have easily been used to save thousands of lives. There were reports of military boats riding by, leaving people to drown or be eaten by alligators and snakes, not to mention the horrific conditions at the Superdome, which resembled slaves in the bottom of a slave ship piled on top of each other, eating, sleeping, defecating, and urinating in the same space that they laid. The word dome is a greek word that means, place of the Gods. Thousands were housed at the Superdome, or "supreme" place of the Gods. Domes were designed to generate energy the same a way that a pyramid does, making the Superdome into a giant antenna for anyone trying to harness that energy. To the average person, this may not make sense, but for those who deal in the occult, this type of energy (fear, despair, misery) is actually fuel that gives life to a given ritual. Our people were then tranferred to another hell hole, the Astrodome, which became another energy center for those who wanted to zapp our power to use as a battery for some other wicked scheme. Those who were fortunate enough to make it to safety into the neighboring town were quickly turned around at gunpoint by officials who were positioned at key points to protect those areas. And they call this a rescue operation? I would hate to see what it would be like if they were trying to kill us.

Now let's look at the situation from an even deeper occult perspective. This view of what happened is pertinent because when dealing with high level government officials, most of them are part of some secret society that has a totally different agenda that the public is not aware of. George W. Bush himself has long been rumored to be a member of a secret society called The Skull and Bones, which originated out of Yale University, where he went to school. These secret societies deal heavily in occult sciences; the word occult means hidden. What they're hiding is well cloaked in their satanic rituals, blood sacrifices, and devil worship. New Orleans has long been known for its Voodoo influence in the United States. Tales of the supernatural are common around these parts, it's a magical place. It may very well be a sacred place for those who practice magic, therefore it needs to be evacuated at all costs so that these wicked occultists could have a safe haven during the last days of this paradigm. Or perhaps New Orleans sits on an energy grid line; these grin lines that run through the earth's core serve as veins that send energy to different sections of the earth. An occultist's prior knowledge of the location of such a grid line can put him or her in position to harness this power using the proper rituals to do

267

so. These types of rituals are usually heightened by massive deaths. This could very well have been a blood sacrifice.

Now the rebuilding processes begin and guess who has the contract to do so, The Halliburton and Bechtel Corporations, which are the same construction companies that helped rebuild Iraq after America's retaliation for the September attacks. The Halliburton Corporation just so happens to be partly owned by Vice President, Dick Cheney. A lot of money will be made by the very same people that caused the destruction, it's the American way. When New Orleans is finally rebuilt, it will be off limits to its previous residents. It will become the new Vegas. They are already offering two thousand dollar checks to anyone who is willing to sell their property. The city of New Orleans will never be the same; those who are guilty of causing this atrocity will pay the price for the role that they have played in destroying God's children. We must never forget what has happened, and learn from this tragedy. America continues to prove that it doesn't care about its so called citizens, and it will stop at nothing to continue to reduce the population of the "useless eaters" at all cost. Look for more tragedy in the near future.

The Hip Hop community has stepped up big time to show support during this crisis, but could very well be a part of the problem when we examine the situation in greater detail. Even though most of the residents of New Orleans didn't have a choice whether they would stay in the city or not, there was a portion that could have left but chose to stay rather than leave their material possessions behind. This obsession with material assets can partly be blamed on the Hip Hop videos that show rappers who care about their cars, houses, and diamonds more than life itself. Since rappers are the only ones who seem to be making any money and constantly dominate the television, this has a greater influence on the minds of the people than one can imagine. It is not enough for rappers to just donate money, but they must begin the process of restoring value to things in life other than material objects, so that if we find ourselves in a similar situation, our priorities will be about saving lives rather than looting for material possessions.

The truth about what really happened in New Orleans will soon come to the forefront, including reports of police officers shooting dead bodies that floated to the top of the water to ensure that they stayed on the bottom, the official death report which will be closer to 20,000 rather than 400, the Red Cross conspiring to steal most of the donations, the military firing on the police department, and the fires actually being set by the government. This information will not be available through the mainstream media, one will have to search alternative sources for the truth. These are just a few of the sources that will lead you in the right direction: FEMA tells first responders not to respond until told to do so, FEMA news 2005, Aug 29, FEMA won't accept Amtrak's help in evacuations, FEMA news Aug 29, 2005, offer of helicopters for rescue work is rejected, Narcosphere Sept 1, 2005, FEMA blocks 500 Florida airboats from rescue work, Sun Sentinel Sept 2, 2005, FEMA to Chicago: just send one truck, Chicago Tribune Sept 2, 2005, FEMA bars morticians from entering New Orleans, Tri Valley Central Sept 3, 2005, FEMA blocks 500 boat citizen flotilla from delivering aid, Daily Kos Sept 3, 2005, Homeland security won't let Red Cross deliver food, Post Gazette Sept 3, 2005, FEMA fails to use Navy ship with 600 hospital beds onboard, Chicago Tribune Sept 4, 2005, FEMA cuts local communications phone lines, Meet the Press Sept 4, 2005, FEMA turns away experienced firefighters, Daily Kos Sept 5, 2005, FEMA turns back Wal-Mart supply trucks, New York Times, Sept 5, 2005, FEMA prevents Coast Guard from delivering diesel fuel, New York Times, Sept 5, 2005, Navy Pilots who rescue victims are reprimanded, New York Times, Sept 7, 2005, U.S. government turns back German plane with 15 tons of aid, Star Tribune, Sept 10, 2005. This may come as a shock to some, but the primary function of FEMA, Homeland Security, and the military is to protect the government in a time of crisis, not protect its citizens. This is one of the main reasons that it took so long for help to arrive. The coming days ahead will shed new light on the government and its intension for its citizens in the near future. Hurricane Katrina is just the beginning.